King's Shilling

Mike Lunnon-Wood was born in Africa and educated in Australia and New Zealand. Based in the Middle East for ten years, he now lives in West Sussex and has a young son.

D0806360

MIKE LUNNON-WOOD

KING'S SHILLING

HarperCollins*Publishers*

HarperCollins*Publishers*
77-85 Fulham Palace Road,
Hammersmith, London W6 8JB

A Paperback Original 1998
1 3 5 7 9 8 6 4 2

A catalogue record for this book
is available from the British Library

ISBN 0 00 651162 7

Set in Meridien by Rowland Phototypesetting Ltd,
Bury St Edmunds, Suffolk

Printed and bound in Great Britain by
Caledonian International Book Manufacturing Ltd, Glasgow

For the people of the Elsted area, who made me so welcome, and those who have the watch, that we might sleep safely

ACKNOWLEDGEMENTS

Many people helped me with my research, too many to thank individually. The most help came from the wonderful people aboard HMS *Richmond*, a happy ship, unashamedly the inspiration for the fictional HMS *Beaufort* of this story. Her Captain at the time was Commander Andrew Underwood. He, along with his Executive Officer, Lt Commander Richard Brooks-Bank, and Ops Officer, Lt Commander Simon Howell, gave up many hours to help me try to get it right. Lieutenants Tracy Langrill, Graham Smith, 'Harry' Palmer and Paul Marshall all gave freely of their time, as did every officer in the wardroom and every rating on the ship. Michael Hill at Northwood was hugely helpful, reading the manuscript, and Major Cawthorne RM and my brother, Squadron Leader Tony Lunnon-Wood RAF, deserve mention for technical advice freely given. Any mistakes are mine, not theirs.

While you attempt to create entirely fictional characters, sometimes people you meet elbow their way into a novel by sheer force of personality. If Richard Brooks-Bank, 'Bob' Langrill, 'Tex' Marshall or Chops(M) Rolfe see bits of themselves appearing in this story, either standing alone or as elements of other characters, I apologize and hope I've done them justice.

Prologue

Splif cradled his weapon and, sitting back on his thin haunches, sucked deeply on the gigantic marijuana cigarette. Rolled in newspaper, it funnelled out towards the end dropping burning cinders, but he didn't notice that or the flies that buzzed round a weeping sore on his bony leg. There had been no real food for two days now; they were going out later and would find some. Take some from someone.

He was fourteen and wore nothing more than a pair of shorts and plastic flip-flops, but he had his gun and he had his comrades. His name wasn't really Splif. It was the one he had adopted when he joined Ulima-J to fight for the freedom of his country, but there wasn't much freedom and he wasn't really sure who they were supposed to be fighting because most of the time he lived in a drug-induced haze. They were supposed to be after NPFL, but that didn't happen very often. They just fought skirmishes with whoever they came across and raided across the countryside to find food, killing as they went. He had killed many people. Women. Children. But yesterday they had clashed with ECOMOG, the Nigerians at Tubmanburg to the east, and there were stories of dead and captured. He had never met General Roosevelt Johnson, the leader of the Krahn Ulima-J, but he had once seen Alfredo Garlo, the Chief of Staff. He wanted to be like him one day.

Splif looked across at his friend Bang-Bang. He was only eleven, but he fought like the veteran he was. Bang-Bang rolled cigarettes with a mixture of marijuana and the scrapings from expended cartridges, the burnt gunpowder

1

giving his smokes their own distinct smell. He preferred dugees, smokes laced with heroin, but you couldn't always get those and so he smoked burnt gunpowder and his eyes would go red and he was fearless using his machete afterwards. He would sometimes cut the hands off people they found and once he had eaten a liver they had taken from a woman, saying it would make him powerful. Bang-Bang wore special amulets and charms to ward off the bullets – they all did, but his were different. He had some-one's dried-out severed ears threaded on a piece of dental floss, along with a miniature surfboard someone had patiently carved from a section of a toothbrush and a pro-peller from a child's toy aeroplane, although they didn't know what either of those two items were.

The word was they were on the move. Their section of nine boys was part of a larger unit with a sixteen-year-old major in command, themselves a tiny part of the might of Ulima-J. Monrovia. They were taking the Nigerian pris-oners and marching on Monrovia to kill the NPFL and their leader Samuel Taylor.

He took another drag on his cigarette and tried to remember his mother's face, what it looked like before the attack. He remembered it vividly afterwards. The jaw hanging sideways, separated from the rest of her head completely down one side where the machete had cleaved through. He was eight then. He tried to remember her before, the way she looked as she cooked the evening meal for him and his brothers and sisters. He couldn't, but he didn't care. He was Splif, a soldier, and he didn't care about anything.

1

South Atlantic

It was the forenoon watch. The sea was undulating, oily and smooth on the surface of the big swells that rolled under the ship's bows, gently lifting her grey bulk before she eased down the other side. Lieutenant Jamie Buchanan was bending over the plot table, the officer of the watch's binoculars, identified by their red braided rope sling, swinging in time with the movement of the ship. The rating on the wheel was feeling sick. He was not used to the long, climbing and falling, fore-and-aft motion, and half an hour earlier Buchanan had sent him down to take two Stugeron motion sickness tablets.

Frigates are stiffer than most ships, designed so that with the weather on the beam they will flick back to the upright as fast as possible so that the weapon systems can bear. It took some getting used to, Buchanan reflected, but once you were accustomed to it things were fine, unless of course you were ploughing into long Atlantic swells when there was no flick back, none of the frigate feeling. The long, lazy, up-and-down motion of the ship along her fore-and-aft line as she crossed the swells in baking sun would have its price, and he knew that there would be many in the ship's company feeling queasy.

He worked the calculation quickly. The satnav gave them a precise position and beneath the clear perspex surface of the semi-automatic plotting table a set of little motors silently moved an arm that shone a tiny red dot upward, showing exactly where they were on the chart, but Buchanan checked it again. The navigator had laid off the course and in a few minutes, just before the watch changed, he would bring the ship round another five degrees to starboard, the most economical route home. He walked forward to the bridge windows and lifted his binoculars. Radar had picked up a vessel out ahead of them, crossing their track westbound, and she would be visible for a few minutes. Slowly he swept the horizon on the bearing, move an inch, stop and look, move an inch, stop and look, as he had been taught. There. His eyesight was good. A smudge on the skyline. He tried to guess her journey. Outbound south-west from some African port into the Atlantic, to Buenos Aires or Rio de Janeiro perhaps. He lowered the glasses to his chest and looked at his watch. His relief was due any minute and he was looking forward to going down to the cool wardroom to eat. The bridge was air-conditioned to an extent, but every time someone moved in or out of the bridge wing doors a blast of hot air rolled in and even wearing tropical rig with shorts, the starch put in by the Chinese dhobi men keeping the creases sharp, it was still warm.

He looked down at his watch. 'Steer three-three-five degrees,' he ordered.

'Aye aye. Steer three-three-five,' the quartermaster confirmed back to him, turning the small butterfly-shaped handle slightly to the right till the course indicated was correct.

Buchanan smiled to himself. As a seagoing officer in the Royal Navy he got to play with big boys' toys and he loved his job. He was among other things the ship's diving officer and genuinely liked risk. He was demolitions trained and got a buzz from the more dangerous end of the Navy's tasks. At his age it didn't get any better than this, watch-keeping on his ship.

'Permission to enter the bridge?'

'Sure,' he answered. It was the oncoming duty QM, the seaman rating who would relieve the QM at the wheel. A few moments later another figure moved up.

'I suppose you want me to relieve you?' she said, with mock exasperation.

4

He looked across and smiled. Sarah Conway, also a lieutenant, had the 1200 till 1600 watch.

'Yes please.'

Standing at the plotting table Buchanan began his hand-
over, bringing the oncoming watchkeeper up to date on
course changes, the navigator's instructions, daily and
standing orders.

They moved back to stand by the central compass bin-
nacle, Sarah's eyes automatically taking in course and
heading and the radar picture of what lay out in the seas
around them from the array of instruments and displays.

'Okay, the course is 335 degrees, the speed is 130 revolutions. You have a course change mid-watch. Currently
you have traffic on the horizon off the port bow . . .' he
bent and looked through the gyroscopic compass '. . . on
321 degrees. It's 1202 and you have the ship.'

'I have the ship,' she repeated.

He took the binoculars from round his neck, filled out the
last of his log entries and a few minutes later stood upright.

'Done. What's for lunch?'

'Ummm, cheesy, hammy, eggy or tagliatelle,' she
responded, adding, 'The pasta wasn't bad.'

'Bollocks,' he grunted softly, dropping down the two steps
towards the ladder. He didn't really like either of them.

She smiled and slipped on the binoculars. Lieutenant
Sarah Conway had the watch in HMS *Beaufort*.

Beaufort was a Type 23 frigate, one of the Duke class of
warships. The newest ship on the Royal Navy's active list,
she was 133 metres long and 15 in the beam. Her crew
was sparse by any navy's standard, only 185 people of
which 21 were women. The small complement was only
possible because *Beaufort* was state of the art. High technology allowed minimal crewing and she was very hi-tech
indeed. Her fighting capacity was impressive. She could
deliver more firepower than older generation warships
twice her size.

Her close-range defence system comprised Seawolf missiles. Sitting in their silos on the foredeck below the bridge, they could engage aircraft or incoming missiles, and as further protection from aircraft she deployed a 30-millimetre cannon either side of her waist. For offensive operations she had Harpoon anti-ship missiles and Stingray torpedoes and, dominating the foredeck, a Mark 8 Vickers 4.5-inch gun that had been upgraded from the original GSA 8 Fire Control System to offer a laser sighting system. With laser, radar control or optical local area sighting, she could fire a 4.5-inch shell every second and a half with devastating accuracy.

She also had an attack helicopter on her flight deck. The Lynx, sonar equipped, could drop depth charges, carry and fire torpedoes and launch anti-ship Sea Skua missiles.

Originally frigates were light, fast warships with a single gundeck. Too small and lightly armed to stand and do battle in the line, they were used as scouts, to seek out the enemy or carry messages for the fleet. In time some had a second gundeck and they were classified as fifth or six rates, but by the mid-nineteenth century the class had all but disappeared. Re-emerging just before the Second World War, they had become general purpose warships, slow but with a good range and designed for convoy escort duties, usually in an anti-submarine role. In modern times the term frigate became a generic term for a general purpose warship and the Royal Navy's, while still specialist submarine hunters, could now, like modern destroyers, bring the firepower of a cruiser into action. But unlike a destroyer, designed as an area defence platform to defend the fleet from air attack where everything happened incredibly quickly, frigates were best out hunting. Their prey of choice were submarines. She was a thinking man's warship. She could run fast and silent, so silent on her big diesel electric motors that submarines couldn't hear her coming and once she had found them, her delicate sensors seeking them out, it was all but over. Her torpedoes and helicopter-launched weapons would do the rest. The Royal Navy had long been viewed by other navies as having the best anti-submarine capability in the world and the Type 23s were the latest in the line of sub killers, quieter than any surface ship since sail, with a stealth capacity to reduce their radar signature down to that of a fishing boat and complex electronics and weapon systems. Submariners were terrified of them.

The type had two power options. The twin diesel electric motors were housed in sound-proofed units mounted on rubber to limit vibration to the hull, but when she didn't need silent running and wanted speed she spooled up her twin Spey gas turbines. She could race along and then shut down the gas and move into a target area on electric power, silent as a ghost, listening for her prey. Her sensors were impressive. Below water she had the 2050 hull-mounted sonar with its omni-directional medium-range capability enhanced for passive listening and she also had the 2031 long-range towed array sonar. Above water, looking out, she had 966 radar for long-range three-dimensional video display data to the weapons systems and the 1010/11 positive identification of target system. Finally she had UAT, an electronic warfare system giving command information on hostile or friendly radar emissions.

Down in the Ops room, the nerve centre of the ship, things were routine with just a training exercise going. A week before it had been very different – full live firing exercises with the South African navy in the Indian Ocean – but now they were on their way home to Portsmouth, their fleet oiler a day out behind them. RFA *Gold Rover* had left earlier, but, plodding along at seventeen knots with a bearing problem, had seen them overhaul her two nights ago. Yesterday they had spent a few hours in company, transferring bunkering lines and taking on fuel oil. The other supplies had come across by helicopter, the big Sea King that was aboard the oiler. The helo had just finished the last hop when it had its own mechanical

7

problem, and when the *Beaufort* eased up the gas turbines and *Gold Rover* turned eastwards towards Libreville to collect equipment that was being returned to the UK, it was in their hangar, its gearbox being stripped down by the artificers.

Forward elements of Ulima-J were now only sixteen miles from Monrovia and moving forward in a steady if ragged advance, some walking through the bush, others along the roadside, others still in a collection of old heavy commercial vehicles and Japanese pick-ups. It was the usual advance of rebel armies who lacked communications equipment and effective command structures and leadership. Forces that were effective when operating as independent units with a common political aim were often the worst when brought together because they lacked the infrastructure and the discipline that regular military units depend on. Ulima-J was no different, part of the brutal meat grinder that was Liberia's political system.

Run by the Krahn warlord Roosevelt Johnson, they were one of six factions that had been at each other's throats in Liberia for the better part of six years in one form or another. Two other powerful factions controlled other parts of the country. The stronger of the two was Charles Taylor's National Patriotic Front of Liberia. It was Taylor that had ousted Master Sergeant Doe, who himself had overthrown his predecessor and then disembowelled him on Monrovia's waterfront.

The veneer of political intent was thin, almost transparent. The warlords were simply out to maintain enough power to loot and plunder over their area of control, but six years on there was little left to take. In the Krahn area there were mines and Roosevelt Johnson had raked them over as far as he could while keeping some semblance of production running, extracting huge bounties for everything going into the mines and everything coming out. The last pickings were in Monrovia, the capital, and that was held by Taylor, but they also knew that Taylor's people were fighting the Liberia Peace Council, George Boley's armed faction down in the south-west, and Boley would only need to turn his gunmen to the north to be pressuring Taylor's stronghold in Gbargna.

An old Bedford tipper truck looted from a mine rolled to a stop on the track, its engine pouring steam. Splif and Bang-Bang, who sat resting in the bush beside the track, looked up at it longingly. They had found food yesterday, but had eaten it all and were hungry again. Their leader had said they wouldn't be moving again till late in the afternoon so they were free for a few hours. Splif got to his feet. The road wasn't far away, maybe a mile or so. There would be cars and people. Someone would have food they could take. They moved fast, dropping into the rhythm of the march, confident as only a heavily armed gang could be in a land where they could do what they wished, a gang of children, their cruelty and callousness untempered by either maturity or understanding. Splif knew that if they moved quickly they could set up a road block ahead of the main Ulima-J elements and have first choice of the pickings. Food, money, other things. Last month up near Tubmanburg one of them had taken a big yellow toy truck off a white man they had stopped on the road, an aid worker. They knew about aid. It always meant rich pickings, much better than the crowded vehicles of locals where at best you might get a chicken or some sorghum, handed over with fear in their eyes, real fear, wide-eyed jabbering terror if you lifted the gun barrel or fingered the handle of your machete. He liked that. The power. But aid workers were better. They always had money and with money you could buy dugees, the heroin-laced smokes they loved. The seven of them broke into a jog. Bang-Bang had been smoking all morning, big marijuana smokes laced with the cartridge case residues, and his eyes were red and angry. They would find someone who had food.

Sasstown and Paynesville were only four or five miles

distant and they had been through there before, looting and raping before going back to the bush with their booty.

Lieutenant Conway raised the binoculars and looked out at the seas ahead, then crossed back to the plotting table. On the large-scale chart the west coast of Africa ran down the right-hand side. Out there, off the starboard bow, some 320 nautical miles away, was the Ivory Coast. Their course would take them northwards deep-sea, then closer in until they had Cape Verde, the westernmost tip of Africa, and Dakar, the capital of Senegal, visual.

Senegal. The thought didn't appeal. Not after Durban and Cape Town.

It had been a good trip. The shore leave had been great. Three days ashore was long enough to do something other than carouse with the others, so when the Beau tied up in Durban she and two of the others had rented a car and driven out to a private game park. After the evening game drive, all crowded into a Land-Rover with two Americans and a French couple, they had sat round a huge fire while the staff barbecued food and they had slept the night in a *rondavel*, a round, thatched structure. It had been great fun. They spent the last day on the beach back at Durban, but the high spot was the game park and – she smiled at the thought – the rather attractive young chap who had taken them out in the Land-Rover. He was tall, clean-smelling, blond and brown from the sun, with impeccable manners and a ready smile. That evening as he had entertained them by the fire, showered, his hair wet, in clean shorts and shirt, his eye had caught hers several times and they both knew. If she weren't married it would have been on, she thought to herself. Oh yes, I would have gobbled him up. She smiled again.

Someone moved up behind her. 'Wotcha.'

'Hi,' she replied. Paul Morris, the navigator. As always, his eyes took in the course and speed in a second. He didn't need to check his instructions. Thanks to a phenomenal

10

memory, on most voyages he knew every stage he had planned, the course changes and the times they were scheduled for. Invariably he had plotted alternates, nearest landfall at every stage, nearest point that they could operate the Lynx ashore. After a quick look at the plotting table and the satnav readout he wandered over and stood beside her.

Out on the bridge wing two of the lads were painting, touching up the inboard side of the screen where rust was already showing through around the bolts securing the weatherproof intercom panel. They worked stripped to the waist, enjoying the sunshine. One laughed at something the other said.

'Ah, a happy sailor,' Morris said with a grin. 'He won't be when he hears what the Buffer and the Jimmy have planned for tomorrow.'

'What might that be?' she asked.

'The hangar inside roof.'

'The Buffer' was the age-old term for the ship's professional sailor. A Petty Officer, he was traditionally the chief bosun's mate, but modern ships had no bosun and he reported direct to the Executive Officer. He was responsible for the seamanship on the decks, the handling of lines and warps when berthing, the seaboats and suchlike. At sea most of his day was taken up with routine matters and maintenance. The hangar formed the bulk of the aft superstructure and was big enough to get the Lynx inside once the rotors were folded in. It was hot in there and up against the roof it would be worse.

A figure appeared on the other bridge wing. 'Talk of the devil,' Morris said.

It was the XO. Peter Kitson was a Lieutenant Commander, but he had not got there by the normal watch-keeping route. The Executive Officer is the ship's First Lieutenant and is tagged 'the Jimmy' by most, the name coming from King James I. In the modern navy seaman officers come from various specialist disciplines and Kitson came off the flight deck. He was an aviator and by all accounts a good one, and not just good at flying. As a naval officer he was tipped for the top, but only if he could manage his outspokenness, his only failing and one consistently mentioned in his superior officer's reports. Short, stocky and always wearing a rather battered cap, he was popular with the lads and known as scrupulously fair. Thorough yet creative, he was an inveterate writer of lists; his colleagues, while appreciating his thoroughness, tagged whatever list he was working through as the 'hymn sheet'.

Although most of the crew chose to live somewhere near Portsmouth, Kitson's family was in Falmouth, which meant a long ride whenever the ship was home. He was divorced with two daughters, both the image of their mother, an attractive and well-educated woman who had never learned the elusive secret of how to be a good naval wife. She had been gone three years now, having run off to find herself in South America. She lived in Lima with an American she had met there.

The girls lived with her parents. He loved being home, and would take long walks with the girls, the dog, a cross-bred floppy-eared, hairy thing salvaged from the RSPCA lolling along with them. His other love was his sole real indulgence, an 1100cc water-cooled Yamaha that he commuted on, wearing a set of Kevlar reinforced leathers that Judith had bought him for the last Christmas they had together. The girls loved the bike and also wanted leathers, but Kitson drew the line there as he had done with jeans. The eldest, Lucy, old enough to be fashion sensitive, was now wearing jeans and it had taken years to get that far. Kitson hated jeans, and while he had given in to his daughter, he had never owned a pair and wouldn't have them in his wardroom. The others mocked him, tagging denim as 'the devil's cloth', but gently because he was the Jimmy, and because they knew there was a strength in him which could be ferocious.

He loved his daughters and he loved his ship, but he could never watch a helicopter lift off the stern without wishing he was flying it and it was so obvious that no one ever commented on it. Most civilians thought of naval helicopters as primarily things involved in rescues, but that wasn't half of it. They were the long reach weapon platform. A Lynx fully loaded with fuel and the right mix of ordnance could kill submarines or surface ships with equal ease. She could reach out hundreds of miles from her mother ship, like some giant, prehistoric, ever-so-deadly dragonfly, scan the seas and skies and deliver firepower that was awesome.

In cruising watch, the normal state of readiness, as the First Lieutenant he stood no watches, but worked a normal day. Once the ship went on to defence watch, on *Beaufort* six hours on and six hours off, he was still flexible, deciding his working pattern with the Captain. If the ship was at defence watch for an extended period, then eventually he would command one watch and the Captain the other, but for now it was officially from 0800 to the first dog watch. He had a meeting in a few minutes, heads of departments in the wardroom, but first as was his custom he would smoke a quiet after-lunch cigarette on the bridge wing. The wardroom was his: he was the chairman and determined the rules of conduct, dress and behaviour, so he could smoke in there if he wished, but was considerate enough to those who disliked the habit to restrict smoking in the wardroom to after supper.

He looked through the windows on to the bridge. The officer of the watch, Sarah Conway, was enjoying a joke with the navigator. He smiled to himself as he lit his cigarette, recalling the day she arrived in *Beaufort*, the first woman on board and for nine months the only one. Some wag in the wardroom, a *Blackadder* fan, had remembered the programme where Blackadder's new servant turned out to be a girl who dressed up as a boy to get the job and called herself Bob. The joke went round, and even her

13

name badge read Lieutenant Bob Conway. Like everyone else in the Navy, Kitson had been concerned that they get it right when women were accepted on active service. They had got it right with Bob. A graduate entry, she had come from a family with four brothers, played rugby for the varsity women's team, and was a competitive animal. Her degree was in history, a respectable upper second. She was pragmatic, reliable and tough without having lost any of her femininity, and she fitted in immediately. The others in the wardroom admitted that she added something, too, a normality that softened the all-male environment.

The relationship was odd. To an observer she was part of the wardroom, one of the complement of officers on one of Her Majesty's warships. But it was also a microcosm of society at large where she filled a part of every role filled by women. She was part little sister, part mother, part platonic friend, part girlfriend, part sexual fantasy, part agony aunt, confidante to many on board the Beau. She was a first rate watchkeeper and a fine officer, but never lost her 'girliness' as one of them once described it. She was popular with the lads, too. As the only woman on the ship until recently she had to walk a careful line, always professional but without distancing herself too far. The incident with the lads was a classic.

They had been tied up in the Thames and ended up en masse in a London night club. After quite a night, she had gone on to another club where she had promised to meet some of the crew, mostly her division, for a drink. Half an hour after she arrived a man in another group asked her to dance and when she declined said something unpleasant. As they were leaving in a few minutes anyway, they finished their drinks and moved towards the door.

The trouble followed them out on to the pavement and one of the trouble-makers, a pony-tailed bond dealer with too much drink in him, walked back over from his sports car and insulted her again. A bony fist flashed over her shoulder and the dealer went down as if poleaxed, his mouth dripping blood. It was one of her lads, an Electronic Warfare Technician who wasn't going to have his divisional officer take that sort of shit from a civilian.

The bouncers moved in and she was there in the thick of it, holding back her own people and assuring the doormen that it was over. The dealer, blood all over his expensive suit, was getting to his feet as a police car on patrol stopped.

'Out of here, ma'am,' one of the crew members said. 'Quickly now.'

'No,' she replied. 'You're my lads.'

She argued the case with the police, who wanted to take in the punch thrower and a few of the others for questioning and advised her to go back to the ship in a taxi.

'I will not. That man insulted me and insulted the Royal Navy. My shipmate simply came to my defence when he thought that that . . .' she pointed to the dealer, who was holding a handkerchief to his mouth, '. . . nasty little oik was going to go from verbal battery to physical battery and actually assault me. These people report to me. They are my division and as such I am responsible for their welfare . . . as they,' she added with a rueful smile, 'seem to be for mine. There was real provocation here. We just want to go back to the ship peacefully, no problems to anyone. But you take any of them in and you'd better take me as well.' She was getting nervous. Over their shoulder she could see two of her lads doing something to the sports car.

Eventually a compromise was reached. She would return to the ship, but she would take her people with her, all of them. 'Just to make sure we will give you a lift,' one of the policeman said acidly, indicating the police Transit van that was pulling up.

'Fine,' she replied, moving her people to the van quickly. The dealer dropped the handkerchief from his mouth. 'No way. I want someone charged. Look at my suit!'

'Shut it,' one of the policemen snarled, moving up to

him. 'There's ten of them with one story, sunshine, and you and your two mates all with different ones. By all accounts not only did you have it coming, but you got off lightly.'

She sat with the men on the way back to the ship, two of them grinning. 'And you two!' she said exasperated. 'You zapped it didn't you! The car. You zapped it!'

They nodded and chorused a reply. 'Yes ma'am.'

'You're a pair of bloody prats, right? What are you?'

'Bloody prats, ma'am,' one replied.

There was a pause and then she asked, 'It was a Porsche, wasn't it?'

One of them nodded, unable to stifle his giggle and then they were all at it, Sarah as bad as any of them, the two policemen in the front looking back, wondering what on earth was going on.

Most regiments, air force squadrons and navy ships have their crest or coat of arms reproduced on small, sticky-backed bits of cardboard the size of a fifty pence piece. It's a familiar calling card and military units take great delight in 'zapping' another unit's vehicles, buildings and equipment while no one is looking.

While the police had been talking to everyone the two had sneaked across to the dealer's Porsche and 'zapped' it with fifteen or twenty HMS *Beaufort* crests.

It was all over the ship by morning: the Wren officer was okay. The lads stuck by her and she returned the loyalty, defending her divisional members like family.

They were in an ageing Peugeot 504 estate. Three nuns on their way back to Monrovia from trying to visit the mission at Kle, being driven by a young aid worker in Liberia with Save the Children. They had been turned back by an NPFL section at a big roadblock two miles back. Unusually there were adults in the group, and they were disciplined to an extent, so when they were turned round they accepted it, thankful that all they parted with was some money. The nuns had been planning to drive up on their own, but there were reports coming through of gunmen moving south and the young man had insisted on accompanying them.

Dave Culverhouse had been in Liberia for almost two years, a lot less than the nuns, but he was considerably more street-wise, because although he was travelling on a British passport he was a Zimbabwean by birth and upbringing and that made him, as his boss said, an old Africa hand. He had a deep love for Africa, and an instinct in dealing with its people. Being fluent in both Shona and Sindebele wasn't much use up here, but growing up in a black African culture was, and the moment he saw them step on to the road he knew it was trouble. Not NPFL and they were young, too young. You could reason with an adult, he had said the weekend before to an American girl at their Embassy, but the kids were tougher and if they were stoned it could get very terminal very quickly. With six or seven AK47s pointed at them, and one boy waving them to stop he began to slow the car.

'OK, ladies, here we go,' Culverhouse said, thinking: Ulima. They look like Ulima.

'O sweet Jesus,' one of them uttered softly, crossing herself.

'Do as I say. Don't challenge them and don't get excited. Whatever they want we give them,' he said, drawing the car to a halt.

One walked to his open window and gestured, lifting a hand to his mouth. Shit, he thought, they want food. We have nothing. He remembered the orange that he had taken from the house this morning, but not eaten. He shrugged and smiled, passed the orange through the window, then gestured around him with lifted shoulders, the international sign language for: I can't help any more. I'd love to, I really would, but see, I don't have what you want. He took some money from his shirt pocket, there since the last roadblock and as he went to hand it over there was a commotion from the back. He turned, a door was open, one of them with wild red eyes was leaning in, reaching for the crucifix round Sister Helena's neck. Instinctively she raised her hand to protect it and he said, 'Let him have it, let him have it,' quickly and softly, smiling all the time, but the boy didn't wait. He stepped back and swung his rifle barrel up.

Culverhouse's shouted plea was drowned by the muzzle blast and in the next second, with the nuns screaming and other boys bringing their weapons to bear, he gunned the accelerator and slipped the clutch. The one in front, darting to the side, was too slow and went down under the wheels and the young Zimbabwean shrank in his seat, tearing up through the gears, rounds hitting the car until the next bend, Sister Helena, silent, going into shock, the other in the back seat also hit, screaming, but trying to help, Sister Michael in the front leaning over the seat trying to pull them both down lower.

As they took the bend he flicked a look over his shoulder. They were out of sight.

'Who's hit?'

'Both of them,' Sister Michael replied. 'Oh, mother of God, the blood. Pull over. We must stop the bleeding.'

'No. Not for a few miles yet. There might be others. We have to keep moving. Do what you can.' They had a doctor on their team. He looked at his watch, thinking fast. Three-thirty. The small Save the Children clinic was this side of town, but in the afternoons the doctor was at the big clinic on the Robertsfield road. The main hospital in Monrovia was very basic and although they had seen more than their share of gunshot wounds the facilities weren't up to this. There was the ConLib medical centre. Too far. He looked over his shoulder again. Blood everywhere. Stabilize them. We must stabilize them. The Americans had their own doctor with a small but well-equipped surgery.

'We'll go to the US Embassy,' he said.

They pulled over three miles further on, just for four or

five minutes, to better staunch the bleeding in both of their patients, Sister Helena, her white habit splattered and red with her blood, still holding on to her crucifix, but going into deep shock. Sister Marie, younger, stronger, but still with two bullets in her was holding out better, staunching the blood from her thigh wound with one hand and holding her habit over the wound in Sister Helena's chest with the other.

Three decks down, almost below the bridge in E section on 2 deck, the small Chief Petty Officers' mess was smoky and crowded. Off to one side the Chief Petty Officer (Missiles), known as Chops(M), put down his big mug of tea and reached for a biscuit. Some of the others were drinking beer, but he never drank during daylight. He tried to drink very little at sea, a little discipline he had set himself, like the seventy push-ups he did on each arm every morning. Dave Wilks was a career man, had worked his way up from the bottom. Lean and hard, he spoke out of the side of his mouth with a voice like gravel. He was thirty-eight years old, the senior rating in the ship's offensive complement. His demeanour was not that of a sailor and many who saw the way he moved, his stature, the way he came to attention, the way he commanded, thought he was in fact a Marine. A woman visiting the ship had said as much once. Wilks, who disliked Marines as much as he disliked Pompey football club, looked at her with a look that would have shrivelled gorse and said, 'I'm not a Marine. I'm a real sailor. The fact I'm wearing blue is the give-away.' He cut himself off there, but she got the message.

He was salty. His beret, worn with age, dropped down almost vertical over his ear and the Chief Petty Officers' badge was always highly polished. When the ship was at action stations he sat at the missile and gun control console deep in the Ops room, but he was also responsible for the ship's small arms training and the skills of the boarding parties. He commanded the detachment that took the salute on the bridge wing as the ship entered and left port: the rating with the bosun's pipe and the other raising and lowering signal flags and ensigns, the yeoman. He knew every ship in the surface fleet, who commanded her, their seniority and the web of protocol, traditions and rules that caught the unwary. Woe betide any of his people who screwed up, as those on other ships did regularly. A signal missed, a pipe mistimed, or the worst sin of all, forgetting the five minutes to sunset rule – for five minutes before sunset a whole different set of protocols took over, further confusing things – and then, jaws clenched, one word would be uttered from the side of his mouth as he thought he saw his beloved Navy slide into mediocrity.

'Cunts.'

As a youngster living in Portsmouth he had always been close to the Navy. Having left school early, and finding it tough to find work, he had skirted the edges of crime, knocking off the odd car radio. When his best mate was arrested and banged up he saw the flashing amber light and within a week had joined the *Andrew*. He had married young and his wife had been killed in a car crash, but his two sons, raised by his parents while he was at sea, were fine boys, one having just joined up and in *Brave*. The other was at university, the first in his family, and Wilks was so proud of him he embarrassed himself.

Twenty years on he was a veteran. He had been in the Falklands, on board *Sheffield* when she had taken an Exocet and woe betide any man jack on his ship who didn't take fire drills seriously. The new ships were better. The lessons had been learned. There wasn't thicker armour – there never would be in a small warship – but there was everything you could want to fight a fire, and then some. Fearnot suits, breathing apparatus, extinguishers everywhere, a halon gas system and built-in redundancy in sea water mains meant they could take on fires that would have killed older ships and many of their crew.

After his cup of tea he would be having a chat with a

rating who had ignored the fire drill. Off duty. Didn't want to get involved. The officer hadn't seen her, but he had. He wouldn't tell the DCO, a wanker in his book. For Chops(M) the Supply Officer, who became the Damage Control Officer the moment they went into action, was okay for issuing stores, but bugger all good for much else. He would deal with this.

Tommy Godshall was working bare to the waist as he stripped down the starboard 30-millimetre gun, enjoying the feel of the sun on his skin. There had been a problem with its traverse on the exercise and he thought he knew what the problem was. He was lean and wiry and a tattoo of a swooping eagle took up most of the space between his shoulder blades. Godshall, a weapons artificer, had been made up to killick, or leading seaman, a rank roughly equivalent to a corporal, for the third time. He was always getting into trouble ashore and getting bust down, but today it wasn't his troubles that bothered him. He was worried about his mate. Dave Tomkins was normally a happy-go-lucky bloke, but he had been withdrawn of late. Silent. Moody. He knew what the problem was, but neither of them was much good at talking about serious things. Dave just threw himself into his work down in the Main Communications Office, the MCO. Even when they had been ashore in Durban he hadn't really let his hair down and relaxed with the lads.

He and Dave Tomkins were mates. Born within a mile of each other in Rotherhithe, they had only met on the ship and found they had drunk in the same pubs, shagged the same birds and, in spite of the six-year age difference, knew the same people.

They were opposites. Dave was gentle. Gentle as a lamb, whereas Godshall was a fighter. Born the last of six, he had had to take whatever he wanted – it wasn't going to be given to him. Once when unemployed he had earned money on Saturday nights as a bare-knuckle fighter out the back of the pubs in his area. He was shy with women, where gentle Dave was charming in his boyish way and pulled more than his share. But not in Durban. He was cut up. Worried sick by what had happened, but he shouldn't have been, Godshall thought. It wasn't his fault.

Splif had let go half a magazine at the car and Bang-Bang more. They had all fired as it tore away, but it hadn't stopped and now they still had no food and the money they had taken, five American dollars, wouldn't buy anything out here except maybe some dugees if they found one of the boys who had some. Snoopy was dead, run over by the car. They called him Snoopy because when he joined them he had a Snoopy tee-shirt. They stood over him and looked down, his thin chest crushed by the wheels, lots of blood in the dust on the road. They took his gun and his magazines and one of them took his flip-flops, because they were better than his own and then they left him there and moved off into the bush again.

Splif looked at Bang-Bang, angry with him for shooting too soon. If he had waited till they were all ready then he could have shot the man before he had time to drive away. He had a watch on his wrist that he had wanted. Whites always had more to take. Monrovia. There were whites there. There would be plenty if they got in soon, before the main Ulima-J forces arrived.

They fought over the orange like a pack of dogs until Bang-Bang pulled out his machete and then Splif took control long enough to suggest they peel it and share it out and Bang-Bang lowered the heavy blade. His eyes were still red and angry and he was smoking again as they moved through the bush. Several hundred yards away were others of their section and they were all moving in the direction of Paynesville, with some elements now on the main road. Eight or nine thousand of them, an advancing front covering some eleven miles across.

* * *

22

The captain's quarters on a modern warship are always basic. On *Beaufort*, directly below the bridge, he had a small night cabin, with a bunk, as narrow at twenty-two inches as any on the ship, over lockers and drawers beside a hanging locker. The door, next to the small head and shower unit, led to the main day cabin which was as personal and cosy as Waterloo station. There was a desk against the interior bulkhead with a PC and comms unit that constantly babbled. A long table, seating six or eight people and topped with plastic wood veneer, dominated the centre of the cabin. A sideboard stood under a hatch to the captain's pantry, where a steward would prepare his meals, and along the seaward bulkhead was a long bench seat and a single steel-framed easy chair. They were covered in a floral fabric of greens and yellows that should have looked summery and bright but instead just looked incongruous and, against the MoD carpets, wood veneer finishes and steel walls covered in yet another patterned wallpaper, it verged on bad taste. The wardroom had the same fabric covering their chairs and the story was that it was chosen years before by a senior Air Force officer's wife and then left in the MoD stores as stock. Never willingly requested by any of the three services, it was eventually forced on whoever needed furnishing fabric from stores. It was the Air Force's big joke on the other two services.

Commander Nick Bennett, *Beaufort*'s Captain, sat in the tubular steel chair and read through the latest batch of reports from his heads of departments and the disciplinary paperwork for the following morning's Captain's table. Every now and then a knock on the steel outer bulkhead would precede someone's entry, the ship's secretary, the junior supply officer, or a department head.

The ship was split into four departments. The executive department, Operations, dealt with watchkeeping, seamanship and warfare. There were two engineering departments, Marine, responsible for the propulsion, generators, power supply, water and utilities, and Weapons, a specialist department of highly trained people simply to keep the complicated weapon systems operative no matter what. The last department was Supply, the ubiquitous pursers who keep the ship supplied with everything from toilet paper to jam to engine spares, ammunition to electronic circuit boards, ballpoint pens to fresh fruit. Modern management gurus call it matrix management, but the Navy has been doing it for years. Every officer alongside his or her primary job function may have a secondary role and then a third, the welfare, training and development and counselling responsibility for a group of ratings. This is their division. They might be advising one sailor on the best way to clear up a debt, keeping an eye on a fellow who has problems at home, suggesting to others the next courses they should apply for and standing advocate for another in trouble and about to appear at the Captain's table for disciplinary action. The system works, but makes for confusion among observers, especially as a plethora of titles, all abbreviated to initials and acronyms, are used constantly.

Commander Bennett was expecting his EWO at 0900 the following morning, with one of her division who was up before the table for insolence. The EWO was Lieutenant Sarah Conway, who admitted she knew little about electronic warfare, nowhere near what her team knew, but wore the Electronic Warfare Officer's title because they were her division. Also up before the Captain in the morning was one of the Deputy Marine Engineering Officers, from the DMEO's division, with an artificer who had taken a swing at another in the K section ratings' mess.

Nick Bennett was a full career officer. He had got his third stripe and this ship at thirty-nine years of age, young in a Navy where there were good seagoing officers awaiting their first drive at forty-two or forty-three. He was the product of a naval family and a good public school, immersed in enough tradition to have kicked against it when young but now old enough to appreciate it. He was married with three children, the family home in the shadow of the South Downs in the West Sussex hamlet of East Harting, just half an hour from the naval dockyard at Portsmouth. His brother was a successful businessman and his sister was married to the local MP, but while he was a seagoing officer he saw little of either of them, preferring to spend his rare shore time with his wife and children.

He looked up as his steward put a tray down on the table. It was one of his eccentricities: he only drank tea in the afternoon and then it came in a pot laid out on a tray, as it should be, with bone china cups that he bought himself. As the ship moved beneath him, he poured his tea, pleased that they were homeward bound after a safe, successful deployment.

Sister Helena died on the way in, but Sister Marie lived long enough to get to the US Embassy compound where their doctor, a man in his fifties who had been in Vietnam and who had seen many many gunshot wounds, did his level best. She died that night with renal failure, the direct result of a 7.62 intermediate bullet having hit the pelvic bone and tumbled upward through her body lodging in the kidney.

David Culverhouse, still in bloody clothing and drinking Heineken straight from the can was being interviewed at the British Embassy. Leaning over a map, he showed them where the incident happened.

'You're sure the first roadblock was NPFL?'

'Ya. That's confirmed.'

'The second one about here?' the man asked, pointing to the map.

'Ya. At least two miles, maybe two and a half, further back this way.'

'They are through, then,' the man said with some finality.

'They were Ulima,' Culverhouse said. 'Definitely.'

'We had other reports this afternoon. They moved

25

through the bush. While NPFL were on the road Ulima came round the side. They'll be in Paynesville by now.'

'Shit . . .' Culverhouse shook the beer can beside his ear. Still some left. 'You think they are coming all the way here, into Mon?'

One of them nodded. 'The Americans are trying to talk to Johnson. Get him to negotiate, but as usual it's difficult to find him. NPFL are redeploying. But yes, I think they are going to come in this time. They'll be here by this time tomorrow.'

'Well there's nothing for them to stop for in Paynesville. They went through that place a few months ago,' Culverhouse said finishing his drink. 'You know, I like kids, eh? I mean, I'm here with Save the Children, but I tell you, if the rest of them are as bad as the little fuckers we met today, then the sitrep here is shit.'

'You say you ran over one?'

Culverhouse nodded, his eyes narrowing for a second, the memories of the feel of the wheels going over the boy vivid. The third secretary smiled. He liked Dave Culverhouse. The young man had provided him with a lot of intelligence over the last two years, and debriefing him after one of his frequent trips up country had become a pleasure.

'Couldn't be helped. You and Sister Michael are alive and well. You would all be dead if you hadn't acted when you did.'

'Ya,' Culverhouse said, 'but maybe I should have acted sooner. Then we'd all have walked away.'

'Hindsight is always twenty-twenty. You have talked your way through fifty, maybe sixty roadblocks. There was no reason to think this one would be different. Go home, get cleaned up, then let your people know. I'm going to talk to the Ambassador. He's in a meeting just now. I believe he will be contacting British and friendly nationals by tonight, advising them of the situation and suggesting

26

they might want to move into the compound. The Americans have started and ConLib have closed three of the access routes into the village.'

Culverhouse nodded. Consolidated Mining Liberia was the single largest business in the country and employed thousands of local people as well as several hundred expatriates. The expats were housed in a huge compound the size of a small town in the west. When Consolidated Liberia Mining closed access to their self-contained residential village with its admin block, shopping centre, cottage hospital, and club and rec facilities, things were getting serious. There were four roads in, but if they wanted to tighten security they normally closed two by simply moving a huge trailer across the road behind each of the gates. On the outward side the trailer had been given a skirt of six-inch railway sleepers that dropped to the ground and a foot out from that was a screen of wire mesh, a lesson learnt after a rocket-propelled grenade had been fired at the compound in '94. He had never heard of them shutting three gates. This would be all they needed, he thought. The word was that the renegotiations for the vast mining concessions were almost complete, and security and the ability to do business was always high on the joint venture partners' agenda come the renegotiation time.

An hour later, using sophisticated communications gear, the British Ambassador contacted the Foreign and Commonwealth Office in London and two hours after that, a series of hurried meetings over in Whitehall and some contingency plans dusted off, a senior official of the FCO contacted the Ministry of Defence at Northwood.

Northwood, long-time operational headquarters of the Royal Navy fleet operations and one of only two MoD facilities equipped for full NATO command, had more recently been given a wider role. It was now the home of the Permanent Joint Headquarters and consequently its staff included Royal Air Force and British Army personnel.

PJHQ was currently under the command of an army General but it was to the Director of Naval Operations that the MoD went, to explain the worsening situation in Liberia and to see what support the Navy could offer if it became prudent to evacuate British nationals and those of friendly countries. The DNO, a Commodore, immediately contacted ACOS Ops, the Assistant Chief of Staff, Operations, at Northwood. The huge hi-tech deployment board showed the disposition of the fleet, Her Majesty's warships, submarines and auxiliaries scattered across the globe performing one function or another. In the Arabian Gulf the Armilla patrols continued, there was the frigate, HMS *Brave*, on guardship duty in the Caribbean, the ice patrol ship HMS *Endurance* was on routine patrol in the South Atlantic and the aircraft carrier HMS *Illustrious* with her squadron was supporting the NATO presence in the former Yugoslavia.

HMS *Fearless*, the old assault ship, had just arrived in Gibraltar for an exercise with her company of Marines and there was a clutch of movements in and around the base for the fleet in Portsmouth and the Channel.

But the eyes of the Fleet Operations Officer were drawn to the warship that was off the west African coast northbound for home. HMS *Beaufort*. Nick Bennett's drive. 'Sorry chaps,' he said aloud. 'Looks like a little delay for you.'

He went into his office and looked up the mobile number of one of the staff of the FOSF, the Flag Officer Surface Flotilla. They were all on their way back to Portsmouth after a visit to Whitehall and the staff all carried newish digital phones, but even so nothing would be said over the air. It was answered a few moments later.

'Hello, Philip? Roger Witchall. Good day? . . . excellent, excellent. Look, something's come up. Can you get the boss to phone in please?' That meant a land line or a secure telephone somewhere.

*   *   *

In the wardroom the evening meal, supper unless an occasion demanded increased formality when it was called dinner, was run over two hours. The early sitting was for those going on watch or who had duties that required their presence. It was just as well, because the wardroom table only seated ten and there were sixteen officers. Kitson as the chairman of the mess tried his level best to prevent there ever being an assumption that the more senior people, the heads of departments, mostly Lieutenant Commanders, took the later time, but inevitably the second sitting was top heavy. They had opened the wet bar and had a couple of drinks while the first bunch, mostly in working rig, ate. Kitson walked in, hair still wet from a shower, to a burst of laughter from the group seated by the bar. It was always the same when homeward bound, loved ones and friends getting closer.

'There's too much morale in here!' he called, taking a can of beer from the small fridge by the door and joining the others. At the table as early diners finished the places were cleared and relaid and the second group, in evening seagoing rig of open-necked shirts and cummerbunds, made their way to their places, Kitson as the First Lieutenant and chairman sitting at the head of the table. Protocol demanded that, whatever time he sat down, his place was left vacant until he had finished and only then might another take his seat. In these modern days wardroom dining was by comparison very relaxed, but some traditions were still observed. As people sat down they took their table napkins in rings from the pigeon holes and carried them to their seats, the steward hovering ready to serve soup. Kitson sat down at the head of the table.

At his right sat Aubrey Montagu. Known as 'Orbs', he was a watchkeeping Lieutenant and also the ship's Communications Officer. Montagu was a throwback. From fine noble blood, he was a superb seaman with a wonderfully sardonic view of the world. His family, although burdened by death duties and crippling running costs like all the owners of England's ancestral homes, were still seriously wealthy, which made him a man who was at sea because he loved it and this was reflected in his dry humour. Next to him was Lieutenant Steve Mayberry the P1, pilot on the Lynx helicopter, and round again was Lieutenant Commander 'Jack' Denny, Ops and Principal Warfare Officer, or PWO. Lieutenant Commander Charles Fripp, the Marine Engineering Officer, MEO, and his number two Lieutenant Ian 'Tex' Marshall, the Deputy MEO, came next, sitting at the far end. The two engineering officers got along famously, and even spent leave time together, rebuilding an ancient S-type Jaguar.

Robert Scott, also a Lieutenant Commander, the Weapons Engineering Officer or WEO, came next and next to him Lieutenant Andrew Therdy, the Supply Officer. Gordon Dow the PWO(U), the specialist anti-submarines officer, was in the middle, with Sarah Conway sitting on Kitson's left. That put Sarah at roughly the opposite end of the table from Tex, the DMEO, but the banter started immediately.

'Looking forward to getting home, Bob?' he asked.

'Yeah. Like all of us, but I won't be phoning ahead when I arrive,' she replied. It was an old joke, the sailor who has arrived home to find two large black fellows in bed with his wife, vowing to always phone ahead first in future.

'Ah yes. Winston and Leroy,' he smiled.

'No just Winston. Leroy is over at my place,' Mayberry said morosely, looking at his soup as though it contained something alive. 'Grindy pepper, please, and the chilli wine. Give this some taste.'

The chat continued and it was just after the second course arrived that the main broadcast system cut in.

'*XO, Navigator and Comms to the bridge.*'

Someone raised an eyebrow, but Kitson merely looked at the steward as he stood up. 'Keep it warm, please.'

Montagu stood as well, neatly folding his napkin. 'Me too, please.'

As the door closed behind them Sarah looked down the table, but no one seemed any the wiser. The Jimmy, the Navigator and the Communications Officer meant something was happening. New orders and a course change at least, and something that required Orbs in the comms suite (MCO) with his division of ratings. That was not routine. That meant coded traffic coming out of Northwood. She looked at her watch: 1900 Zulu. After hours.

'Bugger,' someone said softly.

2

Commander Bennett was standing with Lieutenant Morris in the navigator's area behind the bridge when Kitson and Montagu arrived. The area was curtained off with heavy black drapes to keep the light from ruining the night vision of those on the bridge and as they squeezed in Morris was spanning a set of dividers across the chart on the table.

Wordlessly Bennett handed his XO a printed message from the MCO and as Kitson began to read it Morris looked up from his calculation. It matched that from the Global Positioning System's computer to the minute.

'At twenty-eight knots, helo distance by 0400 hours tomorrow. We can be standing off by 1100.'

'Very good.' Bennett looked across at Kitson as he handed the message to Montagu.

'Peter, I might want you to go ashore in the helo. You will be bringing someone out to brief us. While you are there get a good look at the layout, the geography as you go in, with a view to a possible evacuation. It might be our only chance to overfly the area. For this exercise assume no local support or clearances. You will drop into the compound and then out again the same way.'

'I could borrow a video camera from someone,' Kitson suggested.

'Good idea.'

'Who are we bringing out, sir?'

'Third secretary,' Bennett answered. Montagu smiled, thinking: third secretary, bollocks, he's a bloody spook. Bennett went on. 'Aubrey, let Northwood have our position. Let them know we are changing course now, standing off Monrovia 1100 hours tomorrow. Then raise the Embassy there. Use secure comms. Let them know we are under way and that our helo will be there in the morning – let them know exactly when later. Ask 'em if we need clearances or anything. The Americans use helicopters into their compound all the time and there's probably no civil authority who would be bothered answering anyway, but ask the question. Clear?'

'Sir.' Montagu nodded. He had two ratings in the MCO and they would be getting to the end of their watch. Not enough. It was going to get busy in there.

'Right. Pilot, new course please. Peter, I want officers for a briefing at . . .' he looked down at his watch '. . . 2200 hours. In your wardroom, if I may.'

'Of course, sir'

'And get your P1 up to speed if you will.'

'Captain, any chance this is going to mean armed blue-jackets ashore?'

'We've seen this sort of thing recently in Albania, and only three months ago in Sierra Leone. Quite possible.' He nodded.

'I think it might be a good idea to bring Chops(M) into the loop.'

'You're right. Get him along as well.'

Back in the wardroom Kitson slipped into his seat and waited till the steward brought his plate back before looking down the table at Steve Mayberry, the ship's helicopter pilot. 'Get together after supper please, Steve?'

Mayberry nodded and put his hand over the top of his glass. Stop drinking? Kitson nodded and the exchange was seen by everyone, so he came clean.

'Monrovia,' he began. 'Liberia. It's gone pear-shaped. Two, maybe three armed factions about to meet head-on in the capital. There's much toing and froing, but we may have to stand off to evacuate British and friendly nationals. All officers, Captain's briefing in here, 2200 hours. The navigator will hold the watch. Pass the word, please.'

He took a mouthful of food and chewed slowly. Get a ride in the budgie, if nothing else he thought. Talk Steve into letting him fly back to the ship and get a couple of hours in.

Chops(M) found the rating he was looking for on 'Burma Road', the main passageway that ran the length of the ship on 2 deck outside the Wrens' accommodation space in J section.

Kate Wallace, like the other Wren ratings, had been in *Beaufort* for nine months. She was a southerner, from the New Forest, and had come to the ship as a trained weapons artificer. She was, as her friends agreed, one of those girls who always attracted the wrong kind of men, but cheerfully acknowledged they were normally more fun. And when ashore, with her dark curly hair down rather than tied back in the short pony-tail she wore at sea, she was pretty enough to keep them coming. She was smart, ambitious, but too lazy ever to excel, too ready to duck out of things where she could have shone. When the Chief Petty Officer (Missiles) pointed a finger at her and said 'You', out of the corner of his mouth, she knew she had been caught out.

'Your mess deck.' Wilks jerked a thumb towards the door. She led the way back in.

'Permission to enter the mess,' he snarled.

'Yes.'

The door closed behind them. There was one other girl reading a book in the living area, but he ignored her. This was as private as it was going to get.

'Fire drill on the noon watch. You pissed off.'

'Wasn't me, Chief,' she began.

'Don't fuck me about,' he snarled. 'I saw you. Do you think I need glasses?'

'No, Chief Petty Off—'

'Do you know what will happen to you if you get Captain's table?' he cut in.

'No.'

34

'No. Well let me tell you. You are out. Through. You will be put ashore in Pompey. The Captain will not have anyone on this ship who does not take fire seriously and neither will I.'

'Yes, Chief,' she said, but something in her voice told him she was just going through the motions, looking over his left shoulder. He hadn't made his point.

He pulled his shirt open. 'Look at this! Fuckin' *look* when I tell you!' She looked down at the ugly scars that covered his chest and shoulders. The scarring made by burns and subsequent skin grafts. 'You have never seen one of these burn. I have. I was in *Sheffield*. It gets hot. Heat that melts plastic, skin, eyes. Everything burns. There is nowhere to go. Nowhere to run to.' He paused for a moment before continuing, his voice low, intense. 'You get a fire. You fight it. You put it out. If you don't put it out, shipmates die and you get burnt. I was lucky. I lived.' She was looking at the scarring. 'Eighteen operations. You never get used to the pain and no man would ever look at you again.' She swallowed and nodded. 'Happens again, it's Captain's table. Understand?'

'Yes, Chief Petty Officer.'

After he left she sat down on the seat and the other girl put her book down. She had seen it all. Cheryl Simpson was a chubby, rounded individual who lacked confidence in everything she did but remained a happy young woman. She rarely had anything unpleasant to say about anyone and was forever smiling. In her first weeks on the ship she was seasick at the slightest motion, but continued working with a stubbornness that earned respect. The two girls were as different as chalk and cheese. Hardworking, rather plain Cheryl, daughter of a school dinner lady and an Oxford garage owner, who had only ever had one boyfriend and had agonized over the decision to let him go all the way on a weekend coach trip to Bournemouth, and Kate who was brighter, prettier, lazy and used her sexuality like a tool. The bond had grown over the months and each girl, forced to live alongside someone they would never have socially chosen, found something of themselves in the other. Of the twenty women ratings in the mess, they were the odd couple.

'Never mind,' Cheryl said. 'It could have been worse. He could have reported it.'

'Oh, piss off,' Kate snapped. Cheryl said nothing, but understood. The Chops's message had sunk home. The anger was that of realization, but it faded quickly.

'Sorry, I didn't mean that,' Kate mumbled.

'It's okay,' Cheryl said, pleased. The apology was unusual. Kate usually came off the back foot fighting. 'Let's get a video out. What about *Backdraft*?'

They both started to laugh. Pompey was only days away now and they were looking forward to getting home.

The British Ambassador in Monrovia was not the typical professional FCO career diplomat. Liberia was not a fast track posting, the sort of place that one expected to see as in the formative years of a diplomat's CV. Nor was it a sleepy backwater, undemanding of intellect, skills or ability. It was a posting that required consistency, toughness, experience, bags of common sense and a good deal of instinctive response. As the country spiralled into its nasty civil war after the death of Doe, it was not just another African dream turned sour: this was Liberia, with its heavy African-American influence and massive funding making it more interesting to any commentator. Then it slipped further into a brutality that would rival Rwanda or anywhere else in Africa, surprising even the most jaded observers, who watched as the warlords, following no agenda but their own, began to fight over the spoils. The country had been looted by the factions, who displayed the attributes of armed robbers or plundering invaders rather than of political parties. The warlords tagged their groups with 1970s revolutionary names like the National Patriotic Front of Liberia or United Liberia Movement, but they were solely intent on becoming powerful enough to take whatever they wanted as if by right. By 1996 there was nothing left to loot. Anything of value had been stolen, sold or destroyed and the people of Liberia lived in fear of anyone and everyone who came to their villages and homes. United Nations peacekeepers in the form of ECOMOG tried to keep the factions apart, while teams of weary negotiators, usually American, tried to broker the next ceasefire or the next election, but nothing changed. The only intervals of peace came when the combatants were too weary to fight and the faction leaders spoke of free elections and jobs and peace while planning their next move.

Any western ambassador in Liberia needed the patience of Job, mental and physical robustness and an understanding and acceptance of the gritty realities. Like William Black, the British Ambassador. The Embassy had only reopened two years before and again there was discussion in Whitehall as to whether it was required at all. He had a very small team, just four full-time people: James Aitcheson as second secretary, Tony Wisher, a nominal third secretary who didn't really report to him but was the intelligence officer, an aid co-ordinator and the wife of one of the Brits at ConLib, employed locally to manage consular affairs, do some typing and deal with any remaining tasks. The building was busy, however, with a clutch of aid workers from various charities occupying offices. They would rather have been in their own villas and compounds, but here they could at least get a telephone line that worked, assist each other and, simply by their presence there a couple of days a week, subtly exert the Embassy's influence to get shipments cleared through the ports, permits arranged and suchlike. The Ambassador officially looked after the interests of nationals of Ireland, France, the Netherlands, and many Commonwealth countries, but in reality any westerner whose country did not have representation in Liberia could call on either the British or American Embassy for assistance.

Black knew West Africa well, having come to Liberia after a posting in Ghana. While he had suits in the wardrobe he habitually wore open-necked short-sleeved shirts, with a tie in his desk in case of need. An advantage of his rank was that he rarely wore shorts, although he was happy for the rest of his people to do so if they wished. He was an energetic man who would never sit in one place for long and if he had to he was still in constant movement, leaning forward then back, rocking on his chair. It was something others found unnerving and he used it. Sandy hair, receding, glasses, medium height and build, made up a very average appearance which concealed a formidable intellect. While at university he had jokingly completed a Mensa application test, which his room-mate had secretly sent off. The response from that august institution of people with very high IQs described him as 'seriously bright', even by Mensa standards, and implored him to become a member. He never did. He hated clubs and institutions and spent his university years playing rugby and cricket, both badly, squash rather well, and to no one's surprise was awarded a double first in History. Alongside good French, he spoke passable Spanish and fluent Portuguese, and he married a nurse whom he met while recuperating after falling off a friend's motorbike and breaking his leg.

Maggie Black was the anchor around which the Embassy swung. Solid, practical and still for her husband the only woman in the world, she would be cutting sandwiches for an aid team that had just arrived from up country, with bread she had baked, and fifteen minutes later, a smear of lipstick on, hair brushed and a clean dress, she would be greeting guests for an informal function. She was discreet, loyal and the perfect foil for Bill, who they both knew would spend his career in trouble spots round the world, doing what he did best: representing the interests of Great Britain in hugely demanding circumstances in places that many wished they could just forget. She was happy at the moment. Her sister Poppy was with them for a month. Nine years younger, Poppy was very like her older sister, leggy and full-breasted, with the family's wide smile, but she was heavier, more curvaceous. The other difference in appearance was that Poppy was blond, her hair almost white, where Maggie's was a rich chocolate brown.

Bill Black was on the telephone with a meeting waiting to start. It was informal, just him, James Aitcheson, a bright youngster put there to learn his craft, and Tony Wisher. By the nineties MI6 was a lean organization and quite simply did not have the resources to staff every foreign mission as they might wish. Embassies that should have had three intelligence people had one, many that needed one had nothing, but Tony Wisher had arrived in Monrovia two years before, along with Black, as the situation there worsened. He was there not so much to feed classic military or economic intelligence back to Britain as to keep a close eye on the ever-changing moods and agendas of various warring Liberian politicians, his concern the safety of British interests and nationals. Black had never understood the need for an intelligence officer: feeding information gleaned from a network of locals back to London could have been done equally well by a military attaché; but he appreciated the extra pair of hands and Wisher's peculiar interpretation of events. He was often right, and in diplomacy, a gift for accurate prediction was essential.

A few minutes before, the lights had flickered and dimmed and then, as the power went down, the stand-by generator had cut in. It wasn't big enough to power all the air conditioners, so they limited night generator use for air-conditioning to bedrooms and a fan swished slowly overhead.

Black put the phone down and leaned back in his chair. 'Right, Tony. What's the latest?'

'Ulima have stopped for the night. They are north and west around as far as the Gbargna road, but the main concentrations seem to be Brewersville and Paynesville.

There are reports of fighters in Careysburg. Taylor's still here in Mon, but his people are on the move. These people don't fight pitched battles, as you know, but they will certainly be in contact and there are reports of fighting where they are. The interesting one is the sightings in Careysburg. That could be LPC. If it is, then Taylor has got them coming from both sides.'

'Planned?' Black asked. Did it matter, he wondered, even as he asked. This was West Africa. Anarchy was always only a shooting away.

'Who knows? Unlikely, I would have thought. If it is LPC then it might just be Boley capitalizing on the instability. Taylor will have to turn his attention to Gbargna.'

Black nodded. With Johnson's Ulima-J in a ramshackle, undisciplined, but nevertheless military advance from the north and Boley now flexing his muscles in the south, Taylor's NPFL central Liberian stronghold of Gbargna would be exposed. Taylor had the biggest faction, but if he had to split them to hold both the capital and his tribal areas he could be outgunned in either. He looked at Wisher, appreciating again his ability to make a plausible appraisal. He had just come in, having been out on the streets, and was grimy, dusty and sweaty. He came and went as he pleased and Black knew he had a network of local contacts and the use of a battered old Series Two Land-Rover that had been rebuilt and was now powered by a new engine. The vehicle belonged to a local man who owed Wisher favours; sometimes it was prudent to move about in a vehicle that was less obvious than the Embassy car with its diplomatic plates.

He looked at Aitcheson. 'So what's the count?' he asked.

Aitcheson looked down at his list. 'Including the Médecins sans Frontières people on their way in from Kakata and the Dutch who have just phoned in from Buchanan, it's two seventy-six.'

Black thought about that. If the normally stoical Dutch aid group in Buchanan, a fair way to the south, were

40

prepared to move into the diplomatic enclave in Monrovia, then things were very tense in the port city. That confirmed Boley was on the move, because Buchanan was NPFL held and usually functioned in its own ramshackle way whatever was happening around the country. Two seventy-six British and friendly nationals. The Americans would have more, mostly ConLib people. Their mission was larger, with fourteen full-time staff and eight Marine guards, stepped up from five the year before. The compound was also much larger and sported a real helicopter landing area, rather than the mown Kikuyu-grass lawn that the British had occasionally used – which bought Black to his next point.

'FCO have been at work. There is a Navy ship, the ah ... *Beaufort*, close by. She is on her way as we speak, to assist in getting people out should it come to that. Be here tomorrow morning. Their helicopter is coming in at first light. James, can you do your thing with the lawn again? Mark it out somehow? Good. Tony, you will go back out to the ship and brief them. I'd like a very visible presence. Obviously, if we need to start moving people out then the port would be best, but that may not be possible, so can you discuss with the Captain where he might best position himself to be seen by all. The Americans are beefing up their guard detail with people from Sierra Leone tomorrow lunchtime.'

Wisher nodded. He wanted the meeting over. He wanted to get out again. On the way back in he had seen three heavy vehicles towing trailers moving round to the south of the diplomatic enclave. The equipment looked as though it came from the remnants of the National Army, but they had all but been disbanded. The Liberian government was nominally controlled by a council of six men, of whom two in fact led warring factions, Charles Taylor and Roosevelt Johnson. Because no one could trust who the army might support in this period of chaos, the army, in the absence of a true government, reported to no one. Not paid for

41

over a year and restricted to barracks, many soldiers had simply deserted, walked out and joined the factions, where at least they could take what they needed at the point of a gun. If they were National Army and being deployed, then he needed to establish who they were out for, because that represented a shift in the balance of power.

'What news from ECOMOG?'

Wisher shook his head. 'None. I spoke to their liaison officer here this evening, but he's got nothing useful for us. He was hoping we could enlighten them. They are trailing a big Ulima element, but understandably they aren't too keen to try and get in front of them and halt the advance. They are trying to contact Taylor and Johnson to get them to agree a ceasefire, but both are incommunicado.'

None of them envied the Nigerian-led ECOMOG peace-keeping mission their task. It was thankless, dangerous work and Africa's first attempt at policing their own countries on behalf of the UN. The Nigerians were going at it with all the right intentions, but were defeated by the complexities, rather as the UN effort in the former Yugoslavia had been for so long. Wisher personally thought that European or preferably American contingents would have had more influence, but it was time for Africa to try and sort its own problems out. There was another factor in the stakes: credibility. Wisher had witnessed that problem two months before. An ECOMOG officer had been trying to move a band of Ulima-J fighters back from the road and one of their leaders, a political type with a cutting logic, looked at the Major and said, 'And you. You are Nigerian. Are you a role model for us? Are *you* from a fine democracy? Are *your* hands bloodless?'

'I'll try my NPFL contacts,' Black said. 'One of them must know where Taylor is.'

The door opened and Maggie came in with a tray of cold chicken and salad on plates. 'It's me, I'm afraid. I let Maxwell go off. He's worried about his family.'

Black nodded. Maxwell was the Embassy cook and he wasn't surprised that he wanted out. Africa was an odd place. In other parts of the world when trouble flared embassies usually knew that staff would want to bring their immediate families into the compounds and they made contingency plans for that, but not here. Maxwell's people were in a village some distance from Monrovia. He would go home and if it wasn't safe, then he would do what they had done since time immemorial: go into the bush and hide till the trouble passed. The gardener wouldn't be in tomorrow, either. He would have to keep an eye on the gate and the two bored policemen who were responsible for security. As the trouble got nearer Mon he knew they might just decide discretion was the better part of valour and evaporate.

'How are the troops?' he asked.

'My girls are just fine,' she replied. 'Poppy's on the phone and Philippa Davis has joined us. We only have a few to go and it's been on the World Service.' Black smiled. Maggie and 'her girls' were manning the phones at the two desks in the boxy little office that was the consular section, tracking down British nationals and others and advising them of the worsening situation. Someone had brought in a bottle of gin and sliced lemons in a little Tupperware container and raided Maggie's shrinking supply of real Schweppes tonic water.

'We have about forty in already. They have all brought picnics and what have you, but that won't last for ever. We've been telling people to bring plenty of food with them. I have had a couple of calls about the sisters,' she said. 'Will there be a funeral?'

Wisher shook his head in resignation. Some people, he thought.

'I doubt it. Not at the moment, anyway,' Black responded.

'That's what we told them . . . Oh and Tony, young Mr Culverhouse called in. Said you might want to give him a ring. And lastly,' she looked back at her husband, 'Ted Brooks is on his way over.'

Black nodded his thanks.

Beaufort's wardroom was gathered when Commander Bennett strode in followed by Chops(M), who had waited until the Captain arrived before entering the officers' wardroom: not that he would have been unwelcome before, but he was aware this was their space and respected that, just as they respected the CPOs' mess.

Kitson had got a steward to get a flip chart up from 2 deck and Bennett briefed them as well as he could, finishing by asking for questions.

'The Embassy grounds, sir,' Mayberry asked. 'Do we have any idea how big they are?'

'No, but they have had a helicopter in there before, apparently. There is an alternate at . . .' he looked down at the sheaf of paper he held '. . . the US compound, four blocks away. We are told that is much bigger with a sealed surface.'

Mayberry nodded. Fair enough. If they have had an aircraft in there before then no problem. They had no flying maps of the area, or even road maps with basic geographical features, but the Embassy was in the left centre of the diplomatic enclave: a main building with two smaller buildings either side like outriggers on a canoe, and the main building had a flat roof with a large GB painted on it in red. Should stand out like a dog's balls, he thought.

'Will we be taking them all the way home, sir?' the Supply Officer asked. It was his stores and facilities that would have to cope with the people who came aboard, and 280 extra people would stretch his stocks of food, drink, medicines, blankets, everything.

'Not sure. Probably not. We will drop them somewhere where they can fly home, I would think.'

'We can manage a day or two without too much trouble,' he responded, 'but any longer than that and things will start getting bland.'

'They're bland now,' someone muttered, and a few of them laughed.

Chops(M) raised his head so he was looking squarely over the Captain's shoulder. 'Sir. Will the XO be armed?'

Kitson and the Captain looked at each other. They had enough to think about and this detail had obviously escaped them. Chops(M)'s look at his Executive Officer said it all.

'Ah, yes. I think I might,' Kitson responded. Like most pilots his view was if you were close enough to use small arms you were probably buggered anyway, but this was different.

'Might it be a good idea if I come along, sir?'

'No, Chops,' the Captain replied, 'you have work here. I want the shore party selected and I want them up to speed. Begin at first light. Targets off the stern. XO?'

Kitson stepped forward. He had been in his cabin thinking it through: what he wanted in terms of resources ashore, enough, but no falling over each other. They were limited by weapons. The initial party might be only half a dozen, but even in a worst case scenario they only had thirty rifles on the ship. 'If it happens and we go in, there will be a shore party. Hopefully only five or six, but let's plan on needing more. Lots of presence. Thirty ratings. Three officers. Chops and myself. It will comprise three teams of eight with a PO and an officer. Chops(M) and I will float. We will look at detailed orders nearer the time, but our objective will be to go ashore, either by helo or by seaboat, and if necessary evacuate approximately two hundred and eighty civilians back to the ship. Officers will be Lieutenants Montagu, Buchanan and Conway.'

He had thought about that very carefully and Bennett had agreed when he had asked for the Wren officer. There were women and a handful of children in the group and she would add a woman's touch, maybe bring a bit of balance and understanding to the proceedings.

'We go ashore, and if we have to bring them off we do

it nice and quietly, hopefully without even seeing anyone who means them harm. No gung-ho, no bloody heroes. Remember, safety first. Small arms refresher training will take place at 0500 on the aft deck. Chops, who do you want?'

'You are going ashore armed before then, so I will have you in half an hour, sir.' His tone was saying: this is not negotiable, enjoying it. 'The others, all volunteers of course . . .' he began with a grin to name names, the ship's sec writing them down, all men he knew, their strengths and weaknesses apparent in the close confines of a warship, every now and then an officer commenting on someone they knew, one of their division.

Captain Bennett had assumed the worst case scenario, that they could not go alongside the hard in the port and would be bringing people off the beach. He knew the task would take time and time meant exposure to risk. Even using the helicopter, and with both of their rigid inflatable seaboats shuttling back and forth, it would take hours to move that many people. The *Beaufort* would have to be in close, and with each seaboat cramming people in with the two crew, five minutes out, five buggering about alongside as the boat was hoisted inboard (he didn't want civilians trying to use the rope boarding ladders), then seaboat away again and back to the beach – fifteen minutes a trip. The charts showed that most of the coast was exposed to the Atlantic. There might be a place or two where sandbanks or other features calmed the seas, but he had to assume that the beach nearest the diplomatic enclave was exposed to deep water and therefore there would be the chance of surf. The seaboats could cram in ten or twelve with the crew in good conditions, but if there was surf breaking then they would limit each trip to eight. Two boats would give them sixty-odd people an hour coming aboard. The helicopter, also bringing eight at a time, could probably manage six or eight trips an hour, maybe ten. Without breakdowns or hold-ups, everything running like a Swiss watch, three hours minimum. Allow for snafu. Double it. Too long.

Back in the hangar the ship's flight engineers were stripping heavy rack-mounted electronics from the Lynx. The gear, essential for finding and attacking submarines and surface ships, was unnecessary for the run ashore and certainly redundant weight. If they began lifting people out, that represented another person each trip.

Chops(M) was still calling out names, so Bennett looked across at Montagu and crooked a finger at him. The Lieutenant rose and moved across to his Captain who was standing by the door.

'Raise Northwood. See if they or the FCO have found anyone else in the area. If this goes off I want another helicopter, preferably something bigger than a Lynx.'

Bennett suspected he knew the answer. If there was another Royal Navy ship they would have known about it. The RFA *Gold Rover* was two days behind them at least, and her Sea King was being stripped in their hangar as they had parted company. If it had been repaired and was operable, then it could fly up to them and operate from their deck, but that would mean two aircraft operating off one limited landing and maintenance area, with all the risks that involved. Still, it was an option if things got worse. After all, he reasoned, they themselves were just moving in to stand off in case they were needed. The situation would have to escalate before the FCO were on the phone seeing which countries had ships nearby to assist. Wait and see, he thought. It will probably come to nothing.

The DMEO moved towards the door. 'May I be excused, sir? We have starboard seaboat engine stripped at the moment. I want to get it reassembled.'

Bennett nodded. 'Of course.'

Ted Brooks sat in the back while the driver, a local fellow, took the last half-mile slowly and carefully. They had stopped at their house to pick up more videotape and left again, leaving the morose producer and technician behind to disassemble the satellite transmission gear and pack it into the spun aluminium cases. It was a full van-load. They were tired, all of them. Brooks, his cameraman and the sound man had been on the road for thirty hours, trying to piece together what was happening and hoping for an interview with Johnson, but not even getting to see his usually urbane press secretary. Beginning to suspect why, he had headed back for Monrovia to try and contact Taylor, another man notoriously difficult to see, knowing also that with Ulima on the advance the main story would come to them – if he was right, then oh boy, wouldn't it just. The producer had met them at the door, telling them the embassies were phoning round and things were hotting up.

Brooks wasn't surprised. He had been born in Africa, Southern Rhodesia as it was then, of a British father and so had a British passport which made moving round the continent much easier. After training in Johannesburg he had immediately moved to London and worked on a broadsheet before being seduced by an offer from Reuters to go back to Africa and, based in Nairobi, cover the east coast. He had covered the Kenyan elections, the fighting in Eritrea, the famine in Ethiopia, the ongoing story of the Sudan. Reuters selling their news exposed their journalist to the American media who liked his pithy, no bullshit style and his extraordinary understanding of the African continent. He managed to explain it with a clarity and a humility that xenophobic middle America loved and CNN made him an offer he couldn't refuse. Now he had been CNN's West Africa correspondent for four years.

Without being aware of it, Ted Brooks was the archetypal foreign correspondent, right down to the forty Gauloises he smoked each day, the cream linen jacket he habitually wore, the alcohol he consumed, the jaded look of a man who had seen too much of life's brutality. He was doing the only thing he knew. He didn't know if he loved it, but he knew he would miss it if he stopped, because he was bitten by it, bitten when he was five or six years old. He had lived with his parents and two brothers in a small house in Salisbury. The neighbours were different, with things going on. It was a big flat-roofed house with a big garden and a swimming pool which he and he brothers were allowed to use and they, as children are, were fascinated by the residents. Two men, noisy, laughing, confident men, lived there between comings and goings and, with tut-tutting and disapproval from others who knew, they lived with two women. Women from Europe, who wore little, were big-breasted and attractive, who sunbathed naked, so it was said, on the roof of the house. You didn't do that in Rhodesia, not with servants wandering around. He had been up there once to take something across for his mother. The steps up to the roof were round, like a stack of coins leading upward, and there were thin mattresses and one of the women was there, with a tray of drinks and a record player and a thick paperback book face down beside her, its spine cracked, its pages worn. Robert Ruark. He had seen it before – his parents had a copy. She covered herself, slipping on her swimsuit top and walked back down with him and gave him a cold Coke from the fridge.

The men would arrive home and there would be laughter and giggling and parties and noise and for Ted and his brothers it was a wonderful thing, these larger-than-life men with their noisy, raucous, sexy women. He didn't know it then, who they were. They just smiled at the boys, ruffled their hair, one of them German, big, with a beard and flashing white teeth. He was Klaus and the other, the American, was Tom. Ted Brooks didn't know it at the time, but looking back he had been bitten then, bitten by the life those men led: that was what he wanted to do. Then one day, a day he remembered as though it was yesterday, there was crying and screaming from the house and he

49

and his brothers knew something had happened, because their mother went over and that was the end. There was no more laughter, no more parties there, the pool went green and the grass went uncut and the big house with its huge, semicircular steps up to the roof was silent.

It was a couple of years before he found out what had happened. Tom and Klaus had worked for CBS news and were covering the trouble in the Congo. They had got themselves attached to Mike Hoare's commando of mercenaries and Tom, the journalist, had had his head out of an armoured car, looking out, as they had rolled through a village. He had taken a bullet in the head and Klaus, his friend and photographer, sitting beneath him in the vehicle, had held him as he lay dying.

He looked out of the window at the dirty, tired streets, the sights so depressingly similar to the last big stories that he had covered on this coast. Sierra Leone back in June. A coup by the usual junior army officers followed by anarchy. Murder, butchery, rape and theft. And then the Congo, the Rwandan refugees who were chased into the forest never to be seen again. Africa. Brutal, beautiful, but unforgiving of the weak.

The edgy, nervous guard opened the gates when he saw the white faces inside the car and as it rolled down the short drive, Brooks could see lights on all over the compound and what seemed like lots of people. He looked back at his crew.

'See if you can find yourselves a cup of coffee or something. I'm going in to try and see Bill Black. Then get the gear out and get some footage of these people. We will do an update piece if nothing else.'

Two or three minutes later he was with the Ambassador and Tony Wisher, who Black had asked to remain behind. Black was prepared to do an interview, but only under certain conditions.

'You know the score in these situations, Ted,' he said. 'We shut the door and we share what we know.'

Brooks wasn't surprised and he knew that if he breached an off the record conversation his sources would dry up. One call from Black or someone like him and there wouldn't be a diplomatic mission on the west coast that would co-operate with him. And he suspected that Tony Wisher wasn't just the third secretary.

'Fair enough,' he replied. Wisher left the room and came back with bottles of cold beer from the fridge. Brooks took one and drank from the bottle, wiping his mouth as he finished.

'Right, we came back from Gbargna this afternoon. Lots of people on the roads, moving east. I spoke to people who had come from the north. Ulima is still rolling forward, but it's different this time.' He stopped to take another mouthful of beer.

'How do you mean?' Wisher asked.

'It's got a . . . a purposefulness it hasn't had before. You've seen it. Roving gangs that could have been an advance, stop, retreat, talk, haggle, loot, stop, change direction. It's usually without strategy. Not this time. This time it's driven.'

'What's your reading of that?' Black asked.

'Supposition only,' Brooks said carefully.

'Of course.'

He sipped his beer again. 'No one has seen Roosevelt Johnson for a while. I don't mean just westerners or journalists, but no one. Usually when he has dropped out of sight Garlo, his Chief of Staff, is around. Visible. But no one has seen him either. Ulima-J will function for a few days without them, but this? This advance? Unlikely.' He paused and pulled a packet of cigarettes from his pocket and lit one, carefully picking the loose tobacco from his tongue, his French brand untipped.

'Ever heard of Marriot Bokia?'

Black said nothing, but Wisher nodded imperceptibly. 'Rings a bell. Let me get my notes.' He was back a moment or two later, with four secretary's notepads bound together with a rubber band, and Black asked the journalist to continue.

'Again, only hearsay. Rising star in the Ulima ranks. Young, extreme. Word has it he hates Taylor, whites and Ameri-Liberians. Only twenty-nine. I think I saw him last year. Dangerous. Very dangerous. The hate came off him in waves. This fellow, if it's the one I saw at Johnson's camp, is very probably unhinged. Well,' Brooks continued, 'I was up above Tiene a week ago. The crossing into Sierra Leone?' The two diplomats nodded. 'Tracked down a man, seventeen going on sixty. Had enough. His eyes were back from the dead. Flat. Anyway, he was going across the border to look for his family, he said, but it was more. He was shit scared.' He shrugged. 'But money talks. Now again it's unsubstantiated, but he said that there was a bomb. Road bomb, he said. A land mine. Took out Roosevelt Johnson's car. I asked him which one. Long silver one. The boys kept everyone away from the scene. But this guy heard the blast and later his friend who had seen it confirmed it.'

'The Buick,' Wisher said.

'The Buick,' Brooks confirmed. 'Apparently Alfredo Garlo was with him.'

'So, the Ulima-J leader and his Chief of Staff. That is very interesting,' Wisher mused.

'Oh . . .' Brooks said, swallowing the last dregs from the bottle, 'it gets better, or worse. The vehicle hadn't even started to move. From what this guy told me, someone had dug the mine in under the wheel. The moment it rolled forward, kaboom. And the reason our friend at the border was so shit scared? The friend who saw it, who is no longer of this world, says Garlo at least was still alive after the dust settled, and guess who, allegedly, went in to finish the job with a machete?'

'Marriot Bokia,' Black answered succinctly.

'Correct. I was sceptical when I heard the tale. But now, as the days go by and this advance shapes up . . .' He shrugged. 'Any more of these?' he asked, waving the empty bottle gently, holding the narrow neck between thumb and forefinger. Black nodded at the tray of cold ones on the side table.

Wisher looked up from his notepads. 'It does ring a bell. Spoke to an American aid nurse a couple of months ago. A fellow arrived in her hospital demanding treatment. She remembered him not only because of the armed gang with him, who she described as disciplined, her word, but because everyone was terrified of him – the local staff, the patients. Gave his name for the test form but never came back for the results. She remembered the name too. It's unusual.'

'What was it?' the journalist asked.

'Syphilis. Advanced stages.'

'It fits,' Brooks said, thinking it through.

'Oh good,' Black said dryly. 'So, gentlemen, if your information is correct, we are now potentially dealing with a man in the advanced stages of syphilis who we believe hates African-Americans and whites, who has taken command, with a bomb and a machete, of the second largest armed faction in the country and who is advancing on the capital. Tony, do me a favour, phone Doctor . . . no, hang on. My wife was a nurse and her sister still is. Maggie?' he called. A few moments later it was not Maggie but Poppy who put her head round the door.

'Syphilis,' he began.

She smiled. 'Something you haven't told Maggie?'

He ignored her good humour. 'What can you tell me?'

'Oh . . .' she stepped into the room '. . . still a social problem. Treatable with drugs if caught early. If it's not treated it's usually fatal. Some years on,' she qualified. 'Starts with the normal STD-type indications, but they disappear as the disease settles in and slowly spreads. It's highly infectious at some stages.'

'Effect on reasoning, logic, behaviour?' he asked. He knew, he just wanted confirmation from someone.

'Eventually catastrophic. In advanced syphilis it affects the brain. Delusions, dementia, paranoia.'

'Are we talking about brain disease that would make someone dangerous, certifiable?'

'Oh yes, I would say so, but I'm not a doctor . . .'

'But you have seen it?' Wisher asked.

She nodded. 'It's unusual these days. In the west, that is. Early treatment. Good health education, awareness is the best solution. But I have seen it.' She paused. 'It's awful.'

The Embassy, like all official British missions, had a secure telephone link to London. It wasn't the line that was secure so much as the high-speed digital encoder that scrambled the voice at one end and allowed its sister machine to unscramble it at the other. When Wisher dialled a number in London, he knew that no prying ears were listening. Forty minutes after his call went through to Century House, the headquarters of MI6, a call came back through to him. His desk officer who had been sitting with friends in a Covent Garden restaurant glanced at his pager, excused himself from his party and took a cab back to the office. Once there he telephoned Wisher and they spoke for fifteen minutes. The desk officer thought for a few minutes, then made a call to the FCO, where at that moment a permanent secretary was talking to William Black. He said he would call back and the desk officer then rang his superior, the head of the African desk, to bring him up to date. The senior man thanked him and said he would talk to the FCO, suggest they apprise Joint Staffs at the MoD.

They did so and they also stepped up the game two levels and telephoned the Foreign Secretary, to brief him on the new intelligence. He in turn asked for a morning briefing from the Security Service and the MoD and telephoned his counterpart, the Minister of Defence.

At Northwood a three-man team headed up by ACOS, the Assistant Chief of Operations, a Rear Admiral, looked at the developing scenario and made a contingency decision.

HMS *Fearless*, the veteran amphibious assault and command ship currently in Gibraltar, would be advised of possible new orders and to prepare for deployment. Her Captain responded within fifteen minutes. Many of his crew and contingent were ashore on leave. They would need to be contacted. They were also due to take bunker oil and supplies on the following day, but he could move everything forward and be under way by 1200 noon.

On board *Fearless*, or more correctly, based on board *Fearless*, but ashore in the bars and night-spots were the 120 men who made up Zulu Company of 45 Commando Royal Marines. Equipped for an exercise they could be issued live ammunition and ordnance from *Fearless*'s stores and deployed if required, but at the moment that seemed very unlikely indeed.

Northwood were well aware that she was an old ship and her top speed of twenty knots was slow by modern standards. Even if she ploughed southwards with every old rivet shaking, that still put her three days away. It wasn't ideal. She would prepare to leave and if they reviewed the situation in the morning they could always order her to stand down. In the meantime they would prepare to support HMS *Beaufort* with some specialist personnel, a resource appropriate to a warship that might need to put bluejackets ashore.

The Royal Marines liaison officer was telephoned at home and within a few minutes he was heading back to Northwood. He had declined the offer of an official car: it was quicker to drive himself.

At Northwood he was quickly briefed and he in turn contacted Northwood's senior Royal Marines officer, currently a Colonel on the Operations staff. The Colonel listened to the liaison officer, asked two or three questions and then responded.

'Fine. I'm coming in. I think we should get a recce troop ready. Get on to Condor. Advise 45 that their recce troop is to move at . . .' he looked at his watch: get to Northwood, see what's happening, an hour, advise HQRM '. . . 0500 hours and report back if there is a problem with that. You say that *Beaufort* is standing off by tomorrow. Getting them in to the ship will be the problem. We'll want air liaison.'

'He's here, sir.'

'Very good. I'll see you shortly.'

The Marines liaison officer then telephoned the Officer of the Day at Condor Barracks, the Royal Marines base in Arbroath in Scotland, currently home of 45 Commando and the Commachio Group.

At that moment twenty men, none of whom had any idea of the situation in Liberia and most of whom would not have known exactly where to find it on a map, very tired men, were throwing their bergens and kit into the backs of two trucks. They had been out for five days on an advanced survival skills course. They were young, very fit and highly trained. It wasn't a long drive back to camp. The course location had been chosen deliberately so the men could be recalled and back to camp inside an hour, but that hadn't made it any easier, and as the truck engine braked its way down the steep Scottish road towards their barracks the men were beginning to relax, looking forward to a hot cup of tea and in a few hours a hot breakfast. For now the main galley would have soup and bacon sarnies for the lads coming in, something their young officer had made sure of organizing when he pulled the rug from under them and added the extra miles to the exercise. His lads had sworn, bitched, rehitched their bergens and yomped the rest of the way in four and half hours, this after five days in the field eating lichen, nettles and other vegetation, which wasn't the best thing to keep blokes happy. Lieutenant Andrew Gordon was chuffed. His lads came through as he knew they would: he'd expected nothing else. They were Royal Marines. The best. The recce troop of Support Company of 45 Commando, in barracks at Condor with X-Ray Company and Yankee Company, currently the fleet standby rifle company.

The fleet standby rifle company was just that: the Royal Marines element trained and designated to support the fleet wherever and whenever required. But any move by the fleet standby rifles would be preceded by their commando's advance element. Part of the support company and on two hours' notice to move, the advance element was the recce troop. There were various specializations in the troop's strength, including men who were mountain and cold weather warfare trained, men who had done demolitions courses, a couple who had done a tour with the Special Boat Squadron, and all were parachute trained. The recce troop could provide a number of highly skilled Marines, a small formation, its size determined by the task, to be deployed in any number of scenarios from first arrivals in a disaster zone to a full escalating military operation or, as in this case, to support other resources in a specific incident. Both at Northwood and at Condor, a basic contingency plan was activated and the Colonel, the Commanding Officer of 45 Commando, was with his Support Company Commander and his Intelligence Officer.

When the two trucks rolled into Condor with Lieutenant Gordon's platoon he was a little surprised to see the lights on in both the company offices and the main block, the OC's car outside. The Corporal in charge of the guard detail on the gate waved his truck to a halt.

'Lieutenant Gordon. Report to the company commander immediately please, sir. He's in the HQ Building with the OC. Your men to remain in company lines.'

He nodded, thoughts going through his mind. Something's on, but the lads won't be pleased having to wait here. Many of them were married and lived down in the 'patch'. They wanted hot showers, clean kit.

'Thank you,' he responded, nodding to his driver.

Four minutes later, dirty and tired, he knocked on the door and walked in and saluted.

'Excuse my appearance, sir.'

'Come in, Andy,' the Colonel replied. 'Good exercise?'

57

'Very good thanks, sir.'

'Good.'

'You're under notice to move from 0500,' his company commander said, coming straight to the point. 'May want you down to HMS *Beaufort* with your troop. She's off West Africa. We are just putting it together now. Get over to the mess, get cleaned up and join us back here.'

Gordon nodded and flicked a look at his watch. Twenty past one. 'Sir, my lads are sitting over by the transport. Main Galley is expecting them. I'd like them fed.'

'Good,' the Colonel said, smiling. Health and welfare of one's men was paramount. This young officer had used his initiative and called a favour to get the Main Galley open. 'Send them over. Then let them go. Everyone back by 0430 hours. By then we will know who you are taking with you.'

He couldn't resist. 'What's the job, sir?'

'Probably nothing, but it may happen. Monrovia in Liberia. It's looking like we will be evacuating nationals. It's likely that *Beaufort* will have to put crew ashore to assist.'

He said no more, but he didn't need to. Gordon nodded. Sailors were good on ships. That's what they did. They were not trained or equipped to be deployed ashore. They would do it, but they didn't like it. That was why there were Marines. Had been for over two hundred years.

Beaufort's twin Rolls Royce Spey gas turbines were pushing her as fast as they would go without stressing her design limitations. In some civilian ships it was called 'top of the green', that edge on a revolutions counter before the needle went into the red. Her diesel electric motors, designed for stealth, were shut down and the officer of the watch, had her 'up on the gas', the twin turbines each delivering 20,000 horsepower down the shafts, turning the propellers 195 times a minute. (Frigate officers, unlike those on faster destroyers where power was ordered in percentages of what was available, call for the number of revolutions of the propellers they want and from what source.) She could go to over 200 revolutions before the MEO began threatening that things would break, but he didn't need that. The sea state was calm and this 29 knots would have her on station on schedule.

Other than the bridge and engine room people on watch, the ship was largely silent in her cruising state, the captain's orders clear. Everyone to get their rack time, everyone except two weapons artificers who were stripping, cleaning and checking the contents of the armoury including the four big general purpose machine guns. Chops(M) had looked at them, thought for a second and said, 'Get 'em out, too.' The GPMGs were the same model as the army's section weapon firing the old NATO 7.62 mm long round rather than the lighter, smaller ammunition fired by the newer SA80 rifles. Although they were on warships to provide a close-in anti-personnel defence capability, they did have bipod legs and straps and could therefore be taken ashore.

The two artificers, Leading Seaman 'Chalky' White and Kevin Baker, a killick, chatted easily as they worked, discussing the captain's address to the crew over the main broadcast system earlier.

'You reckon you in this mob, then?' White asked.

''Course I fuckin' am,' Baker replied. 'Other than Chops himself, and Godshall, I can handle these things better than anyone else on the ship.' He paused for a moment. 'Well, I better be,' he added. It hadn't occurred to him that he might be left out.

'Know soon enough, sunshine,' White said. 'Don't fancy it myself. Going ashore in Umbungo bungo land when the locals is 'ostile. What was that movie? Yeah, *Zulu*. Ever see *Zulu*? Thousands of the black buggers charging at the lads. Michael Caine as the toffy git officer. I'm more yer Stanley Baker type.' He looked up from the workings of the SA80. 'You know, up from the ranks, 'ard but fair. Officer of

Engineers. That's me.' He stripped the working parts back quickly and expertly, running his thumb over the firing pin, feeling for spring tensions. 'Na, those days are gone,' he continued sadly. 'This, this will be more like yer *Dogs of War*. Christopher Walken. Mercenaries in some banana republic.'

'Bollocks,' Baker replied. 'You watch too many videos, my son. Go ashore, pose a bit, bring off the bloody civvies so they can get in the way and puke everywhere and that'll be that.'

'Mind you,' White mused, 'might be some fresh totty amongst it. They might be grateful. You know, for being rescued by the brave jacks of the Beau. Reward us with their favours, like.'

Baker looked at him. 'You're a sad bastard, Chalky. Now get that weapon finished.'

White grinned, quickly reassembling the rifle, stacking it to one side and taking up another. 'That bird you pulled,' he said.

'What?'

'That bird you pulled. The one from the Blue Lagoon. She was a bit of all right.'

'Mmm,' Baker replied, looking down a barrel.

'D'ja see 'er again? I mean, she saw you right din' she? Out the back?'

'Mind your own fuckin' business.'

'You did, you bastard!' White grinned.

'I saw her out the next evening,' Baker said, slightly defensively. This was always the problem. You might pull someone, actually like her afterwards, and then the lads all know you had her within two hours, think she's a slut, and either want a crack at her themselves or think that no one should actually want her as a regular girlfriend because she was too easy, or both. Girls that were too easy or too physical were not good partners for sailors who were away so much of the time.

''Ere? That was the letter you got, wasn' it?'

Baker nodded.

'She were tasty,' White said, thinking back to the night in the club. He looked at Baker. 'You gonna see 'er again when you're back?'

'Dunno,' Baker responded. He looked up. 'She's probably shagged every jack in Pompey,' he said bitterly. It had been troubling him.

'But maybe not,' White said. 'They're not all like that.'

'*She* was!'

'Only once that you know of. You shag her the next night?'

Baker said nothing.

'Well?'

'No. Wouldn't let me. I dropped her at home. Said she was pissed the night before.'

'Well then. Give her a ring when we get back. When we've conquered the dark continent again.'

'It'll be volunteers only,' Baker said. 'If Chops asks. You coming?'

'Know what they say. Never volunteer,' White responded.

'You serious?'

'Naaa . . .'course not,' he replied, grinning. 'Bit of a run ashore. Get some local fags. A few rabbits from the voodoo trinket salesman. Yeah, I'm on for that. Anyway 'ose gonna look after you, ya soft git. You'll be paying too much for everything like in Monserrat. 'Ere, remember the XO?'

Baker grinned and nodded. Kitson had been going back to the ship with two of the other officers, Baker and White behind them, when he had found a turtle on the jetty. Caught by a fisherman, it was on its back, still alive, its little flippers up in the air. Kitson, a real softy with animals and something of a conservationist, turned it over and dropped it back into the sea and the fisherman, who suddenly appeared from down in his boat, was complaining and shouting, wanting the police. But for fifty dollars he would not call them. White moved up to them and suggested to the Jimmy that he just return to the ship. He would negotiate the compensation. A fiver and twenty Bensons later it was done.

If it came to it he would go ashore with the lads if he could, White thought. They couldn't be trusted on their own.

3

At 0557 local time the Lynx lifted off the deck and turned
her stubby snout north, running parallel to the coast. *Beaufort* was still 120 miles away from Monrovia itself, but the
Liberian coast was only forty miles off the starboard beam
and the Lynx could now safely get in and back without
needing fuel. Behind the aircraft against the rail Chops(M)
was running his weapons familiarization for the officers
and ratings that might be required to go ashore, the rounds
going out into the sea behind the ship. As the Lynx was
ready to engage rotors, the people shifted round towards
the ship's waist alongside the hangar and then, as the helo
lifted off, they moved back to the rail, one of them lugging
a bunch of yellow plastic containers tied together like
balloons on a string.

Lieutenant Mayberry, the P1, unlike in a civilian helicopter, was sitting in the right-hand seat, his observer on
the left. As they gained height, Kitson, sitting in a fold-
down winch operator's seat side-on behind them, watched
enviously Mayberry's right hand on the control column,
his left caressing the cyclic that rose like a huge handbrake
from between the seats with a motorcycle-like twist grip.
A strop had been connected to the frame above the sliding
door and lashed along the back wall was one of the ship's
four machine guns, with two full ammunition cases
beneath the seat on the other side and a rating, one of
the boarding party, dozing alongside the gun. The army's
Lynxes, Kitson knew, were equipped with 20mm cannon
and the weapon could be mounted on special hardpoints
in just over an hour, but the RN didn't use Lynx as a

ground attack platform so a borrowed machine gun hanging off a cargo strop was the best they could manage.

An hour later they were coming in the last mile, fast over the water, the waterfront suburb that was the diplomatic enclave spread out before them, the city and the port to the south. Kitson was at the door with the video camera he had borrowed, recording it all as Mayberry was lining himself up, coming in two-thirds of the way up the sea front.

There, over the land, power coming off, bleeding off speed, looking out, the observer's gloved finger pointing a little to their right. Mayberry saw it and began flaring out, long wall, grass, people, masses of bloody people, some waving, cars, GB on the roof, white pitch paint or something down on the lawn and someone waving the people back to the drive, away from the machine that was coming in.

Mayberry landed the Lynx on the marked cross and, as Kitson undid his lap strap, removed his helmet and prepared to jump out, he leaned across and looked at the XO, running a finger across his throat. Kitson nodded and waited for the pilot to shut down his engines. Then he dropped to the ground and walked towards the main building, where someone was coming out towards him, the sidearm on his belt feeling very conspicuous.

Some of the people who had been sleeping in their cars were grinning at him, raising thumbs, very pleased indeed to see the Royal Navy helicopter, others with a concerned look on their faces. Why were the Navy here? Did they know something? Maybe it was worse than they had been told? Kitson saluted and took the outstretched hand.

'Hello. I'm Aitcheson, number two here. Welcome to Monrovia.'

'Peter Kitson, First Lieutenant, HMS *Beaufort*.'

'Come in and meet the boss.'

Aitcheson was making the introductions when Poppy came in with tea for Black and Aitcheson. 'Oh, I'll bring another, shall I? How do you . . .'

Kitson smiled. 'White. No sugar.'

The meeting was quick and business-like, winding up with William Black asking if Kitson wanted anything from them.

'You don't have any local area maps, do you? The city, the port, surrounding area. Tourist things will do, if that's all that is available.'

'Tourists?' Black grimaced and smiled. 'Never been many of those. No,' he continued, 'we can do better than that . . .' the door swung open and Tony Wisher came in. 'Ah. There he is.'

He introduced the two men and went on: 'Tony has a full set of everything that's available. Some of it's quite new, produced by the UN for ECOMOG, some of it was done by ConLib . . .' Wisher raised his hand for quiet, cocking his head, and then they heard it, like fire crackers far away for two or three seconds before it died away.

They looked at him and he shrugged. 'Two miles away at least.' He grinned at Kitson. 'What the news will no doubt call a fierce clash.'

Black stood up. 'Your chaps have probably finished their tea. You will want to be getting back to your ship. My compliments to Commander Bennett. We appreciate his swift response. I'm sure Tony's briefing will answer many of your questions. The rest are probably unanswerable.'

'Can I ask you something, sir?'

'Of course.'

'Your diplomatic status here. Is it respected?'

'By and large, yes,' the Ambassador answered. 'But if you are asking are the people inside these walls safe, the answer is that the situation here is fast approaching anarchy.' He left it there.

'What is your security structure?'

'What you see. A decent wall, gates that close and lock and a two-man diplomatic protection detail.'

Wisher cut in there, the grin returning to his tired face. 'Local police. Not what you understand diplomatic protection to mean.'

'If a bit of a presence will help, I could if you wish have the helicopter return with an officer and some armed ratings,' Kitson suggested. He looked at his watch. 'They could be here by about nine.' As if to strengthen his point there was another distant crackle of gunfire.

'Thank you, Lieutenant Commander. I'm sure everyone would appreciate that. Give 'em all some peace of mind if nothing else.'

Four minutes later, Wisher in the helicopter with them, it lifted into the air and, staying low over the trees and rooftops, picked up speed heading seawards. Kitson had Mayberry fly north-west up the beach for two minutes, then south-east again, all for the camera, recording what he could – the sea front, the port area, buoys, channels and markers – before he nodded and pointed seawards.

Black had come out to see them off and was now walking round the people, stopping at each small group and chatting for a few moments, reassuring them. Some were disappointed to see the helicopter, their link with the outside, leaving and two men, one of them heavy, paunchy and florid, his face already perspiring in the morning sun, walked over to where Black was talking with a group of people.

'Can you please tell us,' the sweating one said, his tone insulting, 'why that helicopter left half empty? Not only did it leave half empty, but it seemed to be evacuating embassy staff, while we, all British . . .' he was about to say 'taxpayers', but stopped himself; that was why he was here: no tax '. . . subjects are left standing around?'

'They were here to assess the situation,' Black answered. 'It looks as though we will be evacuating and, if we do, that will begin later this morning when the ship is much closer than she is. Until then . . .'

'But if we are going to evacuate then why did it go half empty?' the man interrupted.

There were people gathering round them now, drawn

by the raised voice. 'It is not confirmed that . . .' Black began, his tone level.

'Look here, this isn't good enough,' he puffed. 'I am not dealing with you. I want to see the Ambassador, William Black. I've met him on many *official* occasions, and I'm sure he will see me.'

Black had never spoken to the man before, only shaken his hand in a reception line, but he had been pointed out by Aitcheson as a middle manager type at ConLib.

'Everybody is doing the best they can under trying circumstances. Please be patient. We will . . .'

'I want to talk to . . .' the man said, raising his voice.

'The Ambassador, William Black. Whom you have met on many official occasions.'

'Yes.'

'I am William Black, and I have never met you before. If you want to see me privately, make an appointment.' He turned and walked away. Some of the people who overheard began laughing; one man looked at the florid, sweating man and shook his head. 'You prat.'

The southern annex was the residence and most of the people were now spread out under the shade of the trees that formed the bulk of its garden. There was some order there now, with the camp beds people had brought with them set up in rows. The downstairs lavatory was the men's while the ladies were assigned the one upstairs. Aitcheson and Wisher had both given up their quarters in the northern annex to families with very young children, and a woman visiting her grandchildren from England was now in the Blacks' spare room suffering from malaria. Two doctors from Médecins sans Frontières, both French, had arrived very early that morning and diagnosed her condition immediately.

Maggie was round the side by the kitchen door, where with some of the wives she had organized a rudimentary catering facility. The young French manager from

Monrovia's only decent hotel had supplied big pots, pans and utensils from his kitchens. He had also raided his cold room and stores and the hotel's old van was now parked in the embassy driveway loaded with food. In the kitchen four or five people working in concert were now producing a meal of sorts from whatever people had brought with them to be added to the communal larder. There were now 250 people in the compound, the last stragglers still arriving every few minutes. Black walked over to where Maggie was, her sister Poppy beside her, leaning over a table slapping butter on to slices of bread. The slide in her hair had slipped and there was a dark smudge of something down her neck. She finished the loaf and looked to where one of the young English aid workers was slicing the bread, ran the back of her hand across her forehead as he approached.

'You've been looking again, haven't you?' he said softly with a smile.

She looked up and laughed gently. It was an old joke of theirs. Years before, after a reception where one local dignitary had punched another, a third had vomited all over the hall floor and the caterers had run out of ice, gin and soda water within the first half-hour, she had bent down and peered at the floor. 'What are you doing?' he had asked. She looked up and said, absolutely deadpan, 'Oh, you know. Diplomat's wife. Embassy parties. Beautiful people and all that. I'm looking for the glamour. It must be here somewhere.'

'How are we doing?' he asked.

'Just fine,' Maggie answered. 'Everybody is mucking in.'

Poppy looked up from her buttering. 'And here was I expecting to have a lovely, idle holiday,' she mused.

'Silly tart,' Black said fondly. 'You should have known better.'

'I should.' She smiled back. Black was about to move away when she went on. 'Bill. That naval officer,' she asked casually. 'What's his name?'

'Why?' Maggie asked with a raised eyebrow.

'Oh nothing really. I think I may have met him somewhere.'

'Porky pie.' Poppy smothered her grin. Bill always knew when she was fibbing, always had done. Maggie had stopped buttering and looked across with a smile.

'You fancy him, don't you?'

'No I don't,' she replied, too quickly. 'Don't be silly.'

'His name is Peter Kitson,' Black replied, knowing otherwise and trying to fathom what made men attractive to women. He knew he was bright, but this eluded him. She had only seen the man for a few moments when she had brought tea to the office. 'First Lieutenant on HMS *Beaufort*.'

'He seemed very nice.'

'He'll be married. The nice ones always are,' Maggie said sensibly.

On *Beaufort*, down in the depths of the ship in the Ops room, the helo controller took the radio transmission from Kitson and patched it through to Commander Bennett, who looked across the bridge at Jamie Buchanan, the officer of the watch, as he talked to his XO. He put the handset down and spoke quickly to the rating with the quartermaster. The rating repeated the order and spoke into the main broadcast system microphone.

'*Do you hear there? All executive officers to the bridge. Chops(M) to the bridge.*'

Bennett spoke to his watchkeeper. 'James, I am putting you and shore party in on the helo as soon as it's back. Briefing here in two minutes. Get ready, if you will. I have the ship.'

'You have the ship, sir,' Buchanan replied and was on his way down the steps to the officers' flat. He was back inside two minutes with the small bag he had packed earlier, in it a couple of garments from the purser's store. The other officers were there, as was Chops.

Bennett briefed them quickly and because he was about to lose the first of the four officers who would be going ashore, and this would affect the watchkeeping schedule, he moved the ship on to the first stage of active footing a few hours earlier than he had intended.

'Right, we were going to go on to defence watches as of 1200, but we shall move that forward to 0800 hours. Ops?'

The Ops officer, the XO in Kitson's absence, nodded.

'Begin with the port watch, change at noon, six on and six off thereafter.'

'Very good,' Bennett said. 'Mr Buchanan, your party on the helo deck ready to go as soon as it is refuelled. Anything you want?'

'I'll leave the choice of the party to Chops, sir, but I'd like to have comms separate to that of the Embassy. Mobile comms, both back to the ship, and if my party is split.'

'Take one of the Clansmans, and a couple of handhelds. Happy?'

'Sir.'

At the edge of the group the yeoman grinned to himself and when Buchanan arrived down at the hangar he was there in the party.

'What are you doing here?' Buchanan asked.

'Comms, sir,' the yeo grinned, looking up from the big radio set he was bent over. Buchanan looked at Chops, who rasped, 'There is always one wanker who thinks he is indispensable.' He passed him a rolled-up webbing belt with a sidearm in a holster. Buchanan took the kit and looked down at the machine gun.

'Do we need it?'

Chops shrugged. 'Never know. But if we do and we don't have it we are going to feel like a couple of cunts . . . sir.' Buchanan nodded.

'Everyone eaten?' he asked. They all replied in one form or another. 'Everyone happy?' Again the affirmative. 'Right, the helo is fifteen minutes out. I'll see you on the aft deck in ten minutes for a briefing.'

He got permission for the machine gun and went back up to the wardroom to get his kit and snatch some breakfast. Sarah Conway was at the table next to Tex, the DMEO, and she couldn't help but notice the heaviness of the rolled-up webbing that he dropped into his bag.

'Quick as you can, please. Muesli and toast,' Buchanan said to the steward. 'I'm going out. I . . .' he looked at Sarah, his face long and drawn like a forties movie hero. 'I might be a while. Bunty, I say, Bunty.' He reached across and took her hand. 'If . . . if anything should happen . . .'

'You're not taking this seriously, are you?' she remarked, pulling her hand away.

'Ha!' Tex said, joining in, throwing his head back and flicking an imaginary scarf. 'We laugh in the face of danger!'

She couldn't help herself and laughed and Buchanan grinned as the steward arrived with his cereal.

'I may not be, but Chops is. He's got a bloody machine gun out there.'

'And that's not all,' Tex chimed in. 'He's got thunderflashes, some smoke grenades . . .'

'See? Don't worry, Sarah, Chops will have the rebellion quelled and the natives at peace by the time you get there. Just like Beau Geste.'

'Bollocks,' she retorted.

'What time you coming in?' he asked through a mouthful of muesli.

She raised an eyebrow minutely, her version of a shrug. 'We'll be there elevenish. Sometime between then and twelve, I suppose.'

'Mmmm . . . seaboat. Hellish on the hair, darling. Never mind, we'll do lunch!' He finished quickly and, jamming two pieces of toast together to make a sandwich, stood up. 'Places to go, people to see! Must dash!'

'Oi, tosser,' Tex said, 'if you get shot can I have your skank?'

'Tex!' from Sarah, not appalled at the tasteless remark

or even surprised, but determined to try and maintain some standards of decency. Most of the men on the ship had top shelf magazines, skank, what one had described as 'the only way to remember what women look like'.

'Sure,' Buchanan replied, lifting his bag. 'But only if I get shot in the togger. Otherwise I'll need it.'

'That's not fair. How the hell will they ever hit your togger? It's smaller than a thimble,' Tex protested.

'Naa it's not. Ask your wife,' Buchanan retorted.

'One-nil, I think,' Sarah said as Tex winced a smile and dropped his head in acknowledgement of the finesse.

'See you later,' Buchanan said and stepped out of the door. Sarah, just for a second, felt a flicker of fear, a premonition of something. She shook it off and finished her breakfast.

Fifteen minutes later Kitson was leading Tony Wisher up the steps to the bridge to meet Captain Bennett and by the time the Lynx was lifting off again, with Lieutenant Buchanan, Chops(M) and six ratings, the briefing had begun.

Wisher had stuck the maps and several of the aerial photographs to the wardroom wall with Bluetack. He explained the latest intelligence to the core of senior officers gathered at the table, the remnants of breakfast barely cleared away, and finished up by pointing to the blown-up photograph on the right.

'So, I think the port is out of the question for the moment. It's too far, five miles away. We don't have transport and the exposure in trying to cover that distance with this number of people is extreme. Secondly, there is no one to give you permission to enter, or to handle your lines once you are in. Thirdly, I'm not sure it is secure anyway. I'm no seaman, but I'd have thought you are at your most vulnerable when tied up somewhere unfriendly.'

'Well put,' Bennett said dryly. 'Options?'

'One. The beach, for want of a better name – sand

mostly, rocks and litter and flotsam – is only three hundred yards from the compound. Round the corner, down the road, past the old Kenyan Embassy, past the USAID office and a few others, four sleepy intersections and you're there. At the bottom, here . . .' he pointed to the photograph '. . . is a deserted villa still owned by the Italians. It's close to the water. If anyone gets hostile we can bung people in there till it's over.'

'What about the beach?' someone asked. 'Does it shelve steeply? Is it wide? Is there surf?'

'There's a lip as you get to the high-water mark. About eighteen inches or so. Then grass, shrubbery and vegetation. The water isn't too deep. You can see the locals out fishing on calm days, maybe thirty yards out, chest deep. There can be surf, though. Never thought about it in terms of how big. Nice weather, no more than two feet at most, I'd say. If you chaps can manage that end of things, then let's hope for the best. On the up side, the fighting has never yet come into the enclave as such.' Wisher put down his marker pen.

'But you now suspect that the leadership has changed and we may be dealing with the unknown,' Bennett confirmed.

'Yes,' Wisher replied.

'There is a small detachment of Royal Marines coming to assist. An officer and twenty-odd men. They will probably get as far as Sierra Leone today and then if things are still tense, join us tomorrow.'

Buchanan, bored with looking at the sea, swept his eyes around the inside of the helicopter cabin. They were crammed in, eight of them plus a rating on the door gun, stretching the Lynx's total weight capacity to the limit. They could probably have squeezed in one more, but Mayberry had every pilot's respect for fuel load and, operating off a ship without alternative places to put the aircraft down, he wanted every pound he could put into his tanks; an extra person meant less fuel. Chops seemed to be dozing, his eyes closed. Buchanan smiled. There was no way the Chief was asleep. He knew this was the one weakness the man had. He hated flying, but to his credit he dealt with it as he dealt with everything. Head on. The yeoman was chatting to Baker, who had the machine gun across his lap, and on the other side the other three rates seemed happy enough, excited even. There might be a twenty-four hour delay in getting home, but this broke up the monotony of the voyage. Godshall, the weapons artificer who had earlier been working on the starboard 30 mill, sat against the other door lintel, his eyes closed. All were wearing camouflage smocks and seagoing working rig blue trousers. A pile of gear, including the radios, some rations and ammunition boxes, took up the space at their feet.

As Mayberry began his turn in to the beach, starting to lose height, he reached back to get Buchanan's attention, pointing to the north of the city. Three different palls of smoke rose from the area. Buchanan nodded and looked out of the front windscreen trying to get his bearings. Below them the water looked good and deep, deep enough for the Beau to come in close, and the beach seemed unobstructed. There was a heavy old wooden boat up on the sand and half a mile up the beach to the north he could see a figure in the water casting a net. He knew the tide had turned just after six so it was coming in, and by the look of it high water would have the seaboats almost up against the scrubby vegetation.

The helicopter crossed the beach and a few buildings and immediately began to slow, its nose rising up, flaring out and dropping into the walled British Embassy compound.

Buchanan was out first, the others following with Chops last, making sure nothing was left behind. With the men clear and Mayberry just about to lift off, Aitcheson ran out from the main building holding up one hand and moved over to meet Buchanan.

74

He leant close to the naval officer's ear and shouted, 'We have a stretcher case,' pointing to the helicopter. Buchanan thought for a second. As far as he was aware the evacuation hadn't yet officially begun, but if it did they wouldn't want a stretcher case that would have to be manhandled. If he called it wrong he might get a bollocking, if he called it right then he would be saving them a lot of trouble later. He nodded and leant forward. 'We have no doctor on board.'

'Malaria,' Aitcheson responded. 'We have tablets for her.'

Buchanan nodded and jerked a thumb at the helicopter. Two minutes later the sick woman was on a camp mattress in the back of the Lynx and Buchanan looked round the people. He saw a couple with two small children. Bugger it, he thought. Hung for a sheep as a lamb. He looked at the woman and held up three fingers, then pointed at the children and waved them forward. The husband didn't hesitate, but pushed them forward with an overnight bag. Buchanan looked at the people who were moving forward. He cupped his hands: 'Six more children! Six children!'

People ran forward with their children, shouted words to the mother in the aircraft, a name passed, a phone number, collective parenting there in time of need as ever. Then the door shut, Mayberry increased power and lifted off.

The father of the first two children watched the Lynx fly away and looked at Buchanan. 'Thanks for that. I feel much better already.'

'Don't mention it. Kids love helicopters. They might be flying back in a few hours,' he responded.

'Not this time,' the man said, shaking his head. 'This is going to be Sierra Leone all over again. This time it's for real.' He walked away.

Buchanan swallowed. The remark had surprised him. He turned, looking for his people. They were grouped against the wall by the gate and he walked over to them, thinking: Christ, it's hot. He was sweating already and he noticed that two of the men had stripped down to dark blue tee-shirts, but he wouldn't do that. He lifted his cap and wiped his brow, squatted down.

'Right, here's what I want you to do. Yeo, raise the Beau. Let them know we are in. Chops, have a look around. Take one man and have a wander round outside. See the lie of the land. Two men on the gate, one down to the back. Baker, you do that. Wait for me there. Remember, our task is to secure the Embassy compound. Rules of engagement are you may only fire if fired upon, or on my orders, or if you, your mates or any of these civvies are in mortal danger. Everyone understand? Remember we are not here to start anything. Safety first, remember your drills. Okay?'

Everyone nodded.

'I'm going to see the Ambassador. Then I will walk the wall. Chief, back here in ten minutes, please. Then we can deploy correctly and set up watches.'

Everyone nodded again.

Buchanan threaded his way through crowded, humid rooms. People were seeking refuge from the heat and the sun in the air-conditioned interior, but the system wasn't doing very well and people were still hot, fanning themselves, everyone's eyes on him, some smiling. He found William Black in his office, a telephone to his ear, waving him forward and pointing to a seat as he continued talking. When he finished he stood up and introduced himself.

'James Buchanan. I'm afraid I jumped the gun, sir. Took the opportunity to put some children on the helicopter. I hope you don't mind.'

'Mind? Nonsense,' Black responded. 'Initiative. Still valued. Nice to have you here.'

'I have my chaps looking around. We will set up under the tree in the front corner there, if you don't mind . . .'

'Wherever you think best, Lieutenant. You know more

76

about this than me.' He seemed distracted, his mind else-where.

'Brilliant . . . ah, I'll get on then,' Buchanan replied, sur-prised at the easy attitude. He didn't know what he was expecting, but it wasn't this complete delegation from a civilian.

'Let me know if there is anything you need,' Black said, but he was concerned about something, his expression distant.

'You all right, sir?'

Black looked at him and smiled bleakly. 'No, I'm not. That call. Someone just arrived at the American Embassy compound. Travelled through the night. The mission at Boplulu was attacked last night. The nuns, twenty-seven in total, two British, another twelve of them French and Belgian nationals were raped and murdered.'

He picked up the receiver again, but this time he looked at it, replaced it and lifted it again. 'It's down.' As he finished speaking the air conditioning spluttered to a halt.

'Power cut,' he said. 'The generator will kick in in a few moments. I'll leave our security in your capable hands, Lieutenant.'

Buchanan nodded and, picking up his cap, threaded his way through yet more people to the back door and into the garden. He found Baker, who had climbed on to the flat roof of a small structure in the north-east corner of the compound. One room with a shower and a cooking area, it was obviously basic living quarters for a local member of staff. Baker looked down.

'The cook's gaff, sir. Can see into the gardens on the other side. Good viz for about thirty yards both ways, then trees and stuff. There's another gaff over the other corner. That's the same except you can see the road that comes along the front.'

Buchanan jumped up on to the oil drum that Baker had used to climb up and hoisted himself easily the last five feet. The top of the wall was now waist height and he looked out over it. It was a good twelve feet high on the outside: no one was coming over that without a ladder. There was the sound of weapons fire, little more than a rattling, sustained crackle from a long way away, but they both knew what it was. Nuns. They had raped and killed nuns. Bastards. Buchanan wore a grim smile.

'You might earn your pay this day, Baker. Okay, come with me.'

Chops was back when they arrived and the yeoman and Godshall had been busy. He had already suspended a groundsheet from two rings in the wall, put there by the gardener long ago, and a rake leaning outward held the groundsheet up, forming a canopy from the sun.

'What have we got?'

'Didn't you say there were two policemen on the gate?'

'Yes I did,' Buchanan replied.

'Not any more. They've scarpered. Streets are clear enough. No one much is out. Only saw one car moving. Found the road to the beach. Don't like the cars out front. If we have visitors then it's giving them cover.'

'We'll move those we can,' Buchanan said. Many of them must belong to people inside the compound and so the keys would be available, but he knew that the owners wouldn't want the cars moved too far for fear of having them looted.

'That corner there,' Chops continued, pointing to the far corner of the front wall where a big bougainvillaea grew along a trellis. 'Behind that screen is a garden shed. The gun should go up there. Command the street both ways. Back that van,' he pointed again, this time to a Transit van, 'up against the gates on the inside. We need to get started. Need to strengthen the position.'

'On the inside?' Buchanan asked.

'These walls are breeze block,' Chops continued. '7.62 long will go right through a six-inch tree trunk. Seen it.'

'Will they have long? I thought they used intermediate?'

'We use small calibre, but we have long,' Chops said

patiently, jerking his head at the GPMG. 'They might, too.'

'Fair enough,' Buchanan replied. 'We've got firing steps in the other corners. Loopholes will be easy enough if we need 'em. We want one of the Land-Rovers backed into this corner for us to stand on. These cars,' he pointed to the fifteen-odd cars parked in the drive and on the lawn, 'loaded with stuff and backed into a line to form a second protective wall. Then if some bastard fires something that punches through the wall the round will have lost its speed, be tumbling and nearly spent when it hits that barrier.' There was another crackle of rifle fire followed by a dull thump. Buchanan looked at Wilks, who shrugged. 'Landmine maybe,' he said softly.

'Okay. Let's make it happen.'

Aitcheson got together a working party and with four sailors guarding them, men began to move cars away from outside the Embassy walls, others on the inside helping to move cars into the line. Ted Brooks's camera crew were recording now, their satellite dish set up on the Embassy roof, but neither Buchanan nor his shore party seemed to notice. One man, thin and tall with grey hair, left his wife and walked up to Buchanan.

'I am the president of the ConLib shooting club and as such am familiar with weapons. If you want someone on the walls with your chaps . . .'

Fucking great, Buchanan thought. A gun nut. That's all I need. 'Thanks, but we only have enough kit for ourselves.'

The man smiled, went to his car, opened the boot and took out a canvas gun case, an old leather overnight bag and a floppy bush hat with fishing flies in the brim. He came back to where Buchanan was standing.

'I can judge distance to within ten metres, with or without the spotting scope I have in this bag. I have a pair of 10 x 50 binoculars. I have a Remington .3006 in a free floating stock mounted with a Unertll ten-power telescopic sight. I can place a round into a dinner plate at eight hundred yards nine times out of ten. I was in Malaya in the emergency. Before you were born,' he added pointedly. 'I hoped I would never have to shoot at anyone ever again, but needs must. So, Lieutenant, where do you want my rifle?'

Although there might be no fighting nearer than that they could hear, Buchanan was also acutely aware that his shore party was small and if anything happened they would be very stretched. He understood the infantry's basic man management principle, that your never put green men on their own. Minimum unit was a pair and if the threat moved nearer then he had insufficient men to cover the corners of the compound and the gate in pairs. It could be three or four hours before *Beaufort* managed to get more ratings ashore. He had already made a decision, that if the fighting moved close then he would request another Lynx load of men regardless, but they were at least an hour away from the first request. 'I'll let you know as we deploy. In the meantime can you do something for me?'

'Of course.'

'My Chief tells me that bullets will go through these walls.'

'He's correct. Some certainly will.'

'I'd like to get some protection for my men on that roof there with the section weapon. Can you round up something we can use as sandbags, get them filled?'

'I'll get right on it.'

The Royal Marines officer, Lieutenant Andy Gordon, was with roughly half of his men in a Royal Air Force C-130 Hercules heading south-east. He had eleven from his own troop and would meet up with the rest of his command, a further nine from Zulu Company who were on HMS *Fearless*, in Gibraltar. The men had been chosen for the skills they possessed and training they had completed. The planners at Condor and Northwood had been busy but the only way to get support to *Beaufort* was by airdrop. The twenty men, sixteen marines, three corporals and a sergeant, were all parachute trained.

For the duration of the operation Gordon and his own support company men would become attached to Zulu Company's command structure on *Fearless*. The Hercules had flown up from its base in England to collect the men from RAF Leuchers, refuelled and was now en route to Gibraltar. Gordon's men were busy. They had drawn the equipment they needed, enough to also equip the nine men who would be joining them from Zulu, and were re-sorting it in the air and packing it into bergens. The extra stores would go into the waterproof canisters that were lashed to the central roller track that ran down the fuselage.

Because they would be stopping in Gib first, they wouldn't finish the job. Each of the men joining them would repack his own bergen, check his own parachutes and personal weapons. Only then and after they had changed into their drop gear would they seal the canisters. Eight feet long and cylindrical, they were only ever filled to half of theoretical maximum capacity, the remaining space taken up with inflating air bladders that would keep the canisters afloat till they were recovered by seaboat or towed in to a beach. The seals had been checked and checked again and Gordon was happy that their kit would arrive and be recovered in working order. If it happened it would be a medium level descent into warm water beside a friendly ship. No need for thick wetsuits or complicated survival kit. This was unusual and he was looking forward to it. Normally the SBS blokes had the monopoly on wet jumps and this would be bloody good experience for his lads. He made the final check with his men and at 0940, knowing that they had had no rest the night before, he stood them down and told them to get some sleep. They made themselves as comfortable as they could, some in the fold-down canvas racks, others nestled among the piles of kit on the floor.

In Gibraltar the OC Zulu had selected the best nine men he could offer Lieutenant Gordon. Four of them were slightly hung over from the run ashore the night before, but they were functioning and sorting personal kit and weapons while someone up in Ops was trying to establish from Condor what the recce boys had brought with them.

The corporal took the bleak option, decided that it could be a compete fuck-up, and with his troop commander lobbied the OC to let them go assault equipped or, as the corporal put it, 'well tooled up'.

The OC agreed. Time was of the essence. The bunkering barge was alongside and the stores had come aboard first thing, *Fearless*'s Captain pulling favours all night. She would, as he had promised Northwood, be ready to slip her moorings before noon and head south to support *Beaufort*, although the jokers were already saying that if the civvies had to wait for *Fearless* they were really in the shit. There was also a lottery running on at what stage something would break down, the most embarrassing slot, just having cleared Gib harbour, gone in a flash.

The nine Marines, because they were armed and there were protocols to be observed, would be transported from the harbour to the airport by the Military Police, technically in transit. There, because they had none of the routine troop movement clearances, they would wait with the vehicle that would rendezvous with the Hercules on the pan. The corporal, Mick Doughty, was a short, wiry marathon runner driven by the Marines' very simple code. Never give in. An excommunicated Mormon, he had been driven from the church of his family's faith, not by lack of conviction and not by the lure of alcohol or coffee or drugs, from which he still abstained, but simply because, as he would tell people with an appealing little grin, he couldn't keep his willy in his pants. He wasn't normally a ladies' man, but he did favour the dusky look of the maidens of the South Pacific and when in New Zealand doing his time as a missionary he had a wonderful time in pursuits that didn't please the church elders. They thought he should take a wife, honour her before God. His view was different. His own personal code of never give in brought them converts. He took to the role as he did everything, with a dogged determination that brought success, but the growing numbers of unhappy local girls, members of the congregations who fell for the self-effacing tough fellow, spoke of a man who wasn't taking the church elders seriously.

He was returned to England and had a few days with his mates winding up the local police and then, without discussing it with anyone, decided to join up. But who? He flipped a coin. One side was for the Royal Marines and the other was the French Foreign Legion. The Legion won, but he spoke no French and the frogs were crap at football and ate shit like snails so he joined the Marines. He was everything they were looking for. Tough as old leather, resourceful, fit, determined, with a single-mindedness that his instructors found unnerving, but with a fast, ready, self-deprecating humour that became more apparent the more pressure he came under.

Sometimes his attitude got him into trouble. While deployed on an aircraft carrier on a goodwill visit to the USA, he had gone ashore with half a dozen of his mates, all Marines. They hired a car and drove into the countryside, eventually stopping in a small southern town. A couple of the lads had taken the piss out of the rednecks standing at the bar, one calling them pooftahs. Someone slipped off, made a phone call, and within fifteen minutes pick-ups with rifle racks and Confederate flags were pulling up outside the bar. Now they were vastly outnumbered the Marine who had started the trouble thought he'd better extricate them and smoothly talked his way out of it, apologizing and being congenial. They all made it to the door except for tough little Doughty, who had said nothing to anyone. He sat where he was, his feet up on the table, looking at the gathered men, twelve or sixteen of them in feed caps and overalls.

'You goin' with your scrotum head friends?' one asked.

'I am,' he said, standing. 'Not staying here with you bunch of fucking faggots.'

He got the crap kicked out of him, as he would admit later with his trademark little grin. When someone asked why he had stayed, wasn't it foolish, the smile dropped and he explained, 'Marines never give in. Never.'

Corporal Doughty got his 'well tooled up' section loaded and, lifting two fingers at the lads on *Fearless*, they set off for the airport.

Beaufort had arrived two miles offshore in 36 metres of water. The navigator having conned her in past the three mile limit, Bennett tried to raise someone ashore to advise that she had no hostile intent. This was protocol only. William Black had been trying to get a response from someone in authority since dawn, until the phones went down.

Commander Bennett, out on the port bridge wing, was looking at the shoreline through binoculars. He dropped them to his chest and looked at his watch. It was now just on 1100 hours. The ship was on a defence watch with half the slightly depleted crew closed up, and special duty seamen were ready at the seaboats either side of the waist. The remainder of the shore party were gathered on the weather deck by the entrance to the citadel waiting for orders to go and he looked across at Kitson. There had been almost constant communications with the Embassy, but he wanted to give his efforts to raise someone ashore another five minutes.

'*Bridge, engine room.*' Morris recognized the voice of the MEO and he stepped across and lifted the microphone from the comms panel beside the QM at the wheel.

'*Bridge, go ahead.*'

'*Bridge, I've got a problem on the starboard shaft. Overheating and the torque balance is all out. I think we may have fouled something. I want to shut down. Now. Over.*'

As he was speaking Morris was looking out, at the sky, the shore line, thinking about tides and depth, and then

Bennett was suddenly there at his shoulder and took the microphone.

'*MEO, Captain. Stop starboard. Dead slow ahead on port. I'm coming down.*' He looked at Morris. 'Maintain station on port engine only. Depth?'

'Thirty-six metres, two knots of tide running, two to three winds from the east.'

'What's the bottom?'

'No idea, sir. It should take the hook . . .'

'Right. Get an anchor party ready.'

'Diving officer is ashore, sir,' Morris reminded him.

'I know. Bugger it. I don't like this, Pilot. Can you get me further out?'

'It shelves very quickly, sir, from here down to a hundred fathoms. No lee shore. Tides manageable for the next hour at least. Clear skies. The options are here, shallow enough to drop the hook, or ease out into open sea.'

'*Engine room, Captain.*'

'*Engine room.*'

'*Captain. Can you give me revolutions to get to sea?*'

'*I'd rather not, Captain. If we have netting or rope round the starboard shaft then it could be tightening round the port side as we speak.*'

'*I'm coming down.*'

'Close up the dive party,' he said to Morris and went for the steps.

'*Do you hear there? Buffer to the bridge. Anchor party to the foc's'le. Diving party close up.*'

It was Baker who saw them. On the staff quarters roof in the south-east corner of the compound he could see through the neighbouring garden and up on to the road, a view unobscured by trees unlike that from the south-west corner, actually on the road. A small band of armed men, young men. He thought at first that they might be carrying implements of some kind, but then very clearly he saw the familiar curved magazine of Africa's most commonly found weapon. He looked down the wall at the other southern corner. They weren't watching that way. He could see them clearly, five or six of them there behind some of the cars that had been moved, talking to each other. He could hear nothing, but there were animated gestures of disagreement. At the opposite end of the compound they had seen movement, but not the band that Baker had spotted.

There was a vehicle moving down the road that ran parallel to the seafront, a white Land-Rover, barely slowing at intersections, the driver gunning the engine to speed up again as he passed through each one. At the back of the compound Baker heard it, the high-pitched engine note of the four cylinder and the road hum familiar to anyone in the forces.

He looked down at the people below him. A woman caught his eye. 'Get my officer please, ma'am, quick as you can.'

Buchanan was down on the ground at the gate, waiting to get it open in case this was another arriving national.

'Hello! Hello,' she called, running to him. 'Your chap at the back wants you to . . .'

There was a burst of gunfire from right outside the walls. Six or seven weapons on automatic fire and behind that incredible noise – screeching tyres from the vehicle on the road. Buchanan dropped instinctively and ran forward, pulling the woman down, bedlam inside the compound as people gathered up children, ran for cover, dropping behind the row of cars as they had been told to do, one woman screaming.

The two ratings on the south-west corner were only forty feet from the source of the firing, but could see nothing through the thick foliage of the trees that lined the road.

Baker from his vantage further down the wall could see the gang firing. He wasn't sure if this constituted grave danger or defence of the Embassy compound, but certainly someone was under fire and this was the diplomatic area. He shifted his barrel half an inch to the right, ducked up, sighted on the main group behind a dark blue Renault and opened fire. His first burst put five or six rounds into them, starting low at their feet, ending up at head height of the crouching attackers, and then he dropped into the way he had been trained, no more than two shots, then resight and fire again. The surprise was absolute. There was such a volume of fire coming from the attackers that they didn't hear his rifle and by the time they realized they were themselves under fire the damage was done. Baker's rounds had torn into them. Two were down on the ground, a third holding his face, and two more were swinging round looking for the source of the fire. He aimed and fired again and then Chops was beside him, taken up on to the roof in a mighty vault off the shoulders of one of the civilians who was crouching at the bottom.

'Where away?' he barked.

'Blue car!' Baker fired again at the last two who were now running backwards, dragging a comrade by his webbing.

'Cease fire,' Chops ordered.

He squeezed Baker's shoulder. He was shaking, the adrenalin coursing through his blood, his breath coming in short sharp pants.

'Good lad. Stay 'ere now.' Chops nodded. He slid down the wall and ran up the compound, his beret square on his head, his rifle like an appendage to his body. He dropped down beside Buchanan who was by the gate waiting for his report.

'Baker clocked 'em. Engaged after they attacked. Seven or eight, about thirty or so yards down the street that way. There's some down. The rest have run for it.'

'Everyone all right?'

'No rounds came in our way,' Chops answered. 'They were all up the street.'

Buchanan nodded. 'Yeo?'

The yeoman dropped from the north-west corner and scuttled over to where the two were.

'Raise the *Beaufort*. Let them know the shit has now arrived in the enclave. We have had one light engagement. No casualties on our side. Extreme, I say again, extreme caution for any personnel from this time. This area is hostile. Got it?' The yeoman nodded.

'Right, Chops. We need to have a shufti. See who was in the Land-Rover. I'm going out. If anything happens, cover me from the wall and I'll be back in like a frightened rabbit.'

'Alone isn't smart, sir. I'll come with.'

'No. I'll call you if I need you. I'm going over the side wall. Get that ladder out of the shed and get it ready to drop down on the other side.' He cocked his side-arm. 'Let me have a rifle, please.'

'At least change out of the whites,' Chops said, passing his rifle and webbing over. 'You look like a fuckin' ice cream salesman . . . sir,' he added with a grin.

Buchanan smiled and Chops slipped his camouflage smock off and handed it to him, jerking his head to the right. Buchanan turned. The Ambassador was coming towards them.

'What's happened?' he asked.

'Someone came under fire outside the gates. Someone, we assume, trying to get here. Ergo a national or a friendly. My people returned fire. I'm going out to see if they are okay . . .'

'Do you think that's wise?' Black asked.

'Probably not, sir, but needs must,' Buchanan answered lightly. Thirty seconds later he dropped off the back wall into the garden of the neighbouring house and began to work his way round to the front.

The yeoman looked up at the Chief Petty Officer as he pulled the headphones on. 'Chief, one day your disrespect for Her Majesty's naval officers will get you into real shit.'

Wilks smiled. The yeo always prattled when nervous.

'It has before, Yeo. Most of 'em are wankers ... but him,' he jerked a thumb in the direction that Buchanan had gone, "e's all right. Good lad. Get that message through.'

He then moved round the wall, briefing the men on what had happened and advising them that Lieutenant Buchanan was now outside and not to bloody shoot him by mistake. He finished up back at the gate and together they rolled the van back and waited.

'Message from the shore party, Captain.' The comms rating handed him the flimsy signal and waited for a response. The anchor was down and the diver, a killick seaman, was down. *Beaufort* was lying two miles out, port side beam on to the beach, gently swinging on her cable, and in the seaboat bobbing at her stern were the coxswain and another diver there as sentry. While a diver was down the ship went into a well rehearsed set of safety drills, including locking the propeller shafts, but there was always a sentry, whose sole task was his safety. The diver would be attached to the diveboat by a rope and they had a system of communicating with tugs to the line.

'Christ,' Bennett muttered to himself. He looked up.

'XO to the bridge.'

As Kitson arrived Bennett handed him the flimsy. 'It's started. Use the helo. Get yourself ashore with another party quick as you can. Seaboats will deliver the remainder of your group when the divers are up. I estimate in an hour or so. Consolidate your position and then we will decide what to do. All right?' Kitson nodded, but he knew it would be fifteen minutes before they could be airborne.

Buchanan crept round the wall and moved very slowly and surely up through the garden towards the road. He couldn't see the Land-Rover. From the sound of the brakes it would have stopped somewhere off to the right and he moved that way, pausing every now and then to listen.

He got to the road and then moved parallel to it down towards the intersection, still in the gardens of the houses, peering through the hedge as he went. Something landed in the bushes to his right and he heard a voice. He dropped, turning around, raising the rifle, his heart pounding in his chest.

'Don't shoot,' the voice said, a hoarse whisper. 'Over here.'

'Who are you?' he called back.

A figure crept round the side of a low wall. Young, white, with a cocky half-grin on his face. 'Royal Navy,' he said, taking in Buchanan's cap. 'You from the Embassy?'

Buchanan nodded. 'You?'

'Dave Culverhouse. Save the Children. I was heading back to the Embassy and got revved.' He crawled further round and Buchanan saw he was carrying a semi-automatic shotgun.

'White Land-Rover?'

Culverhouse nodded. 'Yeah.'

'You okay?'

'Yeah, the windscreen's a bit fucked, though.' The lad's grin was infectious.

Buchanan grinned back at him. 'On your own?'

'Yeah.'

'Have you come far?'

'No. Not that dumb. The US compound. Phones are down. It's four blocks that way.' He pointed to the north-east and looked back at Buchanan. 'They gone?'

'We returned fire,' Buchanan replied. 'Let's go in. We will go,' he pointed, 'round the front nice and quick and then you in the gate.'

'Where you going?' Culverhouse asked.

'Down the wall to the end where they were. Make sure they have pulled out.'

'I'll come too.'

'I want you inside.'

'Two's better,' Culverhouse said. He pointed over the

90

street. 'That's the old Zimbabwean mission there. I know it well. We can go down the inside of the wall, cross back behind where they were.'

The man who had offered his help to Lieutenant Buchanan climbed up on to the staff quarters roof with Baker. 'You don't mind if I join you, young man?'

Baker shook his head. He was still watching out over the wall, but his hands were shaking and sweaty. The man lifted his binoculars from a wide pocket in his soft bush jacket and looked out at the scene of the contact. He then settled, his back against the wall, his rifle cradled across his knees.

'They're all dead, aren't they?' Baker asked hesitantly, his voice small.

The man shook his head. 'One's moving. You all right?' he asked softly, packing a pipe with tobacco. Baker nodded silently, then looked at the older man.

'No. Actually I feel sick,' he replied honestly.

'That's normal enough. I remember my first time,' the man said, lighting a match. 'It's one of those things. There's you and them. You do what you have to do, or it's you lying out there, or your friends. Just think of what they could do if they got inside.' Holding the match to the tobacco he puffed on the pipe before shaking it out. 'The sick feeling. It passes. It gets easier.'

'I can still see it,' Baker said.

'You will.' He held out his hand. 'I'm Reg Johnson. Jonnie.'

'Kevin Baker. What mob were you in?'

The older man smiled. 'Green Jackets. It was a long time ago.'

'Where were you?'

'Malaya,' he replied, puffing his pipe, 'but I wasn't with the regiment. Attached to special branch.'

'Intelligence?'

'No,' he replied softly. 'I was there to shoot.'

'A sniper?' Baker asked.

The man nodded and the conversation faded as Baker, looking out over the wall, thought that one through. Then he spoke. 'There's movement.'

Johnson rolled to his feet, reaching for his binoculars. He looked out for ten or twelve seconds.

'It's your officer and someone else,' he said. 'Cover them now. Keep the left in view, hard left. Look for movement. Also, keep an eye out behind. They may come that way again, but it's more likely they will see that it's not a good idea. Come from another direction.' He spoke steadily, his voice even, the experience evident. He passed the sailor his binoculars and dropped down again, puffing on his pipe.

Baker was feeling much better. He watched Lieutenant Buchanan move forward with the other bloke. They didn't wait long, but pulled one of the men he had shot round by his webbing and began to drag him back towards the gates. One of the Médecins sans Frontières doctors ran forward as they came in. The casualty, young, maybe sixteen years old, had taken a bullet through his thighs. The entry wound was high on the right side, just below his pelvis, and the bullet had exited the right thigh and entered the left where it had lodged. He was bearing his pain with stoic strength and considering the blood loss it wasn't surprising that he was going into deep shock. 'This way, please,' the doctor said. In spite of his best efforts the young man would die twenty minutes later, but Culverhouse carried him towards the main building and Buchanan watched as Chops started the engine and reversed the van back in front of the gates.

Culverhouse was back out a few moments later.

'I came over to see Tony Wisher, but apparently he's out on the ship.'

'That's right,' Buchanan said, thinking quickly. If it was enough to risk being on the roads then it might be important. 'If necessary we can raise him on the radio.'

Culverhouse thought for a moment. 'Dunno. I have been trying to talk to him since last night.' He looked at the officer. 'I was out last night. Saw trucks towing guns. They were on their way down towards the port, but this morning they were out heading past the enclave to the north.'

He looked at Buchanan, who was trying to make something of it.

'The field guns are held by the national army,' Culverhouse explained. 'If they have handed them over to one of the factions, then they have sided with one. It's a whole new scenario.'

'Fair enough.' Buchanan turned. 'Yeo, raise the Beau, please. This gentleman wants to speak to the third attaché.'

The yeoman bent over his radio and began talking, looking up a few moments later. 'Sorry, sir, he's on the helo. It's just lifted off with the Jimmy and some of the lads.'

There was a muted call from the wall, the front corner where the Land-Rover was backed in. 'Sir!' Buchanan looked up and one of the two ratings jabbed a finger down towards where Baker was. He ran down the garden and this time the man the Chops had used as a step was waiting with a grin on his face, two hands down, fingers intertwined. Buchanan put his foot in and the man lifted him up.

'Thanks,' he called. 'What have we got?'

Baker pointed down the road to the edge of their vision. 'There. Ten o'clock under the water tank. Three hundred yards.' Buchanan lifted his binoculars.

'Can't see anything.'

'They're there,' another voice said. It was the old bloke with the rifle. He held up a long black tube. 'Use this.' Buchanan took it. It was a telescope and looking through it he found there were grading marks down the sighting reticle. He swung slightly to the left. There. Two faces peering out and behind them a man on his haunches. There may well be others out of sight, he thought.

He swore under his breath.

'They are not approaching,' Johnson said.

'No. But I have a helicopter inbound.'

'Aah. That's too juicy to ignore. Do you want to divert it?' Johnson asked.

'Not really,' Buchanan replied. 'It's got more lads on it, but I'm not bringing . . .'

'Can I suggest you request your pilot to come in fast and low from the north-west, rather than directly from the west?' Johnson interrupted. 'Young Kevin and I'll give them something else to focus the mind upon. There will be nobody in the group sticking their heads out. Give us thirty seconds' warning.'

Buchanan looked at him, thinking. One automatic and one sporting rifle firing from three hundred yards away? Unlikely to phase veteran fighters like these people. From what he knew suppression fire needed to be volumetric in form.

'I'll get another couple of men down here.'

'Rather you didn't,' Johnson said, looking into the bowl of his pipe. 'It's a bit distracting and there isn't much room up here. Don't worry. We will keep their heads down.'

Buchanan looked at the killick. 'You happy?'

Baker nodded in assent. 'Yes, sir.'

'You understand the rules of engagement? I don't want anyone hurt unless they open fire on us.'

'Sir.'

'Okay. But I want to know if they move forward,' Buchanan finished. 'Here, you'd better have this.' He passed one of the small handheld radios to Baker, then moved back to the gate and the Clansman radio.

In the helicopter Mayberry took the message and thought for a second or two, then swung the nose of the Lynx to bring it in as requested from the north-west. He nodded to his observer, then looked back and got the attention of the XO. Kitson moved up and Mayberry briefed him quickly, pointing out the way he was now coming in.

94

Kitson nodded and stepped back. He spoke to the rating who was manning the door gun and he cocked the weapon. The Lynx was lightly armoured. Small ball ammunition wouldn't come up through the floor, but nevertheless he had four of the men sit well back against the aft bulkhead and moved two men so they were lying on the floor, their weapons pointed out of the door to return fire at the ground if it became necessary.

On the staff quarters roof Johnson tapped out his pipe, put it in his pocket and then, reaching into another pocket, brought out a box of ammunition, brightly coloured. He slid it open and there, individually nestling in cardboard tubes, were bright ends of brass cartridges. He pulled five out, inspected each in turn, put them to his ear and shook, listening for the sound of smooth-flowing propellant. Happy with each he slid back the bolt on his rifle and loaded the five rounds into the magazine. He took another five rounds and dropped them loose into his right-hand jacket pocket. The bolt action half-closed with a round half into the breach, he slipped the covers of the telescopic sight and, putting his soft floppy hat on the top of the wall, leaned the rifle on it and waited.

'Right, young Kevin. I'll shoot left to right,' he said. 'Once I stop, it may not be necessary, but be prepared to lay down your fire. Until then I'd like you to spot for me. You are looking for anything I might not have seen or that appears. If you see another target left or right of where I am aiming, call it out. Describe it, by geography, with reference. Under the tower, left of the shed and so on.'

Baker nodded. His hands were sweaty again, and shaking. Then they could hear it, the dull whumping sound of the rotors.

'Aah. Won't be long now,' Johnson said.

4

The radio squawked into life. 'Baker, Buchanan. You have about thirty seconds.'

Johnson was already leaning forward, peering through his telescopic sight, the rifle butt into his shoulder. Three hundred yards away he could see the fighters. There was talk, animated gestures, hands pointing. They had heard the helicopter.

Baker was watching also, through the spotting telescope. Don't do it, he was willing them, just leave us alone. In the briefing they had been told that one of the factions had hijacked a helicopter once, held it for a few days before giving it back, but they hadn't shot at one yet, not that anyone knew of, anyway.

They were up, moving. Which way? Shit! He inched the telescope round. A wall. Nothing. He grabbed the small yellow handheld radio.

'Lieutenant Buchanan, Baker. They heard the helo and are moving. I say again they heard the helo and are moving.'

'Which way?'

'They headed towards the road again, sir.' He thought for a second. 'West, over.'

Johnson, still peering through his scope, saw a flash of movement. Men running past a gap in trees. 'I have visual,' he said. He sighted and waited. The next man moving was carrying a plastic bottle, a big one, its Coca-Cola label faded. He held his breath, leading the target, and squeezed and the big rifle kicked back into his shoulder as the report echoed round the compound. The water bottle was ripped from the youth's hands, exploding as the heavy bullet hit it, and he, with some experience of being shot at, dived into cover. No more men ran across the gap. A head peered round the thick trunk of a tree on the far side and Johnson, aiming six inches above the head, fired again. The bullet hit before the report reached them with a solid thump like a hammer blow, ripping a chunk of the bark away. The head disappeared.

'That should stop them being too inquisitive,' Johnson called. Moments later, the sound of the rotors a solid beat, the Lynx settled on the lawn in front of the main building.

Kitson and Wisher came out of the door together, six more armed ratings following them out on to the dry grass. The people previously selected to go back on the helicopter were in a huddle together, but Kitson was already moving over to them to explain that they wouldn't be going. The decision to land the vulnerable helicopter had been the pilot's. He had assessed the risk and with only a handful of rates ashore and the situation worsening he wanted them reinforced as much as anyone. But lifting off again the machine would be at her most vulnerable. If anything went wrong he wanted as light a load as possible, and no civilians at risk, certainly not women and children.

He pointed out through the plexiglass in the direction of the armed men outside the walls, looking for confirmation that he had it right, and as Buchanan gave him a thumbs up he put power on and lifted the Lynx off the ground into a hover six inches above the grass and turned it round so he was facing to seaward, the rating in the door shifting his strop so that he could hang the gun out of the port side door, the direction of the threat. That done, Mayberry lifted off, staying low, going for airspeed as he skimmed the treetops, running for the beach and the *Beaufort*.

Kitson watched it fly away and then turned to Buchanan. 'Right. Well done, Jamie. What's the sitrep?'

'Had a contact a short while ago.' Buchanan quickly

briefed his XO, finishing, 'Got a civilian down in the far corner with Baker. He seems a useful type. Ex-mob. Shoots. Got his own rifle. Knows how to use it. Let go a couple of rounds to keep heads down as you were coming in.'

Kitson's look said it all.

'I know what you're thinking, sir,' Buchanan responded, 'but I had lads on their own and Baker had already been in the shit. The results of his initiative are out there. He can see them and is feeling awful about it. The old bloke, he . . . he has a steadying influence.'

Kitson thought for a second or two. 'All right. I'll go down and meet him later. The rest of the shore party won't be in for another half an hour or so at least, but I want a small recce party to go down and guide them in.'

'Chops has seen the road down. I'll go down with him and one other.'

'Fair enough. In the meantime, you now have another six lads. Get them briefed and deployed.'

David Culverhouse had found Tony Wisher and told him about the movement he had seen that morning and when Kitson, threading his way through people to find Black, approached them, Wisher caught his eye and nodded through the doors into the office suite.

Brooks was there, also waiting to see the Ambassador.

'Lieutenant Commander Kitson, isn't it?'

'Yes, sir.'

'Ted Brooks. I'm with CNN. Can we get together? I'd like an interview.'

'I'm sorry, but not now,' Kitson responded. 'Maybe later, and then only if the Ambassador and my Captain agree.'

'I'll not be here later. I'm going across to the US compound if we can get there. My employers always want an American perspective,' he finished dryly.

'Mr Brooks, I wouldn't encourage anyone to be moving round outside at the moment. You know the situation better than I.' Kitson removed his cap and went through into Black's office as the door opened and Aitcheson came out.

Below the *Beaufort* the diver was just finishing the freeing of the propeller shaft. It was fishing net, new, nylon, incredibly strong, the sort of stuff the Koreans and Japanese used for their infamous 'wall of death' drift nets. He had got halfway through and then had to go back to the boat for bolt cutters as the trailing edge of this section, wrapped tight round the shaft, had a wire rope core. He wasn't aware of the big Asian boats fishing the coast of West Africa, but it could have been drifting for months. He finished cutting, pulling each piece clear and watching it sink as he did so, the last bits with the steel core sinking faster than the rest. It had taken over forty minutes and he was tired. He began making his way back to the diveboat.

There was plenty going on. The small group of civilians that had come back with the helicopter were down in the Wren ratings' mess, now converted by them into a mini crèche. The ship was still on defence watch and on the bridge the special sea quartermaster was waiting at his post at the wheel. The watch was closed up, Lieutenant Morris, the officer of the watch, was on the bridge wing with the captain looking at the diveboat as it bobbed near the stern and further up in the waist the next shore party was gathered. Some of them were getting into the second seaboat, ready to be lowered to the water for the run ashore.

Lieutenant Conway, the officer with this group, had been looking forward to getting ashore and on with the job, but since the word had come down that the lads at the embassy had returned fire it was becoming a little more complicated. She would now wait for the second boat, the one the divers were using, to load the last of the shore party and then with Orbs Montagu as the senior Lieutenant they would head for the beach together, where the XO would have someone to guide them in to the best place. She looked back. The helicopter was coming in, three or four hundred yards behind the ship, slowing down and getting ready to flare out.

'Bloody hot, isn't it?' Montagu said. He wiped a hand across his brow and replaced his cap. 'I was on *Britannia* when we lifted some people out of the Yemen. There were three ships and we were nearby. People being shuttled out to us. We dropped them off in Djibouti.'

'I didn't know you had served on *Britannia*,' Sarah said.

'Just the one trip. Watchkeeper got the clap or something. There was me, waiting for a ship.'

He plucked at his shirt. Normally at sea there was a breeze across the deck, but here with the ship at anchor there was hardly a breath and his shirt was sticking to his skin.

'Have you met her then?' Sarah said.

'Her Maj?' Montagu smiled. 'No. Trade trip.'

'Seaboat's coming inboard, ma'am,' someone called.

'Right, PO. Let's get 'em loaded,' Montagu said.

His party moved round to the other side of the ship and as the diver climbed clear with his sentry, the coxswain and his mate stayed in the boat and the armed ratings began to climb in. The big, rigid inflatable was in her cradle, still attached to the hoist, and as the last man, Montagu himself, climbed in, the boat was swung outboard and began to lower to the water.

On the other side Sarah Conway and her group were just six feet off the water when there was a dull thump and three hundred yards from the ship a column of water rose up.

'What the fuck was that?' someone demanded.

'Shit!' someone else said. 'Some bastard is shooting at us.'

There was another thump, this time closer, and another column of water shot into the air. For a second it seemed unreal, but they had all seen shot fall, the older ones on exercises, the younger ones in movies, and as the column of water began to fall back to the surface Conway grabbed her radio. Whatever was happening ashore was now secondary.

'*Bridge, Conway, seaboat. We are under fire, repeat we are under fire.*' She looked up at the rating on the winch motor, twirling her finger in the air. 'Bring us up! Now!'

The man looked over questioningly, the boat still descending.

'UP you cunt!' the Petty Officer yelled, jabbing his finger upwards. 'UP! UP!'

'*Bridge, seaboat, the ship is under fire!*' The winch stopped and then started again. This time they were going up. Morris and the Captain left the starboard bridge wing, colliding as they rushed through the bridge door.

'*Bridge, Ops! Fast inbound track bearing 045 degrees!*' crashed through the speakers from the Ops room. '*Sound action stations! Assume condition Zulu.*'

Bennett took it all in in a second and as the third shell landed, still about two hundred yards out, he was weighing up his choices. Command was broken into three key priorities, fight, float, move. The ship was afloat and still undamaged. She needed to move and she needed to fight, in whatever order he could manage.

'They are ranging,' Morris said.

'Sound action stations,' Bennett snapped. 'Seaboats back inboard! Break the cable!' He snatched up the intercom. '*Engine room, Captain. We are under fire, repeat we are under fire. This is an emergency. Get the shaft locks off. Get me under way NOW!*'

The action stations klaxon began to blare around the ship.

'*Captain, MEO. That will be five or six minutes minimum.*'

'*Make it one!*'

'*Anchor party, close up. Break the cable, repeat, break the cable.*'

'*Captain, Ops.*'

'*Ops, Captain, what have you got?*'

'*Captain, Ops, fast small inbound from 045 degrees.*'

'*It's artillery,*' Bennett responded. The anchor party, with the buffer in charge, were racing up to the foc's'le now, to go through a well tried and trained routine, but one they had never actually done – shearing the anchor cable. At various points along the cable there were shearing points where they could snap the pin on a shackle-like link, jettisoning the anchor and whatever chain was out. It was very expensive and very, very dangerous, but much quicker than trying to get the anchor off the bottom and the ship free to move in the conventional way.

Another shell landed in the sea, this time on the far side of the ship.

'We are bracketed,' from Morris, calling the fall of the shot. Bennett was thinking fast. The action stations call demanded that certain things happen in a given sequence, but at anchor and stopped in the water some roles were confused. The buffer, using his initiative, was up with the anchor party, while his rates were closing hatches and vents to take the ship to Zulu condition, closed down for action in the worst case scenario, that of NCB warfare. She was floating. She would be moving as soon as they could humanly get the shafts unlocked. Rules of engagement were open. The ship was under attack, attack initiated by the hostile party. Command imperative. Fight.

'*Captain, Ops.*'

'*Captain, go,*'

'*Helo reports seeing muzzle flash. He has visual . . .*'

In the Lynx, Mayberry, who had seen shot fall many times in training, had seen the first shell land in the sea and immediately aborted his landing, power on, turning the helicopter to seaward and then round to become the ship's eyes. Another voice crashed on to the bridge over the speakers.

'*Bridge, port TDS. I can see them!*'

'*Port TDS, Captain, keep watching! Ops, prepare to engage with gun.*'

As crew all over the ship ran for their action stations

the captain of the gun bay, a Petty Officer Weapons Engineering Mechanic flung himself back into his kingdom. He
had been at the head and when the klaxon had gone off
he ran the length of the deck to his position: whatever
the threat, his fast-firing 4.5-inch radar controlled Vickers
Mark 8 could be needed. As he entered the gun bay he
saw his number two scrabbling to unlock the emergency
stack of live ammunition. They had eight HE rounds in
the rack and two star shells.

'*Gun bay, Ops! Load HE!*'

Sweet mother of Christ, we're going to fight!

'Load 'em,' he snarled. Two ratings began carrying shells
across the two feet to the semi-circular feed ring, where
an electric hoist would pluck a round and deliver it up to
the automated gun turret. This was the gun's limiting factor. It could fire a shell every second and a half, guided
visually, by radar or by laser, but it still required that men
manhandle the shell into the auto-loader feed ring. He
watched the rounds loaded into the mechanism and
switched the load lift to the central position from single to
automatic. He snatched up the intercom. '*Ops. Gun is ready!*'

His heart was pounding. HMS *Beaufort* was going to
engage, gun to gun, across barely two miles of sea. The
captain of the turret hurtled past him with a set of keys
and in seconds the hatch from the main magazine hoist
was open.

'Cheers,' the gun bay captain called. They now had
ammo. As much of it as the gun could fire.

'*Brace! Brace! Brace!*' over the main broadcast system from
Ops.

The next shell hit the *Beaufort*.

It struck high on the port side, just at the base of the
funnel, blasting the funnel structure apart, huge pieces of
steel flying through the air and taking down aerials and
masts. On the bridge wing Captain Bennett was almost
blown off his feet and was left dazed, bleeding from the
ears and a small cut under his eye. Morris was on his feet.

Immediately aft and below the blast on the top of the citadel superstructure where the local area sight was located, the leading seaman sitting in the TDS seat, the man who a few moments ago had called that he could see the shore battery, took a shard of steel into his side. His life was undoubtedly saved by his flash hood and helmet – something had hit him on the head hard enough to have knocked the helmet off – but he was still wounded and slumped in the seat. The rating on the far side, manning the other TDS, picked himself up and looked astonished up at the gaping great hole where the funnel had been, then heard the cries. He ran across, dragging his mate out of the seat. Incredibly, he was still aware and still had his mind on the job.

'I had 'em in the sights. Fuck . . . I *had* em.' The other rating lowered him to the deck and he looked at him, holding the back of his head. 'Get in the seat. On the shore line in the trees. The big clump of trees. I'm all right! Do it!'

He jumped into the seat and plugged in his own comms plug, staring through the graduated gunsight. He inched it right. There!

Up on the fo'c'sle the buffer's party finally broke the links in the anchor cable and with a thundering roar the last few feet of chain crashed out of the eyes. Further aft the seaboat party were now inboard and running for the action stations, Sarah Conway not dropping through the citadel door but going straight into the 2 Echo area through the officers' flat and down the steps, sliding on her hands down the handrails. She took the last ladder the same way down into 3 Echo and the hubbub of the Ops room where as EWO she had her battle station.

'*Bridge, fo'c'sle. Cable is broken.*'

'*Port TDS, Ops.*'

'*Ops, port TDS, go.*'

'*You OK?*' Someone was thinking down there.

'*No. Need a medic for Taffy. I'm Lewis from the starboard*

side. TDS is sighted on target.' There was a puff of smoke from the trees. *'They've fired again.'*

'Help is coming. Hold on the target!'

In the Ops room Bennett's voice came crashing in. *'Take it with gun!'*

'Aye aye,' from Ops. *'Weapons director, visual spotting, directing follow TDS port. One round – fire!'*

Three feet away from him the leading seaman missileman, sitting in the seat that the Chops(M) would have usually been in, selected the gun and pressed the foot trigger.

Up on the weather deck the Vickers Mark 8 4.5-inch gun swivelled to the left, its massive barrel tracking the TDS sight and fired.

'On target! On target! Fire for effect!' from Mayberry in the Lynx.

'Brace! Brace! Brace!'

'Ten rounds – fire for effect. Engage!'

Then the second shell hit them.

It entered through the port side above the waterline on 2 deck, through the ratings' mess and dining area, crossed above the tables, ripped through the main passage, tearing out comms cables and junction boxes, passed through the internal bulkhead on the starboard side of the main passageway and crashed through the MCO, all in a millisecond, finally exploding as it hit the starboard side outer steel bulkhead.

The ship shuddered, every person feeling the blast. On the deck the gun faltered for a second as the TDS shook, and then the rating, with commendable focus, found his target again, laying the gun back where it should have been.

On 2 deck some of the blast had ripped back up the passage, but the bulk of the explosion had been absorbed in the MCO, expended on heavy racked mounted comms gear and decoding equipment, where flames now belched out of cracks round the door, now hanging on its hinges, and the entry hole. Cheryl Simpson, still running for her station, was the first on the scene, sweet kind Cheryl. She did what she had been trained to do and more: she yelled 'Fire!' and snatched an extinguisher from the wall. Someone was inside, someone still alive, screaming, and without waiting for the fire teams, who were pulling on Fearnot suits and running from both muster positions fore and aft, she slammed the base of the extinguisher into the door, smashing it open, and entered the burning comms suite. Two ratings who had been passing the mess that the shell had seared through saw her disappear into the flames and the thick, billowing smoke. It was black, acrid, coming from burning insulating plastic around communication cables and electronic circuit boards. Pulling a hose reel from the bulkhead mounting they threw out the 'water wall' from its nozzle. The main fire teams arrived then, twenty seconds from the time of the blast, concentration of expertise, four men in fireproof suits and breathing apparatus, pushing their way past the ratings with the hose. They were blind. The room was thick with smoke, the fire now out, the 'water wall' from the hose spraying them and it took them a few moments to find her. She was there, her extinguisher empty, her hair smouldering, badly burned, covering, protecting the still moving form of someone alive beneath her.

The ship's technical people were gathering back in the main control room, there to provide expert knowledge to any given problem. They rerouted fire water around the ruptured pipes, stepped up the ventilation system and isolated the area where they believed the fire still burned. Although it was just along the passage from where they were, the ship was shut down into watertight and fireproof sections. It was another fifteen seconds before the on-scene emergency officer Tex Marshall, down on his knees looking into the room, gave the first damage report to the Damage Control Officer.

'DCO, DMEO. Shell exploded in MCO. Fire is out, repeat fire is out. We have casualties, over.'

'DMEO, confirm fire is out.'
'That's confirmed. Fire is out. Need medical assistance.'

They both heard it. Buchanan walked over to where Kitson was standing and on cue they heard it again.

'Field gun?' Buchanan muttered, with a raised eyebrow. 'Sounded like one.'

Others in the compound had heard it too, the flat, cracking blasts.

'I bloody hope not,' Kitson replied. They listened again for a few moments. 'Where's Wisher?'

'Inside somewhere.' There was another crack. 'The kid I brought in this morning. He said he needed to talk to Wisher. Something about trucks towing guns. The national army having crossed over or something.'

Small-arms clashes is one thing, Kitson thought, but if they are now firing artillery at each other then that changes the situation considerably.

'Go and find him, if you would,' he asked.

There was the sound of another gun firing and this time they heard a hit somewhere and then the much louder, flatter, thumping crack of a bigger piece opening up from another direction and at the same moment the ground beneath their feet trembled as the flat c-a-r-r-u-m-p of the blast reached them.

'Sh-i-t,' someone said slowly. People were looking at each other now, worried at this change in events. Then it started, rapid fire. Only one gun on this continent could fire like that. 'That's the Beau!' Kitson shouted, running for the radio. 'They were firing at her! She's engaging!'

He was squatting down by the radio as the last sounds faded, with the yeoman trying to raise the ship, when the Lynx came past fast and low. He looked up. Shit. One-sixty knots. Helo recce. Trying to see if they have done the business.

'Sorry, sir. No response.'

* * *

107

On the bridge of the *Beaufort* the comms speakers issued a steady cacophony of noise, reports, orders and commands.

'Bridge, MEO. Locks are off, repeat shaft locks are off.'

'Get us out of range,' Bennett said to Morris.

'One-eighty revolutions on the gas,' from Morris, the navigator. *'Steer two-sixty degrees.'*

Present her stern to the shoreline, reduce the target profile for enemy gunners, if any were still capable of firing, and get further out. 'Comms are down, sir,' a rating said. 'Can't raise the helo.'

Comms are down. Of course the bloody comms are down, Bennett thought. The MCO has taken a direct hit.

'Use VHF,' he replied. *'DCO, casualty report and comms status? Let me know immediately you have it established.'*

He knew he had to get on to Northwood as soon as possible. He had the standing sea emergency parties closed up, everyone at their stations and he knew the engineering officers would be waiting to enter the MCO after the casualties had been brought clear, trying to establish what was still operative, what could be salvaged and repaired. The injured from 2 deck were on their way to the sick bay and there were people heading towards the wounded rating back at the port TDS. Getting him down would be a bitch. They'd have to use a Neil Robinson stretcher. Vertical ladder twenty feet to the deck, but he knew that Lieutenant Montagu was there managing the task with the buffer – Montagu, who by rights should have been in the MCO when the shell hit.

Down in the Wren space the children who had made up the first party of civilians from ashore were panicking. They didn't know what had happened, but they could smell the smoke and the running round and noise frightened them. Kate Wallace, who had surprised herself by offering to stay with them when the ship went to action stations, along with the one adult, tried to calm them. She gathered them round in the small area by the video.

'Don't worry. See, it's all finished and the ship is moving

now. Can you feel it? My friend Cheryl will be off watch soon. She knows lots of sailor songs you can sing.'

Unknown to her, at that moment, barely thirty feet away up the main passage, the Leading Medical Assistant was standing over Cheryl Simpson as two first aiders helped the others. He had fired morphine into her, as much as he could, to deal with the pain and now he went to work, looking up every now and then as people came in the door. There were other casualties coming in, a rating who was on his way down from the TDS and one other being the most serious, but for now he just had this Wren and the man she had been covering, Dave Tomkins, who was dying on the other table. Tomkins had taken shell splinters or something, because he had puncture wounds in his chest and was now bleeding into his abdominal cavity. The LMA had given him something for the pain, but knew he was dying; there was nothing more that could be done for him, so he concentrated on the burned Wren. He had never done time in a burns unit and this was a job for a specialist, but there was no one else. He began to try and peel the burnt clothing back from her skin.

On the bridge Bennett's mind was racing. Who the hell had fired on them? Why? This was a humanitarian mission. But what had started as a simple 'stand off and prepare to lift out civilians' had become something more as that first shell had hit. He had crew ashore, civilians under the protection of his ensign, and the initial rules of engagement were now blown to the wind, blown away along with the lives of members of his crew. Someone ashore must know and he must raise Northwood somehow. The game had just changed. Someone had initiated hostilities against them, and without communications with Northwood he was on his own in terms of decision-making. Many Captains would envy him, longed for the independence of the days of sail, before radio, when Royal Navy Captains were absolutely alone in their decision-making, often interpreting policy and His or Her Majesty's intent with little more than an outdated understanding of the politics and a firm belief in what they saw as Britain's greater interests. In some ways little had changed. He had a task. He had Britain's interests to consider. He had the lives of five hundred-odd people to consider.

Bennett looked down at the second Clansman radio in its usual place in the corner of the bridge. They were heading out to sea. Out of range of the radio any minute. The XO would be trying to discover what the hell was going on.

'Get that Clansman up. Raise the shore party,' he said.

'Yes, sir . . . Sir you are bleeding.' The rating pointed, his hand shaking. Adrenalin. Bennett nodded, the blood now congealing in the cut above his eye.

'Got 'em, sir!' The yeoman held out the handset and Kitson came over. 'They want to know if we are secure.'

They moved into the comms room in the building, the yeoman setting up the Clansman on a table top, and Bennett briefed them on what had happened. William Black and Tony Wisher were there and listening, as he had requested.

When Bennett finished Kitson asked him to stand by.

'Well, any ideas?'

'Not the national army functioning on their own,' Wisher answered. 'Very unlikely. Taylor? It's possible, but again very unlikely. If the army were going to cross they would have before now, and he knows where the lines are drawn and where the aid comes from. The others? Not in the same league, but remember Marriot Bokia. If Brooks' sources are correct then he is a maverick. Mostly unknown and what we do know tells us that he is the most likely to carry out something like this.'

Black nodded. 'I agree. I shall immediately protest and the usual things, but I'm not sure that there's anyone to listen. I need to talk to London.'

'As do we, sir,' Kitson said. 'Your facility here is now

our only way to communicate and we will need to act as relay for the ship. I must advise Northwood immediately and I think we need to advise the US Embassy.'

'As you know, the telephones are down. This equipment,' Black pointed to the embassy's secure communications unit, a keyboard, VDU and satellite uplink, 'never really functions very well with the generator supplying power. It should, but never seems to.'

Kitson looked at the set-up. It doesn't rain but it pours, he thought. He was tired, his eyes grainy. He hadn't got to bed at all the night before and he knew that there wouldn't be much sleep that night.

'Excuse me, sir,' the yeoman said, 'but Willard is a radio artificer. Perhaps he could have a look at it, and Jonesy is a mechanic.'

'Thanks, Yeo. Give 'em a shout, if you would,' Kitson said. He looked back at the Ambassador and Wisher. 'You said you had some medical aid workers here. Would there be a doctor?'

'There would,' Black said. 'There are two that I know of, Médecins sans Frontières people. And there's a Dutch chap who might be here with the group that came in early this morning.'

While Willard, a tall, thin fellow from Nottingham, was having a look at the rack of equipment in the comms room, Kitson found the Médecins sans Frontières group and introduced himself in very bad French. 'We all speak English,' a woman said. She had short hair with three earrings in one earlobe and was wearing clogs.

'My ship was fired on by a shore battery. There are injured and we only have a medical orderly. I would like a doctor to be in the next party we transfer to the *Beaufort*. We could use some help.'

'Of course,' the woman said.

It didn't take Willard long. The generator lacked sufficient power to keep a consistent voltage running through to the equipment. The comms unit was a keyboard with a screen that encoded the message to be transmitted. Willard bypassed the main junction board with the lights and air-conditioning and took the generator power cable direct to the comms room circuits, then fired it up. The unit worked fine and ten minutes later Kitson was at the screen typing in his message for Northwood to be sent in the same encoded burst as Black's message to the FCO.

He finished and got up from the chair to let Black in to put his message on the screen. The US Embassy, he thought. Need to advise them that things are hotting up. They would have heard the guns. VHF. If they have a helicopter that comes in then they might have VHF. He took the Clansman radio through to Black's office, where he found a woman sitting in an easy chair in the corner. She had long, almost white blond hair piled up in a bun on her head. She was busty, curvy, the sort of woman who in time would struggle with her weight, but for now every curve was in the right place as she sat with her feet tucked under her on the chair, smoking a cigarette. Her piercing sky-blue eyes narrowed as she smiled at him. He remembered her. She had brought him a cup of tea that morning. Was it only that morning? Seemed like an age ago.

'Just grabbing a moment's peace,' she explained. 'If I ever see another sandwich I will scream. I'm Poppy, Maggie Black's sister.'

'Aah, right. Peter Kitson,' he introduced himself.

'Do you want me to go?' She pointed to the radio he had put on the desk. Kitson shook his head. If she was the Ambassador's wife's sister, then she was deeply involved and very much part of the inner core of events anyway.

'No. Stay put.'

'You look tired,' she said. 'When was the last time you ate?'

He smiled. Last night? No. Never finished it. Didn't sleep, either. 'I'm okay,' he replied.

'We've got some ham still. On the bone, from the hotel. I'll make you a sandwich and get you a cup of tea.'

'I'd rather coffee, if you have any,' he replied, suddenly realizing he was hungry. 'I thought you were going to scream if you saw another sandwich?'

'Oh, you'll hear it,' she said, standing up, smoothing out her dress, the wide smile again.

He powered up the Clansman and firstly advised the *Beaufort* that he had passed the message to London and that there were trained medical staff among the civilians. He then selected 243 megahertz, the aviation frequency on which he thought the Americans would have a listening watch, and picked up the handset.

'US compound Monrovia, US compound Monrovia, this is Beaufort two.'

He waited a few seconds and was about to repeat the call when there was a response.

'This is the US Embassy Monrovia. State your callsign and go ahead please, over.'

'US Embassy, this is Beaufort two at the British Embassy compound. Can I speak to your Ambassador, over?'

'Aah . . . bo-fit two, he is a little busy at this time . . . Aah bo-fit two, did you hear that firing earlier, over?

'That is what I need to talk about. Can you identify yourself please, over?' The door opened and Poppy came back in carrying a plate and a red china mug. She put them down beside him and sat down again quietly in the corner chair.

'Bo-fit two, I am Corporal Stowitz, United States Marines.'

'Corporal, I am X-ray Oscar of HMS *Beaufort*,' he spelled it out phonetically. 'She is standing off the coast at this time and I am ashore with a party in the British compound. We have been under fire. Now I need to speak to someone in authority in your location immediately. Do you copy that? Over.'

'Ahh, affirmative bo-fit two. Stand by on this frequency. Sir, for your information we have a helo inbound in about fifteen minutes and we will need this channel, over.'

'I understand . . . ah, suggest you advise your aircraft that there are hostiles in the area.'

'Stand by.'

He looked across at her. 'Thanks.' He was sipping his coffee and about to reach for the sandwich when the radio squawked.

'Bo-fit two, bo-fit two, this is Lima Oscar, stand by.' Another voice came on. 'This is Charles Davis, first attaché. Who am I speaking to?'

'Charles, my name is Peter Kitson.' He explained again who he was. 'The shelling you heard was my ship coming under attack from shore-based artillery and her response. In addition we have been under small-arms fire here at this location. Be advised, the enclave is now hostile and I suggest you take all precautions. We will be evacuating this area sometime today, over.'

'Aah, thank you, Commander. I will advise the Ambassador immediately. We are expecting . . . added resources any minute.' He was being very careful what he said, aware that it was an open channel. 'Can I ask the . . . man in charge to speak to you direct on arrival? I believe he will want your view of things.'

'Affirmative. Beaufort two out.'

The message that came in on the Foreign and Commonwealth Office decoders was hand-carried by messenger round the corner to the MoD in Whitehall. There a ranking naval officer was waiting to receive it and he took it straight to his office where Northwood were waiting on the telephone line. He read it to them twice, and then gave it to a second messenger who would arrange to have the hard copy delivered. The Defence Minister was advised and he in turn put a call through to the Prime Minister at No 10 at about the same time as the Foreign Secretary was tracked down to his constituency where he was about to open a new factory built with Korean investment.

At Northwood a naval operations group quickly convened in a meeting room. The standard scenarios were now out of the window. One of Her Majesty's ships had come under fire, an act of war, and while the politicians in Whitehall and Westminster discussed the options they had a simple task: to support one of their own until the political types came back with policy.

The meeting had begun when the C-in-C arrived. Admiral Sir Michael Spalding was lean, hawk-like, in his early fifties and the very image of the modern navy. He was previously FOSF, the Flag Officer Surface Flotilla, with every ship in the surface fleet under his command and that was fine because he hated submarines. He had commanded one once and, standing six feet three in his stocking feet, had spent his life avoiding banging his head on pipes and valves and door lintels. Now as C-in-C he had them in his fleet, but his Chief of Staff (Operations) was also FO Submarines so he managed to avoid them. He had been C-in-C for eighteen months and many said that he would be First Sea Lord before he retired.

With him was Captain (F) Davis, not only commander of his own ship but of the six-frigate flotilla to which HMS *Beaufort* belonged.

'Morning, gentlemen,' Spalding said, taking control. 'Hope you don't mind my butting in. I have brought Guy Davis in. He was in the building and the Beau is one of his ships. He also drives a 23 so he knows more about them than the rest of us put together. Sitrep?'

'Sir,' the fleet Ops officer, a commander, began, '*Beaufort*, standing off Monrovia under orders to help execute an evacuation if deemed necessary, was fired on by a shore battery. She was two miles off, anchor down, shafts locked while a diver was down clearing a propeller shaft of netting. She took a hit, commenced return fire and took a second hit before, we believe, her four point five neutralized the battery. Commander Bennett believes it was neutralized because in the further few minutes before the shaft locks were off and the cable was broken so she could move, there was no further fire.

'The first shell hit high in the funnels. Superficial damage. The second exploded in the MCO. We have four dead ratings and ten injured, two of those critical, two serious, six walking. The XO is ashore at the Embassy with a party. More to go in. Airborne out of Gibraltar,' he looked at his watch, 'twenty minutes ago is a recce troop of Marines to support the bluejackets. *Fearless* in Gib is slipping her lines as we speak.'

'Netting. Fishing net?' Spalding asked.

'Yes, Admiral. Fishing net.'

'Of all the places to get fouled.' He shook his head in amazement. 'Options?'

Another officer looked up. '*Nottingham*, *Southampton* and *Richmond* are all on the Tanus exercise in the channel. *Gold Rover* is nearest and now under way and heading for Monrovia as quickly as she can. Still three days away, and then she can only offer space. Nothing else nearer.'

'Air?'

'*Invincible* is thirty hours from serviceable.' This was an aviator speaking, aircraft his speciality. 'Turbine work in Portsmouth. *Illustrious* is still in the Adriatic. Too far to offer support. But *Ark Royal* is one day out of Fort Lauderdale. She has been working with F14s and F18s out of NAS Oceana in Norfolk. They will be well worked up. With a bit of careful planning and mid-air refuelling she could launch Harriers with a half-decent load by late tomorrow.'

'What's your view?' Spalding asked the aviator.

'Without clear targets and clear objectives . . .' he paused '. . . it would be little more than an armed recce. If there was nothing to let the ordnance go at, they would have to jettison it anyway, to lighten the load and make it back to the refuelling point. Unless there is something for the boys to attack, and a clearly desperate situation for our people on the ground, enough to warrant risking the lives of these pilots, then I'd say it's a last resort.'

They were running over other various options when a rating knocked on the door and spoke to Admiral Spalding.

'Sir, telephone call. It's the FCO.'

Spalding went to the telephone on the side table, listened for a few moments and said, 'Again, please.' Finally he hung up and turned to the room.

'Yet to be confirmed by the Americans, but on our comms link with the Embassy in Monrovia. An American helicopter has just been shot down as it was coming in to the American Embassy compound. The crew and personnel, Marines who were going in to reinforce the Embassy guard, were all killed.'

'Oh Jesus,' someone uttered sadly.

Spalding looked at the group. 'This is now something for the fast response committee. We need to establish who else has ships in the area and contact *Ark Royal*. Advise she is to await fresh orders, but for now she is to proceed with all speed to place herself able to launch aircraft into the theatre of operation.' Spalding knew that for the moment that simply meant a ten or twelve degree course change and he was well within his remit to order that in advance of any word coming from Whitehall.

He thought quickly about the two Type 42 destroyers, *Nottingham* and *Southampton*. They were fast. With speed well in excess of thirty knots they could be down there in four days and they could offer naval gunfire support to the Marines and bluejackets ashore. They could also offer refuelling and staging for *Fearless*'s troop-carrying helicopters if necessary. But four days? This situation was worsening by the minute.

Kitson was outside when it happened, briefing Chops and the three ratings he would be taking down to the waterfront to meet the incoming seaboats. Baker and the civilian Johnson were still watching the group on their side and Kitson was planning a nice, peaceful stroll to the beach when he heard it. The heavy whumping of a big twin rotor transport helicopter. He looked out, knowing he would see it any minute, the sound of the rotors familiar. It was a Chinook, standard workhorse of both American and British forces. He felt better suddenly, knowing someone had the resources to get a big helicopter into the area: a Chinook could land a lot more people than their little Lynx.

'Now that,' the yeoman said, listening to the beat of the rotors, 'is a bloody big budgie.'

Kitson smiled. It was that. He was feeling better. More friendlies in the area. There. He could see it now, coming in from the sea. Big, slow, its nose lifted as it approached its LZ in the familiar tail-dragging way. Then suddenly, bright lights arcing up at it, red and green tracer rounds, the crackle of small arms and a dozen or more weapons began shooting at it from the north. There was a gasp from the people watching, the scene unreal, like something from a film.

Oh shit. Abort. Come on, abort, he was thinking, power on, abort the run-in, come on, come on, then the pilot reacting, the discs forward, the whine of the power settings increased and then a bigger gun opening up. A big 30-millimetre or maybe an old fifty calibre, heavy rounds slamming into the helicopter. They were close enough to see the strikes, bits of plexiglass and darker bits of the fuselage being blown away. She was hit, mortally wounded, falling on her side as the pilot tried to correct, and just before her rotors hit the trees and she dropped from view there was a massive blast as incoming fire hit a fuel tank, a fireball of fuel above the rooftops. She hit the ground with another blast and a mushroom fireball of orange rolled upward, no more than two hundred yards away. The heat wave rocked them back, shaking leaves in the trees and Kitson was on his feet and running for the gate.

'Mr Buchanan! Cover us. You men, with me!' Chops and the other three took off after him.

Someone started the van and pulled it away from the gate and as Kitson was about to open it the French doctor, the one with the earrings and the clogs was suddenly there with them. Kitson didn't argue. If anyone survived that then they would need her. One of his people threw him an SA80.

'Let's go.'

He moved them quickly from cover to cover down to the intersection and then across to the far side of the road. The flames and pall of smoke rose from their ten o'clock and as he paused and went down on one knee to look ahead, Chops came past him expertly and they began to leapfrog each other, the other four moving up behind them. Ammunition began to cook off, rounds exploding in the heat of the flames. This was Kitson's worst nightmare. Aircraft down. He was a pilot. He was there in the cockpit with them. Two blocks up Chops stopped and peered round the corner. They weren't going to have long. Whoever had done this would be wanting to survey their work, loot the wreckage – or what was left of it.

He was up and moving and then they were in amongst it, bits of debris and wreckage on the ground. A body, blown naked by the blast, hung in a tree, another almost whole on the road splayed out. There was a lump of something further up the road. Wilks, the Chops(M), looked back at them. Ammunition was still going off.

'Stay 'ere,' he said to the lads and he crawled round the edge of the wall with Kitson. The French doctor moved round past where Kitson knelt. He went to take her arm to hold her back, but she pulled away and moved into the smoke, alongside him but down on her belly like Wilks. They were gone a full ten minutes and when they returned, the woman's eyes were glazed and Chops was pale. It had been carnage, a vision of hell, flames, smoke, bodies and parts of what had been people, limbs torn off.

'Ammo is going to be going off for hours. Let's move out,' Kitson said to everyone. One of the ratings was being sick. He had seen the lump of something up the road and realized what it was. It was a human lung.

Kitson was talking to Buchanan on one of the small yellow handheld radios, advising him of what they had found and to get on to Northwood, when the rating nearest the road junction whistled softly. Kitson looked back and the fellow pointed up the main road ahead of them. He and Wilks crossed the road and moved up to the corner where they could peer round. There was movement. Chops brought his weapon up to his shoulder and a few moments later lowered it. 'Septics,' he said.

It was three young Marines from the Embassy, even their sergeant seemed to be barely shaving to Kitson, who quickly briefed them, finishing: 'There's no point going on. I think you would be better back at the compound. Who is your commanding officer?'

'I command the detail, sir. There's eight of us. That was our buddies in . . .' he trailed off.

Kitson could see his discomfort. It wasn't just the loss, the shock of losing his comrades, but he was also having to deal with the fact that he was now it. He was the senior Marine on the post and as the situation was deteriorating their link had been cut.

'Let's head back. I want to meet your senior people anyway.'

Three minutes later they were slipping into the US Embassy compound through a small Judas gate. At least three hundred people crowded down the shady side of a large grass area and the mood was sombre. The situation was similar to his own compound, the place crowded, most of the families gathered in the shade where they could, with possessions, luggage, several portable barbecues, even one or two bikes and toys and a few vehicles scattered around, but the people were shocked, quiet, and some were crying. One group of about thirty were standing together with small bags and Kitson knew they would have been going out on the Chinook's return journey. He was very obvious in his cap and uniform, now getting grubby; people began to look at him and point and he understood immediately. They were frightened and had just seen a representation of their country, young men, their Marines, their protectors, their link with law and order and home blown out of the sky within yards of where they stood. They were alone again, vulnerable, and suddenly he was standing there in a naval officer's uniform.

Two men came towards him, the younger, taller one putting out his hand. 'Charles Davis,' he said, taking in Kitson's shoulder tabs. 'Commander Kitson, is it?'

'Lieutenant Commander. I am sorry, Mr Davis. All dead, I'm afraid. We got there as quickly as we could. We couldn't get right inside the wreckage, flames and ammunition going off. Everyone we saw was dead. Inside no one could have survived.'

'Oh my God.' He recovered quickly, pointing to the man on his right. 'I understand. This is Edward Alberry, the Ambassador.'

Alberry shook hands. 'It's Ed. You have just come from the wreckage?'

'That's correct, sir.'

'And in your opinion no one could have survived that?'

Kitson shook his head. 'I am sorry.'

'Sweet Jesus . . .' he bowed his head for a second, appalled by what had happened, then looked up. 'Son, did you see it go in?'

'We did. From the British Embassy compound.'

'In your opinion, as a serving military officer, what caused the crash?'

'I'll go further than serving officer. I am also an aviator. I fly helicopters. That Chinook was intentionally shot down by ground fire.'

Alberry nodded and looked away for a second or two. 'Three crew and forty Marines. Forty-three dead kids, Commander. Murdered . . .' he trailed off, then looked back. 'If they shot down that helicopter, they could hit another? Right?'

'Absolutely.'

'That helicopter was going to begin evacuating people. I think we'd better go into my office.'

The building was bigger, two-thirds as big again as the British Embassy, festooned in American flags and pictures of Bill Clinton, with a walk-through metal detector and proper glass-screened security desk. It made the British mission seem very low-key and casual. Alberry's office was big, with a full lounge suite on one side and big windows that overlooked the private back garden that was also full of people.

'Your ship is standing by?'

'She is. Damaged by shell fire. We too have dead. But the Beau will remain on station,' he added with some pride. 'I have an officer and twelve or so armed rates ashore now, with another group on their way any time. Our intent is to have thirty armed ratings ashore today, supported by a recce troop of Royal Marines hopefully by tonight, and to commence moving people out to the ship as soon as we prudently can.'

'I have eight Marines headed up by a sergeant. You met him out there. They are good. They do their job, but they are now stretched to the limit. I think we may need to see how we can co-operate.'

'Of course,' Kitson replied thinking quickly on the implications. Two compounds, several hundred yards apart, double, maybe triple the number of people. He had been thinking through the logistics of moving those in the British compound out to the ship in terms of seaboat trips, eight or nine at a time, from a secure defendable area. Two hundred and seventy-odd people, thirty crew. While the faction fighting was this close, and they were prepared to fire at neutral aircraft, nothing short of a major operation would allow airlift. It would need suppression or neutralization of ground fire by support elements, either men on

122

the ground rolling out a perimeter some miles, or ground attack helicopters suppressing the enemy forces long enough to allow the heavies in to load and get out again. A major military operation in anyone's book.

'How many people do you have here, sir? In total?' he asked.

Alberry had been thinking about his commercial VIPs. The timing of this escalation was not advantageous. Three very senior people from CDL, the US partner in the ConLib joint venture, had been working on the three-yearly concession negotiations. They had influence, enough lobbying power in Washington to make people sit up and take notice. One of them had been at college with his wife and was staying with them at the residence.

'Eleven staff and...' Alberry looked at Davis, who responded, 'Four hundred and seventeen nationals and friendlies.'

Kitson thought back to the last families' day in Portsmouth. They had had over seven hundred visitors on the ship that day and while people were falling over each other, it was manageable.

'On your request, we will of course lend all assistance and if necessary evacuate your people to the *Beaufort*. Of more immediate concern is keeping things safe for the next few hours.'

'I agree. The phones are down, but you and Charles have talked on the radio already. I think I should raise my people in Washington and talk to Bill...' he looked at Kitson: 'Bill Black.'

'Can I suggest, sir, that you are careful choosing your words. VHF is open channel.'

Alberry smiled. 'We will get through it. We play Trivial Pursuit together and I know the way he thinks. Bill speaks pretty fair Spanish, and so do I. He also did Latin at school, as did I. We will endeavour, son, not to drop you in the do-do.'

*   *   *

Lieutenant Andy Gordon and his recce troop of Royal Marines were now outbound from Gibraltar in the Royal Air Force Hercules. Flight planned to cross Morocco, move out over the Atlantic and then run down the West Africa coast, they would be overhead the drop zone just after 1700 hours Zulu. This long-haul-equipped aircraft had very long legs, but even so the Foreign and Common-wealth Office were still trying to get permission to refuel in Sierra Leone on the return journey. A contingency plan was already in effect, with a mid-air refuelling tanker out-bound from her base in southern England and a second tanker, an American aircraft, sitting on Ascension Island. If necessary she would go straight on to meet the 'Hercy bird' at a mid-air rendezvous to be determined, trail out her hose and nozzle and pump fuel back to the hungry tanks of the four-engine heavy-lift turboprop.

But that wasn't Lieutenant Gordon's problem. He knew that his lads would get a half-hour warning. Approaching the drop zone the Hercules would depressurize slowly as she lost altitude, finally lowering the big aft ramp doors as the red light came on. All things going to plan, it would be in the last hour of daylight and they would see the ship below them, recovery boats out waiting, flares burning in the water. If the wind wasn't too bad they should all be able to land within one or two hundred feet of the flares. They could get closer with the new parachutes, but with thirty canopies and seven canisters in the water there was every chance of hitting something on landing, getting tangled in lines or, God forbid, striking a canister, and you wanted to land softly into clear water.

Then aboard ship, break out the gear, get briefed – they had heard nothing since departing Condor early that morning – and then get ashore and do the business. Ninety per cent chance this whole job would come to nothing, but with a dusk drop into the water, with canisters and a seaboat recovery, it was better than an exercise and they could all log the jump.

He looked down at the men who had joined them in Gibraltar. He knew three of them, Corporal Doughty best of all. He was pleased Doughty was along. With his bubbling good humour and a wonderfully irreverent view of life, officers and women, he was always good company. He was also a bloody good Marine commando and ready to make sergeant. He was sitting wide awake, telling a story to two of his oppos, his cheeky little grin there as he spun out the tale. The lads from Condor were all dozing quietly, trying to get some rest after their night out on the heather. The gear was all checked and stored, the canisters closed and, if anything, they were over-equipped, Doughty having prised two section machine guns and a bunch of shoulder launched missiles, LAWs, from the armoury on *Fearless* in addition to the kit they had brought from Condor. He almost wished they didn't have it all. Lots to lug around, get wet, clean and be accountable for till it was back with the QM.

He closed his eyes and tried to sleep.

On *Beaufort*, Commander Bennett, his officers gathered round him on the bridge, was finishing a meeting. They were all there, the engineering team, supply, and the executive branch of watchkeepers and warfare specialists. All had briefed the captain on their departments, their functions, reviewed their operational capability in the aftermath of the attack, and aired problems. For Bennett it boiled down to his command imperatives again. Float, fight, move. They were floating, they were moving. There had been some degradation of power since the hole was blown through the funnels, but the MEO had a team up there now patching the damage and compression would be back to normal by nightfall. Their ability to fight had not been impaired. They could not, however, communicate with anyone, other than their shore party with the Clansman radio. Had London ordered an evacuation, stepped up the game? They had to assume the evacuation was now a reality. Therefore they had an objective, a clear task, but in vastly different circumstances. There might be another shore battery, so coming in close in daylight carried some risk, although under way and therefore a moving target and with her own firepower ready to respond, the risk was bearable. There was also increased risk ashore. The mission had been all but under fire and the streets were a no man's land.

When the news about the American aircraft came through there was a stunned silence on the bridge. 'Well,' someone said, 'that's it, then. It's on,' almost as though he had not believed all that had happened to them in the last hour. A couple of them looked at Mayberry, who had turned and was staring out the window at the sea. He was appalled and shocked, saddened and angry and wishing that his Lynx wasn't a softskinned marine variant but an attack helicopter, ground-attack equipped. The weapons and electronics suite designed to offer the ability to hunt and kill submarines or ships was about as much use here, he thought, as tits on a bull. Oh for a thirty mill and rocket pods. Then we'll see who sticks their heads up.

'Right,' Bennett said. 'Tasks.' He looked at Montagu, his Comms Officer. 'One, raise the Embassy. They are to advise London of our VHF frequency and let us know of the drop point for the Marines. We will be there. Two, remaining shore party to go ashore at dusk, earlier if we need to be on station to uplift the recce troop. First seaboat back to have a doctor on board. Three, raise the US mission. Offer all assistance.' Mayberry was next. 'You get some sleep, if you would. Then your helo ready for operations by dusk or the Marines, whichever is first. You will be airborne for that, with divers. Ops, I want to drop back to defence watch. Short ones. Three on, three off. Let the lads get some sleep. It's going to be a long night. Back to action stations at dusk, the ship ready to take on civilians and, if necessary, fight. Everyone happy?'

He wanted to get down to the sick bay. See his people.

126

One of the wounded had been asking to see him and it was the least he could do.

Down on 2 deck in the Wrens' mess area, Kate Wallace had finally settled her young charges. The children were now watching a video. It was a grown-ups' movie, but had enough of a huge, ugly, slobbering dog tracking down its master's killer to keep them interested. One of the other Wrens came through the door and, stepping over little brown legs, went for a cup by the sink where Kate was standing.

'How is she?'

'Who?' Kate responded.

'Cheryl.'

'I don't bloody know. She was supposed to give me a hand with these little sods,' she whispered.

'Oh f—' The Wren caught herself. 'You didn't know?'

'Know what?' Kate hissed. 'I'm in here doing bloody Blue Peter,' she added with a grin.

'Cheryl. I heard she was in the MCO.'

Kate was at the door in three strides and as she swung it open and ran into the passage the other Wren smiled weakly at the mother.

The sick bay was only a few yards up the passage and as she went through the door she stopped. Cheryl, please no, not Cheryl. It was crowded, injured people seemingly everywhere, five first aid trained ratings working under the direction of the Leading Medical Assistant, who was still leaning over Cheryl Simpson. Her body was covered in a sterile sheet, only the burn he was working on exposed. Kate swept her eyes round the room, looking at the people on bunks and chairs, some bandaged, some lying flat, looking for her friend. There was only one form she couldn't see. The leading medical assistant, the nearest thing they had to a doctor on the ship, was leaning over someone, his back to her.

'Out of here,' one of the first aiders said. 'We're busy.'

'Cheryl,' Kate said. 'Cheryl Simpson?'

'Out!'

'Please . . . she's my mate. Please tell me . . .'

The LMA looked round at her. His eyes said it. His eyes over the surgical mask he was wearing. He turned and pulled it down. He shook his head. He had just lost her.

Leading Weapons Artificer Cheryl Simpson was the first woman rating to be killed in action since women were allowed to serve aboard a Royal Navy warship. For her selfless courage in entering the burning communications suite and shielding the body of a shipmate with her own, she was also to be the first woman to win a medal for conspicuous gallantry above that normally expected of a British sailor in the face of the enemy.

She would not be the only one that day.

5

Kate held back the tears long enough to reach the rail. With the ship at action stations there should have been no one on the weather deck, but she ignored that and stood looking out to sea from the starboard rail and let the tears come.

Lieutenant Morris, the navigator, who still had the watch, saw her and was about to send her back into the citadel, but he knew that they were about to go on to defence watches and he could see she was upset and he hesitated. Bennett was thinking the same and shook his head. 'Leave her,' he said. He had just been advised that LWA Simpson had died of her wounds.

The ship's company knew. The news spread like wildfire. Another of their own was dead. But something extraordinary was happening. The mood had changed. This time it was not just a shipmate but a Wren, one of their 'girlies'. They had all wondered about going into action with women, what their reactions might be, but it had been a distant, passing thought. Few of them ever believed it would ever happen, really happen. Men in the process of getting used to serving aboard ship with women might slag them off, tease them, sometimes resent them, but they were theirs. *Their* Wrens. Their bloody shipmates. They were angry. Someone had killed one of their girlies and this was now personal.

There were differing manifestations of the mood, all intensely individual. In the gun bay, where there were four live rounds in the feed ring, a rating without being asked or told, or seeking permission, loaded more, filling the ring to its maximum sixteen rounds. Down in the main control room the senior rating nearest the engine control station felt the levers. The bridge called for revolutions, but they could never get it exactly right because they didn't think in revolutions but in power settings. The bridge might call for 120 revolutions and they knew where to push the levers to give 'em roughly 120 turns of the propellers every minute, but it was never exact. Today it was. The senior rating, an engineering Petty Officer, eased the gas turbine throttles forward a hundredth of an inch. Exactly what his instincts told him was 120. This was all he could do, but by Christ it would be right. In the Ops room a man watching the 966 radar plot cranked it out, seeking a threat, seeking something he could lock on to, and the men in the hangar waiting to go ashore gripped their weapons closer, checked magazine loads and fidgeted. They wanted to go. Fucking get stuck in, as one said. Get it sorted.

As Kate stood at the rail, wiping away her tears, the activity below her was furious, the MEO's people rough patching the hole blown in *Beaufort*'s side, the blackened steel edges punched outward a full twelve inches by the blast.

At the British Embassy compound, Ted Brooks was frantically busy. Accepting that he was not going to be able to get to the US mission he had decided to operate from where he was and his producer and techie were still setting up the satellite dish on the roof and getting the system fired up when the American Chinook had been coming in. His cameraman, professional to the core, had been recording, the scene dramatic enough, but when the ground fire began to hit he zoomed in closer, capturing everything on tape. This was now a huge story and Brooks knew that the moment he could get the satellite uplink functioning, CNN in Atlanta would interrupt whatever was running for his breaking story and the dreadful news and pictures he had for them. He was working to camera, doing the background, when the vehicle in front of the gate was quickly reversed out of the way and Lieutenant Commander Kitson and his patrol ducked through the gates, the cameraman seeing it in the background to the shot and panning left to catch the armed sailors coming in. The dramatic sight said everything. No longer was this the normal image of the naval officer in the tropics, whites crisp, clean and gleaming. Kitson entered last, his camo smock now grubby and carrying an SA80 assault rifle. With the cameraman following, Brooks began walking towards him, talking to the camera as he went.

'As you can see, the patrol made up of a shore party from the Royal Navy's HMS *Beaufort*, at present standing off the coast waiting to take the foreign civilians inside these walls to safety, the patrol that watched with us in horror as the helicopter plummeted earthwards and raced out, we believe, to where the aircraft went in just half an hour ago has just returned. The officer is Lieutenant Commander Kitson and we shall now try and get some update on events.' He held the microphone to Kitson's face and Kitson knew that, given the circumstances, he would have to make some statement.

'Commander, we all saw the helicopter come under attack and falling. Can you tell us what you found?'

'We got to the crash site. As everyone witnessed, the aircraft, a US military Chinook, exploded before it hit the ground, so the wreckage is scattered. It is still burning and there is ammunition going off, as you can hear, so we were unable to go into the two main sections of the fuselage, but no one could have survived in those two areas. The wider area we could get into, we did. Regretfully, we found no survivors.'

'No survivors at all?'

'That is correct.'

'How many people do you think were on board? What could an aircraft that size carry?'

'We returned via the US mission with US Marines of the Embassy guard detail who also came out. I am advised that there were forty military personnel, United States Marines on their way to reinforce the guard detail, and three crew on board.'

'We all saw the ground fire, Commander, fire aimed directly at the helicopter. Is there any indication of who committed this act? Of who fired?'

'I can't speculate on that. There is fighting to the north of the enclave and the situation is very confused. Now if you will excuse me.'

By now the American Ambassador had been in touch with both his Department of State in Washington and the Embassy in Sierra Leone, nominal contact point for the US military logistics team and operating base and the point of departure of the crashed helicopter. He strongly advised that any further attempts to fly into his location in Monrovia be suspended until the situation eased, explained the worsening security situation and relayed the Royal Navy's offer of assistance.

State moved quickly. The Pentagon and the President were advised and while the White House press aides organized a quick press conference, CNN on the television sets in their offices, the Pentagon got to work. There were no more Marines in Sierra Leone: the staging area there only had one supported platoon for its own security and they had been in the Chinook. The nearest trained personnel were in Germany, at a base not far from Frankfurt, but the decision was taken to deploy a more specialist unit from the Marines base at San Diego. They were given three hours' notice to move, but even so it would be twenty hours before they could be on the ground in the Embassy in Monrovia. The US Navy aircraft carrier USS *John F. Kennedy*, known as 'Big John' to her crew, had slipped her moorings that morning from Dublin Bay in Ireland after an astonishingly successful goodwill visit and was under way towards Southampton when she got new orders. She was retasked and, at top speed, turned south with her small battle group. She had helicopters and there were currently 76 marines deployed in her group, but more importantly she could at least offer some defence of her transport helicopters and tacticians were already working on the methodology. She was at least three days away.

Twenty minutes before the press conference was scheduled, Brooks got his link and an aide rushed into the Oval Office and turned on the television. The President watched the videotaped footage in horror and the following interview with the British officer who had attended the crash site. As he watched, a security aide slipped from the room to make a call.

Splif, Bang-Bang and the others in their little band were still moving. Either side of them small units of Ulima-J, more gangs than military formations, were closing on the city. Thousands of them. The sprawling advance through the bush had become columns of men and boys, the semi-circular array covering a front miles across. Every now and then they would stop, to rest, to forage, to take some food at gunpoint if there was anyone to steal it from. One of the younger boys had found a book. This was one they liked. It was big and soft, easy to fold and had stories told with many pictures, of a man in a black cape and mask, with a long black car with big wings at the back. One of them could read a little and he said the man was called 'Betman'. They wondered whether this was the same kind of bats as they had, one of them translating for a younger boy who spoke no English, but they were all agreed, the car was good. They all wanted one of those.

Bang-Bang, his eyes red, stoned out of his head, in a moment of clarity knew they never would have a car like that. Not now. Not tomorrow. Not ever. The best they would ever do was something like the car they had stopped yesterday. That was good. Lots of room. Maybe one day he would have one of those and he could run a taxi service. That car could maybe take ten people. He thought briefly about the nun he had shot. There was no remorse. No regret. He was strong, she was weak. That was the way it was. In front of them they could see the skyline of Monrovia itself. It was maybe only three or four miles away. Booty. Money. Women maybe, some white ones. He had heard they were different. Their hair, down there, was long. Not the crinkly tight black curls he had seen on their women. He was hungry. With dugees he forgot about food, but he had not had heroin smokes today. Money, they had said. Plenty of money in Monrovia. They would fight. He liked that. Liked shooting his gun. Fight and take what was there. Money to buy dugees, food, maybe even a car. How much did a car cost? He didn't know. If he couldn't have a car, he would get a bicycle with saddle bags and a light, and maybe some sunglasses.

At the British Embassy the encoder link with London was running constantly. Aitcheson pulled off the latest page from the printer and handed it to the rating at the Clansman radio with Kitson, who was at that moment talking to the ship. The XO had expressed his concerns and wanted the remainder of his party ashore forthwith and while Captain Bennett was assessing this new risk, he looked down at the message. It was for *Beaufort*, details of the drop point for the Marine detachment and a formal request from Whitehall, routed through Northwood and then back on the FCO encoders, for HMS *Beaufort* and her company to lend all assistance as required to the US mission. This had come through incredibly quickly, he knew that much. Someone at the US end had got their act together. A formality, really, but one Kitson knew his Captain would appreciate. More importantly, in the second section was a change to RoE.

The new rules of engagement, obviously authorized after

the attack on the helicopter, opened out Bennett's brief and allowed him to take whatever action he thought necessary to protect the wellbeing of both British subjects and all other foreign nationals as he saw fit, in the course of evacuating them to a place of safety.

Kitson, assuming that their conversation was being listened to, had been very oblique in his references till that point, but he read that message to the Captain verbatim and repeated it twice. There would be no way of getting hard copy out to the ship, so a writer took it straight on to a pad, checked it twice and then Bennett read it back to him, word for word, punctuation perfect. This was critical. There was no room for error in a commanding officer's understanding of his rules of engagement when his ship was operating in an environment such as this.

'That's correct, sir,' Kitson confirmed.

'Thank you, Beaufort two. Advise that we have the Romeo Oscar Echo, that we have the Romeo Victor for our friends. Your other request. Do you remember what time Baywatch starts?'

'Ah, certainly do, Beaufort.' Kitson grinned. Morris. Morris was feeding the boss with the gen. Six o'clock. Eighteen hundred hours. The hallmark of a good navigator. Finding an anchorage where you could pick up Baywatch by 1755 hours without fail.

'Three hours before that at the place you described. Happy? Over.'

'Ah, yes. Can we backload, over?'

'Affirmative, Beaufort two. Can we expect a medic in the first transfer, over?'

'That's confirmed.'

Kitson signed off. Fifteen hundred hours at the beach at the bottom of the road. He looked at his watch. It was just before 1300. He wanted a patrol out soon. Recce the route again. Then move down – how many? Cram them in. Eight adults no problem, go for ten in each. Twenty adults. No kids yet. Do that after dark when we are in strength.

He was thinking it through when the generator outside

spluttered to a halt and the decoder and other equipment died.

'Oh shit,' Aitcheson muttered wiping the sweat back from his face.

'Willard.' Kitson turned to the radio artificer who had rerun the power cables in the first place. 'Have a look, will you?'

Willard was back in fifteen minutes with Jones, the mechanic.

'Not good, sir. It's been leaking coolant from somewhere. Overheated. Seized. With the right kit we could get it opened up, but . . .' Jones shrugged.

'We've been expecting this,' Black said. 'When we reopened the mission two years ago we bought this generator as a temporary measure. Second or fifth hand or whatever. We were told that it needed replacing recently. The new one's due in next month.'

'Well . . .' Kitson replied, thinking: this is all we bloody need. Enough frigging about. 'Then we run without it. Sir, can you talk to the American Ambassador? I can't defend two locations. I'd like to move the people from their compound down here as soon as we can after my recce troop is here. This is the first strongpoint. We go from here in managed groups to the beach. There we will have the second and final redoubt. I will have a shore party to support his guard detail there by 1530 hours and I would like his people ready to go by 1800 hours.'

'I'll talk to him now,' Black promised, but his tone said: it's his call, his decision.

Kitson nodded, pulled his cap on and went out to find Buchanan.

But what is the command structure, he was thinking. Will their Marines drop into my structure? Be allowed to? Or will they run independently, loose allies. He thought they might respect his rank, but there might be a problem once he very happily handed command to the officer in charge of the Marine recce troop, likely to be a Lieutenant.

Personally he couldn't wait for a solid-ground type. He was an aviator and a seagoing officer. This ground-based scenario wasn't his line of expertise. Then again, it might be the opposite. They might be happy to report to an officer of Marines, even if he was a Royal Marine, and not to him. He shrugged it off. Worry about that later. Right now he wanted water for his lads. It was stinking hot and they were sweating. And tonight, the insects.

'Sir, I don't suppose you have any mosquito repellant? Enough for my ratings?'

Sarah Conway looked across at Orbs Montagu. They had stood down their parties to get some food and something cold to drink, leaving a couple of ratings guarding the stack of weapons and gear in the hangar, and were back up in the wardroom sitting at the table. He was miles away. When the steward put a plate of big, sensible sandwiches down for them and left she reached forward and took one.

'Penny for them,' Sarah said softly. She knew what he was thinking, but unlike most men Orbs did talk. Was prepared to voice his feelings.

'I should have been in there. My station, my division. But no, I was larking about in a rubberdub.'

'You were under orders,' Sarah reminded him objectively.

'That's not the point. The point is that I had a responsibility to my lads. There's me happily volunteering to go ashore and suddenly they are in it. I should have been there.'

'You should have been following orders, which is what you were doing. No one could have known we were going to be attacked. There was no warning, nothing anyone could do.'

He looked at her. 'You're right . . .' she pushed the plate towards him and he shook his head '. . . but I still feel like shit. It's ironic. Here we are on the newest warship in the world. State of the art systems. We can hunt and kill just about anything that floats, flies or dives, and yet here, today, none of it is worth a pinch of shit. We are back to Jack putting down a marlin spike, drawing a cutlass and boarding seaboats.'

'Well, that's what we do best,' Sarah said dryly. 'After all, this is the Royal Navy. The defence of the realm and all that. It's what we do.'

He smiled. The phone rang and the steward who answered looked at them.

'Bridge. It's for both of you.'

She stood up. 'Come on, Mole. Let's go mess about in boats.'

Beaufort had begun a long, curving course that would put her three miles off the beach, all weapons systems operative in time to put seaboats in the water at exactly 1445 hours.

Captain Bennett would have liked to increase the size of his shore party, but they were limited by *Beaufort*'s small arsenal and he wasn't convinced that putting unarmed people ashore would add any value to justify the increased risk. He studied the shoreline as he had done for hours now. There was a smudge of smoke over the entire area, not enough wind to shift it, three or four palls rising to the northwards. The whole place looked flat, angry, hot and hostile.

Buchanan led the patrol. It was small, just him, Chops(M) and two ratings, both useful lads under pressure. One of them was Baker, the man who had been involved in the first contact with the fighters. It would do him good, Buchanan thought, to come down from his eyrie for a while. The other was Godshall. They slipped over the wall at the back of the compound and came round to the road the long way, taking it slowly and surely. Then, instead of going past the four blocks down the road to the beach, they moved through the gardens and trees alongside the road, stopping frequently, feeling for any threat either to them initially or to the civilians who would make up the first boatloads back to the ship that they would soon be escorting down the same route. Chops was out in front, twenty yards ahead of them, the other three covering his advance, so it was slow. Buchanan stopped by a pile of garden rubbish, settled on to one knee and looked back the three yards to where Baker moved as tail-end charlie, facing backwards much of the time. But now Baker was looking at him, noticing something.

'Stay quite still, sir,' he said softly, his eyes fixed on a point just behind the officer. He edged forward and then suddenly lunged his rifle out like an extension to his arm, his other hand reaching up to pull Buchanan a few feet forward.

Buchanan looked down as he turned. Baker's rifle muzzle was holding down a snake, its length across four fat coils as thick as a man's arm at their widest and the flat arrow-shaped head of some sort of adder or viper that had been basking by the pile of leaves and compost.

'Fuck!' Buchanan breathed. 'I never even saw it . . . I hate bloody snakes.'

'You'd hate this one, sir,' Baker whispered knowledgeably. 'Looks like Godshall's chopper.'

Up ahead Chops hissed at them. Baker lifted the gun barrel and the snake struck at it, faster than the eye could see, coiling back away from it and striking again but missing again. Buchanan had seen the hint of a smile on Godshall's face at Baker's little joke. Godshall, a lean, tough individualist, had been very matey with one of the lads killed in the MCO and this was the first time he had smiled all day.

'That's his problem,' Buchanan whispered with a touch of sarcasm. 'We are bringing people back this way. Get rid of it.' Baker looked appalled. He was a conservationist.

'All right,' Buchanan conceded, 'move the bloody thing, but I don't want it anywhere near here. Drop it over that wall or something.'

Baker did that. But she was a female and the pile of litter and leaves in the corner contained what was left of her brood: seventeen tiny but highly venomous puff adders.

A few minutes later they were in the old Italian chargé d'affaires' garden. Buchanan looked around. The wall was low to seaward, but higher round the other three sides, chest height, with shrubbery that was overgrown. They fanned out, the two ratings pausing in one corner and Buchanan and Chops going carefully into the house to search it. It was clear. Baker, using his initiative, rigged a series of telltales as they left, carefully erasing their tracks and leaving areas of the brown dirt round the house ready for any footprint and a leaf in the gate catch that would fall to the ground if anyone came in through the gate in their absence.

'Good thinking,' Buchanan said. 'Where did you learn that?'

''E was a Queen's Scout wasn' 'e?' Godshall, an East-ender replied. 'Got his fire-lighting badge 'n' all.'

It was Godshall who, in the lead on their return journey, just fifty yards from the Embassy gate settled to one knee and waved them softly down, raising his rifle to his shoulder and peering through the sight over the bonnet of a car, one of the cars they had moved.

Oh shit, Buchanan thought. Here we go. It's on again. They were all outside the gate, exposed to some extent, the wide road on either side of them. He moved forward slowly.

To the north some eighty yards down the road, over the intersection and under the pall of smoke that rose from the still smouldering helicopter, were three young black men, locals by the look of them. They were all carrying rifles and looking towards something further up the road, away from them.

Buchanan lifted the little yellow radio. 'Beaufort two, this is two one.'

The yeoman came back immediately.

'Beaufort two, we are outside the gate fifty yards to the north. We have visual on hostiles. Figures three, further up the road. They are after something the other way. If you hear fire outside the gates it's us. Repeat, if you hear fire outside the gates it's us. Do not fire. I repeat, do not fire. Over.'

'Two one, this is two reading you fives. We will not fire, over.'

Buchanan put the radio back in his pocket and peered over the top of the car wishing he had a pair of binoculars, something always within reach on the ship. Chops was there as well. He looked at Buchanan. 'They've heard or seen something.'

Buchanan nodded.

'Could be their mates,' Chops went on.

'Could be friendlies, too.'

As Buchanan finished speaking a car came round the corner above the three men and immediately accelerated hard, its old engine revving. The men fired at it as it passed them, an ill-disciplined burst, but some of the bullets hit, and as it gunned down the street towards them Baker was talking out loud. 'Come on, come on. Floor it!' willing the driver. After what seemed an age it cleared their field of fire, Buchanan snapped 'Fire!' and the three sailors opened up, single shot rapid fire, as they had been taught.

The three fighters caught in the open all fell, the two on the right going down first, the third following them, dead as he hit the tarmac. The first two were alive, trying to crawl into cover and Godshall was sighting on them when Buchanan called the ceasefire. He let go one last bullet, but Buchanan was looking at the car which had come to a stop by the Embassy gates.

A black man was slumped in the passenger's seat and the woman who was driving was clawing her way towards him.

'Two, this is two one, open up. We're coming in.' Radio

in one hand and rifle in the other, he looked at the others. 'Chops, cover us. You others, let's go!' he snapped and darted across the road to the car. Inside the gates he could hear the van being moved and as Baker and Godshall dragged the wounded man from the car, Buchanan grabbed the woman's arm. She pulled it back and snarled at him, her eyes wide with fear. 'Royal Navy,' he snapped. 'Inside. Quickly now.'

She looked at him bewildered for a second, taking him in. 'My driver . . .'

'We got him. Move it.'

The gate was open and two ratings appeared from inside, picked her up bodily and carried her in, the other men following, Baker and Godshall being as gentle as they could be with the passenger, who had been wounded. There was lots of blood, some of it congealed and dark. Not in this incident, Buchanan thought as they carried him past, this happened earlier, surprising himself a little at his clarity of thought. He lined his rifle up on where the wounded fighters had dragged themselves into cover and signalled Chops who crossed over and they moved through the gate together.

Inside the yeoman was on the radio, answering the Americans who had called in having heard the firing, and Kitson was waiting. One of the French doctors ran forward as the wounded man was lowered to the ground, the woman close to him.

She was wet, her dress clinging to her body, the smell somehow familiar, her eyes blank now, her expression dazed.

Buchanan quickly briefed Kitson.

'Only two?' the XO confirmed.

Buchanan nodded, sipping water from a bottle someone passed him.

'Your route?' Kitson asked.

'As safe as it's going to get, sir.'

Two contacts, Kitson thought, we came off best in both. Luck always plays a part, he acknowledged, but their original strength was undiminished and they were about to be reinforced.

'When you go back for the RV take six of the lads. See the civvies away. Once you are back here, we will split the party. I want you to go over to the US mission. They have eight Marines there. Take ten of our lads. Enough?'

'I hope so.' Buchanan grinned. 'If that's not enough then I want my mum.'

'Once the recce troop is in they will come straight up to you and then you will move everyone back here. It will be tight but manageable. From here down to the beach.'

'We'll have to get that right, sir. The house is quite small. Wouldn't get more than a hundred in there at a time. Small groups of a hundred down to there. I was thinking. Each big group is split into seaboat loads. If we get going as soon as the Marines are here we will still be shuttling . . .' he quickly worked it out: twelve per load, two boats, twenty-minute turnarounds, seventy an hour, ten hours, allow for snafu, twelve hours '. . . at lunchtime tomorrow.'

'I don't like it any more than you do. I'm going to see if we can get hold of another couple of inflatables. I was thinking that maybe the Americans have some wherever that chopper was based. They could drop them to *Beaufort*.'

'Why not pussers boats?' Buchanan challenged. 'If they left now we could have them sometime tonight.'

'Not just a pretty face are you?' Kitson said, pleased with the idea and at the same time pissed off he hadn't thought of it. 'Comms are the problem. We will have to get a message through the Americans.'

Northwood had thought of it already. People paid to plan, second-guess needs, think ahead of what the tactical people on the ground might need. When the Americans accepted the offer of help and effectively doubled the numbers of people that needed to be moved out to the ship, Northwood stepped it up a notch.

They were not just looking to drop a couple of inflatable

143

boats to *Beaufort*. Four Gemini inflatables used by amongst others the Special Boat Squadron were now on their way to the military end of Gibraltar's runway. With fully sealed forty horsepower outboards they could do twenty knots fully loaded. They could be dropped by parachute and were going to be loaded into a waiting RAF Hercules that was equipped with long-range tanks. She could get all the way without refuelling and would be met on her homeward leg by the same tanker that would refuel the aircraft delivering the Marine recce troop. The Geminis weren't going alone. Eight men, members of the Special Boat Squadron, would parachute in to operate the boats and bring their own special skills to the situation.

There was a second aircraft preparing to depart. When the FCO had failed to get messages through to their Embassy they had established through the Americans that the British mission now had no electric power and therefore no way to work their communications equipment. With *Beaufort*'s comms also disabled, and knowing of *Beaufort*'s XO's intention to move the Americans nearer the embarkation point and into the walls of the British compound, they knew that by 1800 local there might be no communications at all, unless someone, someone very vulnerable, remained at the American compound to use their encoders. It wasn't ideal and the communications between Northwood and the Pentagon had been running constantly.

At RAF Kinloss in Scotland, 206 Squadron's standby Nimrod was being readied. The Nimrod was a four-engined hunter. It hunted anything from lost people in a search and rescue role to enemy submarines, flying long maritime patrols, its electronic eyes and ears sweeping out around it. It had very 'long legs' and on long patrols, as the aircraft lightened, the pilot could shut down two of the engines to conserve fuel. Usually its sorties weren't dangerous, just long and boring, and whenever they took off the thirteen crew all secretly hoped that something would happen to enliven the trip. But for anyone lost or in trouble deep-sea, or people who were lost in the air, there was no more comforting thought than knowing that an RAF Nimrod was airborne and looking for them. Because they would be found. Enemy submarines took somewhat less comfort from that same ability.

This one had extra crew. The flight deck team of two pilots, two navigators (one route and one tactical) and one engineer was to be supplemented by another two pilots. Two full shifts. Take-off was timed for 1600 hours. This would be a long sortie, eighteen hours in the air, and although they could take on fuel indefinitely the limiting factor on flight duration was engine oil. Pushing the operation towards the maximum twenty hours meant that they might have to stop somewhere on the way home and this meant taking ground technicians, men capable of servicing the Nimrod's four jet engines.

Camp stretchers were loaded, extra food and drink ordered from the catering department. The off-duty crew were called to man the new stand-by aircraft and planning preparations went ahead. She would fly for seven hours, meet up with a tanker, take on 40,000 pounds of fuel, locate HMS *Beaufort*, and then go into a long loiter overhead, flying in a long figure eight, an airborne radio relay, moving messages between Northwood and the warship. In the unlikely event that whoever had fired on *Beaufort* had something more sophisticated, then the Nimrod could use her big eye and see out hundreds of miles round the ship below, identifying any air, surface or submarine threat with the most sophisticated radar in the world, radar that could find a periscope in an ocean.

Up the back the air electronics officer would be working overhead *Beaufort*, but the three drymen, the people who manned the electronics screens, and the three wetmen, who operated the sonar buoys, would have a long, boring trip. They were already borrowing paperbacks and other reading material.

There was also an American Boeing AWACS aircraft

145

being readied at Andrews Air Force base. Its departure would be timed so that it arrived overhead HMS *Beaufort* as the RAF Nimrod reached the limit of her duration and the AWACS could take over the relay. A second AWACS was also on the pan. She would go straight on to Sierra Leone and be ready to take over from the first. From 0300 hours the following day the USAF would have aircraft overhead the evacuation constantly until the arrival of the US Marines and later the carrier, 'Big John', or until the evacuation had succeeded.

Buchanan's second trip down to meet the incoming sea-boats went off without a hitch. With twenty civilians, six-teen of them children and one the French woman doctor, he was praying that they would just be left alone and they were. They thought they had been seen once, by a group of armed fighters up the street where the last contact had been, but they showed no hostility, one of them even watching through a pair of binoculars. They crossed the gardens down the route they had established before, one man out in front, four with the party, and Godshall trailing as tail-end charlie. Godshall, who had been promoted up to killick and demoted back to seaman three times, was usually something of a handful, expressed by a PO as a 'gobby idle bastard'. Invariably if the police or shore patrol delivered men back to the ship after a problem ashore, he would be involved somewhere. But Buchanan had seen something of a change. He had volunteered for both trips to the beach, and his natural aggression, which normally just pissed people off, had a vent here.

He had settled at the base of a wall, letting the group move ahead of him, alone and exposed in a hostile environment that would normally make people bunch up and take comfort in others around them.

Buchanan, looking back, could see the expression on his face and the look in his eye. He was thoroughly enjoying the whole thing.

At the old Italian villa, Baker moved ahead to check his tell-tales and finally waved them in.

The seaboats were crammed with men. One over the maximum they were technically overloaded, but with almost millpond calm water the coxswains knew they could deliver their shore parties safely to the beach. They also knew that by the end of the day they would have broken all records for numbers of people crammed into an inflatable. The logistics were complex. Bennett insisted that normal safety measures be observed wherever possible, so the incoming armed ratings were all wearing lifejackets which would be removed and put on to the people going back to the ship. There would be a stack of them at each end. In addition to the boarding ladder that was being rigged on the starboard side, safe only in calm water, the MEO's people were helping the buffer build and rig staging platforms that could be lowered from the seaboat davits. The normal method of entry would be to hoist the boats inboard, unload on the deck and then lower them back to the water, but that would take too long. The platforms were being made from wooden pallets with a welded steel framework and sides made of webbing mesh taken from the helicopter landing deck safety rail. Shackled to the davit winches and lowered to water level, the platform would receive the civilians and be hoisted up while the seaboats were heading back to the beach after refuelling down there if necessary.

Lieutenant Sarah Conway was in the lead boat and half a mile from the beach. She settled back against the rubber sides of the boat and lifted her radio to her lips.

'Two one, two one, this is two two.'

'Go two.' Buchanan's voice.

'Two one, you should have us visual, over.'

'We see you. Come to the right. There is a big tree with a grey red-roofed building in front of it. We are fifty yards to your left of that, over.'

147

A few minutes later the boats were rubbing their bows gently on the sandy beach and the lads were baling out, carrying various bags of gear, Chops directing them up into the villa as others of the original party herded the civilians down to the inflatable, shoving lifejackets over heads as they went, and then the boats were away. As they disappeared out of trouble's reach Buchanan looked at Conway and Montagu.

'So, the gang's all here.'

'Sorry we're late,' Sarah said casually. 'We were a bit busy earlier.'

There was a crackle of gunfire away across the enclave, a sustained burst from something fully automatic followed by other fire that died away. It was more or less constant now, bursts of fire that were long and sustained enough to warp barrels.

'So were we,' Buchanan replied.

'We heard,' Orbs Montagu said dryly. 'The best laid plans and all that.'

Buchanan ignored him and turned to where Chops had gathered the new lads. The other six were out in a defensive picket, and he briefed them quickly and succinctly.

They were back inside the compound gates twenty minutes later, Buchanan having taken his time leading them in, letting them see the lie of the land that they would be covering that night, many times.

Within ten minutes of getting back he was on the move again, with Chops(M) and nine other men heading towards the US compound, one of them humping one of the machine guns. The fire they had heard had been along the street by the Embassy and had stopped when the US Marines had opened fire for the first time. Somehow Godshall had got himself selected for this task, too, and when they left the gates of the British mission he took the point, leading all the way, past the still smoking helicopter, till Buchanan moved up.

'Let's make sure they know we are friendlies,' he said.

148

He stopped them there, spoke into his little portable radio and had the yeoman contact them on the Clansman.

'Tell 'em we are coming round the corner thirty seconds from now. They are not to fire.'

He was last through the gate and found that people all over the compound, very pleased to see friendly allied troops armed to the teeth, had begun clapping. Buchanan was mildly embarrassed as were the others.

Kitson sat down, realizing that it was the first time he had done so since arriving that morning. He had been given an anteroom off Bill Black's office to use as his own space and the chair, old and creaky, was comfortable enough. He took his cap off and wiped the sweat from his face. Conway and Montagu sat opposite him and he was very conscious of the fact that with Buchanan and Chops(M) at the US compound, for the next few hours at least all that day's command experience had gone with them. These two were fine officers, but neither had been blooded as such and for a second he regretted sending both Jamie and Wilks.

'Get around the lads. Be seen. There is at least one of the original bunch at each corner. That should steady your teams. Down in this back corner,' he indicated out of the window, 'is an old civvie bloke that hooked up with Baker. He's useful. Got his own rifle and can use it better than any of us. Remember the RoE.' He looked at his watch. 'It's coming up for four. As soon as the recce troop are in we are going to move the people from the US compound down here and almost immediately start groups from here down to the beach. There are thirty of us, eight US Marines and the recce troop – how many is in one of those?'

'It varies,' Montagu replied. He had done a familiarization course with the Royal Marines, spending a week with them in Devon. He had been impressed by what he had seen, the sheer professionalism of it all. 'From memory it's about half a platoon. Twentyish?'

'That's about sixty of us. Should be plenty.'

'Sir,' Conway began, 'are we handing command on to the Marines?'

'I think so. I will be in charge, but it's what they do, so tactics, defence and who does what I will let their officer sort out.'

On *Beaufort*, Captain Bennett was running his own meeting. He had sent Morris below with orders to sleep: the navigator had been on watch effectively since midnight, and he would be needed later. Lieutenant Commander Denny, the Ops Officer, now XO in Kitson's absence, had thought through the issues for that night and was offering them to Bennett and his senior colleagues from the wardroom.

'Weather tonight is two to three, some cloud cover, but we will have moonlight breaking through. Cages on the davit hoists will be ready. I suggest that we lie bows on to the beach if the weather permits. That will reduce our target profile and mean we can bring in a seaboat to either side. It will also mean we can use the gun if we need to. God forbid the weather turns, because if we need to be under way and bringing boats into the leeward then it could slow things down. If that happens we will stagger the boats, one going in one out. Once the other boats arrive we will need both cages running and signals of some sort. MEO, your rates on that?' Denny asked.

'Yes.' The MEO, Lieutenant Commander Fripp, looked up from his notes. 'They are almost finished. Hand-held signal lamps. Hooded down, with smaller bulbs and coloured with spare filters for the running lights. Will give us a red or green at the landing cage. If we are under way, then we will have a secondary set that will indicate status both sides, the upper lamps always being the other side of the ship.'

Bennett was imagining it as he listened. The lamps would, like traffic lights, indicate to the boats coming in which side to approach. 'Good,' he said. 'ETA for the Nimrod is 2200 hours. What about comms?'

Mayberry looked up, but the MEO carried on. 'We have managed to salvage nothing meaningful from the MCO. We can use the Clansman, but any alternate will need to be through the budgie, sir. We can talk to him on 243 megahertz. I'll look at running an intercom line to the cockpit. That will free up a handheld.'

'Unpluggable, I hope?' Mayberry said.

'We'll use a jackplug,' the MEO responded, 'but the aircraft will need to be out of the hangar on the deck.' Mayberry shrugged. Weather was okay.

'The doctor is on board?' Bennett asked looking round. He had watched the civvies come up in the seaboat and none of them looked like a doctor.

'Yes, Captain.' It was Thurdley, the Supply Officer who responded, answering the Captain's unasked question as well. 'She's the one with the short hair. Sort of a suede head. Earrings. She's down with the LMA now.'

'I'll go down and see her after this,' Bennett said.

'Sir, what about the bodies? They are in the laundry space at present. We have got . . .'

'Empty one of your fridges,' Bennett said.

'I thought, sir,' Thurdley pushed gently, 'with all the civvies coming on . . .'

'I said empty one of your fridges,' the Captain interrupted. He paused and then said in a tone that would brook no discussion, 'I'm taking *all* my crew back to Pompey.'

Down on 2 deck in the Leading Medical Assistant's area the doctor, Renée Bujould, had worked through the casualties one by one, looking at the work done by the LMA and the first aiders. A body, that of Tomkins, lay covered. He had died shortly after the Captain had been down to see him, but had yet to be moved. She isolated three of the less seriously injured where she wanted to remove and replace sutures, but for now they could wait.

151

One of the seriously injured was stable enough, but the second, the man who had taken shrapnel on the TRD platform, wasn't doing well at all, drifting in and out of consciousness, and the third, a seaman with burns and broken ribs, was now in respiratory distress.

'You 'ave done well. Good work,' she said to the LMA, 'but now we work again, eh? This one needs a chest drain. I am not a thoracic surgeon but . . .' She shrugged and told him what she needed and while she scrubbed up the LMA found her enough equipment to work with. Ten minutes later she opened a small hole in the man's chest and fed a drain tube into the lining between the chest wall and the lung, explaining to the LMA what she was doing as she worked, using him as a surgical assistant. As the pressure came off the man's lung his condition instantly improved, his ragged shallow painful breathing eased and the change in atmosphere in the crowded sick bay was palpable. As they were cleaning up Captain Bennett stepped into the sick bay.

'Doctor Bujould? I am Nick Bennett, the Captain. I wanted to thank you for volunteering to come out and help us. Is there anything else we can get for you? Anything you need?'

'Yes. Drugs. Analgesia. There is only enough morphine for another few hours. Broad spectrum antibiotics also. Saline, too. I shall make a list. The Americans in Freetown, eh? Ask them. They 'ave a dispensary that will 'ave most of what we need and they 'ave helicopter.'

'Can these people be moved?' he asked quickly. The LMA's first report had been that they needed stabilizing first.

'No. Not for the time being and . . . aah . . . not to Freetown. There is no 'ospital at the base. Just a clinic. We have one patient who needs a neurological unit. Until we can stabilize him he should not be moved. The other problem is the drug we need they will not 'ave in Freetown. It is something you only get in big 'ospital.'

'What is the problem?' Bennett asked.

'He took a blow to the head. He is slipping in and out of consciousness and it is getting worse. This is caused by intercranial haemorrhage and cerebral oedema.'

Bennett looked blank.

'There is a build-up of fluid on the brain. The pressure builds up under the skull, eh? Causing secondary brain damage and death.'

Bennett nodded.

'This can be eased by a drug called dexamethasone. A steroid. But it is not something that the dispensary would 'ave.'

'Write it down for me. I will do my best. These other men,' he indicated the walking wounded, those less serious. 'Can they travel?'

'Sure. But they don't need to.' She shrugged. 'We can care for them adequately here.'

'I am sure you can, doctor. It's the . . .' he was wondering how to say it, how to explain that he wanted space, beds freed up, that the fight had only just begun, that there could be more broken, bleeding, dying carried below before the day was out. There was much that hadn't changed since Trafalgar. He was saved by a killick, one of the men injured in the shelling.

'Sir, if it's all the same to you, I'd like to stay, like . . . with the lads, like. You others?' There were nods of assent. 'We'll make space when the time comes.'

"Ang on!' another said, having visions of civvie nurses and good food. 'I . . .' He trailed off under the glare of the others.

'Speak your piece,' Bennett said gently.

"Sall right, sir. It was nuffink.'

Bennett turned to the doctor as she handed him the list. 'I'll get your drugs.'

'What about this?' she asked, gently touching the cut over his eye.

'It's all right.'

She smiled. She had seen it all before. 'It needs cleaning and closing up or you will 'ave unnecessary scarring.'

'I'm busy.'

'It will take five minutes, or are you a big baby and frightened of the needle?' she challenged, glaring at him.

He sat down. 'You have five minutes,' he said frostily, while the others in the sick bay grinned at each other. It would be all over the ship in no time. The French bint had called the Captain a big baby.

Kitson had relayed the message to the US Embassy, checked on his people and was back in the little anteroom off Black's office. His cap was on the tabletop, a band of clean skin across his forehead above his grimy, soot-streaked face.

He was making a list, things to remember to do, a sequence of things in chronological order, with a schematic diagram, one of his hymn sheets, and was almost finished, as finished as he would ever be because conditions were constantly changing, when Poppy put her head round the door. She was holding a mug, and a long hank of ash blonde hair had fallen down one side of her face, framing her blue blue eyes.

'Hi.'

He looked up. 'Hello.'

'Coffee. It's the last of the Gold Blend, so appreciate it.'

'I will,' he smiled.

'Can I escape in here quietly for a few minutes? I promise I won't disturb you.'

Kitson looked at her, thinking: disturb me? As beautiful as you, you disturb me just being in the same hemisphere, which, considering that she simply wanted him to notice that she was young, single and half attractive, was a good result.

'Of course,' he replied. 'I'm finished for the time being.'

She sat in a chair against the wall, put an ashtray on a low filing cabinet and lit a cigarette. 'Want one?'

'Yes. I will, thanks.' He took a cigarette, lit it with his own old Zippo and leaned back, sipping his coffee. 'Bliss,' he said with a little grin and sipped again. They talked for a few minutes about Monrovia and then got on to his lifestyle.

'You must miss your family when you are away.'

'I do. I have two girls, one twelve and the other fourteen. They have moved on from pre-pubescent boy bands and are in the process of introducing me to Oasis.'

'Ah, the pleasure of the real teenage years to come. Deviousness. They wrap their daddies round their little fingers, women's bodies and surging hormones with only a child's experience. Tears and joy, confusion and angst.'

He laughed. 'You have got them, obviously.'

'*Moi?*' Mock horror. 'No, I'm unattached. Yet to bear young.' She smiled, her eyes twinkling. 'That was all my own memories. I was a little minx, so my parents say.'

'My sister was older than me,' Kitson said. 'She largely ignored my existence, so it's difficult to remember if she had my old man round her little finger.'

'Fathers never notice. Mums do that. Their mum no doubt does,' she probed gently.

'That's unlikely. Their mother lives in South America. Lima. Doesn't see much of them.' Much of them, he thought. One letter in three years.

'Oh, I'm sorry.'

'Don't be. It wasn't your fault.'

'So,' she said, 'you must have a girl in every port.'

'Girls in ports may be nice, but they're usually short timers,' he replied with a smile. 'So far I have resisted the temptation.'

There was a burst of gunfire and then the sound of mortar rounds, but this time closer, appreciably closer. 'That's my wake-up call.' He stood up and finished the coffee in two gulps.

She stood too. 'I'll see you later, then?'

'Yes,' he replied absently, 'that would be nice.' Then,

155

realizing what he had just said, 'I'm sorry, I didn't mean it like . . .'

'That's okay,' she laughed and then, thinking: shit, I'm the wrong side of twenty-five to be coy, she met him halfway. 'Umm . . . I'll look forward to it, too.'

'Good,' he said softly.

The Royal Navy Casualty Co-ordination Centre, the central repository of records for next of kin, had supplied the requisite information to a small group of officers at HMS *Nelson* in Portsmouth. Guy Davies, the Captain (F) in command of the flotilla of which HMS *Beaufort* was part, had urged them to get next of kin informed with utmost immediacy, channelling his request through the offices of the commanding officer at HMS *Nelson*, a Commodore. The news embargo on the names of the dead and injured was under huge pressure since the CNN broadcast and it would be lifted at 1730 hours, in time for the early evening news. Extra staff were already at the RNCCC taking the phone calls that had been coming in since the news of the attack on the ship was broadcast and this would accelerate after the television news when their number was given out.

In Oxfordshire a blue Mondeo pulled into the forecourt of a garage. A woman and a man both wearing naval officer's uniform got out, leaving a third in the car, and found the owner. The radio was usually on in the workshop, but on his trips in and out he had missed the news bulletins.

'Mr Simpson?'

'Yes. That's me,' he said cheerfully. 'What can I do for you?'

Get it right, they had said, always check and double check.

'Is your address 44 Holmhouse Way?'

'Yes,' he said. The smile had gone.

'My name is Sue Carter. I am with the Royal Navy at

HMS *Nelson.*' She produced her ID, in spite of the fact she was wearing uniform and the two and a half stripes of a Lieutenant Commander.

'What's this about? My daughter is in the navy.' His voice was dry, dusty, flaky, dying as he said the words.

'I know,' she said gently. 'Mr Simpson, I'm afraid I have some very bad news for you.'

'Is she hurt? Where is she? How bad? . . . Oh no. Please, no . . .'

'Cheryl is dead,' she said softly over his plea. 'I'm terribly sorry.'

He seemed to crumple then, back against the table in the office, his hands to his face. Shock. Denial. Disbelief. One of the mechanics was coming out of the lube bay, wiping his hands, and the man who had waited with the car came forward. He intercepted the mechanic, who listened, nodded and came to the door. The other person in the room was a naval chaplain. The bad news was Sue's job, but this was his. Ministering to his flock in time of need. He had seen a fax of the flimsy copy of her Captain's message through to Fleet. 'Regret to advise that LWA Simpson died of her wounds.' Her service number was there, but the last words on Bennett's message were the most poignant: 'Greater love hath no man.' He didn't know the details – no one would till it was over – but for a Captain to send that . . .

'She was brave, Mr Simpson,' the chaplain said softly. 'Oh so brave. You must be so proud of her. Then you must be brave, too, because we are going to have to tell her mother.'

He looked up. 'Are you sure it was our Cheryl? There could be some mistake. Are you *sure* it was . . .'

'We are sure.'

They left him quietly for a few minutes and then the chaplain crossed over and stood with him again. 'Come on. We'll take you home now. Is there someone here who can lock up?'

The mechanic nodded.

'Her mother. I must tell her. She's at work . . .'

'We'll take you,' the chaplain said.

'She wasn't well last year . . . she . . .'

'We have someone with us who can give her something.'

'Thank you. Thank you for coming to tell us.' He began to cry then, great silent tears running down his cheeks, and Sue turned away, her own tears coming. Sometimes she hated her job.

It was about then that the Prime Minister caught the eye of the Speaker of the House. She nodded and called his name. He stood at the dispatch box to read a short statement to the House of Commons, bringing them up to date on the situation in Monrovia and harshly condemning the attack on one of Her Majesty's ships in the performance of a humanitarian mission. After reading the statement written by the Naval Secretariat at the MoD, he paid tribute to the courage and dedication to duty of the personnel.

Meanwhile in his office the Armed Forces Minister looked up from the flimsy at the people gathered round the meeting table.

'We have got mission slippage.'

Mission slippage was the euphemism for the dynamics of a deployment that, having begun modestly, as events or policy dictate sees ever increasing resources thrown at the problem. The American intervention in Vietnam was the classic example. What began with a handful of advisers ended up with half a million men under arms in a protracted war they could never win. What had begun this morning with a ship standing off in case an evacuation was necessary now had an American carrier group racing that way.

He was looking at a request from Northwood routed through the Joint Chiefs of Staff to give Zulu Company of 45 Commando, already en route on the *Fearless*, official orders. The support company's recce troop were already nominally attached to Zulu, but this order would commit the rest of the company, some 120 men.

'We have, sir, but Northwood feel, and we and the Joint Chiefs concur, that it's necessary and will all be over very quickly. Mission remains the same. Get our people away. Everything going to plan, by this time tomorrow they should all be heading home.'

'Better be.' The Minister stood up as one of the press officers entered the room. Now that the PM had told the House he, flanked by the First Sea Lord, would hold a press conference in the ground floor concourse below them. A podium would have been set up and the area could accommodate well over a hundred media people. Then it would be across the road to the Millbank studio for the in-depth television interview.

In Portsmouth two young women, both with their men serving in *Beaufort*, knocked at the door of a third. She was older, the wife of a Chief Petty Officer. She brought them into her front room and took over, allaying fears.

'Look, if they were hurt we'd know by now, right? Right? So stop worrying. Jen,' she looked at one of them, 'where are the kids?'

'With me mum.'

'Yours?' she looked at the other.

'School. They're at school.'

'It's gone time. You should be collecting them. You go and get them and we'll put the kettle on and then I'll phone up. Okay? Then we'll do something. Go for a drink, eh?'

'I want to watch the news,' Jen said. Both her brother and her husband were in *Beaufort*.

A few miles away a girl working in a shop listened to the radio and thought about the young sailor she had met in a night-club called the Blue Lagoon. Her friend had buggered off with some bloke and there was this guy. He was from the *Beaufort*. She remembered thinking that name sounded French. He was nice. She had had a few drinks and when he slipped his hand up her skirt she let him. First time she had been out in a year and she must have been drunk because they did it in an alley near the club. When she saw him again the next night she felt like a slut for having let him have her up against the wall like some dockside tart. Wrote to him once after he sailed and he replied. She wondered if he got her last letter, posted just a week ago. He was nicer than the others, who were usually just after one thing. She didn't mind that. That was normal. They were men. After all that was what it was all about. Finding someone you wanted to be with and everything, that was part of it, but there had to be more. This one said he would take her out when they got back. Take her out properly, like, for a meal. Imagine if they fell in love. She looked out of the shop window dreamily. Mrs Tracey Baker. Sounded nice. Maybe write again tonight, but maybe not, she thought sadly. He would have thought she did it with everyone. He would never know he was the first.

At the base, Sarah Conway's husband, a Lieutenant Commander now attached to a training department, took a call.

'Is that John Conway?'

'Speaking.'

'Hello. It's Sally Shaw. I'm a friend of Jamie's, Jamie Buchanan. We met . . .'

'Yes. I remember. How are you?' She was tall, leggy, he remembered. Doe-eyed over young Jamie. Sarah had said that if Jamie had a regular girlfriend this was her, but that she spent most of her time living in hope. Besotted, she was.

'I was wondering . . . um . . .' He knew. He knew how she felt. Distanced. Apart. Alone.

'Fancy a drink after work?' he said. 'We can talk.'

She wasn't the first to phone. Jack Denny's wife had called. Wanting to know what they would be doing, where they were, what was happening, reassurance. The kinship of those whose waited. He always thought it was melodramatic shit until now, but it was real enough. He was worried too.

6

Chalky White scrabbled his way up on to the low roof where Baker was back with Johnson the civilian, guarding the wall.

"Allo, sunshine,' he said, dropping down beside them, his eyes taking in Johnson and his rifle. Baker grinned at him. 'Hello, Chalky.'

'Fancy a cuppa?' He held up a plastic shopping bag. 'Amazing what ya find, innit? A frigging 'Arvey Nichols bag in the middle of mbungo land,' he said, taking out a Thermos flask and three cups.

'Where'd you get it?' Baker asked with a smile. Chalky was a great procurer.

'Ponced it off some old dear,' he grinned, pouring tea into the first cup. 'She were lovely.'

'Actually, she *is* lovely,' Johnson said.

White looked up.

'You *ponced* it,' the older man said, carefully pronouncing the word, 'off my wife.'

'Ah.' White's face was a picture, a sheepish, embarrassed grin, and he was only saved when Baker burst out laughing.

'Jonnie, this is Chalky. If there's a way to stick his foot in it he will do it.'

They sat on the roof shaded by a big tree on the other side of the wall, drinking the tea, pleasant and welcome even in the heat, and it was Baker who raised the subject.

'How was it?'

'Bad. Fuckin' carnage in the MCO. Topsy. Dave Tomkins. Killed a Wren too. Cheryl. You know the one? Big lass.'

161

Baker nodded. They had heard that. 'The lads?'

'Pissed off,' White replied. 'Marines coming in later, apparently.'

Baker raised an eyebrow. 'They'll be wanting to yomp about with Union Jacks 'anging off radio aerials, reliving Port Stanley. Well . . .' he paused, looking away, at the plumes of smoke that drifted over them, the sounds of weapon fire a short distance away to the north. 'They can have this place. It's a fucking shithole.'

'All be over soon enough,' White said. 'More boats coming, too. Be back in Pompey for the weekend.'

Baker sipped his tea and thought about that. Getting ashore for a few days' leave, a decent pint or two. The girl he met, Tracey. He liked her. Liked her a lot. Got her letter with its big looped girlish handwriting. Chatty, nice, but he thought it was written to justify her actions to herself rather than to him. She wouldn't want someone like him. A matelot. Better not trying than getting blown out. It had been, what, six weeks now. She would have someone else sniffing around. Someone else would find her lonely after three gin and tonics, just like he had done. But that bloke wouldn't be sailing two days later.

At the small US logistics base in Sierra Leone they had received the relayed message from HMS *Beaufort* and two assistants were putting together the order of drugs from their dispensary. The base was busy. They had put aside the loss of their aircraft and people as best they could and now the feeling of impotence was gone. There were things they could do. A second helicopter, a Sikorsky CH-63E Sea King, was being prepared on the small flight line, and preparations were being made to receive incoming aircraft, a Lockheed tanker and a Boeing AWACS, later in the day. For once fate had smiled on them. Transiting the base on their way to the Gulf was a collection of personnel, among them a small US Navy surgical team. The base commander contacted C-in-C Atlantic and requested their orders changed; now ready to travel down to the British warship was a highly rated 38-year-old 'bone man'– an orthopaedic surgeon – an anaesthetist and two Marine medical corpsmen who were skilled enough to assist with surgical procedures.

They had plundered the base for what they wanted, the surgeon smiling, hearing the anaesthetist's shouted 'Yo!' as she came upon something she had never thought to find in a small clinic. They now had three bulky bags of equipment and supplies for the clinical management of trauma. They were ready to go, keen to do what they had been trained for. Twenty minutes later the Sea Hawk lifted off, its long-range tanks loaded with every drop of fuel they could take.

At the US compound Buchanan had settled in. He had looked at the preparations made by the sergeant in charge of the Marine guard and acknowledged them as being as good as could be expected with the resources available. The young man had eyed the GPMG with relish and he and Chops(M), with what Buchanan thought was very cordial détente considering Chops's view of Marines, agreed where it should be best sited. The ten British sailors were then deployed and settled in for a hopefully peaceful wait till nightfall and the arrival of the Royal Marines recce troop before they broke out and headed for the beach.

There was a lot of activity behind closed doors in the Embassy building, comings and goings, but Buchanan, who had made the small outer office that housed the Marines' radio and admin area his command post, kept his thoughts focused on his immediate problem. One of the Marines was passing a message for *Beaufort* back to the Brit compound and a civilian, seemingly one of the embassy staff, had appeared from nowhere and was listening in. He was a tall, thin man with ferrety little eyes and sandy hair daubed down with gel and Buchanan thought the braces and how tie he wore with a short-sleeved shirt looked ridiculous considering where they were.

He looked at Buchanan.

'Hi there.' His smile, big and toothy, had all the honesty of a politician's. 'Dave Kreutz. How you doin'?'

Buchanan took the offered hand. The shake was dry and hard.

'We, aah, have a situation and I think you can help us.'

'What's that, sir?'

'As you no doubt know,' he pointed to the radio in the corner, 'there is a helicopter that has just left our facility in Sierra Leone for your ship. A humanitarian mission in the spirit of co-operation.' Again the toothy, shallow smile. 'Well, we would like to get some people away on that bird. Seems a pity to go back empty, now doesn't it?' He looked for some sort of positive response from Buchanan and then continued. 'In that same spirit, we'd like you to get in touch with the ship and have a boat come in and get these people.' He leaned forward. 'Just a handful. Three. It's mighty important . . . if you get my drift.' He all but winked at Buchanan, who remained stony-faced.

'I'm sorry,' Buchanan began. 'For several reasons the evacuation will only be beginning after dark. Then we will begin with women and children. If you'd care to . . .'

'Lieutenant,' Kreutz said, eyeing Buchanan's rank, 'I said it was mighty important. Now correct me if I am wrong, but your orders were to offer any and all assistance. Am I correct?' His tone was faintly threatening.

'Sir, you may . . .'

'Am I correct?' he insisted.

'You are correct,' Buchanan answered. 'Any and all assistance in the evacuation of civilians to safety.'

'Well then . . .'

'The method of evacuation, timing and execution are up to us, for everyone's safety,' Buchanan finished.

'Do I have to go over your head?' the American said,

softly but menacingly, looking quickly back at the Marine by the radio to see if he was listening.

'It would appear you do,' Buchanan replied evenly and walked out of the room.

Kitson was out in the garden, trying to get a feel on the movement of the fighting when the call came through and someone found him. He made his way back to the comms room where the Clansman was set up, the spare batteries that had come in on the table beside it, and picked up the microphone.

'This is Beaufort two. Go ahead.'

'Beaufort two, is this sunray actual?'

'Yes, this is the commanding officer speaking, go ahead.'

'Sunray, please ask any others to leave the room, over.'

Kitson raised an eyebrow and when the yeoman stood up to leave he shook his head, indicating that the rating should sit down again.

'I'm clear,' Kitson said. 'Who am I talking to?'

'Let's just say national security, Sunray. Now, I have a problem.'

Kitson listened to the man at the American compound with mounting discomfort and when the voice finally finished he responded: 'I'm sorry, but Lieutenant Buchanan's decision stands.' He put the microphone down with a muttered 'wanker' and walked out. The yeoman grinned.

Fifteen minutes later Kreutz arrived at the British Embassy's gates with three of the young Marines and a few minutes after that Kitson was asked to join the Ambassador in his office.

Tony Wisher was there, embarrassed and looking out of the window, and Bill Black was standing impassively behind his desk.

'Lieutenant Commander Kitson, I have come over here in the hope that I can personally explain our position.'

Kitson listened, feeling the mood in the room. Black as Ambassador could instruct him to co-operate, but he hadn't done so. Distancing himself perhaps? Staying out of it? Walking the diplomatic line. My call, he thought. When Kreutz finished he put his cap firmly back on his head and looked the American in the eye.

'You have wasted a trip. As I said, Lieutenant Buchanan's decision stands. *Beaufort* is currently some miles off and I am not asking for a seaboat to come back in before dark, when we will have further support. Once the evacuation begins it will be, in the old-fashioned way, women and children first. Now if these people are women or children, which I doubt, I will be pleased to see them in the first few boats away.

'As things stand there will be no one going out to the ship in time for that helicopter.'

'Commander, you are a career man right? This is not going to . . .'

Kitson stepped forward, looking up at the tall American. Kreutz was obviously CIA, but the request had not been channelled through his Ambassador to Black. That made it unofficial. He had had enough of this shit.

'Don't run out your guns at me! Who the hell do you think you are? Take a look.' He lifted a finger and touched his cap badge. 'I'm Royal Navy. Not yours. Now, unless you happen to sit on the Admiralty Board you can't affect my career. I know who you are and what you are and I don't give a shit. So don't lean on me and don't lean on my people. And if I find out you have, then you and your party will be the last bloody people off the beach.'

He turned, nodded to Black, who had the merest hint of a smile on his lips, and stalked from the room.

The Nimrod was ready. The planning session was complete. They had filed flight plans with alternates, the correct charts were on the aircraft and both the tactical and the route navigators had finished their preparations. Waypoints and rendezvous were marked up for mid-air coupling with the refuelling tankers. Being essentially a comms mission, the bomb bay had been left with the usual search and rescue load mix and the crew were on board checking their own stations, the flight deck crew doing their routine pre-take-off checks.

The Captain, a Squadron Leader, unlike most of his colleagues, was one of the few Nimrod pilots who had transferred to the lumbering multi-engine patrol aircraft from strike aircraft. He was a veteran. Trained originally on Hunters at RAF Wittering, he had done tours on Jaguars and Buccaneers. When the Buccaneers had been finally phased out, dreading having to move on to Tornadoes, which he regarded as overrated, and aware that at forty-two years of age keeping fit enough to fly 9G turns was becoming boring, he applied for Nimrod and was surprised when he was accepted. He had always acknowledged that there were two kinds of officers in the RAF. The career men, Teflon backs to which no shit would stick, clean noses, political, right job, right moves, groomed for promotion to Wing Commander and Group Captain, and the others. The pilots. The front-line squadron boys. The guys who loved to fly fast jets, were good at it, and found the thought of flying a desk at High Wycombe or the administrative elements of a job at Wing Commander level crushingly boring or required more arse-licking that they could stomach. It was generally accepted that what made a good front-line squadron or wing commander in time of war were not necessarily the same qualities that were looked for in time of peace. The dependable yet imaginative, tough, talented and experienced natural leaders, often with maverick leanings, who earned the respect of their subordinates in action were often considered unsuitable for peacetime promotion. They were too hard to manage, too individual for the homogenous machine.

Squadron Leader Tim Page was thinking, as he finished his checks with his right-seat man, that he was definitely one of the pilots and the arsehole Wing Commander in the briefing room was definitely one of the politicians. The other pilot, the relief settling in down the back, was okay.

A tough, dark, bald, little Scot by the name of Matheson, he and Page had flown together before several times and in the mess he was a real party animal, always a bonus to any squadron's social life.

Page raised a thumb at the ground crew outside on the pan.

'Start one,' he said.

'Start one,' the engineer repeated.

A naval surgeon had located the nearest hospital with stocks of the drug dexamethasone and a police car, one of the new very fast Volvos, had done the run from Inverness to RAF Kinloss at record speed, the small package on the back seat. But there had been a snafu. The surgeon who had found the drug had asked one of the people in his office, a Wren Petty Officer, to phone Kinloss and tell them an urgent package was coming and needed to be dropped to HMS *Beaufort*. The Wren had been reaching for the phone when someone passing her desk had knocked her cup of coffee over and it had spilt into her lap. She went to the ladies to get cleaned up, and when she came out she was intercepted by someone on the social committee. By the time she got back to her place the message pad had been turned over and dabbed dry by the girl at the next desk. It was half an hour before she remembered it and the moment she did, the police Volvo was crossing under the hastily lifted boom at Kinloss and accelerating towards the Nimrod flight line.

Squadron Leader Page looked out at the matrix of flashing lights on the civilian police car as it came towards him.

'What the fuck?' he asked himself.

It pulled to a halt in front of the aircraft and the driver jumped out and ran over to a ground crewman who then looked up at the cockpit and held up both hands. Stop.

'Shutting down port side,' Page said to his number two. 'I'm going to see what's happening.'

Someone had come out from the Ops room and by the

time he had dropped down to the pan from the belly hatch there were three people animatedly discussing something.

'We can't just drop it. It has to go in a special container, a mail container in the bomb bay.' The Wing Commander was getting excited.

'What's the problem?' Page asked.

The policeman looked at him. 'This is from the hospital in Inverness. It's for the ship you are going to. Haven't you had a call on this?'

'No. We haven't. What's the story?'

Fucking marvellous, the policeman thought, and here's me on a blue light all the way. 'There is someone on that ship who was injured when they were attacked. If this drug doesn't get there he will die.'

Page thought quickly. They weren't equipped for a drop, but it couldn't be beyond the wit of man. 'Done. Give it to me. I am using fuel as we speak.'

'You can't. I mean it's . . .' the Wing Commander said. 'Your mission is comms. You haven't got . . . you can't just chuck it out the window. Group should know.' He turned on the policeman as though it was all his fault. 'There are *procedures* for this sort of thing.'

Page took the small package. 'I'll get it there. We're outta here.'

'Right you are,' the policeman replied.

'But how . . . I mean . . .' from the Wing Commander.

'Initiative,' Page called, already moving. 'We will use initiative, sir,' and before the Wing Commander could challenge further he ran back to the Nimrod. They were taxiing under a minute later.

On *Beaufort* they were busy. As the fighting ashore was obviously worsening Mayberry had offered to do a helo recce, fly ashore and try and establish where the fighting was taking place and how far the fluid front had moved. Bennett had reluctantly agreed. He didn't want his only helicopter damaged, but as Mayberry said, they needed a fix before nightfall, and anyway, when the American Sea King came in, it would need the deck space. The seaboats were back inboard awaiting their next use, to recover the Royal Marines from the water, and from then on it would be busy, very busy. *Beaufort* would move back into shallow water as fast as she could to put the Marines ashore and begin the evacuation under the cover of darkness. Later the second air drop would come in, the SBS men with their Geminis, but after dark and not visible as a target, it would just drop the men and their boats alongside the ship while the seaboat evacuation continued.

It was Kate Wallace who thought of it, took it to Chops(S), who then took the idea to the WEO. They then convinced Mayberry and it was the three men who stood in front of Commander Bennett and asked if they could perhaps make the Lynx a little more offensive than she was.

'Tonight, sir. It could get a bit hairy. We have got the gun, but if there is a concerted attack on our lads, and if Mr Mayberry was up . . . well we thought that we could build and drop a few bombs, sir,' the Chief Petty Officer (Sonar) said.

'I beg your pardon?' Bennett said. 'I thought you said bombs.'

'I did, sir.'

Bennett looked at Lieutenant Mayberry. He wasn't an aviator, but he knew a bit about them and he knew they didn't like things that went off near them, let alone carry and try to deliver something as potentially volatile as a home-made bomb. 'Your view?'

Mayberry had thought of little else since the suggestion, but he knew that if anyone could put together something it was an old seadog like Chops(S) and a handful of shrewd, innovative and highly technical weapons and electronics artificers.

'Well, sir,' he replied, 'I took some convincing, but they reckon they have delayed action fuses we can trust. A

170

couple of them have volunteered to come along and lob them out through the door.'

'What will you use?' Bennett asked the big sonarman.

'Rework the detonators from the practice depth charges. They are pressure activated. We use the timers of the dets from the smoke grenades. There's nine left, sir. Take out the ballast and drop in six or seven kilos of Torpex from a real DC.' He shrugged then, his big shoulders shifting an inch. 'Some bits of metal, old bearings, filings and offcuts and the like. Cut the practice depth charge containers back to something manageable. All up weight forty pounds-odd. The problem is height, but we have worked that one out. If Mr Mayberry is at two hundred feet and moving at one-thirty knots then . . .'

Ops was there then, listening in, appalled at the risk but delighted with the ingenuity.

'Get the workings together. Safety first. Make it so the detonators go in at the last minute. If I decide it's necessary to proceed, then I will tell you. DWEO to oversee. DMEO as safety officer.'

'Sir.' They went away pleased. Pleased because they had already started. Kate Wallace was there already, stripping the detonators from the smoke markers.

Kitson was on the wall in the north-east corner with Sarah Conway, still trying to get a feel for how close the actual fighting was to the enclave. Groups of fighters were moving through, there were the odd contacts between opposing groups, but he was trying to get a feel for where the front, the main contact line between Ulima-J, now probably Ulima-Bokia, and Samuel Taylor's bunch lay. He wasn't having much luck.

It was fluid, moving, swirling, light and heavy weapons fire through the northern suburbs and, it now seemed, round to the east.

Someone appeared and passed him a note from the yeoman. The Beau had been on. They were standing off the rendezvous point to uplift the Marines but had decided on a helo recce in the meantime.

His small handheld radio squawked.

'Two one, two three.'

'Two one, go.' Two three was the north-west corner. He looked down towards them.

'Movement, two one. We have visual. Eight correction nine coming towards us. Slowly . . . aah . . . very slowly and carefully from the north. They seem to be checking cars as they move forward, over.'

'Two three, are they looting?' The previous groups they had seen had been.

'Two one. No, repeat no looting. This bunch look different.'

'I'm on my way.' He looked at Sarah. 'Stay down this side.'

He was halfway there when firing broke out outside the wall. It was close. Very close, the sound different, thuds and ricochets as for the first time bullets hit the compound walls. It was coming from the other way. He broke into a run as the three ratings on the Land-Rover roof covering the south-west corner opened fire, a woman screaming, people grabbing children, shouting, running in behind the second protective screen of cars, the curious hunched-over jog they had all seen on television.

He was almost there when the ratings on the other corner, the first to call in the visual, began firing. He looked across. Montagu was there. He tapped the man on the GPMG on the shoulder and pointed, cool as a cucumber. The big gun traversed a few inches and began to fire, short bursts, so Kitson kept going to the south-west corner and went up the bonnet of the Land-Rover and on to the roof in three steps.

'Sitrep.'

'There's hundreds of 'em!' one of the ratings yelled, letting go a long burst. Incoming fire raked the wall, the bullets knocking off chunks of breeze block, showering them with bits of concrete and dust as they ducked.

'Crap,' snarled the Petty Officer. 'Maybe twelve or fifteen, sir. And you,' he snapped at the rating. 'No more than two shots at a time. Aimed shots. Conserve ammo. Right!'

'But there's . . .' The firing died away but the rating was going to make his point.

'RIGHT?' the Petty Officer barked.

'Yes, PO.'

'Fucking prat.'

'Yes, PO.'

The Petty Officer looked at the XO. 'About twelve, sir. Down in the cars where Baker slotted that first bunch.'

Kitson ducked a look over the wall, but could see nothing. The firing on the other corner had started up again, Montagu there as the machine gun fired three bursts. He looked back down the garden to where Baker, White and the civilian Johnson were. Baker was at stand-to with Johnson, but White was looking back up towards him, pointing over the wall and putting a finger to his eyes. They could see them.

Kitson dropped down and ran down to them, was almost there when the group began firing again.

'Can you see them?' he shouted up.

'We know where they are, sir. See a head every now and then or an arm or something,' Baker called back.

Kitson clambered up on to the now crowded rooftop. 'I don't want them settling in. We are going out of that gate in the next few hours. They can command it.'

'I would say,' Johnson said, turning to look at him, calm, his experience showing through, 'that is their intent. See who's coming and going, perhaps.'

Kitson looked at his two ratings. 'I want them pushed back. Engage.'

'Heavy fire will only make them duck their heads,' Johnson said.

'What are you suggesting?'

'Show them that is not a safe place,' Johnson replied. 'When they break cover you chaps keep them moving.' He turned back to the wall and put his eye to the scope on his rifle. A second later he fired, the big rifle kicking back into his shoulder, his hand a blur on the bolt action, he fired again. He sighted again, fired, and then a fourth shot. Each of the big high-velocity rounds was punching through the thin metal of car doors and panels, hitting targets where he judged them to be on the other side. After the sixth shot they broke, moving back, some wounded, others dragging hurt comrades after them, firing their weapons as they went. One, brave or stupid, having seen one movie too many, turned and retreated backwards firing from the hip. A burst of fire from the south-west corner took him down.

Suddenly, as quickly as it had started, it stopped. Silence. Johnson didn't look back at them, but remained facing forward and when he closed his eyes for a second, from Kitson's vantage he could see the older man raise his hand and make the sign of a cross on his forehead. He wasn't enjoying what he was having to do.

Kitson picked up his radio. 'Two one, sitreps, please.'

'Two two. They have pulled back from here over,' Montagu's voice clear over the sixty metres that separated them.

'Two three. Same here, sir. One lightly wounded.'

He looked behind him to where Sarah Conway was on the other staff quarters roof. She raised a thumb at him. Her corner was fine. He waved a hand and pointed her towards the gates, and as she dropped to the ground he did the same.

The wounded rating was down on the ground by the time they arrived. It was the fellow who had been getting excited. Now he looked pale, his breathing shallow, holding his right hand over a wound on his upper left arm. The Petty Officer was with him and another rating was tearing open a battle dressing. 'Came through the wall, sir.

174

Very small entry wound, it's gone right through, bigger at the back. Armour piercing, I reckon. The small-core thing.'

'Sure?' The PO nodded. Kitson looked at the man. 'How are you feeling?'

He didn't answer, just shook his head. Shock.

'Look at me,' Kitson said gently. 'It's a flesh wound. Little bit of metal this big,' he held up two fingers, 'went right through. It's a bit messy, but you'll be fine. There are two doctors here. They will get you fixed up. Okay?'

'Sir.' He nodded, then looking up, added, 'Whoever said it doesn't hurt got it wrong.'

Conway was there by then, and the other French doctor with two of their nursing staff. He settled down beside the wounded rating and gently made him take his hand away from the entry wound so that he could see it.

'Now lift the arm, please.'

He winced again, but raised the arm so that the doctor could see the exit wound.

'Okay,' he said casually. 'Is no problem,' with a big grin. 'We fix you up, eh? Can you walk?'

He nodded and they led him away into the Embassy building. The first, Kitson thought, as he walked away. Thank God it's minor. Hope it's the last.

Buchanan radioed across for a sitrep and to advise they too had been attacked at their location, by two largish gangs. They were repelled by weapons fire, predominantly by the efforts of two baby-faced US Marines manning the machine gun that the British sailors had carried in. When they had arrived they had carried it away, stripped it and familiarized themselves with it totally and when they used it, from the site where Chops and their sergeant agreed it should go, they were brutally effective. Buchanan had been heartened. They were efficient, each man's role defined, their specialist ground combat training making his ratings look like what they were, bluejackets ashore.

He was talking to Kitson when he saw the Lynx to the south, almost out of range and at height over the city and

175

port where the pilot could see well to the north. He smiled. Mayberry was doing his recce the safe way.

In the helicopter Mayberry's observer had three of the aerial photos that Wisher had given them that morning taped together and lying across his knees. He was marking it with a felt-tip pen, the fires, the obvious points of contact between the factions, but with most of what looked like a six- or eight-mile front silent at any given time it was difficult to see exactly who was where in the buildings. Occasionally there would be a blast, or dust would rise from something going off, but the overall situation was still very unclear. What was clear was that the main Ulima forces advancing from the north were in the north-western suburbs of Monrovia and within a mile of the diplomatic enclave, their forward elements already in the leafy tree-lined streets. He turned and headed back, so that the Lynx could be pulled off the flight deck into the hangar in time for the US Sea King's arrival.

Splif was sitting on his haunches. They were in the shell of what was once a garage with a shop, but it had been stripped, looted before they got there. It was never much of a garage. Old corrugated iron roof, with flattened paraffin tins hammered on to the support poles to make walls. There would have been basic tools once, tyre irons, a few spanners, but now all that was left was a half kerosene tin of sump oil and a couple of sacks that someone had slept on. The shop was just sloping shelving made from wooden boxes where the owner would have sold produce and maybe canned drinks or cigarettes. Bang-Bang was lying down, dozing against the side of the shelving, the others scattered about. There were now ten of them, a smaller group having joined theirs. They had not slept the night before, but at least they had some food. They had happened on a family hiding early that morning. The uncle, terrified of them, had shown them where their belongings were and they had helped themselves. Good food, too. There was meat, fresh meat – goat, one of them thought. Sweet potatoes, bananas and millet or somesuch, still in its UN food programme sack. Bang-Bang had taken the daughter out into the bush and used her. She was much older than him, maybe fourteen, and knew what she was to do, but he was surprised that Bang-Bang did. He had bought her back unharmed, much to her mother's relief, and she had squatted down and cooked the food, always with one of them on guard. They had eaten it, taking the bananas and sweet potatoes for later, leaving the family with nothing.

Now they were waiting for orders. Their section leader, an older boy, would appear every now and then. At dark they were moving forward, into Monrovia itself. Before them somewhere were Taylor's fighters, but while the main Ulima forces engaged them others, including Splif and his section, would move through and break in down the western edge along the seafront. The place was theirs for the taking. He had heard from one of the advance patrols moving back that along that way there were many houses owned by rich people, whites and foreigners. Good pickings. But they had a job to do. The section leader had said they would be searching as they went and there would be fighting. Several had not come back. He hadn't said what they would be looking for, but it didn't matter to Splif. If it got them good looting then that was fine by him and he liked fighting. He wondered if he should have had a go with the girl after Bang-Bang. He had watched from a distance and with nothing said she had raised her skirts and lain down, spreading her heavy thighs for the slim boy with the gun. The problem was, he didn't know what to do. He thought he did, but he wasn't going to get it wrong and have a girl laugh at him, for he was Splif, Ulima fighter and a man, not someone to be scorned. If he got it wrong or failed and she laughed at him, he would have to shoot her in case she told someone else. Better not to bother until he knew what he was supposed to do.

The sun was dropping. They would be moving forward

soon. They could see the rooftops of the houses in the place where the foreigners and rich people lived. He thought about the girl that morning. There might be white women tonight. The thought of being alone with a white woman and then unsure of what he was supposed to do unnerved him. Next time he would watch Bang-Bang more closely. He looked down at his rifle. Now that was something he knew what to do with. They had fought twice that day so far, fast, angry clashes at forty or fifty yards' range. Part of a skirmish line, they had come across a band of Taylor's supporters for the first time relaxing in the shade under some trees. They had killed one of them in that fight, but he had nothing of any value. His rifle was newer than one of theirs so they had taken it and of course they had stripped him of ammunition. Bullets were always a problem. Across the oily earth floor Bang-Bang stirred, sat up and began to roll himself a smoke.

It was at that moment, thousands of miles away in England, in Brighton, that the detectives who had been waiting for the man to recover consciousness got a call from the hospital. In a coma since the night he was brought in, he had died. The detectives who had followed up the next day, taken a few statements, had been waiting to take one from the man himself. As the days had become weeks other jobs had come in and it had dropped down the list of things to do. But with his death the file was pulled. This was no longer a fight outside a pub that went wrong, a serious assault, maybe with grievous or actual bodily harm attached. It was a murder enquiry. They pulled the statements and began to follow them up. A person who had seen something out of the door as it was closing said that he thought the men had been talking to two girls he knew. They were visited at home and one of them fished round in the handbag she always carried when she was out on the pull. There. A beermat with two names written on it. Dave and Tom and a phone number. The number was a bed and breakfast place in Hove. The manager supplied the surnames and the fact that they were off HMS *Beaufort*.

In the RAF Hercules the air loadmaster threaded his way down the aircraft over sleeping men and canisters, leaned over and gently shook the young Royal Marines officer. Andy Gordon woke up instantly. 'Over your drop in half an hour, sir.'

He looked questioningly. 'I thought we were stopping for fuel.'

'Mid-air,' the sergeant said. 'US Air Force transiting Ascension. We RV'd an hour ago.' They must want you there quick, the loader was thinking. They were flight-planned for Sierra Leone, but the Lockheed tanker en route back to the US from the Gulf for its Certificate of Airworthiness checks had been diverted to meet them.

Gordon nodded and yawned. 'Thanks.' He stood up and began to move down the line of sleeping men, noticing that even Corporal Doughty had dropped off. Big night in Gib, obviously, he thought. He shook them awake as he moved down the line. There wasn't much to do. Final check of the loads in the canisters, check the seals. Get personal kit on and squared away. With a bit of luck they could leave a lot of the gear on the ship. The air loader was waiting to check their harnesses. The operation was now his until they went out of the door, his authority aft of the cockpit absolute. The first drop would be for the canisters – no one wanted one of those dropping on them. The moment they were clear the men would go out of the side doors in two sticks. The sergeant began lining them up, port and starboard, his loader checking the couplings on the canisters and pushing them back towards the drop-down aft ramp along the rollers that ran the length of the aircraft's belly.

HMS *Beaufort* was at the rendezvous for the incoming Marines, which was also where she would receive the

American helicopter delivering the drugs they needed. She had turned into wind and was just under way enough to smooth out the ride. The US Navy Sea Hawk flared out and as its wheels settled on the flight deck, the pilot reduced the power setting and raised a thumb back to the crewman who slid back the door.

The ratings on the flight deck under the command of a Petty Officer, expecting to be given a package and then to stand back as the machine lifted off again, were surprised when four people jumped down from the door. All of them were lugging big tote bags and the first was wearing the tabs of a US Navy Lieutenant Commander. The PO saluted and without speaking directed them off the flight deck with an extended arm, one of the ratings guiding them forward.

Two minutes later the man entered the bridge and Bennett met him at the head of the stairs.

'Phil Murphy reporting for duty . . . aah . . . sir. I believe you wanted some medical assistance. I am a surgeon. An anaesthetist and two Marine corps medics travelled out with me. We have the drugs you asked for, so with your permission we'll lend a hand.'

'We weren't expecting you,' Bennett said, taking him in. The Americans were famous for their casual air and specialists like medical people were even more casual. Murphy was tall, lean with bandy cowboy legs and a dark blue Navy issue baseball cap on his head. 'Welcome aboard. We have a doctor that came out in the first load from the beach and I think we are coping. But,' he said wryly, 'the day isn't over. Not by a long shot. I'm sure she will appreciate your help. I'll have you shown below. My sec will organize a bunk for each of you later.' He looked at the ship's name picked out in gold embossed lettering on the cap. As XO on *Nottingham* he had spent several months in the Arabian Gulf on the Armilla patrol. USS *Lasalle* was the American Gulf command ship and she usually sat moored just off Bahrain.

'You from *Lasalle*?' he asked Murphy.

'Hell no, sir. I won this playing cards. My last tour was Bethseda naval hospital.'

By the time Murphy was taken down to the sick bay his team were there and unloading their bags of equipment and supplies. Renée Bujould, the French doctor, was making them welcome while the LMA found stowage for the supplies, drugs and oxygen they had brought out with them. She immediately asked him to inspect the chest drain she had put in. 'Good work, doctor. This looks fine.'

He concurred on her diagnosis of the head wound, reminding himself that in Bethseda there would be a thoracic surgeon to do the drain and a neurosurgeon taking care of the head wound. She was good. 'What's your thing, doc?'

She smiled at him. 'Tropical diseases, but in Africa you end up a generalist.'

'You're a good cutter,' Murphy said and asked the LMA, 'Where's your theatre facility?' Every warship had one somewhere. An area that if required could be converted into an operating theatre.

'Wardroom, sir.'

'Don't call me sir when we are on the job,' Murphy responded, 'You may call me Doctor, or Mr Murphy on account that I am a shit hot orthopaedic surgeon, or after we have worked together for at least, oh, ten minutes you can call me Phil,' he finished brightly. 'Now let's go see the wardroom. Doctor Bujould, we're gonna be working together. Would you like to join us?'

Darkness was falling. Sitting in the helicopter, now back out on the flight deck, Lieutenant Mayberry made contact with the inbound Hercules. The ship was hove to in the water, upwind of the drop zone, the recovery boats out. With four of the ship's handheld radios ashore they only had three left. One was out in the lead seaboat, one on the bridge and one with Mayberry in the Lynx.

'Wind is one to two knots from the north. We are upwind of the Delta Zulu, riding lights on. On your command we shall burn flares in the water around the Delta Zulu, over.'

'Beaufort, Bravo two nine, we copied that. Confirm you have a signal lamp flashing at this time, over.' There was a rating on the bridge wing with the big ten-inch lamp flashing out the Morse code for 'B' every five seconds, its face arced up to the northern sky.

'Affirmative, Bravo two nine.'

'We are approaching from your north-west at 1000 feet. We have you visual and we will be overhead in two minutes. You may light flares, over.'

'Roger, two nine, Echo Tango Oscar two minutes lighting flares.'

Mayberry picked up the small handheld.

'Bridge, P1. Two minutes to the drop. Light flares, repeat light flares.'

He looked out on the water and within seconds two reddish orange flares began to burn on the water several hundred yards out, the light reflecting back off the sea and showing the wake of the seaboats as they gunned back in towards the *Beaufort* to drop one more each side. He increased his engine speed, began rotor turn and was soon lifting off the deck, heading out towards the perimeter of the drop zone, two divers in the back.

'Stand up! Hook up!' the loader called. 'Three minutes to drop!'

The twenty-one men of the recce troop shuffled forward, the blast of warm air and noise from the engines rolling over them as the sergeant and his loader opened the side doors and the aft ramp door was lowered on hydraulic arms. The flight sergeant stood before them, arms spread out, wearing his intercom headset. He watched the lights. He would get a five-second warning from the cockpit over his headphones.

Finally he dropped one arm and pointed to the airman

loader who was looking back towards him. The man gave a push and the canisters began to run back down the rollers, the static lines running down a cable above them. One by one they dropped off the back into the night and as the final canister fell away the air loader pushed both arms forward.

'Red on, wait for it. GO! One and two . . . three and four . . . five and six . . .' The Marines went out of the doors into the dark, the loader moving up behind them. '. . . nine and ten . . . eleven and twelve.'

The pilot had timed the run-in well. The canisters were floating in the water in a ragged line just on the edge of the drop zone, the first of the men in the water already clear of his parachute and holding his small torch aloft. Mayberry hovered over the canisters and with his observer counted twenty-one lights.

'That's them all. Confirm you have twenty-one.'

'Yeah, roger that. Twenty-one,' the observer replied.

Mayberry looked back and jerked a thumb at one of the divers. The man sat down in the open doorway, legs dangling, then dropped into the sea twelve feet below.

The Marines' parachutes, slightly weighted, would be abandoned to sink below the reach of the recovery boats' propellers, but the chutes on the canisters needed to be released by hand before the boat came alongside. The Lynx remained there over the water. If anyone was in trouble he would fly in and drop his remaining diver into the water to assist. By the time the first boat, loaded with men, was at the landing cage, the remaining Marines were piling into the other boat as it stooged along, moving from one torch light to the next.

The first boat then ran back out and began attaching lines to the canisters, the diver in the water sliding into the boat. Twenty minutes after going out of the door of the Hercules, Andy Gordon and his men were in the hangar changing into dry kit and breaking out their weapons and gear. A classic parachute entry and recovery: he was delighted. The trip had been worth while for that experience alone.

The Marines moved fast. They knew their boss would be briefed and he in turn would brief them and they would go immediately. Into what they weren't sure – they had had no news since they left that morning – but from the welcome on the faces of the sailors something was going on. A rating appeared to show Lieutenant Gordon to the bridge and as he disappeared Doughty walked over to a rating in his work area by the missile racks.

'What's the score? We've heard nothing since this morning.'

The rating gave a mirthless grin. 'We got hit, din' we? Took two rounds. Six dead. Ten injured. The Jimmy's ashore wiv some of the lads and by all accounts it's getting shittier by the minute. I'll tell you the score, soldier: the sooner we get these fucking civvies aboard and piss off 'ome the better.'

Now that there was some chance that the wardroom would be needed as a medical treatment area, Bennett had opted to move the Ops to his day cabin. The aerial photos and maps were stuck to the bulkhead with Bluetack and someone had drawn on the wall in a wipe-off felt-tip pen as large a map as possible, showing the position of the *Beaufort* in relation to the evacuation point, the enclave and the two embassies. Resources, *Beaufort*'s people on one job or another, appeared as coloured pins taken from the notice boards. The Captain's secretary, the junior Supply Officer who managed much of the ship's administration, was there to update the board as things happened and present at the briefing were the Captain, Ops, and Mayberry. Twenty minutes later Gordon made his way back to his men.

'Right. Listen up.' He briefed them as quickly and clearly as he could, covering the situation ashore and the task they had to complete. While they finished dumping gear they would not need he took his sergeant and Corporal

Doughty to one side to make sure they clearly understood their jobs.

'You each have one section. Corporal Doughty, you have eight Marines, Sar'nt, you nine. We will be in troop formation a lot of the time, but if we need to we will operate as sections. I'll float. Troop radio operator with me. The two boats ashore together. One section in each. Have your people at the seaboats in . . .' he looked at his watch '. . . ten minutes. Clear?'

They both nodded.

'Questions?'

Both men had a hundred, but knew that their Lieutenant didn't have the answers.

'Kit, sir?' Doughty said. 'The extra section weapons and . . .'

'We take 'em,' Gordon said. 'And every round of ammunition we can carry. As we have heard, they have had seven or eight contacts already.'

The windows of the British Embassy buildings were open in the hope of a breeze to cool things down, but the air was hardly stirring. Maggie Black had found two hurricane lamps in the store room and now one was operating in Black's office, the other in the kitchen. Apart from those two, and an old kerosene lantern that was burning in the small anteroom he had given Kitson, the building was in darkness. Most of the people had moved outside to where it was now cooler, and around the grass and the groups of strangely quiet people candles guttered in the odd breeze that slipped over the wall. There were still bursts of gunfire, measurably closer than that afternoon. Inside the XO sat at the desk, the Clansman radio propped up before him, sweat trickling down his neck in the heat.

'*Roger, Beaufort,*' he finished.

He looked up at Conway and Montagu who had just walked in. 'Right. Sitrep. Recce lads are here. They will be in at the beach in twenty minutes or so. I'll go down and get them. I'll take Baker and Whitc.' I should have kept Chops here, he was thinking. His two most experienced people, Lieutenant Buchanan and Chief Petty Officer Wilks, both blooded that day, were now both at the US compound and he would not ask either of the two junior officers to do something he wouldn't do himself.

Conway opened her mouth to speak but Montagu beat her to it. 'I'll go, sir.' He grinned in the soft light. 'With respect, sir, this is not an XO's job. It's a job for a young, up and coming, but junior Lieutenant.'

Conway rolled her eyes. 'Spare me . . .' she muttered, but Kitson smiled.

'Fair enough. Let Baker lead. He's been down there twice today. Take it slow, very slow, and be careful.'

Baker did. Moving through the gardens slowly they made their way through to the old beach-front villa and settled down, Montagu looking to seaward and the two ratings covering the street wall and the way they had come.

Someone passed her a cup of coffee and Sarah Conway took it gratefully. She had smothered herself in insect repellant, but the mosquitoes were still getting through. She had missed a bit of skin under her hairline at the nape of her neck and she slapped at one angrily. It was still hot and humid and she sweated freely like all the others, her hair lank and dirty. They were at the base of the wall and she was sitting leaning against the Land-Rover's back wheel. Above her a PO and a rating covered the wall, and beside her sat the fellow who had been hit by the core from the armour piercing round. His arm, bandaged and in a sling, was throbbing, but the analgesic tablets he had been given were dealing with that. The rate passed him a cup, too.

'That bird who came in, the one with the wounded driver?'

'Yeah,' someone responded.

'She was raped.'

'Yeah. I heard that.'

'Know what they did after . . . after they had finished?'

'Wot?'

'Pissed on her. They stood over her and pissed on her.'

They were quiet for a moment, no one knowing what to say.

'This coffee is good,' Lieutenant Conway said, to break the silence.

'I dunno about you, ma'am,' the wounded chap said, 'but I could murder a bloody beer.'

She laughed softly. 'So could I. So could I.'

'Cold you know, ma'am, ice cold with condensation on the glass. Like that beer we had in South Africa. Lager it was. Oh, I can taste it. Castle or something, it was.'

She looked at him in the dark, her mind flicking back to the game park, the fire, the cold beer.

'Tell you what. When we get back out to the Beau I'll stand you lads a round or two. There's some of that beer on board. I'll ask someone to put some in the fridge, eh?' The rating laughed, forgetting about the throbbing in his arm, and called softly up to the lads on the wall to tell them that Lieutenant Conway was getting the beers in when they got back.

'Mess will be shut, ma'am,' someone objected.

'Well they can bloody well open it,' she replied, slapping at another mosquito. There was muffled laughter. She was reminding herself to say something to Kitson and then he appeared from across the grass.

'There's too much morale here,' he said dryly.

'Shall we tell you why, sir?' a voice called softly from the gate.

Oh God, Sarah thought. In the shit again. 'I just promised them . . .' she began.

'I heard,' he interrupted. 'You're going to have a hell of a mess bill.'

*   *   *

187

It wasn't Lieutenant Montagu that saw them. It was White. He had shuffled slowly down the waist-high wall towards the sea end and as he looked up the beach towards the north-west the scudding cloud allowed the moon to break through. There they were, moving steadily down the beach. A group of people, men by the look of them, all carrying weapons. Seventy or so yards. The clouds moved over again.

He looked back to where the Lieutenant was. He was looking to seaward, talking softly into his radio, reaching for his torch. It must be them. He's going to signal them in.

'Shsss.' Nothing. He hadn't heard. He picked up a small stone and threw it down the wall and Montagu turned. White pointed up the beach, jabbing a finger.

Montagu peered into the darkness, but could see nothing. White skittered to a halt beside him.

'About fifteen of 'em. Sixty or so yards up the beach coming this way.'

'Sure?'

'Fuckin' right I am.'

'*Seaboat seaboat, two four,*' Montagu said softly, turning down the volume.

'*Two four, go.*'

'*Hostiles to your left from the RV. Sixty yards and approaching. Figures fifteen repeat fifteen, over,*' he reported.

'*Two four, signal your position.*' This was a new voice. Not the rating in the boat. The Marines officer, he realized. '*One flash only. Don't illuminate the sand, over.*'

Shit shit shit. Montagu carefully hooded the torch and made one flash to seaward.

'*Gotcha, two four. Sit tight, over.*'

White was straining his ears, trying to hear the boats. If they couldn't hear them maybe the hostiles wouldn't either. He moved away from Montagu to give himself a field of fire and hunkered down behind the wall, hard against it. He could hear talking now. Soft conversations among the approaching men.

Thirty yards now. Getting closer every second. He could

hear his heart beating. Baker. Where the fuck's Kevin? He wouldn't know. He could come walking down here any moment. He checked the safety catch on his weapon for the tenth time in as many seconds, trying to slow his heartbeat down, slow his breathing. Both sounded like roaring in his ears. Surely they must hear them? The talking loud now, a snorting, snotty sound as one of them blew his nose straight on to the sand. Dirty cunt, he thought, footsteps on the sand, Baker must have heard the snot going. He must have. He would be settling back into the darkness now, silent, watchful, wary.

He came up slowly, remembering the instructor's words: they see movement. The eyes see movement and contrast. Slowly. There. Moving away. The last man four or five yards way. He brought his weapon up to the shoulder, confident that if any of them turned or saw anything he was in a position to react.

It was a full minute before Montagu raised the radio to his lips.

'Seaboat seaboat, two four.'

'Two four, go.'

'Seaboat, they have gone past,' Montagu said, hoping his voice was level. *'You may proceed in, over.'*

'We are in, two four. Sit tight. We are approaching from the north-west along the beach. Do not shoot, over.'

A few moments later there was a low whistle. White dropped down and raised his weapon that way.

'Oi. Stand easy, you tosser,' a voice called softly, 'the Royals are here.'

'About fucking time,' White replied, relaxing. 'We've been doing your job all day.'

A figure moved out of the dark. The man before him was wearing full camouflage gear and humping a pair of rocket launchers in addition to his rifle. The weight of equipment was dragging his webbing down and his bare hands and his face beneath his green beret were blacked out with cam cream.

'Oo the fuck are you then? Rambo?' White challenged softly, grinning at the sight.

'Corporal Doughty. Zulu company, 45 Commando, and seeing you are nothing but a gobshite rate a bit of respect would be nice.' Doughty dropped to one knee and signalled back; others moved out of the dark, silently fanning out through the garden. A figure indistinguishable from the others settled down beside Montagu.

'Hi. Andy Gordon.'

Montagu introduced himself.

'Was it dark when you came down here?' Gordon asked.

'Yes. Yes it was.'

'And you wore a white shirt.'

'It's all I've got,' Montagu replied. He had given his camo smock to someone else earlier and it only occurred to him after they were out of the gates.

Not a problem, Gordon thought. Most of his blokes had already stripped back to their green tee-shirts. 'Sar'nt.' The sergeant appeared from the dark. 'Get this officer a shirt, if you would. Corporal Doughty?'

'Sir.'

'Point,' Gordon said, then, looking back at Montagu, 'Right. Shall we make a move?'

'My chap Baker better go with him. He set up this route this afternoon. Knows it well.'

The trip back was fast, the Royal Marines moving like silent ghosts, astonishingly swift and quiet considering the equipment they were carrying. They moved in an extended diamond formation, Doughty up front with Baker. The Marine corporal at one stage pulled Baker down into cover while he moved ahead to check something, then moved them forward again. It was Baker who pulled the Marine back when they got to the last wall.

'Any further and we get slotted by our own blokes. There's a gimpy on the corner there,' he whispered by way of explanation. Doughty shrank back into cover dramatically. To him the thought of a bunch of sailors armed

190

with SA80s and live ammo was daunting, but manning a machine gun pointing his way?

Montagu came forward, talking into the radio, and a few moments later the gates were eased open and they crossed the road.

There was muffled applause from the civilians as the troop gathered inside the gates. Things were kept in perspective by a few ribald remarks from the ratings on the walls, the usual inter-service digs. Gordon made his way straight in to the building and was shown to where Kitson was talking to the ship, Bill Black with him in the small anteroom.

Black put his hand out. 'Not quite the siege of Mafeking, but you are very welcome. I'm Bill Black, HM's Ambassador to this wonderful country,' he finished dryly. The RM Lieutenant saluted and then shook hands. 'Andy Gordon, sir. Pleased to meet you.' Kitson put down the handset and they began immediately. It was finished inside twenty minutes and Kitson and Gordon walked out into the cool of the garden together.

'I think what I'd like to do, sir, is go out and have a recce. Then we can see how best to deploy. Depending on what I've got to secure, we can make some decisions.'

Squadron Leader Page eased his feet off the rudder pedals and wiggled his toes. The Nimrod was on autopilot. He looked down. Nothing but darkness. Two hours into a twenty-hour mish and he was bored already. The drugs. Go back and work out how to get the shipment out of the aircraft and recovered in one piece. The normal method of dropping things to ships at sea was from the bomb bay. Ship's mail, urgent supplies or spares could be canistered and dropped from the torpedo racks. The other way one could do it, he knew, was down the sonar buoy chute. Both these methods were set up on the ground before take-off and that took time, which was why he didn't opt for them prior to departure. It took about two hours for the lethargic process-driven ground establishment to get something into a bomb bay and his mission was to enable communications between Northwood and the ship asap. No time to be hanging around. This simply required a bit of ingenuity. A bit of initiative. There would be bitching from some of the crew. They had served in the Nimrods long enough to know they were old aircraft and, although they should know better, some of them heard danger in every creak and groan. A case of a little knowledge being a dangerous thing. That, coupled with filling jobs which were often mundane and procedural, where there was a page in the book for every eventuality, made them risk-averse. He knew that whatever he did that they had not seen before, practised before, trained for, they would mutter about. He wasn't going to take any shit from them. He smiled. Phil Matheson the relief pilot would take none of it, either.

He looked across at his right-hand-seat man. 'I'm going back to have a look at that package. You have the controls.'

'I have the controls,' he repeated.

Page climbed from his seat, edged past his engineer and then went down past the two navigators into the body of the aircraft, past the drymen who sat at the radar screens and the wetmen, the sonar chaps, to where the relief crew were sprawled about. There was a pile of magazines and books, everything from the *Spectator*, left by some thinking fellow, to top-shelf stuff like *Fiesta*. Matheson, ever the intellectual, was lying on a camp stretcher reading a copy of *Viz*. His number two, a likeable bloke called Davis, was engrossed in a paperback book. The package of drugs was on the floor by the galley station. Page picked it up and looked at it, feeling it to see how well it was packed. The drugs themselves seemed to be not much bigger than a cigarette packet and were wrapped in bubble plastic. Needs outer protection, he thought, needs to have a retarded drop, needs to float, needs to be seen once it's in the water.

He looked consideringly at the dinghy every Nimrod carried in the cabin, walked back to where the dinghy was stowed and pulled it down. Opened the bag and began rummaging around in the bits and pieces that made up the survival gear. Began to work.

He cut a section from the bag itself, a long strip of the heavy nylon. He took the drugs and packed them in balls of rolled-up newspaper, the pages of someone's *Sun*, then rolled the much bigger package into the nylon outer and secured it with the ubiquitous silver duck tape that was in every tool kit. Matheson wandered over and watched him as he worked.

Happy it was watertight, he then took a lifejacket from the dinghy – they had plenty on the aircraft – and three-quarters inflated it. He settled the package in the space between the two inflated side panels and taped it in, the other pilot helping him.

The lifejacket had a little light that would come on when it hit the water, but that wasn't enough, so Matheson began scrounging round in the survival kit. He came out with a small orange torch.

'Aye. This'll do,' he said.

'Bollocks. It'll sink or break on impact,' Page responded.

'O ye of little fucking faith,' Matheson replied. He walked back up to the galley station and found an empty litre water bottle. He measured the diameter of the torch and cut the top of bottle at the appropriate point on its spreading neck.

'Just before we drop we turn the torch on, secure it in the bottle, and tape it to the vest.'

'Fair enough. What about retarding the drop?' Page asked.

'What about the drogue thing on the dinghy?'

Page looked nonplussed.

'The sea anchor thing. It's like a little parachute.' Matheson was digging around in the bottom of the remnants of the bag. He grabbed something and Page handed him a knife. Matheson stood up holding the drogue, a small nylon shape more like a little parachute than the conical funnel arrangement for bigger boats.

'No. Better idea. Take a retard chute off a buoy. Sorted,' Matheson said. 'Now, how do we get it out of the aircraft?'

Gordon spread his men out and moved off. Leaving his sergeant as 2i/c, he took just four men, Corporal Doughty and three Marines. The cam cream they were wearing had already begun to sweat off in the heat of the evening so instead of matt black they were now mottled, but there was certainly no reflection of white or shiny skin and the rest of the disruptive pattern did its job. As they moved up the wall along the street, leap-frogging each other from cover to cover as they had first learned to do in Northern Ireland, any observer would have had to strain their eyes to see them. In the dark they were virtually invisible.

Every now and then Gordon stopped and, dropping well into cover, snapped on a tiny maglite torch with a red filter and marked something on one of the aerial photographs he had taken; there were whispered exchanges with Doughty while the other three Marines kept watch.

At two points Doughty slipped away and did a lone recce down one of the streets, pacing it out and getting a feel for where they would be visible from, where they could be attacked from. The truth was that the direct route from the American Embassy to the British Embassy, although only four blocks, was very exposed. However, by the time they arrived near the US mission Gordon had a feel for how he could best deploy his men.

He called Buchanan on his radio and a few moments later the five Royal Marines slipped through the gates into the US compound. The situation was almost unreal because Gordon ignored the staring people, again some of them cheering and applauding the arrival of friendly forces, and settled to one knee beside the Marine carrying their Clansman radio. Buchanan came forward to meet them as Gordon finished checking in with Kitson.

'Right, Corporal. Shoot back and get the others, if you will. Take . . .'

'Quicker on me own, sir,' Doughty interrupted.

'Very well.'

Buchanan introduced himself and a few minutes later they were with the US Ambassador in his office. Also present were his number two and the man Kreutz.

Gordon had taken his beret off and above the smeared, darkened bulk of his face was a clear strip of white skin below his blond hair. Buchanan thought he looked like a panda.

'I think the best way will be in groups of a hundred or so. Any smaller and it will take us all night. Any larger and we can't control them if something happens.' Gordon outlined his plan to the four men in some detail for the next few minutes before Ambassador Alberry spoke. 'Excuse me, but looking at what you propose,' he was pointing at the flip chart that Gordon had been drawing on, 'we are a little short on resources. Just how many are you?'

'A troop, sir,' Gordon said lightly. 'Twenty.'

'Twenty?' Alberry said disbelievingly. He had been expecting more. Many more. His own people would have thrown at least a hundred, maybe two hundred, well-trained and well-armed troops into this mission.

Kreutz felt the same but did not have the good grace to hide it. 'What goddam use are twenty?' he interjected. 'Might as well piss at 'em . . .'

Gordon turned to face him, his eyes narrowing, but it was the *Beaufort*'s Lieutenant that stood up.

'If I may, Ambassador,' he cut in. He had been there several hours and had spent some time with the American diplomat. He had also had Kreutz's attitude in chunks.

'It was five this morning when Lieutenant Gordon and his troop left Scotland. Much has changed since then. At five this morning *Beaufort* was simply to stand off. It's possible that our people are now wishing they had sent a larger detachment. It's also quite possible they wouldn't. This is the standard recce troop deployment, and it is my understanding, correct me if I am wrong, Lieutenant Gordon,' he glanced at the Marines officer, 'that the troop normally functions in advance of main elements arriving. They are trained and equipped to do just that. Lastly, Mr Kreutz, do not underestimate what a small force like this is capable of. They are Royal Marines. Commandos. In your structure you would call them special forces. You would be bloody surprised what twenty of them can do. They are also all we have on scene, so I suggest we let Lieutenant Gordon get on with his job.'

'Lieutenant, what is it you would like to start with?' Alberry asked, smoothing things over. His expression wasn't smooth. His look at Kreutz was dismissive, his own anger barely concealed.

'I'd like to break them into four or five groups. Number them. Then start briefing each group in turn. Work it one group on the move, one ready by the gate, one being briefed. Orders,' he flipped the leather cover of his watch face, 'at 1915. Like to start at 1930 hours, have everyone in the Brit compound by 2030 latest. We will redeploy and the first groups then start for the beach and the ship immediately.'

'What else do you need?'

'Chain of command, sir. We can't have two detachments. Your Marines. I can use 'em, but only operating as a cohesive section under my command.'

'You got it. I'll talk to Sergeant Dooley myself. Anything else?'

'A megaphone. I think it's what you call a bullhorn. Do you happen to have one?'

'I think we can organize that,' Alberry answered.

The last question Gordon was going to save for later. He wanted to know which of the houses and villas in the area

196

around the embassies were still inhabited. One of his chaps had been attached to the Royal Artillery 148 battery and done the observer's course. He could call fire accurately into a rubbish skip and if everything went pear-shaped he could call in NGS, naval gunfire support, from the *Beaufort*. But he didn't want to think about 4.5-inch high explosive shells coming in on a civilian occupied area.

Alberry stood up. 'Thank you gentlemen . . .' Then he looked at Kreutz, his expression changing. 'Mr Kreutz, a minute of your time please.'

As they left the room Gordon looked at Buchanan. 'Thanks for that.'

'You're welcome,' Buchanan answered with a grin. 'You're all bloody wankers, but you're our bloody wankers. We slag you off, but that's our privilege.'

'Fuck you, too,' Gordon replied genially.

'Actually, I thoroughly enjoyed it.'

'So did I. Who is that prick?' the Marine asked.

'A spook, I suspect. He had a go at the XO earlier and came off second.'

'Well, I think he's coming off second again now. Alberry is seriously pissed off. What's his problem?' Buchanan told him about Kreutz's request for priority evacuation.

Gordon was explaining what he wanted communicated in the briefings to the groups when three of the embassy staffers came over. One, a woman, had a clipboard. 'Okay. Groups of one hundred-odd?'

She was walking round like a schoolteacher, grouping people, when the US Marine Corps sergeant in charge of the Embassy guard detail walked up to Gordon and saluted. 'Sir, the Ambassador said I was to report to you, sir.'

'Good. Sergeant?'

'Sir. Dooley, sir.' He stood ramrod straight looking past the officer's left shoulder.

'Relax, Sergeant Dooley. Cut the boot camp shit, okay?'

'Sir,' the sergeant looked him in the eyes for the first time, his shoulders relaxing.

'Now, we have a job. Get a bunch of people from here down to the Brit compound, then everyone away to the ship safely. Total seven hundred-odd. I've got twenty Marines and thirty sailors. We all know what we think of sailors, don't we?'

The Marine smiled for the first time. 'They're good on ships, sir,' he said.

'Correct.' Gordon paused there. 'So. I can use you and your men and it's going to be a hell of a lot easier if we work together. You stay together, operate as a section but under my command. Happy with that?'

'Yes, sir. Sir? None of my people have been in the shit before and tonight,' he paused and nodded his head towards the sound of the gunfire, 'I think we're gonna be in it up to our eyeballs.' A warning. His boys and he were green. It was an honest statement and one that Gordon appreciated.

'We all do our jobs the way we were trained and we'll all go home,' he responded. 'They were your mates in that chopper this morning?'

Dooley nodded.

'You want payback?'

'You bet your ass . . . sir.'

'Contain it, Sergeant. Manage your men. No gung-ho. No heroics. And . . . I think you're right. There may be . . .' he paused and smiled, used the American's vernacular '. . . shit tonight. They come at us and we will dish out plenty. Semper Fi,' he said. The United States Marine Corps motto. Semper Fidelis. Always loyal. Loosely translated and understood a dozen ways it always came up to the same thing. Stick together. The Marine smiled back. 'Semper Fi,' he repeated.

The gates were opened and the remainder of the recce troop filed in. They were, as Doughty had put it, 'well tooled up'. Gordon took them to one side and began briefing them, Dooley's men along one side. He had brought the flip charts he had drawn on in Alberry's office

198

out on to the veranda and Buchanan, Chops(M) and four of the rates were there to listen in, leaving just six men on the walls.

Kitson was ready, or rather was hoping he was ready. He had done all the things on his list, his critical path was on track and now he was just waiting for the snafu. The cock-up that was inevitable when so many people were involved with anything this complex. He had worked out what could go wrong, from one boat with a broken engine right through to sustained fighting outside the walls that would prevent them leaving the compound, and thought through what he would do. Now it was time to do it. He looked at his watch. Seven-twenty. Gordon would be deploying his people. The first group gathered at the gate, the second being briefed. The briefing would be simple. Noise to a minimum. No talking. Listen to instructions from the *Beaufort*'s ratings who would be physically herding the groups past the Marines who would be deployed defensively. What to do if they came under fire. If they were hurt. Just how many would remember what to do if it happened was anyone's guess, they all knew that, but hopefully well-briefed they would be better able to cope.

There was a soft knock at the door lintel. Poppy.

'Hello, sailor.' The blonde hair that had dropped down one side made her smile lopsided and in the soft light of the lantern she looked like something off the cover of a *True Crime* magazine.

'Hi.'

She came in and put a plate down on the table beside him. 'Thought you'd like to grab something to eat while you had the chance. We fed your lads and Sarah.'

'That was kind of you.'

'They seemed to prefer what we had to whatever they brought in with them.' She lit a cigarette, remembered her manners and offered him one, but he shook his head.

'Sarah is fond of you,' she said. Kitson raised an eyebrow.

'Well, *fond* is probably the wrong word,' Poppy corrected herself.

'We have shared a wardroom for a while. You get to know people,' Kitson replied. 'She is a good officer.'

'Would I have made it?' she asked. 'I can run a theatre.'

'I think so. You're a nurse are you?'

'SRN. I'm here on a holiday, but I'd rather be in theatre now.' As they chatted, Kitson was thinking about asking her out and wondering what to say. It was years since he had actually asked someone out and he was painfully aware that this was neither the time nor the place to be thinking about such things. His discomfort was halted when Sarah Conway entered the room. 'Oh, sorry . . .'

'I'm just leaving,' Poppy replied, standing. 'Leave you two to get on with things.'

She brushed past Sarah, who took off her hat and sat down at Kitson's indication.

'I was thinking,' she began. 'Worst case scenario. We get someone else wounded tonight. Once we start moving people out we could conceivably end up with all the medically trained people on the ship when we have someone who needs attention here.'

'Go on.'

'Well I was thinking, if it gets really skoshey it's unfair to ask any of them to stay to the last boat, and what's more, they may feel they have to offer. The US surgical team is on the ship, which frees up the LMA. Why don't we bring him in? That will relieve the problem all round.'

'Good idea.' He stood up and reached for his cap. 'Why don't you raise the Beau and suggest that to the boss? I'll be outside with the lads.'

On the roof of the Land-Rover the PO was looking back across the compound. It was a bizarre sight: clusters of people, grouped round candles and what camping lanterns they had brought with them, sitting on the grass, and above them in the sky to the north and north-east the moving clouds reflecting back the flames of fires burning across the suburbs. Occasionally tracer fire arced high enough to be seen over the trees and the noise of the fighting was constant. Every now and then something big went off and they could feel the ground blast under their feet. The people sitting on the grass had become accustomed to the noise now. During the First World War men got so used to their environment that they slept through artillery barrages. These people were the same. Some were frightened, but most of them seemed to be bearing up or hiding their fears.

Kitson jumped up on to the roof.

'Okay, PO?'

'Aye, sir . . . Sir, I was just looking at all that lot.' Kitson followed his gaze. The clouds reflected red and yellow back at the ground and a burst of green tracer speared through black columns of rising smoke. 'Look at it. And what for? What the fuck are they killing each other *for*? I mean, I heard that everything has gone. Everything anyone could take from anyone else has been taken. A bloke over there. He said this place has been looted to a standstill. And yet they fight. They are dying out there. Killing each other. For what?'

'I don't know, PO,' Kitson replied honestly. 'I wish I could answer you.'

It had been bothering him, too. This just wasn't like Africa and certainly not like the Liberia they had been briefed on. Roving bands or individuals would kill for a television set or food and step it up to something with a strategy. Faction fighting amongst the warlords was by its nature a sporadic event, short sharp attacks on each other to gain some short-term advantage.

But this? This had been going on for twenty-four hours. The ferocity, the scale of the fighting, was vast by African standards. Supply lines must have been set up: to be expending ordnance at this rate they were being resupplied. That meant that in all probability they had taken the national barracks and the Army's arsenals. To be fighting this hard for possession of the looted, burning city didn't make sense. There had to be something else they were after. It was almost as if Monrovia itself was incidental. It just happened to be there. The place where Ulima-J and Taylor's bunch chose to slug it out.

Within the Embassy walls they didn't know it, but in the city itself the population had gone. Some of the refugees had scattered into the bush, or headed south into Boley's territory. Others had headed for the port and many were crowded aboard a Panamanian freighter that was bound for Lagos. The Captain, a decent man from the Gambia, hadn't the heart to stop them boarding and now he had a problem – possibly two thousand people crammed on every inch of his decks as he inched out of the port and made for sea.

Chops(M) looked at the group. He and his ten-man section were going to herd them down the street to the other compound, as quickly and quietly as they could, past the defensive positions set up by the Marines.

The array was simple enough. The Americans would remain in their compound on the south-western corner with one GPMG. From there they could cover the southern aspect. From their protective arc of fire the civilians would move down the street past four Royal Marines positions set up at intersections. From those points the British Marines could engage and suppress any attack coming in towards the group. At the bottom, where Chops would herd them left round the corner, was the last RM position covering the road from the beach and the north. Once round the corner the civilians were under the eyes of *Beaufort*'s ratings on the compound wall. Each of the positions would signal with a torch flash for the group to proceed to them and over the intersection into the next safe area. In the unlikely event that anything happened between positions, then one man from each of the nearest four-man positions would reinforce the sailors. Looked sensible enough.

He looked round the group, moving round them, taking stuff that was too heavy to carry safely or that would hold them back from a run and dumping it in a pile. There were muttered complaints, but nothing he hadn't expected. There were kids, at least three babies in arms, and several people well on the wrong side of sixty. What the fuck were *they* doing here, he thought. Not working. Visiting kids, perhaps. The cracker was a disabled bloke in a wheelchair. Chops looked at him.

'Don't worry about me.' The man was young, looked fit enough, and to compensate for his wasted legs his shoulders and arms were ferociously developed, suggesting huge upper body strength. 'I can wheel this chair faster than most of these people can run.'

'That wouldn't be hard,' Chops growled good-naturedly. 'Where's the best place for you?'

'There are no sidewalks. I'm only limited by those in front. That's the best place for me,' he replied honestly.

'Okay, you in front then.' Chops turned and called. 'Godshall?'

Godshall came over and Chops looked at the man in the chair. 'This man will be on the point. Watch him. He will signal back to everyone. Okay?'

The disabled man nodded as a US Marine on the wall whistled down.

'You have a go,' the Marine relayed.

Have a *go*? You have a go. Go what? Chops thought. Bloody septics. Bloody Marines.

The gates were opened and the group filed out into the darkness, Godshall in front and the wheelchair immediately behind him, gliding silently along the road. The leaders had reached the intersection as the last of the group were clearing the gates behind them and Godshall slowed and peered round the corner. A double flash of a torch. Move on.

He led the long conga line round the corner, looking back every now and then. Six of the lads were strung down the line on the roadside, shepherding people against the walls, stopping them bunching up, keeping them quiet. A woman was crying softly, obviously frightened, her husband with his arm round her. Children who had been happily playing in the garden a few minutes before felt the mood of the adults and were silent. A woman near the front carrying a baby and a bag stumbled. Chops took the bag from her and silently hooked it on to the back of the disabled man's moving wheelchair. Another torch flash. Moving without pause. The baby starting to cry, little complaints, the fast, uncomfortable motion, the heat, maybe feeling the tension. Passing the Marines post. They had one of *Beaufort*'s belt-fed machine guns on the corner of a low wall, two men serving the gun facing down the street. Another Marine supported them. Corporal Doughty watched them pass. If it wasn't for the cheeky grin he would have looked like something off a recruiting poster. Beret squared and low on his head, camouflage face veil round his neck, festooned in webbing and equipment with his SA80 at the ready, its butt into his shoulder. Beside him on the ground were tubular objects that looked like cardboard poster cylinders. Chops recognized them as LAWs. One-time-use anti-tank rockets that the Marines loved because they were the 'ultimate bullet'.

Ten minutes later they were there. Chops and Godshall had moved past the gate of their compound so they could join Baker and White to provide additional cover on the street and the first group of Americans streamed into the British Embassy compound.

As the last handful entered the ratings followed and Kitson was there as they came through. 'Well done, lads,' he said. 'No problems?'

'No, sir,' Chops replied. 'Come on, you lot. Next bus is leaving.' One of the men was limping. 'What's wrong with you?'

'Turned my ankle, Chief. Fucking stood on something.' He was obviously in some pain.

'Stupid cunt,' Chops growled. 'Stay 'ere. White?'

'Sir.'

'With us.'

'Thanks for the sympathy, Chief,' the injured man muttered sarcastically. A couple of them laughed and even Wilks smiled. 'Time for that later when I tuck you in your little kip. In the meantime fuck off and find the medic,' he growled.

In a moment or two the ten men were out of the gate and heading back to the US mission. The second group were briefed and waiting for them and they started out immediately, following the same path as the first. They stopped within twenty yards. A woman of some pre-war vintage was having trouble keeping up, her arthritic joints slowing things. Chops made his way back to her.

'It's my hip,' she explained. 'Booked in for a full replacement when I get home.' She spoke slowly and loudly because he was a foreigner and spoke American funny. He took her back into the Embassy and caught up with the rest, and when they came back for the third group he found there were in fact four people who would have trouble walking the four hundred yards, let alone breaking into a run if it became necessary.

'Let's nick that four by four, bung 'em in that,' White suggested, pointing down the street to a dark-coloured Jeep Cherokee. 'They're pretty quiet as long as you don't rev the engine.'

Chops looked at it and then back at the rating. 'Can you start it without the keys?'

'No. But Godshall can. Used to nick cars when he was a nipper.' Chops set them on it and had the US Marine on the radio advise Gordon and Kitson they were having to use a vehicle. The third group set out, the Jeep, Godshall at the wheel, trailing them.

They were halfway when Baker, on the point in Godshall's absence, settled to one knee: the next Marine post had failed to signal them forward. Chops moved up to him.

'Problem?'

'Dunno,' he whispered back. 'They haven't signalled and they are lying very still.'

Chops was moving back down the long line of civilians, quietly urging them back off the road on to the grass and against the garden wall until he could see what was happening, when it started.

Corporal Doughty, down at the intersection, had felt the tap on his boot. He looked back up the road and settled very slowly down the wall in the shadows. Two of his lads serving the GPMG were over the weapon sighted down the street. The third was four or five yards away, prone, like on the range, looking the same way, his rifle to his shoulder.

There was a band of men approaching. Slowly but surely coming their way. The first thing he heard was a muffled challenge. Seconds later someone maybe forty yards away fired a weapon. A short, angry burst at ninety degrees to them. Two groups, perhaps. Challenging each other? His men certainly hadn't been seen. If this group broke and moved the way they were heading they would run right into his four-man post and the civvies. Would they fight? Go the other way? Talking now. Shouts and recriminations. Pissed off at each other. Same side. Which way were they moving?

'Hold your fire,' he said softly.

At the Marine post the civilians had just passed, two of the men had come to their feet and ran fast and silently down the road, past the group cowering against the wall, then slowed and advanced at a jog to support Corporal Doughty's team. He looked back and as they reached the end of the wall he held up a hand to them and slowly pointed down the road. Now they covered both sides of the street.

He looked back at the threat. They were moving now, ten or twelve or them up the middle of the road. They were carrying AKs, the familiar curved magazine and stubby shape a giveaway. Thirty yards. Close enough.

'Stand by,' he whispered.

'STOP!' he yelled. 'DO NOT COME CLOSER. WE ARE ARMED AND ESCORT AMERICAN CIVILIANS! DO NOT COME CLOSER! AMERICANS!'

There was a burst of fire, this time at them, but it went over their heads. A second rifle opened up, yells in the dark, muzzle-flash.

'Fuck this,' Doughty snapped. 'Hit 'em!'

His team opened fire, the gun raking the street, ripping into the bunched-up advancing group. As they scattered the riflemen opened up and, covering both sides of the road as they did, the attackers had no place to hide. No cover worth much. Ten seconds later Doughty tapped the gunner on the shoulder and as he ceased firing he was on his feet and with the two Marines on the far side ran up closer to the killing zone. There was one engagement left. The two Marines on the other side found one gunman with some fight left in him, too terrified or too traumatized to think of surrender, and they took him out. Doughty checked his side and then signalled to the other two and they settled back into cover. He was thinking fast. There was a second group. Would they come running? Or would they think better of it and fuck off? They must have heard his GPMG. They would know it wasn't theirs. Out on the road the wounded were moaning and crying. One was trying to crawl away. Doughty looked out at them. Anyone hit in the initial burst would have multiple wounds. He shook it from his mind. They would have to wait.

He whistled softly and called the two Marines over. 'You two back. Get the civvies past this point right now. Then one of you down to Mr Gordon. There's another enemy force. They may come this way, or they may come down the road parallel to this. I'm going up for a recce. Tell Scott to keep an eye out for me. Goddit? Go.'

As they disappeared into the dark, calling softly to Scott

on the machine gun, Doughty slipped a fresh magazine into his rifle and moved forward.

Back on the main road a Marine dropped down beside Chops. 'Okay. It's clear. Proceed down to the next signal point. Quickly now!' The sailors got the group up and moving. The people had mixed reactions. Some were up and ready to move in a flash, other had to be pulled up from their positions against the wall, some of the children crying. One woman was angry, her fear emerging as aggression and when Chops pulled her to her feet she told him in no uncertain terms that this was all totally unacceptable and she was going to call her Congressman.

'Do you hear there!' Chops snarled. 'Call who you bloody like. They're not here and I am. Now bloody move it!'

The fourth and last group was the largest, 120 people, but also the best defended. It included Alberry and his wife, most of the Embassy staff, the US Marines, now abandoning their post and pulling back, and Buchanan. It was slower, the Marines as a rear guard, one of them a lithe black youngster from North Carolina humping one of *Beaufort*'s GPMGs. It wasn't one of their beloved M60s, but it was a great equalizer.

Doughty had returned to his team. The second group of hostiles he knew were there had disappeared. They were no longer on the road and he wasn't going to start searching gardens on his own, looking for a force of undetermined skills and strength in the dark. He might just find them. Or they might just find him. Heading off into thick cover in darkness on one's own was bollocks, comic book stuff. But they were there somewhere, hopefully confused and scared and settled down somewhere to await daylight. If they moved towards the beach on the road that ran parallel and then crossed over, they would meet Sar' Connors and his section and it would be Good Night Vienna.

He looked back up the road. The last group of civvies

was heading into their control area and he had signalled them towards his intersection. The previous three groups had walked down the other side of the road, but he had been uncomfortable with that. If those fighters were still in the vicinity then he wanted these people down his side, so they could drop down below the low walls on the northern side of the street. There were still wounded men up beyond his position and after this group had passed he would move up, secure the area and see what could be done for them. One of his lads, Scott, was laughing softly. 'What?' he whispered.

The other fellow on the gun, a gifted natural mimic, looked up and impersonating Michael Caine said, 'Don't throw . . . bloody spears . . . at me.'

Corporal Doughty grinned, but mildy rebuked them. 'Eyes front.'

A moment or two later Scott looked up over the gun, peering out into the dark. The other Marine felt the tension and without speaking or questioning Scott he tapped Doughty on the boot again. Doughty lowered himself and looked across at the Marine on the other side of the street. He had seen his corporal move deeper into cover and, using his initiative, stopped any more people moving across.

There was thirty seconds of silence broken only by a cough, but that came from behind them. There were no babies or young children in this group. Doughty and his Marines strained their eyes and ears. They trusted Scotty. If he thought he saw or heard something then they believed him, but it was almost a minute later, when Scott himself was beginning to doubt his eyesight, that something moved in the garden to their left on the other side of the wall.

They're there. They're bloody there in the gardens. How close? Ten metres, twenty?

The foliage was thick, the shadows even in the breaks of moonlight as dark as pitch.

He inched forward and tapped the man lying at his feet on the shoulder and pointed to the wall beside them. The man nodded. Doughty signalled that he was moving off, and skittered like a shadow across the road. The American boys had moved up. He dropped down beside them.

'Listen up,' he said to their sergeant. 'There's a bunch in the gardens here to our right. I want you guys to take that position.' He pointed back to the first RM post. 'Guard the rear. Send them back to me here. Quickly and quietly. Okay?'

The sergeant, to his credit, didn't argue. As Doughty bent over his small tactical radio, the US Marines moved back to their new position and Buchanan and Chops arrived. Buchanan had passed Kreutz, who had looked daggers at him while trying to reassure a small group he was with, but Buchanan ignored him.

'Mike, mike, mike two.'

'Go two.' Gordon's voice.

'Group is stopped around my post. I have hostiles in the gardens to the north. Repeat hostiles in the gardens to my north. Uniform Sierra Mikes now holding the rear and I'm going to do a sweep. Move them out, over.'

'Roger, mike two. Aaaah, stand by. Sunray is on his way.'

Doughty looked at Buchanan. 'Sitrep, sir. They are in the gardens there, behind that wall. We can't leave them there and we can't move. Every minute we are here we risk them being reinforced or having a go. We are going to hit them. Move them back. These people here,' he pointed to the group along the wall, 'they must lie as close to the wall as they can. Cover their ears. Okay?'

Buchanan nodded. 'You're going in there?'

'Yes, sir.'

'Isn't there another way?' Buchanan asked. The thought of climbing over a wall in the dark to look for a group of armed men didn't seem sensible.

'Not really.'

The four men from the rear post arrived at the same

210

time as Lieutenant Gordon from the other direction and he began to brief them.

It was Gordon's call. Doughty, mindful of rules of engagement, had challenged the previous group, let it be known they were escorting US civilians, and been fired on for his trouble. Should they try again and lose whatever surprise element they had? The force could be double their size, maybe more. He couldn't risk a dialogue that would give whoever it was a chance to array themselves better or fire into the civvies, give them a chance to show their intent and then meet their response head on.

Four minutes later the nine men were deployed and got to work. Godshall emptied out his jeep and when they were ready he drove it down the road past the people huddled against the wall, offering what they hoped was a target too attractive to let go. A big Stars and Stripes fluttered from the radio aerial. There was no mistaking the vehicle or its ownership as Godshall, showing what Chops agreed was 'some bottle', gunned it past the wall. Two rifles opened up on it and as it careered round the corner Godshall hit the horn twice. He was okay. Fair enough, Gordon thought. No mistaking your intent.

Three seconds from a command noise they all recognized but no one else would, five stun grenades were lobbed over the wall. The Ulima fighters hiding in the undergrowth were stunned, disoriented, some staggering to their feet. The stun grenades were followed four seconds later by five fragmentation grenades and three white phosphorous grenades, followed immediately by two flares. The frag grenades, spaced down the garden, blew their shrapnel outward and the 'willy peters', the white phos, showered the still hiding men, or those bewildered wounded men, in burning globules of phosphorous. As the flares lit up the scene, four Marines appeared over the top of the wall and poured fire into the Dantean scene as the three others came through the back of the garden. It was all over in thirty seconds, the Royal Marines then sweeping back

211

down through the gardens to make sure they had not missed a threat to the group.

It was brutal. It was efficient. It met the military edict of concentrated force and firepower delivered with maximum surprise.

When they returned they waved the people forward. There was no pretence at silence now. The whole world knew that they were there and it was time to get everyone safely inside the Brit compound. They were there within a few minutes without further incident.

Once in the now crowded grounds, Gordon checked in with the XO.

'So far so good,' he said.

'Didn't sound like it from here,' Wisher replied. The intelligence man was standing next to Kitson, but the XO ignored the remark and introduced the two men.

'I met your counterpart,' Gordon said.

'Ah, yes. Well,' Wisher responded. 'Enough said, eh?'

'We have all met him today,' Kitson said. 'Anyway, well done. That's phase one over. Phase two?'

'Sooner we start the better,' Gordon replied. 'I'm going to get my people deployed in a defensive screen sixty metres or so from the main route. If we have any further problems, then we can hopefully keep it away from the civvies this time.'

'Did you challenge?' Kitson asked softly. 'Sorry. Have to ask.'

Gordon grimaced slightly. Rules of engagement. Always there. 'We did the first time. Not sure they understood, to be honest. It was in English. The second time they fired on us.'

'English is widely spoken here,' Wisher said. 'But there are a couple of Krahn speakers round the place.'

'We'll try them next time. Not sure how much good it will do. Both these engagements were with fairly committed people. In both cases they knew who we were, I'm convinced of that,' Gordon replied. 'But why?'

212

'This is Africa, sport,' Wisher explained. 'What to you and I is logical has no relevance here.'

'Naa.' Gordon shook his head. 'That's a cop-out. There are motives here beyond simply looting and armed robbery. We aren't just caught in the middle, either.'

'You'd better hear about a man called Marriot Bokia.' Wisher began.

Godshall settled down and took the cup of tea offered to him. It was his first drink in what seemed like hours, the first time he had stopped moving. The drive past had been interesting. Two hits on the vehicle, both at the back. His hand was shaking. Not much, just the afterflow of adrenalin. He lit a cigarette and sipped the tea, thinking again about Dave. He had put it from his mind earlier. Dave had been in the MCO. His mate. Lived just three streets apart in Rotherhithe. Bunked alongside each other in 2 Kilo. Pissed together in a dozen ports. Shagged the same women. His mate. Dead. He thought about him with a smile. Gawky, fresh-faced, lived off Big Macs and Cokes and never had a pimple in his life. Bumfluff on his cheeks at the age of twenty-six. A good bloke. Give you the last change in his pocket. Had done more than once. Dave Tomkins and Tommy Godshall. They had written their names on the tart's bum with her own lipstick last time ashore. Brighton. They had gone down to Brighton. The second night it had gone off. They just came at Dave as they were leaving the pub. Picked out the haircut. Thought he was a squaddy, probably. Didn't matter. It was the mob. Army, Navy, didn't matter to these bastards. Dave went down and he turned back and got stuck in. Two of them fucked off, no match for lads off the Beau. But the last had another crack. He had a Stanley knife, swung it at him and then put the boot into Dave, who was still down. When he punched him he went down like a sack of shit. He pulled Dave up and he just turned and let go a boot at the geezer. Like for like. The bloke's head snapped back

213

into the brick wall and he grabbed Dave and they scarpered. Someone was bound to have called the police. Poor old Dave. Never hurt a fly before that. Not even growing up in the East End like he did. Hurt this bastard. It was on the news. He was still unconscious when they sailed on the Monday morning.

He sipped his tea. Cunt had it coming. But Dave didn't. He felt nothing for the people arrayed against them. They had killed his mate. He had taken one down, he was sure of that. Maybe two. Fuck 'em.

The next two aircraft would be overhead within minutes of each other: the Hercules out of Gibraltar with the extra seaboats and their drivers and the Nimrod from Kinloss. Both at about 2200 hours. For now they were limited to two boats and Kitson was talking to his captain on *Beaufort* to begin the transfer. Now that they had abandoned the US compound they had no link with the outside. Until the Nimrod was overhead they were absolutely on their own, but neither Kitson nor Commander Bennett was the least bit phased by that: they had a job to do and, like most people, they liked to be left alone to get on with whatever they had to do. But being out of touch with Northwood wasn't ideal.

The *Beaufort* was at action stations, special duty crewmen closed up, under way at two knots in a figure of eight, in darkness, her riding lights and all exterior deck lighting turned off. Any lighting used would be to seaward wherever possible, until they were expecting seaboats alongside. Bennett was not going to make an easy target of his ship again, not just a mile off the beach as they now were. Lieutenant Morris the navigator, somewhat rested, was back on as officer of the watch and Lieutenant Commander Denny, the Ops Officer and acting XO, roved the ship, the captain's eyes and ears.

It was Denny who had the blinding flash of the obvious. Moving down the length of 2 deck he passed the Wrens' quarters where the children were and they were watching a video. ET, the extra-terrestrial. The endearing little alien who said *phone home* in his little ancient voice. *Phone home*. His kids mimicked it all the time. Prat! I'm a bloody prat!

He took the stairs up to the officers' flat two at a time and ducked his head into the Captain's sec's cabin. There on the little bunkside shelf, its charger running. The sec's mobile. He was always phoning his girlfriend. Northwood. Who's got the bloody phone number at Northwood? The wardroom. The magazines. In one of the RN publications was a number for the fleet public relations guy and he was based at Northwood. He found the number and then went up to the bridge. The phone didn't work, but he knew others on the ship had phones and twenty minutes later he had one borrowed off a PO. The PO bitched to a mate about the cost and the other man said, 'Ah well. You know what they say. Can't take a joke you shouldn't join up.'

'Yeah. But the cost!'

'Pusser will pay. Besides, it's good to talk.'

The operator at Northwood wasn't on the ball that evening. Twice Bennett asked to be put through to Ops and twice she asked him who he wanted to speak to.

'Just put me through, please. It's important.' Bennett was being careful. He didn't know what the technology was, if it was digital or analogue, and he didn't want any eavesdroppers to understand the conversation.

'Who do you want to speak to?'

'The duty officer. Anyone! Jock bloody Slater. Just put me through.' It was the mention of the First Sea Lord's name that cracked it and he was put through to Security where cranks and odd callers were dealt with.

'Who am I speaking to?' he asked.

The Lieutenant gave his name smoothly.

'My name is Nick Bennett. I want to talk to someone senior in Ops, RN preferably.'

'I'm sorry I can't do that. It's after hours and . . .'

'Listen carefully,' Bennett said. 'I'm going to give you a phone number. It's a mobile.' He gave the man the phone number. 'Have the senior naval man in the Ops room phone me back. My name, write this down with the number, is Nick Bennett. Got that?'

'Yes I have, but . . .'

'No buts,' Bennett said. 'You are security? I'm going to give you my pass number. Look it up on your screen, okay?'

There was a pause before the man came back. 'What's your home phone number?'

Bennett told him.

'I know who you are! Are you calling from . . .'

'Yes I am,' Bennett interjected before he could say the word.

'Hold the line sir! Putting you through.'

Bennett heard the next comment clearly. The Lieutenant was having trouble transferring him because he shouted, 'How do I get this call on to 2202? I've got the Captain of the bloody *Beaufort* on the line!'

Listening on the dark bridge of his ship thousands of miles away, Bennett couldn't help a rueful smile.

Ten seconds later he was talking to a three-ringer in Ops, the FOO, Fleet Ops Officer, a man who knew him personally.

'Hello, Nick? James Parsons . . .' The line wasn't great, but Parsons wasn't taking any chances. 'How's Mary and the kids?'

'Wouldn't know,' Bennett laughed. 'Who the hell is Mary? Did you get into that lousy golf club you applied for?'

'Sadly, yes.' Parsons relaxed. 'This is novel. Nice to talk to you. Give me your number before we go on.'

'I'm a bit thick. It should have occurred to me sooner.' Bennett read out the number and by then two other officers at Northwood had come on to conference line extensions. 'Thought you might like to catch up.'

'Love to. Go ahead.'

'Well, everyone's now at our place. The lads from Arbroath helped tremendously there.'

'Ah . . . problems?'

'They kept it contained. No one on our side to worry about. Although they were . . . direct in their treatment of the problem. We are ready to start the next stage.'

'Very good. What's the general situation?'

'Not good. Very confused. The attempts to ruin our evening have been premeditated. There's no doubt we have made the right decision. There certainly would have been tears before bedtime otherwise.'

'Nick, I'm going to give you a direct line number. The same first six digits as the last one you called, then 3702. Got that? Good. Keep in touch.'

The seaboats were fuelled and ready to go, trailing alongside the ship on lines just aft of the cages that were now rigged to the hoists. Boarding ladders ran down to the cages for the coxswains and others of the *Beaufort*'s crew to get down to them and they had practised raising and lowering the cages, the buffer and Lieutenant Commander Denny running the drills so that everyone knew what to do even in the dark.

In the hangar area Kate Wallace and Chops(S), the hefty Chief Petty Officer (Sonar), were building bombs. They had emptied out practice depth charges, two weapons artificers helping them, and cut the drum-shaped containers down. A third person was working with them. The 'Chippy', the Chief Marine Engineering Artificer, a scruffy forty-a-day smoker, at home with his lathes and workshop machinery, was whistling while he worked. He was good. Very good. Could make anything. A central core of Torpex, the high explosive used in real depth charges, had been lowered in the drum and then packed with nuts and bolts, steel filings, and hunks of metal from the engineering workshops. The top half of the drum, cut down vertically four ways, was

217

folded over to hold the charge and shrapnel in place. The detonators and timers could then be inserted through a hole in the top at the last minute. They had converted two of the timers and detonators and tested them over the side. Both had gone the required ten seconds before the nasty flat crack of the initiator told them they had it working.

Gordon's expanded force was deployed. He had positioned teams at either end of the block that the gates opened on to, and further teams down each side road. With a detail of ratings holding the embassy and the beach-front villa, he could position his last two teams on the beach itself and still have a small reaction force that could quickly support any team that needed it.

His last job was to sweep through the gardens inside his extended perimeter and just make sure that no hostiles had got through that far. The southern flank was held by the US Marines where they could operate as a unit, both teams within sight of their sergeant. At the northern flank and at the beach itself, where he was expecting trouble, he placed his own men, who could be supported if it came to it with two rifles from the villa and two from the Embassy. He had chosen them already. They were sailors, but they were ballsy enough. Baker, White, Godshall and their hard Chief, Wilks. Kitson had put his officers out, too. Montagu, the young Looey that had met them when they came ashore, was already down at the villa with ten ratings. Buchanan would run the transfers with ten and Conway, the Wren, would remain at the Embassy, the last to withdraw, with the last ten ratings. Kitson would rove between them as was his wont. He was the boss.

The young Royal Marines officer was ready. The first group was at the gates. It was all women and children; one little boy, an American child that Gordon had first seen at the US compound, was lugging a drum. One of his Marines, a chap all of nineteen who had once thought about the regimental band, had rigged the drum to the boy's belt and was showing him how to hold the sticks. There was room for a hundred in the villa, two hundred if they were crammed inside the building. The tide was out and about to turn.

Time to go. He looked at Kitson. 'I'm ready, sir. If you want to get the boats under way I'll move down with this group.'

The second group of one hundred were just coming in through the back garden when the first boat in stooged in to a stop. A man piled out. It wasn't *Beaufort*'s LMA but one of the two US Marine medical corps men who had flown out to the ship. This had been the surgeon's decision. He needed the Leading Medical Assistant where he was, where he knew his way round the ship's sick bay and the supplies he kept, and conversely the Marine medics were trained to do their jobs in the field. He waded ashore humping a bag of equipment while the first of the many hundreds of people were bundled without ceremony into the inflatable. The second boat edged in behind the first. With the tide out there was a fifty-yard walk down the sand, and when the moonlight broke through one could see down the beach both ways. Everyone knew that there were Marine teams covering the beach, but they were so concealed that no one could pinpoint their position; that wasn't what attracted the yeoman's attention. Up the beach to the north, maybe a hundred yards from the villa, a boat was pulled up on the sand.

'Sir,' he said to Montagu. 'Mind if I nip up there and see if that boat's a goer? We could use it.'

Montagu looked up the beach. He could just make out the boat, but somewhere up there was the Marines post. A bloody good way to get shot was to go up there unannounced.

'Yeah. Make sure the soldiers know you are coming. Take someone with you.'

A few minutes later they were there and the yeoman

jumped into the boat while Jones, the other rating, kept a nervous watch up the beach. The boat was bigger than it looked. Old and of clinker built construction it was probably, he thought, twenty-two or twenty-three feet long. Inside it was almost bare. It smelt of fish, but whatever equipment, nets, oars it needed were gone. It was an old lighter of some type, with solid thwarts and thick hardwood gunwales that were scarred by years of work. Probably pensioned off, it was now, by the smell, still someone's livelihood.

Jones, keeping watch, told him to hurry up. The Marines position was in the trees to their right slightly behind them. Brought up on his grandfather's stories of the Mau Mau and his senses battered by media images of Rwanda and Burundi, to him every black African male adult was a machete-wielding homicidal maniac. He wasn't keen on this at all.

'Oi, Jonesy,' the yeoman whispered. 'Hull seems all right. It's got an engine. Get in here and see if it works.'

'Fuck that,' Jones replied, 'Let's get back.'

'Come on. You're the bloody mechanic. Get your arse in here,' the yeoman whispered encouragingly. 'I'll keep an eye out. Don't worry.'

'Bastard.' Jones came over the side muttering, 'I knew it. I fucking knew it. Never fucking volunteer, right! So what does fucking muggins do? I fucking hate this shit.'

'Shaddup,' the yeoman whispered, grinning as Jones bent over the hole in the floor.

'Well?'

'Wadya mean, well? Ten fuckin' seconds and 'e says well? Just let me get on with it. Right? Gis the bloody torch, then.'

The yeoman smiled. Jonesy was solid as a rock, but easy to wind up and always entertaining. A minute or so later later he popped his head up. 'It's an old Perkins engine. Battery looks all right. I've reconnected the fuel line, but it's only finger tight. There's bugger all fuel and it could use some oil. Shaft's a bit bent by the look of it.'

'I don't want to bloody buy it,' the yeoman whispered. 'Will it start?'

'Dunno,' Jonesy hissed. 'Silencer's probably full of holes, so it'll be noisy as buggery. Let's just fire it over and wait for every jungle bunny in two miles to come and hack us to pieces.' He faded miserably before continuing. 'I think it probably will. But let's wait for the tide to lift her. Then if it does we can piss off in it.'

The seaboats were taking eight at a time and as they ran in towards *Beaufort*'s high grey bulk they throttled back and edged in to the cage suspended just above water level. A rating there passed them a line to run through an eye forward, they were pulled up alongside the cage and people were bundled across, throwing their life-jackets back into the inflatable as they did so. As the boat slipped the line and turned back for the beach the cage was hoisted up to weather deck level and four sailors helped people over the rail. Bennett watched from the bridge wing. It was taking twenty minutes to do a round trip. That was forty-eight people an hour. Too slow. At this rate it would take fourteen hours just to lift the civvies off. They wouldn't have the extra boats till 2200 hours. After that they could step it up to maybe 120 an hour and that was providing there were no cock-ups or delays. Allow for some. It would be dawn before they were through – if they were lucky.

The Marines at the north-eastern edge of their perimeter had been fired on. The four-man team set up behind a wall on the intersection had challenged, the words barely out of their mouths when the approaching group opened fire. This time it was better orchestrated, the fire coming from two points where some of the fighters had obviously advanced under cover and got settled in diagonally across the street.

At present there was no threat to the next group that would be leaving the Embassy, but if the fighters were able to move any further forward their field of vision would take in the crossing point and that would be highly dangerous.

Doughty scuttled back a few feet to where he could see the Embassy walls. If they cross further up, he was thinking, then they can move through the gardens at the back, right up to the wall. He got on the radio and Lieutenant Gordon was with them three minutes later. They had come 'tooled up' and his officer agreed: time to use some of the kit they had brought. With the Lieutenant at his post, Corporal Doughty and another man darted back to the compound, took two heavy plastic cases from the bags they had brought ashore and moved back down the garden to the wall where Jonnie Johnson still sat, rifle at the ready. Another rating was there and Doughty climbed up and looked over the wall into the garden of the next house.

'Got something for that?' Johnson asked him. 'We can't see a damned thing that way.'

'Yeah,' the Marine replied. 'No problem.'

There was no clear field of fire. Shrubs and trees made visibility bad. They could come up this way and, if they were quiet enough, get right up to the foot of the wall.

Two minutes later after talking to Lieutenant Conway – the XO had gone down to the beach – he found a ladder and slipped over the wall with the other Marine. Each of them carried one of the heavy green cases.

They made sure they were alone in the garden and then, with the Marine watching, Doughty bent down and opened one of the cases and removed the outer cover. What was left was a heavy concave item the size of a round bread-board some three inches thick with two legs underneath. Knowing the ground was very soft, he placed one at the base of a tree, its back to the trunk, pushing the two little legs into the soft earth to keep it upright. The second he placed twenty yards away and slightly behind, facing back the same way. Each had a thin wire that he ran back and threw over the wall, the wire unravelling to a command 'clicker' switch on the end. He tied a loose knot in the cable from the first so they would know which switch worked which device, then they moved back and climbed over the wall.

These devices were claymore mines: little more than a charge of high explosive on a backplate. The explosive was packed with hundreds of ball bearings and when the charge was detonated the bearings blew out in an arc, a wall of shrapnel that could cut a swathe through an attacking force. Doughty left the Marine sitting atop the wall with Johnson, the two 'clickers' at his fingertips. The back covered, he took the rating down off the wall for the Wren officer to redeploy and went back to his team where they were exchanging sporadic shots with Ulima fighters.

'Happy?' Lieutenant Gordon asked.

'It's covered, sir,' Doughty responded. As the Lieutenant and his radio operator slithered away he looked out at the intersection. Two bodies lay in the road, slotted by his boys. Fighters brave enough or stupid enough to think they could get past this post. Jesus, he was thinking. They know we are pros. They must do. Why? The line of least resistance is just to let us go. There is something they want, he thought, and it's not women or booty. No one, not even one of these bastards, is willing to die for a shag.

The old motor was roaring away, its throttle a very lowtech string with a loop that the owner probably slipped his big toe through and pulled upward. The tiller handle was long but low, just inches off the deck, and to steer and see over the high prow the driver had to stand in the stern and push the tiller with his foot. To slow the boat he let go the string and a spring reduced the power, but if you wanted to take it out of gear, Jones discovered, you had to bend down and hit the stump of the gearshift lever with a wooden block. Any clutch had long since gone.

The tide had come in and with enough water to float and run through the cooling intake they had pulled the bows round. The yeoman holding her bows into the little waves, Jones had a go. The engine turned twice, coughed, backfired and died. He had another go and then a third and it began to run, surprisingly sweetly considering its ancient vintage and lack of maintenance.

He thumped it into gear and as the yeoman pulled himself over the bow they put out for deeper water and then turned and ran down the beach. Jones was feeling much better: not only was he back on the water, his natural environment, but closer to their comrades. People watched in awe as he conned the old lighter, with both feet and occasionally bending down, swearing and thumping something with a block of wood. He had extended the throttle line with his belt, but it was still gymnastics steering, working the throttle and getting the engine back into gear every time it jumped out. Montagu, delighted with their work, piled eighteen people into the old hull and they set out for the *Beaufort*. Women and youngsters, not small children though, were piled everywhere, and as Jones steered the boat, the yeoman moved among them, shifting them round to get the trim right. A woman that he had seen only two hours before delicately fanning herself and spraying perfume from an atomizer was down with the fish scales and the smell, and what's more pleased to be there. Anything to get away from the flames and the smoke and the fighting that was receding behind them.

'I 'ope someone told 'em we're coming, Yeo,' Jones muttered. 'Or we're likely to get a hot reception.'

'Where's the torch?' the yeoman asked, feeling round at their feet.

'Dahn there somewhere.'

A light began to flash at them, a fast challenge, a warning not to approach. On the Beau someone had seen them and down in the Ops room they appeared as a big blob on the radar screens.

'Who the hell is this? Signal them to stand off and identify,' Bennett said.

'Could be locals, sir, trying to escape the fighting,' Morris offered.

'Could be anything,' Bennett responded. All of his SA80s were ashore and the crew down at water level only had side-arms and one GPMG. 'Prepare the port thirty mill.'

Out on the bridge wing a rating was working the lamp, signalling the approaching boat.

'Reply, sir,' he called, sounding surprised. A torch was flashing back at them. He hadn't expected locals to know Morse. 'Reply is "Got civvies", sir.'

'Challenge again! Who is it?'

The torch light flashed back. It was fast.

'Replying, sir.' Bennett was reading the signal with him and when the rating said, 'It's the yeoman,' he smiled. The message, only three words long had Chops(M)'s favourite four-letter word in it.

Jones brought the boat in very gently. Unlike the inflatables it was big and heavy enough to damage the cage. As the first of the people transferred he was calling out a list of things he wanted, and when the cage was full he pushed off as they hoisted it away. A minute later it was back and the second group passed over the old boat, but they waited then for ten minutes as things were transferred from the cage. Fuel was passed over, engine oil, grease, Jones's own tool kit, a socket set, a bag containing half-inch steel piping in various lengths and other odds and sods, life-jackets and flares. As they slipped their line, Jones looked up and saw Commander Bennett above, watching them. When he raised a thumb at them, Jones's face split into a big grin. They headed back into the beach, the yeoman steering with Jones lying on the wooden deck, reaching down, doing things in the engine compartment. Bennett watched them leave with a feeling of immense pride in his crew.

'The lads,' he said fondly to himself.

He turned to the navigator. 'Those two. Entry in the log please, Mr Morris. Exceptional initiative.'

8

Kitson moved among the people huddled in the villa. It was absolutely dark down here, no lanterns, no lamps, no candles with one exception. As he had decided with Lieutenant Gordon, a single kerosene lamp burned in a broom cupboard where no light could escape: when necessary the door was opened momentarily. People now huddled miserably together, listening to the fighting up the street. They didn't know if it was their boys, as they now thought of them, or another Ulima and NPFL clash, but it was close, very close and they were unsettled by it.

The logistics had settled into a rhythm that everyone understood. The next group to be transferred to the *Beaufort* were crouching against the low wall at the beach end, wearing life-jackets and ready to make the dash to the waterline.

Dave Culverhouse, the young Zimbabwean aid worker, with his shotgun over his shoulder, had taken over the job of managing the people within the villa to free up the forces people. An American woman, the one who had bustled about with her clipboard at the US compound, was helping him. With ruthless efficiency she had identified the groups and the order in which they were to move to the door overlooking the path to the beach. Culverhouse, with undiminished good humour most of the time, kept the peace, gently enforced her edicts and urged the process along. There were exceptions. At one point a British man, an instructor welder from ConLib, was insisting that he be allowed to take a large, heavy tote bag with him.

The woman was patiently explaining that he couldn't,

there was no room in the boat for luggage, but he was bullying her.

Culverhouse stepped round her. 'Where's your passport? Get it out. Any money? Wallet? That sort of thing. Anything else you can get in your pockets, take now.'

'Why?' the man asked.

'Got em?'

'Yeah, but . . .'

'Overnight bag size only. That one stays here.'

The man looked at him, but young David, six feet three in his bare feet and sixteen stone, had obviously made his point.

'I'm going to complain when we get back.'

'Who gives a fuck?' Culverhouse muttered tiredly, walking away with the bag. Kitson, who had watched the exchange from the doorway, smiled to himself and moved out into the dark. Montagu had everything in hand. He wanted to find Lieutenant Gordon and knew where he would be, back up on the corner by the Embassy where the two sides were still exchanging fire.

Even though two hundred people had gone down to the beach, the Embassy compound was still crowded. Bill Black, in his office burning papers in a rubbish bin, looked at his wife ruefully. 'Well, not the most salubrious end to a posting is it?'

'We'll be back,' she said.

'Yes.' He smiled. 'I want you away. You and Poppy. I'll have to stay, of course, till the end, but I'd like you and Poppy away with the other women.'

The sound of gunfire from the corner was constant now. The Wren officer had briefed him. The Marines and *Beaufort*'s bluejackets would hold them, but it wouldn't be long before they came at the Embassy through the back way. Most of the women had gone now, down to the beach villa or actually out to the ship. The last few were in the next group waiting by the gates.

'I'd rather go with you,' Maggie replied simply.

'No,' he insisted. 'Then Poppy will want to stay. Go on. Give me less to worry about. Trudy Alberry is going.'

'She's not. She's saying to Ed what I am saying to you.'

He shook his head. He didn't have to remind her, really. The pact they had made after the Cessna had force-landed in Kenya: never to travel on the same aircraft if possible. They avoided putting themselves in equal risk, so that if the worst happened the children would have someone left.

There was a knock at the door. It was Lieutenant Conway. She had a smudge down her cheek and underneath her camouflage smock her rig was grubby. She looked tired.

'Group's about to leave, Mrs Black.'

'Thank you. You're staying?'

'Believe me, ma'am,' Sarah answered, picking up the tone of the conversation she had interrupted with a smile. 'The moment I get orders I am out of here.'

'But for now you stay?'

'I do.'

'Why?'

'I took the King's shilling,' she said lightly.

'Not every day you get a thumbs-up from the old man, eh?' Jones said, chuckling. The boat was shouldering her way through the water back towards the beach. They had shut the engine down and Jones had done his thing. He had poured in two quarts of oil, greased the prop shaft as far the gland and, using bits from his tool kit, fashioned a handle for the gear shift. He had also deep sixed the string arrangement on the throttle and replaced it with a bit of knotted wire cable that could be eased through the mouth of a pair of pliers he had stapled to the deck and locked off in that position. Now whoever was steering the boat could easily operate the throttle and reach the gear shift.

The beach was just ahead and, aiming to come in alongside one of the inflatables that was almost ready to leave, he turned the big boat and threw it into neutral as her bows came round to point to seaward. Ratings were there to hold them in place and others were bringing the next group down to the water.

'How many, Jonesy?' one of the lads hissed.

'Gis us twenty,' he replied, pulling one woman over the gunwales without ceremony. 'Come on, darlin'. In ya come.'

Another much larger woman was looking at the high sides of the boat and saying she couldn't get up there, she simply couldn't. Small waves were coming in now, lifting the bows.

'I'm too heavy to lift. Can't I wait for the little rubber one?' she said loudly, peering up at Jones.

The yeoman dropped over the side into the water. 'Shssss. We'll get you in,' he responded. He put a shoulder under her vast buttocks and with another rate, timed with the boat's drop, heaved her bodily up and over into the boat, leaving nice big wet handprints on her Laura Ashley bottom.

'You've got a real way with the ladies, Yeo,' Jones whispered. More were coming in now, two or three down the port side, and finally, the boat full and wallowing, Jones pushed the gear shift forward and eased them out into the darkness.

Kitson found Lieutenant Gordon where he thought he would be and the Marine signalled him back, moving towards him. He must have left his radio operator somewhere, Kitson thought: he was carrying a smaller tactical radio like a huge walkie-talkie round his neck, its stubby aerial sticking up past his shoulder.

'Let's head back to the Embassy. I have a man there I want to check on.'

A few minutes later they crossed the road and ran through the gates. Back in Black's office the Marine pulled off his beret and ran his hand through his hair before

229

taking one of the cigarettes Kitson offered him. 'Don't normally, but what the hell,' he said with a grin. The cigarette in the corner of his mouth, smoke curling from the end, he spread out one of the aerial photos on the desk top and smoothed it out.

'Right. Embassy. Villa.' He pointed them out, letting Kitson get his bearings on the photograph. 'I have teams, as you know, here, here and here.' He outlined an oblong box. 'Same on the opposite side. At the moment the disposition against us is concentrated in this top corner. I think they probably have something over two platoons, eighty or so scattered through this area. Thank Christ they're not soldiers or we would have had to support that position an hour ago.' He paused and took a deep drag on the cigarette, then rubbed his eyes tiredly. 'We have to assume that more are arriving all the time.'

'Can we hold?' Kitson asked. 'There must be a point when . . .' he tailed off.

'We draw the perimeter in,' Gordon replied. 'We can hold any point where we can put concentration of force. Covering fields of fire. As it stands we are quite widely spread. If we reduce the perimeter, however, we are actually allowing the hostiles to get in closer. If they then manage to break the corridor between here and the beach then . . .' he took another drag on the cigarette '. . . then we have a problem,' he finished, with a little smile at his own understatement.

'What do you want?' Kitson asked.

'I want to step up the move to the beach. Even if we overflow into the house behind the villa, at least we have all our lambs in one place. I can also support any point in the defence much quicker.' He wasn't going to use words like *overrun* or *breach*.

'Fine, let's do it.'

'They're after something, you know that don't you?' Gordon said softly, looking at the glowing tip of his cigarette and then back at the XO. 'These people don't fight

230

pitched engagements like this. It's just not their style, not their way. They fight for money, they fight for food, loot, whatever. They will ambush, probe, hit and run. This? Shifting a sizeable chunk of resources off the main effort and taking on a bunch of foreign noncombatants who clearly just want to leave the war zone in one piece? Doesn't make sense.'

'The int boys reckon that this Bokia is a section eight,' Kitson reminded him.

'Oh goody,' Gordon replied dryly. 'That explains everything.'

Squadron Leader Page looked at his watch. It was now 2100 hours local overhead the *Beaufort* and they were fifty-eight minutes from her. Somewhere out ahead and slightly to the port side was their refuelling tanker. It was the American again, the KC135 that had turned back from Ascension Island. After she had refuelled the first C130 Hercules she had flown to Sierra Leone, filled her huge tanks and lifted off again. She would give them 35,000 pounds of fuel, keeping back 10,000 for the second Hercy bird that would be overhead about the same time. The tanker would then head back to Sierra Leone, fill up again and meet the Nimrod again before the homeward leg, but that was some seven hours away.

After this refuelling he would contact the C130 and agree flight levels and deconflicting flight plans. Even with their sophisticated suites of electronics, pilots liked to be able to see each other and they would both be illuminated like Christmas trees, with anti-collision beacons and night lights on until the Herc was on the final few miles of her drop run. Normally the air ops people on the ship watching their screens would control the space above them, but without decent comms that would be a bit difficult.

Some of the crew had been muttering. He had thought it through and discussed it with Matheson the relief pilot. They were going to follow the Herc in, low level, very low, power right back to just over the stall, and open the rear door long enough to heave the lifejacketed drugs out of the door. The same recovery boat could uplift the drugs and the extra boats and men that would be coming out the back of the Herc.

He could have been pernickety and held off for a while, but every minute one of the ship's two boats was not on the run ashore people were at risk. One of the crew, a sonarman, and one of the ground technicians had been bitching about it until Matheson stepped in. Page had been explaining the procedure clearly, listening to their thoughts, doing all the modern man management bit, but they were still complaining.

'Sir, I have to say that I have never trained on this manoeuvre,' the sonarman said. 'It's not in the manual and there's no OPs.'

'There's a first time for everything,' Page responded evenly. 'Needs must.'

'Open the door in flight?' the ground technician challenged.

'We depressurize slowly, power off, bleed off the airspeed, nice and slow. It won't be a problem.'

'With due respect, that is not something . . .' the man challenged again and then Matheson had intervened.

'Aah, Christ. I've had enough of this shite,' he had said in his thick Glaswegian accent.

They looked at him sullenly.

'Come to attention.' They didn't move fast enough and he snapped the next words out. 'Did you hear me?'

Heels together, shoulders back, they stood facing him.

'You.' Matheson pointed at the ground engineer. 'You look after engines. Now if there was a problem with the engines, you could warrant getting involved. But this is not engines. You got a multi-engine flying licence?'

'No.'

'No. You don't. This is flying, about which you know jack-shit. This is a command decision, by the P1. Right?'

232

He took the other into his view, now addressing them both, loudly enough for others to hear in case they needed the same message, 'You people listen up. Squadron Leader Page is captain and pilot in command. He has made a decision. If he wants to fly this bloody thing upside down and sideways it's his decision and his alone. He consulted me, which he did not have to do, and as it happens I bluidy agree with him. Some poor bastard down there is dying. That package goes out the bluidy door and that's final. Now get back to your stations.'

They moved off and Page watched them go. 'Thanks, Phil.'

'Wankers,' Matheson muttered. 'We changing again at 2300?'

'If you're happy with that.'

'Oh aye. I'll just get some beauty sleep now then.'

Northwood had advised MoD and the FCO that they had been contacted by *Beaufort*. The silence since the last staff had left the US mission in Monrovia had thankfully been brief and the Nimrod would be overhead with secure comms in one hour. The FCO had advised the US Department of State to keep them informed, but no plans had changed. The Colonel in command was in deep discussion with his number two and his G2, his intelligence officer.

'I don't like it,' he said bluntly.

The Force Reconnaissance Marines, some 400 of them out of the Second Marine Division, were uplifted by the Military Airlift Command, the heavies flying with their equipment out of Scott Air Force base in Illinois. The three-hour window had been met by the Marines, and they were airborne after some delays at the Air Force end of things, a chartered 747 filling the breach. But the planners were still working, both his Force Recon team and at HQ level. The problem was timing and egress. The recon Marines were parachute trained. Getting in was no problem. But by the time they arrived it would be 0700 hours local. If the rescue by the Brits went to plan then almost everyone could be off by then. They would have 400 men sitting in the middle of someone else's fight awaiting someone to get them off again.

The USS *John F. Kennedy* and her group were under way, but still two and a half days away. The chances were that the recon Marines would arrive in time to see the last of the friendly nationals whisked to safety and would be, as one man at State put it, 'rather late for the ball'. On the other hand, if anything went wrong and they weren't there to assist then heads would roll. This was a contingency operation. Like the old saying, someone remarked: the Corps is like a gun. You very rarely need 'em but when you do there's nothing quite like 'em.

The planning had been frenetic, but the entire operation was under way. Nine long-range C130s were loaded with the 'heavy' equipment required by what was an essentially light force and airborne. Without mid-air refuelling they would get to British-administered Ascension Island. If there were technical problems they could leave any sick aircraft to divert and still have space to reload or the redundant capacity to move ahead even if thirty per cent of the uplift capability was unavailable. From there on to Sierra Leone to meet the Marines who were crammed into the chartered 747. They would load into the C130s for the last short tactical stage into Liberian airspace. The force was broken into three rifle companies and a small support and headquarters company. Officer commanding was a full Colonel and he was concerned. This was shaping into what the men of the Corps euphemistically called 'a cluster fuck'.

Intelligence was poor. As a captain he had been as embarrassed as any in the US military at the failure of their attempt to rescue hostages in Iran. Later, as a major, he had been involved in the débâcle of Somalia, where they had been thrown into a no-win situation against local warlords. It was a depressingly familiar scenario, except for one thing: this was in and out. No holding, no peacekeeping, no bullshit.

As the 747 lifted off the planners were still at it. The Brit Marines had jumped to the ship. That was feasible with a handful of men, but not with four hundred. If they had a secure drop zone they could go in, but where in Monrovia was secure? The fighting was so fluid and their intelligence so thin that it was impossible to say where they could be dropped in without attracting ground fire and inevitable casualties. The other option was to go straight in to the airport and land the aircraft on the runways, secure the location and move on to the Embassy by whatever means were possible. But the airport was many miles from Monrovia itself and the diplomatic enclave, there was no intelligence on what vehicles might be in a fit state to commandeer, and they would certainly run the risk of either ambush or sustained fighting en route to the enclave.

The other option was to be dropped direct on to the target. They all knew that because of wind drift they could expect upwards of thirty per cent of their force to be scattered around the DZ, into what they knew was very hostile territory. As good as these Marines were, he knew that any people dropped into the middle of thousands of hostile fighters wouldn't stand a chance and would be killed or captured. The Colonel looked at his watch, then back at his small team gathered in the 747's upper deck. The bar closed for this flight, the cabin crew banished, there were maps spread on the surfaces, clear acetate overlays and coloured markers. Aerial photographs of the enclave were scattered about with various company and platoon level commanders looking at them, familiarizing themselves with the layout.

'I want new int on arrival. Then we have three hours till the tactical lift is in to decide the best options.'

'Colonel,' the G2 said, 'there is no best option. Just a least worst.'

*   *   *

Sarah Conway had gathered them by the gates; the last three groups would leave as one and final preparations were in place. Ted Brooks was sending his last report before abandoning his transmitter van and its satellite uplink.

'One of the officers from the *Beaufort* has just asked us to break down our equipment and join the rest of the people for the short but hazardous journey to the beach. We will be escorted by armed sailors, within a perimeter established by the small band of Royal Marines, to the beach to await our turn in the tiny inflatable boats that will take us out to the ship. All round us now you can hear the sound of gunfire, but the closest is coming from over my shoulder,' he turned and pointed for the camera's benefit, 'barely a hundred yards away, where the Royal Marines post is under constant fire from the fighters, whose identity we can't confirm. We suspect they are Ulima-J and we also suspect they are now under the command of Marriot Bokia who, according to talk on the streets, assassinated Johnson, the Ulima-J commander, some days ago now and has taken control and is sweeping his forces into Monrovia. He potentially commands some ten thousand fighters and . . .'

There was a massive blast outside the wall, then a second.

It was the young Royal Marine on the back wall that heard them. Sitting with Jonnie Johnson, he heard something, saw something, he was never sure what, but they were there. He touched the older man and pointed over the wall. He peered over, confident in the darkness that he would not be seen, and caught movement again. Johnson threw with some accuracy a small but heavy seed pod, of which there were plenty on the roof, across the garden and attracted the attention of the two sailors in the far corner. Just seconds later, when the Marine reached for the clickers, they were ready. He detonated the first mine and followed it seconds later with the second, a flash and a blast, thousands of ball bearings blasting out, cutting a swathe through shrubbery and anything else in their path, then he was up firing into what was left. As the two sailors on the opposite rooftop opened up, he threw a flare, Johnson beside him firing his rifle over open sights. The scene of their attackers down, many wounded, anger, rage, shouts and screams in the harsh white light and stark black shadows of the flare, was something the sailors would never forget. The young Marine gave no quarter: selecting his targets from those still up and fighting, he poured fire into them and the two sailors took their lead from him. Below the sailors four or five came from the side, scrabbling up rubbish piled at the base of the wall.

Lieutenant Gordon, Kitson at his heels, raced from the building. Lieutenant Conway was ahead of them and she scrabbled up on to the far roof, her side-arm in her hand, in time to see a head appear behind the two sailors. She screamed a warning, aimed and fired, fired again at another. The desperate scene was lit in millisecond frames by muzzle-flashes and for a second it looked as thought they might be overrun. She fired again and again, turning to face the front. Another fighter appeared behind her and she was turning and lifting her gun when the man's head snapped back. Johnson had seen him and fired from his side of the garden, putting his bullet twenty inches to Sarah Conway's left, exactly where he had aimed. The three of them were crowded into the corner on the tiny roof, trying to cover both angles of the wall. Another burst. Fire arcing over them, rounds slamming into the breeze blocks, the sailors returning the fire. With no more room on the roof, Lieutenant Gordon, cool, a machine, standing at the base of the wall, pulled two grenades from his webbing and, letting the spoons fly clear, lobbed them both expertly over the top.

As suddenly as it had started it was over, just the dying flicker of the flare and the cries of the wounded attackers.

'New mags!' the Marine yelled across. 'Change your

magazines!' He was pumped up, the adrenalin racing through his blood. But on the opposite rooftop they had other concerns. One of the sailors had been hit. A ricocheting bullet had scored a line down the side of his head, separating the skin, and the wound was bleeding profusely. Kitson looked up at the sailor who was tending the wounded man on the rooftop and, as Lieutenant Gordon scrambled up, turned to look for Conway who, in the scrabbling terror and muzzle-flashes, had fallen off the roof. She was still holding her side-arm, but her left hand was up against her chest, dark blood spreading over her camo smock. She was shaking, pumped up. They all were.

'You hit?'

'I don't think so,' she replied. 'I think I cut it when I fell. Don't know.'

Gordon was talking into his radio and handing the wounded sailor a battle dressing he had taken from his pocket as three more ratings arrived from the gates, Chops(M) in front.

Thirty yards up the compound Brooks, back on his feet, called the camera back to him from where the cameraman was recording the men on the wall. 'There has just been a fierce exchange behind us here – a lone Royal Marine and three sailors, armed bluejackets, fighting off an attack on the Embassy itself. It seems . . . it seems to have gone quiet. Perhaps this attack is over, but one thing seems certain. The people gathered here can expect them back. We are shutting down now, moving with the last of the people from the Embassy down to the evacuation point.'

'How you doin'?' The US Marine medic bent down beside her. It was only four or five minutes since Gordon had picked up his radio and the man had travelled up from the beach-front villa on his own.

'Fine, thanks,' she responded automatically. Then she grinned at the stupidity of her response. 'Well no, I'm not actually. That was silly. I cut myself.'

'Let's have a looky here.' He was a tall, rangy black man with thick-lensed issue spectacles. He peeled the dressing back. 'O-o-okay,' he mumbled, almost to himself, a small maglight torch in his mouth. He turned the hand over and looked at the wound.

'This needs treatment. I'm gonna get you out to the ship.'

'No. It's minor. Just cover it. I'll see someone when we're back.'

He smiled. Frigging heroes. The other sailor had said the same.

'You say you think you cut it?'

'Mmm.'

'I don't think so. This is a gunshot wound.'

She looked at him. 'No. I fell off the roof.'

'You may have done, ma'am, but this injury was done with a bullet. I'm gonna give you analgesia. Clean it and close it. They will redo it on the ship.'

'You're sure?'

'Oh yeah. They'll . . .'

'No. Bullet. You're *sure* I was . . .'

'Yeah.'

She sank back, the realization setting in, the blood draining from her face. 'Oh fuck . . .'

The Marine took her face in his hand. Shock. He didn't want her shocked. 'Hey, look at me. You got it covered. Didn't lose much blood. You said yourself, it's minor. Okay? You'll be fine, ma'am, but I'd rather you went out to the ship.'

'No.' She sat forward, pushing his hand away gently. 'No. I'm not going. I absolutely refuse.'

He smiled. Tough cookie. 'Damn, I love that accent. Let's get you squared away, then.'

'You done this before?' Not: have you treated this sort of thing before? Have you been in a fight? In action. Under fire.

'O-o-oh yeah. I been in the shit. I was in the Gulf.' He

239

grinned, 'So it was mostly Iraqis I was looking after.'

'I shot someone. Two people ... I ... I wasn't me. It was like I wasn't there. It was like watching it from somewhere else. Jesus,' she said softly, almost to herself, the realization sinking in. 'I killed two people. I was so scared.'

'You or them,' the medic said. 'That's the way it is – and believe me, scared is good. Anyone who ain't scared is a danger to their comrades.'

'I never thought ... I mean it was always possible that I would see action, but not ...'

'Not up close?'

She nodded.

'I'm from Alabama. We have a saying. You gotta do what you gotta do.'

He finished in silence and as he stood up, his bag over his shoulder, he helped her to her feet and gave her some painkillers to take. 'Two every four hours. Now I don' wanna see you again tonight. Y'all hear me?' he said, exaggerating the Deep South accent.

'I hear you,' she smiled. 'Thanks, Alabama.'

They moved out five minutes later, the wounded sailor, his head bound, carried on a makeshift litter. There was no discussion whether he was to go straight out to the ship: although he was now conscious that was a given. Even as he protested his speech and reactions were slurred. The medic wanted him under lights with a surgeon and regularly checked his pupils with a torch. This group was large, 300 people, all men, with the remaining sailors from the compound forming a rearguard.

The Royal Marine melted back into the shadows to rejoin Corporal Doughty and Lieutenant Gordon went the other way to pull back the two teams of US Marines and begin reducing his perimeter to something he could support, a rectangular box one hundred yards deep and sixty wide, with the beach as the western edge.

It was 2140 local.

*   *   *

240

The Hercules had powered back and begun its descent twenty minutes earlier, a long, gentle slide dropping 500 feet per minute to bring them over the ship at 1000 feet of altitude for the drop run. The boats would go first. The engines, packed in inflated surrounds, were strapped into the middle of the rigid hulls to keep the centre of gravity correct, and the twin fuel tanks were almost empty, one tank holding enough to get them to the ship. The men would follow, jump on the next run, swim to their boats, mount the engines on the transom and come alongside the *Beaufort* to fill up and get organized and briefed before they started work. The eight men that would crew the boats had brought their personal weapons. They were Royal Marines, but of the Special Boat Service, where specialization and the consequent idiosyncrasies were encouraged. Trained for coastal operations, they were absolutely at home in water, whether on it, in it or under it.

The pilot had made contact with the Nimrod and they had agreed deconflicting flight plans. The C130 would come in first, the Nimrod five minutes behind, in theory giving the SBS men time to get their boats running before the shipment of drugs was dropped. The ship's Lynx, which would be airborne with a diver for the arrival of the men, could recover the package at the same time.

The men were down the back, checking their kit over and over again, laughing and joking as they did so, morale high. When they had left this was to be a doddle, driving their boats between the beach and the ship loaded with civvies. But they had been updated twice by the Nimrod in the last hour. The shit had arrived. Leaving them driving boats wasn't making the best use of their skills. They were SBS, but first and foremost they were Royal Marines, and their lads, recce boys from the fleet standby rifles and Zulu Company of 45 Commando, were taking fire and out-numbered. Three of them were from 45 Commando, and two of them had been recce troop members only two years before. This was personal.

The air loadmaster came back and raised a thumb at them. A few minutes later the rear door lowered and the Hercules powered back on its four engines, flying straight and level at exactly 1000 feet. The red light came on, followed by the green, and the boats were run back on the rollers. As the last boat went out the pilot put the aircraft into a level turn to come round for his second run in half of a figure eight pattern to bisect his original course. There was wind across the landing zone, so he had to drop the men in exactly the same spot to give them any chance to guide their parachutes to bring them down on to the boats. He could see the anti-collision beacon on the Lynx and some dull lights on the seaward side of the *Beaufort* herself. He waited a few seconds, heard the navigator's call and hit the switch for the lights again. Red, green, go.

In the Nimrod, Page was watching the Hercules out of his left-hand window as he ran in on the downwind leg. He wanted to get this finished with and get back up to a height that was fuel efficient for his engines. He was depressurized for low level and ready for his run-in. The moment the Herc began to climb, its job finished, its Captain called him up. Squadron Leader Page let his number two acknowledge and began his turn very low, now dropping through five hundred feet, his engines powered right back, full flaps down, thirty knots over stalling speed. Down the back Matheson was waiting by the door, the drug shipment at his feet. His number two was standing up by the sonar station with a headset plugged into the console. Further up, the tactical navigator watched their position relative to the ship below. She had put her pilot squarely over his run-in with her usual accuracy and the fact that it was clear of cloud at their level mattered not to her. Her eyes were on her screen.

'Stand by,' Page said. 'Open the door.'

Matheson undid the handle and eased the door open inward. Up at the front Page felt a momentary buffeting as the airflow was interrupted along the port side, the roaring noise of the airflow and their engines loud in the cabin. One of the sonarmen was lying on the floor, his foot hooked into a strap, awaiting the command.

'Door open.'

'Stand by . . . three, two, one . . . Okay, let it go!'

Matheson's number two raised a thumb at him. The sonarman pushed the lifejacket out. 'Load gone!' he reported to the flight deck.

'Secure door.'

The package dropped away, spiralling for a moment before the little chute opened. The torch they had turned on and secured in the plastic water bottle spun wildly before settling and below on the ship and from the Lynx they could see it falling. For Mayberry, all things considered, it was fairly accurate, landing some one hundred metres in from the drop zone where the SBS men were in their boats. Two had engines running and one turned and ran in to where the shipment had dropped.

Kitson, watching the second pass from the shore, had an idea. He ran over to where the radio was set up in the hall of the old villa, where Conway and a couple of ratings manned a command post.

'*Beaufort, Beaufort, Beaufort one.*'

'*Go one.*'

'*Beaufort, XO. Captain, please?*'

Bennett came on.

'*Captain, just a thought. Once the other boats start running the landing cage is going to be inadequate. Could we ask the Nimrod to drop us some life rafts? We could moor them alongside as a staging area. That way we can keep the boats running, over.*'

'*Thanks, Beaufort one. Great minds think alike. We had the same idea out here, over.*' He had just finished talking to the Nimrod's captain. Bennett paused. '*Ahh . . . XO . . . heard a rumour out here that EWO is buying beer for your lads later.*'

Kitson grinned and looked over to where Sarah Conway

had suddenly turned round from whatever she was doing. One of the boat drivers had told someone on the deck and it was on the bridge within an hour. No secrets on board a ship.

'Pass a message to her, if you will. They are in the fridge and getting nice and cold. The SO will be pleased to open the mess on Lieutenant Conway's return.'

Kitson smiled. Commander Bennett was a master at morale. His was a happy ship.

'Very pleased to hear it, sir. I shall pass it on. Beaufort one out.'

He didn't need to say anything. Just nodded at the two rates. They would do the rest, gleefully calculating what this round would cost the EWO.

Many people who would not have normally watched a news bulletin switched over to watch the Nine O'Clock News on the BBC. This was the story of the day, the lead story and they had compiled a report using much of the material filed by Ted Brooks for CNN. There was footage of American Marines boarding an aircraft, library footage of the USS *John F. Kennedy*, HMS *Fearless*, and HMS *Beaufort* during her sea trials. The BBC had found a couple of families of crew and filmed them sitting along one sofa, worried expressions, watching satellite television reports. They had a defence analyst on, a retired naval captain, and official statements from both the FCO and the Royal Navy, represented by none other than the First Sea Lord.

Two girls who were watching cared for none of that. They were only interested in the two short pieces of footage early in the report of a naval officer, grimy and sweating, saying something to the camera, the sound of gunfire clear in the distance. There was a second report, filmed a short while before it was said, where they thought they saw him again. Only for the two girls it wasn't just a naval officer. For Lucy and Beth Kitson, it was their dad.

At Commander Bennett's home, his wife had been

taking calls from well-meaning but unwanted callers since mid-afternoon and as she watched the report the phone rang three times. She ignored it.

One woman who hadn't heard anything till she got round to her mother's at eight o'clock watched with real interest. Her Des was a Petty Officer on the *Beaufort*.

'Call 'im,' her mother said.

'No. I can't. 'E'll kill me. Know what it costs? He's supposed to phone me.'

'But you haven't been there 'ave you? 'E may have been calling all day! Go on. Give 'im a ring. Just tell 'im we love 'im and are thinking of 'im. Tha's all,' her mother wheedled.

'Oh all right then. 'Ere where's me book?' She fished around in her handbag, but her mother passed her own, a small, tatty address book, once red with little Valentine hearts entwined on the cover, but now worn and old. 'I'll put the kettle on,' the mother said.

She picked up the phone and dialled the number. It was answered immediately, but not by her Des, and when her mother came back it was all over.

'What happened, love? Din you get through?'

'Na. Well I did, but it wasn't Des. Lent it some bloke who said he was at work. Nick someone.' She was holding the phone, thinking as she spoke. 'He always 'as 'is phone on 'im! Never lends it out.' She paused then and looked her mother in the eye. 'Know what? That was an officer. Spoke beautifully. Posh, you know. Did that . . . naa.'

'What?' her mother asked.

'Naa. Couldn't be.'

'What are you going on about?'

'That news. Said they had lost contact with the ship this afternoon, right? No radio or summin.'

'Yeah?'

'Well, Des is the only bloke on the ship with a phone with a world card, 'e said. I reckon they borrowed 'is phone to call up to home, like.' She giggled. 'I just spoke to 'is

245

bloody Captain. Bloody Nick Bennett.' She burst out laughing. 'Oh 'e's quite dishy, that one. Saw 'im on families' day.'

'Oh. So Des is all right, then?'

'Said 'e was fine. Bloody hell. Imagine that,' she said settling back in the chair looking away dreamily. Her mother was imagining, always up for a chance to make a little extra. She carried two mugs back in, the teabag labels hanging down the side, innocently picked up a copy of that morning's *Sun* newspaper and began looking for something.

On the bridge of the *Beaufort*, Bennett put the mobile phone down near to hand. The Nimrod was overhead so secure comms with Northwood were back on line, but only once she was back at altitude. He lifted his binoculars. She was beginning her run-in to drop the extra rafts.

On the Nimrod they had gone into the well-trained and well-practised routine. Dropping big life-rafts from the aircraft's bomb bays was standard search and rescue stuff. On the racks in the bay there were various S&R load mixes that could be dropped, but the standard deployment was two large rafts and six smaller ones, with rations, food and water. He called up the tactical navigator at her station. From her position she could designate the load to go out of the bay doors and Page told her to select two large rafts only, with standard deployment, and that it would be a pilot drop.

In normal circumstances she would navigate the aircraft using Global Positioning and Inertial Nav systems, bringing the aircraft to do a forward throw, 600 yards off the survivors and 60 degrees off track. She would let go the survival package. First out of the bay would be a container of food and water. Attached to that container was 400 yards of rope which would whip out of the bay pulling two rafts, a short length of rope between them, and another 200 yards of rope before the last container of food and water. In an S&R drop the aircraft would drop the load across the sea upwind of the survivors to drift down on to them. Anyone along that six hundred yards would eventually have at least some rope drifting to them and they could pull themselves along to a raft.

On a clear night like this, with the ship visible, Page had opted for pilot drop. He would run in visually, 200 knots at 300 feet, pickle the switches and let the load go just fifty yards from the ship. The rafts would inflate on hitting the water and drift to her.

'Switches set,' the navigator said. 'You have the drop.'

The building and garden were crowded. On two sides the wall was only waist high, so those outside the house were sitting or lying down and there were people everywhere, but the boats up until a few minutes before had been running like clockwork and Kitson was pleased with progress. A few minutes before he had seen the Hercules come in, just a quick view of an anti-collision beacon through the scattered cloud cover, the aircraft in full view for a few seconds, the dark canopies dropping from the rear. The Nimrod had been a few minutes behind. He knew they would be in soon, the extra boats, and he could step up the evacuation by as much again. He was particularly pleased with LMEA Jones and the yeoman. They were running the old lighter back and forth with solid good humour and professionalism, taking twenty at a time, but even they were holding off for the minute. It had to happen eventually. Some fighters had got themselves a position up the beach from where they could snipe at the boats. No one had been hit yet and the fire wasn't very accurate, but with automatic weapons the chances were they would hit someone eventually and Kitson had suspended operations till he had it sorted.

The two seaboats and the lighter were out there on the water somewhere, invisible in the dark and hopefully out of range.

'Let's have a look then,' Gordon said. He had just returned from the north-east post where their Marines were still under fire. Corporal Doughty's men had withdrawn, leapfrogged back round the other team, who were now the north-east flank, and set up a new position covering the road and the beach front, the villa wall only thirty yards behind them. In front of them was a small two-man post, the men that had watched over the yeoman and Jones as they had stolen their boat, and he knew that Lieutenant Gordon was going to bring them back in. They were exposed, way forward where they could be cut off, and anyway his GPMG in its new position could have a more effective arc of fire.

Gordon arrived at his post with the XO.

'Doughty, you come with me. Quick recce. See if we can see where they are.'

'Bring a LAW, sir?' Doughty asked hopefully. He loved the one-shot anti-tank weapon because it was also a very effective anti-personnel weapon and could clear a position as good as anything.

'Yes,' Gordon answered. This was a job for grenade launchers, but he didn't have any of those. A mortar would be even better. Wishful thinking. He looked at Kitson. 'We'll be as quick as we can. If we aren't back in say two hours, my sergeant will get your people away. Right, Corporal, let's go. We'll pick up the other two as we go past.'

Six of the SBS men had moored their boats and were on the weather deck, helping the rates move a drum of fuel down the deck to the seaward side. The last boat was towing the huge rafts in to the side of the ship, the long lines already passed inboard to be pulled in clear of propellers of both seaboats and ship. The senior man, a sergeant, took the stairs to the bridge two at a time to find the Captain.

Once there he quickly got to the point. 'So, sir, if you have a few lads who can drive boats, we can give 'em five minutes of familiarization on ours and they can run them. I can then take the section ashore and make ourselves . . . useful,' he finished obliquely with a grin. His face was blacked and he was festooned in weaponry and equipment: it looked to Bennett as though they could be very useful indeed. 'Very well,' he replied. He indicated the man on his left. 'This is Ops and acting XO. He'll sort out some coxswains, but how soon we can get you in will be an issue.'

'How so, sir?'

'Boats are coming under fire from further up the beach. Lieutenant Gordon has taken a patrol out to see if he can find 'em.'

'We'll go in anyway, sir.'

Bennett knew they were special forces. They knew their jobs and their limitations. He nodded. 'With your skills, sar'nt, you are the best judge of that, but I am not *ordering* you in till Lieutenant Gordon gives the all clear.'

'My call, sir.'

'Very well.'

The portable phone rang, its electronic beep cutting across the conversation. Bennett answered, spoke for a moment or two and put it down, a curious look on his face. It rang again and this time he was quite curt.

'Excuse me,' he said to the SBS sergeant. He looked across at someone on the dark bridge. 'Have we got comms yet?'

'I should think so, sir,' Denny answered. 'The Nimrod is still climbing back to altitude, but he should have clear HF by now. Helo's back and plugged in.'

'Good. How do you turn this thing off?' Denny showed him. 'Right. Find some people to drive boats. People who have done the course, preferably.'

Lieutenant Gordon inched forward through the dark. Corporal Doughty was to his left and eight feet away, the other two behind them. He stopped to let the corporal move up to him and then pointed into the bush ahead of them. This was, in any soldier's book, meat and drink. Small patrol, in complete darkness, moving forward in complete silence, to try and establish the exact location of a much stronger enemy force. It was also stressful and frightening. They could be on top of fifty or three hundred heavily armed people who had been doing their best to kill them for the last few hours. They had learnt how to do this, covered it in every scenario since basic training. They were good at it. But it was still scary stuff. This wasn't training, with flash bangs and blanks. This wasn't European theatre where you understood your enemy. Where his own discipline required challenges and think through and hopefully some warning of a contact, even if it was only a second or two. This was Africa. Here there was no discipline. Anything could happen. Put your hand on a hiding man's leg in the dark and in a nanosecond it's on. Muzzle-flash and machetes, screaming terror and people dying. They moved forward very carefully indeed. They knew they were better than their enemy, but they wanted to go home in one piece. Gordon was painfully aware that this was a recce patrol, not a fighting patrol. Get the int and slip out again.

He left the two Marines at their egress point, to defend their way out, and he and Doughty moved forward like ghosts, silently, rifle butts up to their shoulders, their feet moving so slowly they were like giant chameleons. In the dark it was sound and movement that gave you away and often the movement was caught in the peripheral vision. Eyes straining, hearing their own hearts beating in their ears, they moved up.

Somewhere in the bush ahead of them was the Ulima position. Men and youths brought up in the bush, who lived in its sounds and smells.

It was fifteen minutes, the longest fifteen minutes of his life, before Doughty settled to one knee, slowly, ever so slowly, and waved Gordon forward. He had smelt something: the smoke of cheap tobacco and something else. He moved forward. There had been no picket that he had seen, no guard protecting this flank, because ahead of them they could hear voices. Several conversations in a language he didn't understand, hushed tones. Gordon leaned across to him. 'Arty.'

Doughty nodded: the silhouetted weapons were unmistakable. He put his lips against Gordon's ear. 'I'll go in behind them. Take a bearing.'

Gordon nodded. He passed him a small black object – a hand-held global positioning instrument. 'Get a fix with this,' he breathed. 'Meet us back at the RV.'

Doughty moved off. There was high ground along to the right. Not much, maybe a hundred feet, but from there he could do the business.

The SBS men cut the motor on their boat three hundred yards from the beach and without the engine noise and phosphorescence from the prop they quietly paddled in. Kitson had been warned to expect them so there was no challenge from his people inside the villa walls, but there was a burst of fire from up the shoreline, sand kicking up further down the beach as bullets hit.

Seven of the special forces men scuttled up the beach and dropped in behind the wall. The last man pushed the boat back out and, starting the engine, he gunned the boat to seaward, getting out into the dark before cutting the power again. This was his judgement call. The boat left in the ankle deep water would have been too juicy a target to ignore and it would have been in tatters within minutes. There was another burst of fire from up the beach, the muzzle-flash clearly visible. Without speaking, two of the men took rifle grenades from their webbing and armed their 203s. They conferred on range, sighted and fired down the beach. Three seconds later the two grenades landed, exactly where the muzzle-flash had come from, each exploding with a nasty flat crack and a flash of white that lit the night. 'That'll have made his eyes water,' one of them muttered.

'Right. Where's your boss?' the sergeant asked a figure in the dark.

'Inside. But the Marines looey is out there, you dickhead. Where you just fired your frigging grenades.'

'I know what I'm doing, sailor,' the sergeant replied testily.

'You better. And it's Chief Petty Officer to you . . . cunt!'

Doughty on his own was quicker and now, knowing what to expect in terms of noise and smells, indications of enemy presence, he was much more confident. He worked his way round through the bush slowly, carefully, checking his compass until he was directly inland of the position. He took a fix on the GPS, pressed the save button, put the LAW down at the base of a stunted little tree and climbed up it and waited, peering into the dark. He looked up. Fucking cloud. Clear, you bastard, clear! She was out there somewhere. It was a minute before the cloud cover scattered and the ship was visible and he quickly took a bearing. Done, he thought. He was coming down from the tree when there was fire from the beach, a burst followed by another. As he hit the ground there were two flat explosions down on the beach. Something was going down.

He was back with the other three twenty minutes later and an hour after they had left they were back at the villa. They came straight into the building, where they could use a torch. In the hall, by the light of the small kerosene lamp glowing out of the cupboard by the radio, Doughty saw the two familiar faces.

'Bloody 'ell! The glory boys are here. What? Your mum let you out, then?'

The two SBS men grinned. 'Fuck you, Mick,' one of them replied. 'Where's your boss?'

Doughty jerked a thumb at the man leaning his rifle against the wall. 'Lieutenant Gordon.'

Gordon turned round and the SBS sergeant introduced himself.

'That you with the grenades?'

'Yes, sir. One of my blokes was under fire.'

'Effective,' Gordon said. 'You took them out. I know because I saw it. I was forty yards away . . .' He trailed off, just his eyes on the SBS sergeant. The special forces man nodded once. He had the message. A few minutes later he was bent over one of the aerial photos with Gordon, Doughty and the Royal Marine who had spent time with 148 Battery on the artillery observers' course. His particular skill was directing NGS, naval gunfire support.

'How many did you say?' the SBS man asked.

'They were scattered in groups . . . Bloody difficult to say,' Doughty replied. 'No less than a hundred, maybe up to double that.'

The Marine specialist had taken the co-ordinates of the GPS and checked them against the compass bearing. The aerial photograph had an automatically produced indicator of magnetic north and he marked out the extent of the fighters' positions from the feel given to him by Lieutenant Gordon and Doughty.

Gordon looked at his watch. It was an hour and a half since they had stopped the boats coming in. 'Corporal Doughty, move your section up to the edge of the wall. Clear field of fire up the beach. If they break on to the beach hit 'em. Let's get it sorted.' He looked at the other Marine. 'It's all yours. Request NGS and call it in.'

A minute later the Marine was ready. He warned the ship, picked up the Clansman, put the straps over his shoulders and moved to the door. He wanted to see it, see it coming in. Two Marines were allocated to escort him, but the SBS sergeant spoke to Lieutenant Gordon and came back. 'We'll go.'

Fifteen minutes later they were in position, well away from the villa and where the observer Marine could see his shot fall clearly.

'*Beaufort Beaufort, Beaufort one.*'

'*One go.*'

'Beaufort, this is one. Requesting November Golf Sierra. Figures seven Hotel Echo. I'll call each. Ready for first co-ordinates, over.'

'Stand by.'

On the *Beaufort*, civilians on the decks had been hurriedly dragged into the citadel or the hangar, the weather deck forward absolutely clear of all personnel, crew or otherwise. Down in the gun-bay the gun captain grinned widely as his orders came through.

'Gunbay, Ops. Load HE! Seven rounds!'

'Yes! Now you get some, you cunts!' he muttered. He watched his lads as they changed the load mix on the automatic feed ring. He grabbed the intercom mike. 'Ops, Gunbay. HE loaded. Gun is ready!'

'Beaufort one. Co-ordinates, please.'

'Beau this is one.' The Marine called the co-ordinates. He wanted the first round in at the northern end and then to walk the fire towards him. 'One round.'

On the deck the massive automated turret had swivelled round to bring the gun to bear. The first co-ordinates had been fed into the targeting computer. This would be the sighting shot, for the artillery observer to see land. From there he could direct fire. In the Ops room there was mounting excitement. Lieutenant Commander Denny was back down in his kingdom, his flash hood and headset in place. They were impotent no more. They were going to fight the ship. Classic stuff. Naval gunfire support.

'Gun, Ops. One round HE. Fire!'

The man sitting in the seat that Chops(M) would normally have occupied pressed the foot trigger. On the deck the four-and-a-half-inch gun fired, the barrel slamming back into the turret, absorbing the massive recoil, and in a split second the casing had been ejected and a new round was travelling up from the feed ring on the hoist. It was collected and slammed home into the breach and the gun was ready to fire again, a second and a half after the first shot.

Ashore the observer-trained Marine was watching where he was expecting the shell to hit. It roared past as the sound of the gunfire reached them and there was a massive blast and a flash of white light in front of them. Direct hit.

'*Fire for effect!*'

The gun slammed again. As the shell hit he was calling in the new position: '*Down twenty. Fire!*'

'*Right fifty. Fire!*'

Back at the villa, just three hundred yards from the incoming shell fire, people instinctively huddled closer to the floor. 'They're ours,' Kitson called. 'It's okay. It's ours.' A woman began to sob, unable to bear the ever-increasing tension. Culverhouse was soon beside her, holding her hand and reassuring her. On the ship people aft in the hangar held their hands over their ears, but up on the superstructure where the crew manned the visual sight and the thirty-mill gun the reaction was different. They were defiant, one punching the air with his fist each time a shell left the *Beaufort*'s gun. Down in the sick bay they could feel the recoil, the ship shuddering each time. A man looked across from his bunk. 'Someone's pissed the Jimmy off.'

There was a burst of laughter.

Up in the wardroom, now a makeshift operating theatre, the American doctor merely glanced up from the head wound he was working on. In the seamen's mess, crowded with people, where the catering staff were hard at work, everyone stopped momentarily. A rating serving hot food to people who hadn't eaten much in the last twenty-four hours, dolloped a ladle of Lancashire hotpot on to a pile of mashed potatoes. He winked as he passed the plate to a child of twelve who was visibly frightened by the muffled sound of the gun and the recoil that she could feel through the deck plates. 'Get that down ya, darling. Don't worry about the noise. It's boys' stuff,' he said dismissively. 'Bang bangs. Treacle tart and custard for pud. You like treacle tart?' She nodded and smiled at him. 'I'll save you a big bit.'

The child moved away to find somewhere to sit and her mother was next in line. 'Thanks for that,' she said.

'No problem. RN cruise where others refuse.'

Another rating beside him joined in. 'The latest in adventure holidays. You couldn't buy this experience. Roll up! Roll up! Lancashire hotpot served with all the drama you could want!'

There was laughter in the queue.

'*Up twenty. Fire!*'
'*Right fifty. Fire!*'
'*Down twenty. Fire!*'

He kept calling the rounds in till he had blasted an area a hundred yards long and fifty yards deep. The SBS sergeant watched the young Marine, cool, professional, his eyes taking in the barrage, marking the shot fall on the aerial photo on his knee with a felt-tip pen, the telephone-like handset of the Clansman to his face. In there, after seven rounds of high explosive there would be no one fit to attack them again.

He was impressed. NGS from a 4.5-inch gun, an area weapon, was usually spread over a much larger 'beaten area'. This fire had been incredibly accurate.

'*Cease fire! I say again, cease fire. Thank you, Beaufort.*'
'*One, Beaufort. We have ceased fire.*'

Bennett, watching with binoculars from the bridge, felt a moment's pity for whoever was under his fire, but shook it off.

Jones, who had been holding his hands over his ears each time the gun fired, finally looked up. The shells had been passing over the old lighter with a loud roar like a train passing. 'Fuckin' 'ell. Wouldn't like to be on the receiving end of that lot.'

'Fuck 'em,' the yeoman replied. 'They started it.' He stood up, looking towards the shore where a light flashed at them. 'We're on again, Jonesy.'

'Know what?' Jones dropped down and started firing up the engine.

'What?'

'I could murder a cuppa tea,' the mechanic replied, turning the old boat's bows towards the shore. The yeoman smiled.

Sarah Conway was sitting with the radio, manning the command post, when a Marine ducked his head round the door.

'Lieutenant Gordon's suggestion, ma'am. You and the others without longs. You might want one.'

'A what?' she asked.

'A long, ma'am. One of these.' He held up an AK47, its bayonet in place and a grubby, frayed set of chest webbing with magazines. 'We snaffled a few earlier.'

The two SA80s left by the two wounded sailors had already been grabbed by Buchanan and Montagu, but if Gordon was arming everyone then things weren't looking good for them. She put out her hand.

'The bayonet won't come off, it's been welded on, but the gat is clean. Magazine release is that,' he pointed, 'that is safety and this is select. First select position is full automatic. I wouldn't use that too much. Overheats. Keep it down on single shot if you can. One of them's got a warped barrel where some bright spark overcooked it . . . Happy?' he asked, his ten-second familiarization over with.

She nodded. 'Yes. I think so. Thank you.'

As he walked away she put the weapon down. Someone had decorated the end of the stock with beadwork and the bayonet blade was filthy with congealed matter of some sort. She shuddered.

9

The pressure on the defensive perimeter was now consistent. Where before it was the north-east corner that was taking the brunt of the attack, on the opposite side the US Marines in their two-gun positions were now under constant fire and had already fought off three running charges, shadowy drug-crazed figures in the dark, muzzle-flash and explosions lighting the scene. Only the two south-westernmost positions, those defending the beach itself, were sporadically silent and those only since the *Beaufort*'s NGS had eliminated the position up the beach. Kitson had recruited civilian men from the villa to help load boats to free up *Beaufort*'s armed bluejackets and they were now deployed in the line alongside the Marines.

The boats running again, the pace was frenetic. They were now two hours behind, they thought, and even with the extra seaboats they would be hard pushed to clear the beach by first light. Chops(M) was down in the water, knee deep, with a powerful torch, signalling boats in either side of him. They had already had one engine failure and the rating coxswain had lost twenty minutes, until Jones, the lighter hove to alongside, crossed over to the inflatable and cleared muck out of the water intakes.

Poppy, Maggie Black and Trudy Alberry, the US Ambassador's wife, were in the last boatload of women to go out to the ship. As fate would have it, it was the old lighter they were ushered towards, the yeoman and Jones pulling people in over the side, men in the water manhandling them up the high sides.

Kitson had been down at the wall and as Poppy had

come past with her sister she paused briefly beside him.

'Will I see you . . .' she trailed off.

'For breakfast, with a bit of luck. I'll come down with you.' He moved down to the water with them, a fast running doubled-over posture, and helped the men there to assist the women over the high gunwales. As he lifted Poppy over the side he could feel her warm skin beneath the thin material of her dress, but there was more. A closeness. He looked up at the yeoman.

'Yeo. Pass a message. The ambassador's wife and sister-in-law to my cabin. Mrs Alberry to Lieutenant Conway's.'

'Aye, sir.'

He looked up at her. 'At least you will have some privacy.' She smiled at him and touched his hand fleetingly.

'On your way, Jonesy!' he said and as the boat chugged out she watched him slosh his way back towards the man with the torch till he was enveloped by the darkness.

'How's it going, Chops?'

'Gettin there, sir,' he growled back. 'We are back to seven boats.'

'Good. That's the last of the women away.'

'Then I can stop being Mr Nice Guy.'

'Anyone here you can hand over to?'

'Got one of the lads. A PO. Rest are civvies, sir.'

'Hand over, then. We can use you up there.'

Lieutenant Gordon sat huddled over a makeshift map in the light spilling from the hall cupboard. The map had been hand-drawn, but showed the villa and every wall, road and feature in their immediate area. He had drawn his defensive array on the map. Eight of the armed ratings had withdrawn into the villa and he had deployed the SBS teams out with his own Marines. The eight ratings were there to reinforce the line at any point that came under a major attack, something he felt was imminent. Montagu was out in the line already, so half the formation he had earmarked for Lieutenant Buchanan. He looked across at

259

the Wren officer. She had a rifle now, but with the bandaged hand he wasn't sure how much use she would be. He also knew that he didn't have much choice.

Buchanan came in and squatted down, lifting a water bottle to his lips. He was sweating, the breeze off the sea doing little to cool the humid night. 'You were after me?'

'Yeah.' Gordon looked at Conway. 'It's Sarah, isn't it?'

'Yes.'

'How's the hand?'

'Throbs,' she replied. 'But it's not debilitating.'

'Feel up to some work?'

'Sure.'

'Good. I've put the SBS lads out and pulled eight of your lads back in from the line. They are a reaction force. I want them split into two groups ready to reinforce my people at any point where things are going pear-shaped. I want each of you to lead one group. If you are happy with that . . . ?'

They both nodded.

'It could get hairy,' Gordon said honestly.

Sarah remembered Tex's words when Buchanan was leaving the ship – God, was it only eighteen hours ago?

'Hah,' she said, flicking the invisible scarf back over her shoulder. 'We laugh in the face of danger!'

Lieutenant Gordon grinned and Buchanan chuckled softly, but it didn't have the same ring it did that morning. There were casualties and it wasn't over yet, not by a long way.

'Fair enough. Any preferences?'

'Chops Wilks. Baker,' she said without hesitation. 'And White if I can.'

'I'll take Godshall,' Buchanan said, and they divided up the eight men.

The rates were sitting along an outside wall, Baker and White side by side. They were tired, filthy, still sweating in the humid night air, Baker sipping water from a bottle. There was no breeze below the level of the wall and he tipped the last bit over his head, relishing the moisture as it

260

ran down his face. Both were so far unhurt, but there had been casualties since nightfall. They knew one of the Americans had just taken a bullet. It had hit the edge of his armoured vest and ploughed into the shoulder, separating the ball joint and shattering bone before exiting through the back. With stoic courage he had put up his own dressing and once one of the SBS men had bandaged him and hit him with a syrette of morphine, he had sat back and loaded magazines for his comrades, holding them between his knees, feeding in loose rounds one by one. The medic had arrived and put up a drip and the word was he was being moved out to the ship when they could bring him out of the line.

Baker looked out at the night, tracer rounds arcing into the sky, flashes in the night as things went off. The whole country seemed ablaze and their immediate area as bad as any.

'Wasn't expecting this,' he said honestly. He had felt fear, liquid and hot in his guts, and he knew others had, others who were silent with their thoughts. They weren't trained for this. He, like all of them all except perhaps Godshall, would have preferred to fight the ship or face every sailor's fear, a below decks fire, something they were trained for and best at. Anything but this close quarters fighting in the dark.

'Me neither,' Chalky replied. 'Thought we'd pick up a few voodoo trinkets. A carving or two for the mantelpiece.'

'Remember this morning. Yesterday morning,' he corrected. 'On the Beau. You were saying it wouldn't be like *Zulu*. More *Dogs of War*? Got that wrong,' he said with a lopsided grin.

'Mystic Meg I ain't,' White replied. He nudged Baker. 'There's Chops Wilks. A quid for the first bloke to make him say cunt.'

'Easy. Just ask him what he thinks of Marines,' someone muttered.

'Or civvies.'

261

'Or the air force.'

'Or the army.'

'Or officers.'

White paused. 'Chief,' he called. Chops(M) looked over at him. 'This being ashore stuff is crap. If I wanted to do this shit I'd have joined the Marines.'

Chief Petty Officer Wilks knew White of old. 'You were lucky,' he growled. 'Someone smiled on you. Took you into the Navy. If you'd joined the Marines, you'd be an even bigger wanker than you are now.'

Someone down the wall spoke then, a perfect impression of the Chief's gravel delivery. 'Rest of you are wankers, too.' Everyone laughed and even Wilks's face split into a fleeting smile.

'Too much morale here.' It was the XO, looming up out of the dark.

Kitson briefed them on what they were to do and before he handed over to his two Lieutenants he looked across at the group. 'Godshall?'

'Sir.' The tough rating was squatting, his back to the wall, his weapon at the ready.

'We have at last found something at which you excel. Mr Buchanan needs a number two in his section. As of now you are acting Petty Officer.'

'Aye aye, sir,' he replied. For the first time that night he smiled. It was a bleak, wintry expression. Kitson moved off and there was a moment's silence while Wilks looked at Godshall. It was no surprise to him. He had recommended it.

'Don't cock it up . . . cunt,' he said.

Chops didn't know why, but there was a burst of muffled laughter and Godshall held out his hand to White.

Two ratings were helping the medic carry the wounded Marine back. The early strength he had found had dissipated and in spite of the drip in his arm he had gone into shock. The medic wanted him medivacced out on the ship 'asap'. They had him in a poncho, the two lads off the *Beaufort* carrying him as gently as they could, but he was heavy and they lowered him to the ground beside a pile of garden rubbish to get a better grip. One of the rates put his hand down to reach for the edge of the poncho and as he was lifting he felt something.

'Shit!'

'What?' the other asked. They were moving already. Almost at the back gate of the villa's garden.

'Something bit me. Stung me, maybe.'

'Let's keep it moving,' the medic said. He was behind them holding the drip. They carried the wounded man down to the beach where three others, the men defending the beach gate, took over the lift, and when they got back to the villa the man looked down at his hand in the darkness. 'Shit. It's hurting now. Throbbing.'

'What?' his mate asked.

'My hand. Something bit me.'

The other rating produced a cigarette lighter and lit it. 'Let's 'ave a look.'

The puncture marks were small and close together, but unmistakable, one either side of the joint between the little finger and the bottom of the hand. Already it was red and swollen, the tiny punctures seeping fluid.

'Ooh. Yeah. Som'ing got ya. Reckon the medic ought to see that.' They caught the US Marine medic as he was coming back up from the beach. He looked at it, a torch in his mouth.

'You bin snake bit,' he said. 'This happen over where we stopped? You see it?'

'No. Just felt it.'

'Godshall,' the other said. 'He said they saw a snake down here somewhere.'

'Find him,' the medic said. The rating scuttled off and was back in under a minute, not with Godshall but with Baker. He looked straight at the man's hand.

'Where did this happen?' he asked.

'Other side of the wall,' the sailor replied.

'In the corner?'

'Yeah.'

'Big pile of rubbish, leaves and shit?'

The man nodded and Baker took the medic's torch and studied the wound.

'We need to know what it was,' the medic said.

'It's unlikely to be the one we saw. A puffy. Threw it over the wall, the other way. Anyway, it was a great big one. A big adult. This bite is too small.'

'They have young 'uns,' the medic said.

Baker looked at him. 'It was a puff adder. Haemotoxin.'

The medic nodded. He knew a bit about snakes, coming from a land where they were common. Because they were unable to inject the sheer volume of venom that an adult snake could deliver, but still needed to hunt and kill prey, the bite of young snakes was much more potent. Haemotoxin was a blood poison. Unlike neurotoxins carried by other snakes the venom would not affect the brain, the nervous system or the respiratory system. This would produce localized swelling, chronic tissue damage in the immediate area, some chance of necrotizing.

'Sure?'

'Positive,' Baker replied. 'The one we got rid of from the same place was a big puff adder. This bite is displaying the right symptoms.' He looked at the medic. 'These things are common here. Every clinic, every hospital will have serum, such as it is. The French doctor who went out to the Beau. She may have some in her bag. She must have treated puff adder bites before.'

He didn't say it and neither did the medic. That the local tissue damage after an intramuscular injection of a potent haemotoxin, such as a puff adder bite, was sometimes so catastrophic that the flesh died. Turned black and died. All too often the solution was amputation of the affected area. This sailor could lose a chunk from the base of his hand and possibly his little finger.

'Okay. You are out to the ship. If the doctor doesn't have serum we will have to chopper some in.' He looked at Baker. 'Can you double back there? Have a look. If it's still there it won't have gone far. I'd like confirmation. Then put that area off limits, or burn it or something.'

Kitson sat by the radio talking into the mike. This was all they needed. They had had another engine breakdown and two of the inflatables, coming in together, were caught in sustained fire. Luckily neither of the coxswains were injured but both boats were seriously damaged and in-operable. He had suspended the evacuation again and out on the water ratings from *Beaufort* were transferring a good engine from one of the useless boats on to the boat with the dicky motor.

Heavy fire coming up the beach from both ends. If that wasn't threat enough, now they had a man bitten by a highly venomous snake. They'd got him on the last boat away, but it was now 0200 hrs and they still had 240 civilians and his own people ashore. It would be light at 0524. The Marines were going to go out and locate the enemy positions so they could call in NGS again, but for the time being they were stuck.

From his position Kitson could see up the hall into the villa's sitting room and in view was Kreutz, the presumed CIA man, sitting with a bunch of people from the US Embassy. Three of them were obviously fright-ened and Kreutz was obviously doing his best to reassure them. Two of them were black men and they lacked the travelled, cosmopolitan air of the many other Africans among the civilians, presumably dual passport holders. Everyone was frightened, but these two displayed it in a manner that Kitson found uncomfortable. All the men had drawn lots for positions in the boats and although Kitson knew that this group had drawn high numbers, somehow they had done deals and got themselves moved up the list. There had been no evidence of intimidation, or complaint from anyone, so he had ignored the matter.

Alberry, a tower of strength, had been moving round his people chatting to them, reassuring them every now and then, but was now with Bill Black in one of the back bedrooms. With morale in mind they had asked if they might have a low light of some kind and Kitson knew that with the windows covered it wouldn't be a problem. They now had a card school running. They were playing bridge, something called Chicago, where players moved round between games. In the main room a game of Trivial Pursuit that had begun at the Embassy had been re-started, this time a transatlantic challenge until someone pointed out that with the US version the Americans were bound to win and they split the players evenly by nationality. Four huge teams now played round the one board. Someone on one of the ConLib teams wished they had Jonnie Johnson, who consistently won the game whenever he played with them, but he was still outside somewhere with his rifle.

The two reaction groups were now ready and one, Buchanan's, had already been used to support a point in the line that looked in real trouble for a few minutes until the attack faded. In that action Lieutenant Gordon had been lightly wounded. A bullet had hit him in the chest and although a magazine for his weapon had taken the full impact and there was no wound, no entry, the force of the bullet hitting the magazine had cracked a couple of ribs. The bruising was livid, blue-black, and he was in some pain, but he was functioning. The Royal Marines motto was 'Per Mare Per Terrum', but the ethos was different. You never, never give up.

He had grinned at Doughty and as he closed his shirt the Corporal had grinned back. 'Tomorrow, boss, that is going to hurt like shit.'

'No kidding,' he responded dryly. 'Right, grab the SBS sergeant and both of you report back here.' Two minutes later he was back with the special forces soldier.

'Time for NGS again. Get out there and get co-ordinates on those positions. Corporal Doughty, you and Toomey the north. Sergeant, your guys can do the southern side. It's right on the beach both ends. Just get a range and come back in and we'll work it out.'

Out in the dark Jonnie Johnson had joined the Royal Marine post at the south-western edge of the beach and settled himself near their foxhole. He had offered his help and Kitson had quickly agreed. His chosen stand had good cover. The Ulima position was a good distance away and any sightings or flash of light were brief, too brief for conventional methods. He got himself settled in, laid out a blanket over his shooting position to keep the sand from his working parts and eventually peered through the scope on his rifle.

A mile offshore *Beaufort* was hove to in darkness, all lights, even her riding lights, extinguished. Commander Bennett had her bows facing the beach, firstly to reduce the target profile he offered any guns ashore and to allow the boats to come in both sides as soon as they were running again. He had opted to come in closer to reduce the transit time for the boats, but the ship was vulnerable so close in and he had stepped up the posture. Down in the Ops room eyes were glued to the targeting radars. The moment anyone fired anything at them larger than a baked bean tin they would know about it. The gas turbines were ticking over, just holding station, and the cages were temporarily hoisted six feet above the water line. Ratings stood ready to let go the rafts. They were ready to be under way in the time it took to give the command. Down below the turret the men serving the gun were ready, ammunition in the feed ring. Topsides each 30-mill cannon was manned and the local area optical sights, the TDS, for the main gun were manned, with the men operating the sights changing every thirty minutes.

Back on the bridge Bennett sat in his chair for more

than a minute for what seemed the first time in hours. Assessing what he had seen in the context of their environment, he had been everywhere, visiting every battle station, stopping at every point where civilian evacuees were gathered to talk to them. The main galley was running full time now, serving food in relays to the almost 450 extra people who were sitting in groups everywhere one looked. Some seamen's mess areas had been given over to families, others to adult women. Many more people had found themselves somewhere on the weather deck and they had been warned that they would have to move into the hangar quite quickly sometime soon. There was no point in limiting people's movement too much. There were just too many of them. Bennett's only limitation was that no one was to go above weather deck level, and no one forward of the citadel or aft the painted circle where the Lynx sat. They were as comfortable as they were going to get, so he concentrated on the other issue. They were critically short of main gun ammunition.

When they had left on this deployment he had loaded a mix of ordnance, most of it intended for the exercise with the South African Navy. They had expended twenty-five rounds of HE at a series of targets and when they had left Durban the main magazine had held the remaining twenty-five rounds of HE and a mix of other ordnance remaining. They had now used twelve. Thirteen left. He had advised Northwood, a standing procedure, but they couldn't resupply him and the RFA with munitions aboard was still at least a day out behind them.

Morris, the navigator, had got his head down for a few hours and now had the watch again and Lieutenant Commander Denny, who had been prowling the ship, was back down in his kingdom, the Ops room, hooded up and waiting to fight the ship the moment they had got the request from the beach. They were as ready as they were going to be.

Someone passed Bennett a cup of coffee and he sipped

it gratefully. He had moved his planning area up to the nav station and for now his quarters were an open wardroom for the use of his officers, most of who had given up their own. Mattresses were laid out on the floor for them to grab sleep while they could and his pantry fed them. The Ambassador's wife, Mrs Black, had gracefully refused his offer of his cabin and had moved into the XO's with her sister. The US Ambassador's wife was in another cabin and three of the others on that flat were given over to post-operative care of patients coming out of the improvised theatre in the wardroom.

Poppy and Maggie Black, both trained nurses, were putting their skills to use. Poppy was in the theatre alongside the American naval surgeon. She had come quietly in while the anaesthetist was bent over the patient and two men stood over his prone form. 'Can I help? I am an SRN theatre sister.'

The surgeon looked up from where he was working on the shattered ball joint of the US Marine's shoulder. 'If that means what I think it means. Where did you train?'

'Where I work. Guy's Hospital, in London.'

For the surgeon this was even better than the offers he had from two more of the French medical people. Both GPs, neither had been close to assisting surgery in a long time.

'Hell, yes. Get scrubbed up.'

She had already showered and was wearing clean clothes: a pair of chinos and a white shirt fresh from the Chinese dhobi men, which she had found in Peter Kitson's chest of drawers. The trousers barely closed over her hips, but the shirt covered her front comfortably. The Marine passed her a disposable smock and with a mask over her face she familiarized herself quickly; the surgeon gratefully stepped aside to let her in closer.

The ship was not short on general medical expertise.

Dr Bujould had left two doctors and two nurses from her team downstairs in the sick bay and took up Maggie's offer of help in the post-operative unit. She had put the man with the snake bite up there. She did have serum in her bag, but it should have been kept cool and she wasn't sure what degradation would occur in twenty-four hours out of the fridge.

'Maybe,' she said. 'If the serum is still good and we have him soon enough . . .' She hit him with a big dose and they sat back to wait and treat the symptoms.

Two levels above them, up on the bridge, Bennett felt the ship move beneath him and felt a kinship with her. Crowded with people, and damaged, she was functioning like the thoroughbred she was.

He remembered that after the evacuation of UN personnel from Somalia in '95, where HMS *Exeter* had performed, the American officer in command of the international task force, Admiral John Gunn, had commented that he compared the Type 42 favourably with one of his much newer Aegis class cruisers. Ha! Bennett thought. He ain't seen my beautiful girl. She makes a Type 42 look very basic: a shit or bust area defence platform.

They were waiting for co-ordinates for NGS. He looked at his watch. Come on people. Let's get this moving.

In Whitehall a small team were spending the night in the Foreign and Commonwealth Office: the Foreign Secretary, a junior minister, two permanent secretaries and a man who had come over from Century House, the home of MI6. They were sitting in leather easychairs, the Secretary of State in his usual posture, one of the long legs that had helped power his rowing eight to victory over Cambridge thirty years before draped over an arm of the chair.

'What have we got?'

'All the women and children and a few men are on board now, but they have been stopped running boats by gunfire from both sides and the attack on their position has intensified. Latest from Northwood, Minister, is that *Beaufort* is expecting to have to provide gunfire support again. The objective to silence or force a retreat from the two positions that are firing on our boats.'

'Mmm. How many did they fire last time?' The Foreign Secretary asked.

'Seven, sir.'

'We know that Captain . . .' he looked down at his notes '. . . Bennett won't use this option unless he has no choice, but I'm mindful of the media response after the initial reaction dies down. All we need is one picture of someone's dwelling looking a bit bashed about, whether it was our fault or not, and there will be cries of "was it necessary?" and all sorts of armchair tacticians saying they could have done it with three shells. Anyway,' he shrugged and moved on. 'Any more casualties?'

'Six, sir, one of them an American Marine, none critical. Two are remaining ashore, both officers. We also have a man being treated for snakebite.'

The Foreign Secretary looked across at the man from Century House. He was head of the Africa section. 'Your people got anything new for us?'

'I don't think so, Minister. We haven't had word out from our man since the comms went down. We have been mulling over a couple of his last reports. I think we must assume that CNN are right and Johnson has been usurped.'

'Did you get that from CNN?' the Secretary asked dryly.

'No, Minister. We had that very early this morning. As you know, our man thinks it's this Bokia who now commands Ulima, a man we think, with some reason, is in the advanced stages of syphilis.'

The Foreign Secretary nodded. 'Taylor. Any news on his whereabouts?'

'No, sir. Boley we know is still south of Monrovia, fighting his way northwards. But Taylor remains as elusive as ever. We have been talking to people crossing over into Sierra Leone. Nothing positive other than many indicators that his hold has fractured. Senior people done a bunk.

This is the interesting bit. Two of the people we think have skipped are two of the very trusted part of the family. They were involved in the ConLib renegotiations.'

'Go on,' the Foreign Secretary said, his eyes narrowing.

Deep inside the command centre at Northwood, without looking at the clocks it was impossible to tell whether it was night or day outside. Deep below ground level, safe from anything but a direct nuclear strike, the outer offices and admin areas were closed up for the night, but in the operations areas people were busy. A communications relay was in place and, via the Nimrod overhead the *Beaufort*, messages were almost instantaneous. The normal tri-service team had been supplemented by a Royal Marines officer, a major who only six weeks before his appointment to Northwood had been 2 i/c of 45 Commando at Arbroath. He knew Andy Gordon and he knew better than any of them the minute by minute tactical considerations that Lieutenant Gordon and his twenty-man recce troop would be facing.

They knew that the SBS people had handed over their boats and were now a fighting patrol under Gordon's command, and they also knew that Gordon had deployed *Beaufort*'s armed ratings out into the defensive perimeter. To have done that, to be using sailors in front-line defensive positions, meant that things were getting bad.

'How many HE does he have left?' the Marines officer asked.

'Thirteen. He also has five star shells, ten WPs and five delayed action.'

The Major nodded. In practice a barrage round a position could form a shield in itself, but it was a hugely costly venture, the guns consuming ammunition at a rate that made any resupply effectively very difficult. In this case even with enough ammunition, with only one gun the barrel would overheat.

The broadsheet dailies, the presses now running for the

second edition, all ran the story on their front pages. All had had access to the Reuters and CNN feeds earlier that day and they all had background material to the reports they had been running for months as the situation in Liberia went from anarchy to chaos. Their reports were given colour by little titbits about West Africa in general. One paper mentioned that the same Nigerian peacekeepers in Liberia, when deployed in neighbouring Sierra Leone the previous year, had allegedly looted street lights and another story, looking back at the scene there only a few months before, showed bodies in the streets.

The graphic artists produced colourful diagrams illustrating the rescue, with little blue arrows showing the direction of the *Beaufort*'s seaboats and the Nimrod overhead with a little jagged yellow line denoting radio messages up to the aircraft and then away over the sea to London. One paper showed a schematic drawing of the likely path of the shell that had killed the crew members and destroyed the MCO, and all papers ran a full colour picture of HMS *Beaufort* and a formal portrait of her Captain. The *Daily Telegraph* had a picture of his wife Lisa, a strikingly attractive woman, and the couple's children, but the journalists were disappointed. Any hopes of worried looks or tears or a woman unravelling were dashed. She had handled them with aplomb and dignity, simply saying that this was her husband's job, he had his orders, and she was sure he would carry them out with the minimum of risk to his crew.

At the *Sun* newspaper the first copies were coming off the huge press, and the supervisor took one from the stack. The headlines yelled from the page: 'We talk to our brave lads!' Further down another headline shouted, 'We sent 'em Sun readers' best wishes.' Yet another story started 'Captain Fantastic' and another 'Phone home'. The caption to the page three topless girl was 'Our stunna says I'll be a Beau for you!' Deeper in, another story had a picture of the wife of the mobile phone's owner, now a bit happier and fifty quid the richer for posing for the picture. The story began 'Little did brave wife know . . .' and beside it another story said 'Cellnet says every ship should have one.'

In Washington DC the White House press conference was timed for 7.00 PM but was late starting. When the press secretary issued her statement she prefaced it with a summary of the day's events. 'We haven't had direct communications with our Ambassador or any of our Embassy staff since they moved across to the British compound. That was seven hours ago. All communication is, as you know, via open channel radio to the British naval ship and then through one of their aircraft back to London. We are timed to have an AWACS overhead ready to take over that link at 0500 hours local. The latest word is that the evacuation is currently suspended because the beach area and the boats that are carrying people out to the ship are coming under fire . . .'

There was a barrage of questions from journalists wanting to know how many people were still trapped and how many were Americans. One journalist, told there were still 300 people ashore, did some quick arithmetic.

'Assuming they get under way immediately, they need to get a hundred people an hour out to the ship. What are their chances of getting that done before daybreak?'

'Currently they can manage about one hundred and thirty people an hour, so this should be well within their scope,' the spokeswoman replied smoothly.

'That assumes that they can begin immediately. Would it be correct to say that any more than an hour's hold-up and they will have people exposed in broad daylight, and presumably the ship will have to move further offshore again?'

'That would be correct.'

'What are the tactical options?'

'We don't comment on tactics. But I can say that HMS *Beaufort*'s rules of engagement allow her Captain some considerable degree of latitude. Secondly, our own Marines will in the area by 0700 local time.'

The journalist wasn't giving up that easily. He was on to something. 'If they are evacuating civilians first and if there are people still ashore and under attack at first light, then it's likely to be the armed services people who are last off?' he said. 'If that scenario happens and the civilians are all aboard the ship, will the arriving US Marines be deployed anyway?'

'Aah . . .' the spokeswoman replied, 'we are still looking at that.'

'So you are saying if that is the case these people might be left, unsupported, to defend themselves as best they can until nightfall.'

'As I said, we are still looking at that scenario.'

A military man off to on side grimaced slightly at the thought. It was the classic conundrum, in a nightmare scenario. Ten or eleven thousand Ulima fighters fighting possibly that many of Taylor's forces. Friendlies caught in the middle and under direct deliberate attack. So leave a handful and hope for the best or throw in more and risk them too? Mission slippage versus the right thing to do. If they put the Marines, airborne at this time, into the enclave in Monrovia then they would be stuck there for at least three or four days and it would be at least a further forty-eight hours before they could be supported by air from the *John F. Kennedy* and her battle group.

State was piling huge pressure on the fragile Sierra Leone government to allow them to step up their logistics base in the country to a full operational station. If that happened then they could have F16s and A10 'Warthog' ground attack aircraft there to lend support by nightfall. That would even the odds till they could be lifted out, the Marines in a redoubt supported by enough air power to make even ten thousand opposition wish they were some-where else. A major western presence might also make everyone sit up and think for a minute. Either way, he was thinking, if the Brits couldn't get everyone away by first light they were talking bodybags. It was gonna be a cluster fuck on a grand scale.

The first woman aboard was still with her two children in the Wrens' mess. She had done an interview to camera, Ted Brooks holding the microphone to her lips.

He had got himself and his crew out to the ship. It hadn't been a conscious decision. He was torn between the options: stay ashore in the thick of the action, but where at least till daylight he could do no to-camera pieces and had no link with the outside world; or move out to the ship where there were related dramas and he could at least film.

When their boat numbers came early it seemed that fate was deciding for him so, instead of offering their places to others, they moved out to the *Beaufort*. Once there he got his people filming background material – crowded passages and mess halls, some dramatic footage of the shell damage to the ship, people in the sick bay and ratings manning upper deck positions in flash hoods. While that was going on he began doing what he was best at, questioning people, and inside fifteen minutes had tracked down the Petty Officer with the worldcard Cellnet phone. He moved up the internal stairs to the bridge, flashed his identification to a rating at the head of the stairs and was asked to wait.

Commander Bennett arrived and Brooks asked if he could have the PO's telephone. 'I want to remain in contact with my people. At least, Captain, you'll know who has got it and that it's being used legitimately. I'd also like to record an interview.'

Bennett was thinking quickly. He had done the press media and public relations courses and knew that journalists were a double-edged sword. Best to arrive at a working relationship. Also, there were areas of the ship that were classified high security and he didn't want a professional questioner wandering around asking questions in a tactical environment.

'With conditions. In terms of the crew, you restrict any serious questions, and you know what I mean, to me or the public relations officer once he is back aboard. You restrict your news gathering to this incident. You bear in mind that this ship is in action and seek permission before entering any operational areas. If in doubt ask. If I say no there is a bloody good reason for it. We will co-operate as best we can. Fair enough?'

'Sounds all right.'

'Have you had sight of the Official Secrets Act and signed to that effect?'

'About a dozen times over the years.'

'Good,' Bennett had said handing over the telephone. 'Bags of common sense and we will get along fine.'

Five minutes later Brooks was tucked into a quiet corner on the weather deck calling his people in Atlanta. This was the single largest breaking news story and as his call came in to the CNN central newsroom the newsreader was stopped mid-flow on a story about urban racoons and he went to air live.

They had forty minutes of excellent footage, shot on the scene, that could be used later in many follow-up pieces and an interview with the woman and her children in the can – classic middle-America stuff. Now he was back on the bridge.

'Captain. The word is that you might be about to use your deck gun again. Any chance we can film it from up here? It's the only vantage.'

You want to film the drama of it. Big gun, recoil, muzzle flash, good action stuff. But it's people dying, Bennett thought. People are dying out there. He nodded sadly and pointed to the far corner of the bridge.

'Stay out of the way.' He looked at his watch. It was 0215 local.

'Beaufort Beaufort, this is one.'

'Go one.'

'Requesting November Golf Sierra at this time. Two targets, I say again two targets, three rounds Hotel Echo and two Whisky Papa at each, then a star shell on the second position. Did you copy that, over?'

'Roger one, two positions, three HE and two Whisky Papas each, one star shell on second position.'

'Beaufort, co-ordinates follow, over.'

Lieutenant Gordon was listening as his Royal Marine observer called in the orders. He had taken advice from the SBS sergeant. It hadn't rained all day and the place was dry. The white phosphorous shells would start fires in the brush that would, with the gentle on-shore breeze, drive the attackers back and hopefully keep them back from the beach for some time. It would also take out any of the fighters who survived the high explosives. That was tough. His intent was not to call white phosphorous in on to personnel – that was against the Geneva Convention – but if they were still in there then fuck 'em, he thought. It was intended to illuminate the position, but if any of the men shooting at them were still in there it would do what white phosphorous had always done: burn. It stuck to the skin and even a small amount would debilitate a combatant. Morale would break down among the remaining men and hopefully they would break and run, look for a softer target.

Commander Bennett heard the order come in. The Royal Navy uses management by veto. The principle allows officers to make decisions, do their jobs, react the way they were trained, instantaneously without the direct approval of their commanding officer. If he, or she, disapproved, then they would veto. White phos, Bennett thought. Sweet Jesus.

He wasn't ashore. He wasn't on the scene. He was not in a position to judge the merits of the need, but he did have 300-odd people there that were his direct responsibility, 34 of them his crew, and another 37 on attachment.

He did not veto the order.

Two ratings began hurriedly clearing people from the weather deck back into the hangar and down in the Ops room Lieutenant Commander Denny called the load he wanted in the feed ring through to the gunbay.

The weather deck clear, the gun loaded and the co-ordinates in the computer for the first shot he thumbed his microphone.

'Beaufort one, Beaufort.'

'Go, Beaufort.'

'One gun is ready.'

'Fire one round.'

The Royal Marine watched the shell hit the north-western position. It was dead on.

'Left twenty, fire for effect!'

'Down twenty, fire!'

'Up ten, fire Whisky Papa.'

'Right fifty, fire Whisky Papa.'

On the sand outside the wall he could see the concussion blasts in the air and felt the ground shake beneath him as the high explosive rounds came in. Then night turned into day, the white flash exploding, chunks of burning phosphorous flying outwards with pretty white smoke trails, showering the bush with burning globules of the chemical. He turned and looked down the beach at the second position.

'Second position. One illumination round. Fire!'

It was the same and as the star shell came in it exploded overhead, letting go a burning illumination flare that swung under a little parachute. Along that south-eastern flank, as the flare lit the night, the US Marines and the ratings with them opened up on the running figures, caught in the open and exposed by the harsh light. The bush was alight, fires burning both ends fanned by the breeze.

'Thank you, Beaufort.'

As he said it Kitson flashed his torch to seawards calling the first boats and soon they were running in. He knew that anyone on either side still in the enemy positions and still capable of firing on them would have no night sight left after the blinding white blast of the phosphorous shells.

'Beaufort one, Beaufort.'

The observer Marine was scuttling back into the gate in the low beach wall when the radio squawked. He dropped down beside Kitson and the ratings by the gate.

'Beaufort go.'

'One XO, please.'

It was Commander Bennett, Kitson realized. 'XO go,' he said, taking the microphone from the Marine.

'Ah . . . be advised that mark eight delivery of initial order is limited. Do you understand over?'

Mark eight, Kitson thought. Vickers mark eight. The gun. His heart sank for a moment. He had forgotten about that, forgotten completely. They had fired seven in the first salvo, six and phos in the second. How many this morning. Four? Five? They were down to, oh shit, down to seven or eight HE rounds.

'Ah yes, Beaufort, I understand, over.'

'One, we do however have something else for you so call when you need it, over.'

What? Kitson thought. The Beaufort's state of the art battle systems were about as much use here as tits on a bull. Sea Skua was radar guided, Harpoons only went after ships, torpedoes liked being in water, Seawolf was okay, if the attackers were coming at the ship at Mach II.

Oh well. If the boss said he had something else then he had something else. Someone out there had dreamed something up. DWEO maybe. No doubt Chops (Sonar) is in the thick of it somewhere. Old school Navy. Ingenious, practical, inventive. DWEO, him and a handful of the weapons artificers could come up with some seriously nasty stuff given the need. He smiled fleetingly.

'Boats approaching, sir.'

'Right, get 'em out and loaded.'

At Northwood the Fleet Operations Officer, a Commander, was at his desk in the Ops room when his Chief Petty Officer assistant carried a signal message through to him. There were two or three others gathered around, one of them the Royal Marine Major. This small band were watching progress, planning, looking to support the *Beaufort* and her people any way they could.

The CoS Ops, the Chief of Staff Ops, a two-star admiral who was also Flag Officer Submarines, and ACoS (Ops), the Assistant Chief of Staff Operations, a Commodore, had been in and out of the circle as the drama unfolded and both had cancelled other commitments as best they could to be available. The CoS was on his way into Whitehall for a meeting at the MoD and his number two was on a conference call with the Pentagon, so it was the Commander currently co-ordinating efforts. This was a Navy-managed task, but they did have an RAF officer who had left his desk at the other end of the Ops room to join them. With a Nimrod overhead on a mission his input was valuable.

The PO passed the A4 signal to the Commander.

Priority Action addressee : Operational Immediate
Priority Information addressee: Operational Immediate
FROM: Beaufort
TO: CinC Fleet
Info: MODUK
FOSF
HQRM
HMS Fearless
Subject: Monrovia: Evacuation
1. Have provided NGS. 6 HE 4 WP 1 SS.
2. Evacuation recommenced this time. Intense fighting ashore.

3. 7 HE remaining. Intend to reserve these for final withdrawal and if necessary use helo to deliver self manufactured ordnance.

'*Beaufort* has engaged again. NGS. Expended six rounds of HE, four white phosphorous and one star shell.'

'That puts her down to . . .' someone began.

'Seven,' the Royal Marines officer said. 'Seven.' His tone was telling. It challenged why a Royal Navy ship, there for the defence of the realm, there to be deployed, put to the use for which she was intended, was on the high seas away from re-supply with so little main armament ammunition. He knew the answer. They all did. But he was thinking of the lads on the beach, his lads, holding a force many times their size at bay. They would be the last off, too. A fighting withdrawal into seaboats the way the Marines had done since the early days of the Empire.

'There's more,' the officer said. 'They have built bombs. They are going to use the Lynx to drop them.'

'They've what?' someone asked.

'Says here self-manufactured ordnance. They have cobbled together bombs.'

'Yes!' the Marine uttered. 'Excellent!'

He was thinking like a Marine. This made eminently good sense. They are in the shit. So what do they do? Improvise. Use what's at hand.

'With what?' the RAF man asked.

'Actually, quite a lot. She has plenty that goes bang bang,' the naval officer answered proudly. 'They'll have stripped some Torpex out of something.'

'Can we get some details?' the Air Force man asked, appalled by visions of home-made bombs being dropped from an aircraft. 'And let's get someone in here who can look at what they've done.' He was from a service which could deliver smart munitions into a chimney pot, had stand-off weapons, retarded drop, who could predict the exact fall and trajectory of munitions and know exactly what the 'footprint' of an air strike might be. The thought of chaps kicking a home-made bomb, probably inherently unstable and with an unknown detonation timing margin, without retarded drop, out of the door of a slow-moving helicopter at low altitude, was horrific.

The Marines officer was already walking to a telephone.

The Commander looked at the distribution on the signal. It was for their action. It was addressed to CINC Fleet. Management by veto: Nick Bennett was stating his intent and it was up to them, thousands of miles away, to veto it. Would they? The whole thing had gone well thus far. All they needed now was to have an accident with dodgy home-made bombs and kill their own people and it would be a catastrophe. He picked up the phone to bring in CoS.

Lieutenant Sarah Conway's small reaction team were on the northern side of the villa, set up inside the garden wall by the gate on to the street. On the other side of the wall just twenty yards away was the first Royal Marines position, with another spanned out to their left. The fire from both positions was sporadic. The Marines were husbanding their ammunition until one of the seaboats brought in boxes of belt 7.62 and smaller calibre rounds for the SA80s from the ship's small arms magazine. For now they were short and the years of training, drumming conservation into the Royal Marines, were paying off.

Chops and Baker were standing to, their weapons over the wall and sighted down the street. From their position they could see the rear of both the Marine posts. Sarah sat at the base of the wall with White to her left, smoking a cigarette. She was going to tell him to put it out, but it seemed pointless. There was a firefight going on just up the street and it was a pleasingly normal thing to have this fellow sitting beside her smoking.

One of the SBS men was just along the wall, a neat row of rifle grenades laid out beside him. He had moved back because he was too close to be able to use his M16-203 grenade launcher. The 40mm grenades could be fired 350 yards, but not tonight. Tonight he had needed to move back a few yards to work to the weapon's minimum range. A few minutes before he had been firing illumination rounds, the Marines on the gun in front then pouring fire into the targets they could see. That had kept heads down. If night was their cover then remove the night. The special forces Marine had been cunning with it. Earlier he had directed three illumination rounds into an area that had only one pool of darkness, one place to hide from the light. The fourth round was airburst high explosive anti-personnel right into the pool of dark: she had thought she heard men screaming and put her hands to her ears. She wasn't enjoying this. It was noisy, dark, terrifying, close-quarters combat and she wasn't trained for it.

'I wish,' White said, 'I was back in Blighty. In some country pub, with a fireplace and a dog and real ale pumped up from the cellar. A place that does steak and kidney pudding.'

'What? You don't like it here?' she replied in mock surprise.

'It's a shithole, ma'am.'

'You can say that again,' she agreed.

'Your old man is in the mob, isn't he?'

'Yeah,' she replied with a little smile. 'He's a two and a half at *Nelson*.'

'He must be worried sick about you.'

She smiled, wondering where he was, what he was doing. Home perhaps, in the little house they had bought near Chichester. Tucked up in bed, lying on her side as he always did when she was away. She felt a rush of love for him.

'What about you? Married?' she asked, trying to place his accent.

'I am,' he replied. 'My wife's expecting our first child. Due on Saturday.'

'Congratulations,' she said. 'Thought of a name?'

He was about to answer when out in front of them the fighting intensified. The snaps and odd bursts became one, the noise furious. Tracer rounds fired by people trying to keep in cover arced up into the sky over their heads and rounds thumped into the wall further up.

'Here we go,' he said. She was up on her knees and peered over the wall. The Marines out on the right were hunkered down and then the MAG responded, opening up in short bursts. She heard the grenade launcher fire and a few seconds later an illumination round exploded sixty yards out from the Marines position. There were running men, not from the front where they had been but coming from the right. Two of the Marines swung right and began to fire at the attackers, the man on the gun swinging his barrel to bear and opening up, but the gun stopped firing halfway through one of its bursts.

'Jam!' the SBS man snapped.

Conway was up on her feet and moving. Without the firepower of their machine gun the four Marines would be overrun and the defence breached. As the SBS man vaulted the wall she snapped an order and took off after him. 'Let's go!'

They moved up the wall in the darkness, running along the storm ditch, Chops(M) firing on the run. It seemed to take for ever to cover the distance and they arrived at the position three seconds behind the SBS man, Conway finally getting the safety catch off on the unfamiliar rifle without a second to spare. The two groups almost ran into each other. The attackers, maybe fifteen or sixteen strong, suddenly realized there was another threat. What developed was a vicious rolling firefight in the darkness. Conway had done what Chops suggested when he saw her weapon, the AK taken earlier that evening. So she would not be confused for an enemy he said she should go for the gun position. She piled into it from the rear and began firing into the oncoming figures. One of the Marines was frantically stripping the gun, but the other three were engaging. She knew her men were spread out to her right and she swung her fire in that direction, adrenalin coursing through her blood, the recoil, the noise, the muzzle-flash merging with the rage and fear. The attackers were among them now and beside her someone began firing a shotgun. An attacker, momentarily illuminated by something, his face blank, his eyes flat like a zombie's, was hit in the chest by a shotgun blast, lifted from the ground and thrown backwards. Someone threw a hand grenade and she became aware that the SBS man was now beside her. She pulled her trigger again. Nothing. He knew sooner than she did. 'Mag!'

She fumbled at the release. He fired his shotgun again and then reached down, snatched the AK from her, his fingers instantly finding the release lever in the dark and dropped it back down to her. She jammed a fresh magazine in, cocked the action and was ready when there was a last fierce exchange over on the right and she rounded on it. The fear was gone. What was there was anger. Cold anger. She was up and moving to where her detachment were, firing into the attackers as she crossed the six or seven metres, screaming like a wild woman, her weapon on full automatic. The rounds cut into them and they faltered, the last of them escaping back into the darkness. 'Cleared!' the gunner shouted, cocking the gun.

One of the Marines scuttled out in amongst the wounded, collecting their weapons and ammunition, and she was talking to Corporal Doughty, panting, her hands shaking, when across where Chops and Baker had made their stand against the wall someone called her name. She crossed over into the storm drain where they were and dropped down into it.

White and Baker were bent over one of the rates, trying to staunch the blood that pumped from his neck and chest, Chalky White pulling the cover from a big battle dressing, but it was too late. The sailor, a Leading Mechanical Artificer was dead.

'Get that dressing on,' Baker said. 'He can't be dead. Jesus!' the frustration welling up in him.

'He's gone, Kevin,' White said.

Conway was aware that Chops had loomed out from somewhere.

'We are secure here again. Let's get him back to the villa. Okay?' she said evenly.

'Not leaving him,' Baker said.

'No. We're not leaving him,' she said. 'Everyone goes home. Do you hear me? Everyone!' she repeated, her voice like steel.

As they stood up, lifting the body, and prepared to move down the ditch, Chops dropped down with them. He took the AK from her hand and handed her the dead sailor's SA80.

'You'll need this.' As she moved away he called her by name. 'Lieutenant Conway?'

She looked back at him.

'You'll do,' he said.

10

'*Do you hear there? P1 and Chief Petty Officer (Sonar) to the bridge.*'

Bennett waited for them, still mulling it over. He had promised his XO support when he needed it and he was now down to very few options. In fact two. The fighting was getting closer all the time. Accuracy of fire was going to be the issue. If he was to reserve some ordnance for when accuracy was the concern, then he needed to find an interim measure; he was back to the classic source, the initiative and ingenuity of his crew. That, supported by the ship's close-in air defence system.

The two men arrived on the bridge.

He looked at the P1. 'How comfortable are you about dropping Chops's bombs from your aircraft?'

Mayberry shrugged. 'I have checked the sums. They seem to make sense. If I can get the run over the target we can heave 'em out. Ground fire will be the risk.' He had been thinking about that. Torpex was supposed to be stable, but he knew little about explosives. For all he knew one round up through the floor – it was only lightly armoured – into one of the home-made daisy cutters and it would blow the Lynx from the sky. With time detonators there could be little or no variation in attack height. He would just have to hope that the fighters on the ground were sufficiently deafened and distracted by the noise not to hear him on his run-in. That had to be accurate, too. With kilos of Torpex surrounded by every bit of steel shit that the MEO could muster going off, the drop had to be right or the risk of a blue on blue, of killing his own people, would be extreme.

He looked at the Chief Petty Officer (Sonar). 'How confident are you that these things will go off?'

The Chief shrugged in his turn. 'All the dets we tested went off with the correct time settings, sir. I'm happy with those. The whole assembly?' He thought for a second. This was no time for bullshit. 'Maybe seventy per cent.'

Mayberry turned back to his Captain. 'I'm prepared to give it a go.'

'Very well. You have how many?'

'Four, sir.'

'Next time XO wants some fire support we use 'em. Get them loaded. Dets out till you are airborne. WEO as safety officer. Who do you want crewing for you?'

'I'll come, sir,' the Chief said. 'And if I might . . .'

'Speak.'

'Wallace, sir. It was mostly her idea. She helped build them.'

'She wants to go?' Bennett asked. He knew that she had been close to Cheryl Simpson, the Wren rating killed in the MCO, and as the Chief nodded it crossed his mind that motives never change. Wanting to hit back. It didn't sound as dramatic as revenge, but it was the same thing.

'Very well. You happy?' he asked Mayberry.

'As I'm going to be, sir.'

The Clansman on the bridge crackled into life and someone passed the handset to Bennett. Mayberry turned away, thinking. The mechanics were simple. Deceptively simple. The WEO had worked them out with Mayberry. The drums kicked out of the door at 200 feet and at 130 knots would fall at increasing speed towards terminal velocity. The fuses would be set to have the bombs airburst, go off above the ground, theoretically at thirty feet. Keeping a helicopter at an exact height at speed was easier said than done. One air current, one updraught or downdraught and before you knew it you were off the mark. Altimeters were set in hundreds of feet. These helos had RADALT, radio altimeters, accurate to within ten feet plus or minus, but even so, in attempting 200 feet he could be at 190 or 210.

There wasn't much room for error in the delivery of this weapon. If it hit the ground before exploding, there was every chance the detonator would be separated, knocked out of the Torpex, and it wouldn't go off at all. Going off too high, too soon, there was the risk that the Lynx would be caught up in the blast. They would run in and drop the drums on to a position marked with an illumination round – someone was talking to Kitson, arranging that – and they thought that if Mayberry gave the command as the illumination round passed under the base of the observation panel by his feet the forward throw would be enough to have the bomb fall roughly on to the flare. As the bomb went out of the door he would jink right, his 130 knots airspeed taking him clear of the blast. Complete a 270 degree turn, a loop, and he would be lined up for the next drop run. Go for a tight turn and lose airspeed or go long and fast, exposed for longer over hostile territory? Three sides of the defence could be covered with an extended turning loop on each of the two corners.

That was skoshey, Mayberry thought. The turning loop would take them out over the guns of potentially hundreds of fighters: hopefully no one would have a heavy gun they could bring to bear. There were two ways to fly a helicopter over hostile ground. One was high. Over the cloud base or out of range. The other was low, very low and very fast, so fast that by the time they heard you and could bring a gun to bear you were over the tree tops and out of sight. Neither option was available.

'*Beaufort Beaufort, Nimrod Four Eight.*'

'*Four Eight this is Beaufort. Go.*'

'*Beaufort we have reached maximum mission endurance and must now divert and meet a tanker. A US AWACS is twenty miles out and will take station over. Good luck and safe passage home.*'

'*Roger, Four Eight. Thanks for your help.*'

There was silence on the bridge for a few moments, everyone feeling slightly alone at the thought of the sentinel who had been overhead for almost seven hours leaving them.

Mayberry broke the silence. 'I'd like a door gunner,' he said. He didn't know why. The muzzle flash would give away their position, but he just felt better having one there in case.

'There's only one MAG left aboard, sir. That's on the waist,' Chops(S) answered, his tone saying: that's all that's between us and any clever bastard who gets in a boat. So much had happened that night – they would not have been surprised. Behind him Bennett put the radio handset back.

'Chief. We have lost someone I'm afraid. LMA Smith. Pass the word. His body will be coming out on the next boat. Have a detail there to receive him.'

In the villa the early interest in the games had dried up. For the people who had managed to perceive the Marines' and armed sailors' efforts as sporadic exchanges of fire where no one was really physically affected, the death drove the reality home like a bayonet. One of theirs dead, carried down to the boat by his mates, his face and chest covered, and killed literally within a stone's throw of where they were.

Fear is contagious, and what began as a whingeing complaint about space in a boat being taken up by a dead body turned into a challenge. When Kitson, on his way past the villa on one of his constant sweeps between his lines, began taking flak from a group of men, the young Zimbabwean aid worker interposed.

They were frightened, the fear manifesting itself as aggression, and Kitson's requests for calm fell on deaf ears. A man pushed him in the chest with a finger, accusing him of favouritism, and his temper was about to go, but Culverhouse stepped in, using his imposing bulk.

'Not fair, boet. He has a job to do. We have our numbers. We wait our turn.'

'Who the fuck are you? A lightweight do-gooder! You . . .'

'I'm the bastard with the clipboard. I'm the bastard who did the draw for places. And lastly I'm the one with the shotgun! Now you listen to me. You'll get back to whatever shithole you crawled out of to come to Liberia and earn tax free money and live the good life. But you will go in turn! You have a problem with that, you take it up with me. And I'll tell you this for nothing – if you do, you better have plenty of sick leave.' Tony Wisher moved in behind him to provide a little official British Embassy presence, but Culverhouse ignored him. He stepped forward so that he towered over the man and his friends, the shotgun in his hand. 'So? How's it gonna be?'

If they were prepared to challenge the young man then the arrival of Wisher, his demeanour supremely confident down to the flat, hard look in his eyes, tipped the balance. The aggression melted away and Kitson went back to his command post in the hall followed by Wisher and the aid worker.

'Sorry about that,' Culverhouse offered, embarrassed by their behaviour.

'He's a low-life,' Wisher said. He too had been embarrassed, not for the first time by the behaviour of his countrymen abroad.

'Don't worry about it,' Kitson replied.

As Culverhouse walked away Wisher lingered. 'A word. Kreutz. He's gone has he?'

'A few minutes ago.' Kitson had seen his departure with some pleasure. He'd rather not be on the same continent as the unpleasant bullying American.

'Trying to put the pieces together. Bit difficult without my pix.'

'What?'

'Well, it just struck me. One of those chaps with him

292

was vaguely familiar. I thought I'd seen him round their compound. He could be an American, he could be an Ameri-Liberian, or he could be local.'

'One of the black guys?'

'Mmmm. If he was local . . .' Wisher began. 'There are lots of Liberians with American passports. Difficult to say. Any US passport holder would have as much right to the protection of their Embassy as any other. Thing is, I don't think he is a national. It's been busy lately, at both missions. The ConLib renegotiations have had loads of people in and out, but I think he is one of Taylor's people. One of the family.'

Kitson remembered there were two black men with Kreutz. 'The other?'

'Possible.'

'No wonder he wanted them out. They would be chopped to pieces immediately.'

'Altruism? I think not,' Wisher responded. 'Anyway, why aren't these people with Taylor? Why have they pissed off?'

'Could this be what this is all about? Because we are seen to be sheltering Taylor's family?' Kitson asked incredulously.

Wisher's expression said that nothing was impossible. 'Anyway, it's academic now. They are away.'

Kitson jerked a thumb back towards the others in the villa. 'Yeah. But these poor bastards aren't.'

The yeoman and Jones were now old hands at handling the heavy wooden lighter. Each time they came alongside they got better at it, Jones inching the big boat in so it gently kissed the foot of the cage, the rates in the cage hauling people over to them. There was fuel waiting this time, and food. The crew in the main galley had used their initiative: 150 rounds of bacon sandwiches wrapped in tinfoil for the lads ashore. Someone had rounded up empty bottles from the galley, washed them, and they were now

293

filled with water and sealed with the caps bashed back on. Five-gallon jerry cans of water were being lowered. Smart thinking, the yeoman thought. No one ashore has time to think of this shit. The lads and the civvies would be thirsty. They pushed off to make space for one of the seaboats and as they turned for shore and the blazing skyline, Jones bit into his sandwich.

'Bleeding bacon. I 'ate bacon,' he said, his mouth full.

'See that camera up there?' the yeoman said. 'We'll be on the telly, mate.'

''Eroes we are. Bleeding 'eroes,' Jones responded, his tone laced with irony. 'I just wanna be in me kip. I'm cream crackered. Trouble is, I won't have a kip. There'll be some friggin' civvie in there,' he moaned.

'Look on the bright side, Jonesy. It could be a bit of totty. Leaving her perfume all over your pillow.'

'Fat chance. I'd get some big smelly git.'

Tracer rounds streaked above them into the black sky and both instinctively ducked lower in the boat. 'Better get this fuel transferred,' the yeoman said. They were five minutes from the beach.

'Look at it,' Jones said miserably, his tone suggesting that it was always guys like him that got on the shit list, always was, always would be. 'It's like frigging Dunkirk!' He paused and then spoke again. 'Tell ya what, Yeo. I could murder a cuppa tea.'

One hundred and fifty yards from the villa Splif, the teenage Ulima fighter, was lying in some bushes watching the road and the wall. Behind that he knew that rich people, maybe even Americans, had lived. Bang-Bang was beside him, the others spread out in a rough line. There were many hundreds of the boys, thousands even. The fighting had been going on for hours now. They had been urged forward by a Ulima officer with promises of booty and rich pickings, but Splif had never had to fight like this before. Other fights, and there had been many, had been fast-moving attacks, soon over as one side or the other broke and ran. But this? The officer had come back several times, once with some food which was unusual. They normally had to find their own. The second time, before he had them attack for, was it the fifth time? he had given them dugees, the heroin-laced cigarettes. Plenty of them and Bang-Bang had been smoking constantly since then. He had taken a small cross and added it to the little surfboard and the ears he was already wearing round his neck.

They had lost four of their little gang, but others had arrived, one a big fellow almost eighteen years of age who the others said had killed many and had many women. He had been to school, too. He could read and write. But he didn't seem keen on what was ahead. He seemed tired of it all. Splif looked ahead again. The white soldiers were maybe a hundred paces away, round the corner. They were old, with uniforms, but they were brave. They didn't run. He would have, he thought. Any sensible person would, faced with this many of the boys. But they didn't. They were protecting something. Something of great value obviously. Wealth.

They had come here to fight NPFL and other Ulima fighters were doing that towards the east. But the officer had said this was better. They had seen a new top man too. Not Garlo, but another. Much younger. Strong. Powerful. He moved everywhere at a fast pace and others had to rush to keep up with him. His eyes looked wild, like he was smoking dugees, too. Someone signalled. They were moving up again. Bang-Bang was up and moving already, his machete in his hand, a crazy look in his eye.

Captain Bennett was on a walk around, stopping and talking to his crew wherever they were, chatting to groups of the evacuees. He worked steadily from one end of the ship to the other, starting on 2 deck, moving the length of the Burma Road, the main passageway that ran the length of the ship, dropping into the engine spaces and the Ops

295

room, encouraging, sharing jokes, bringing people up to date on the latest information, looking to keep morale high. On the helicopter deck he watched ratings carefully loading the four cut-down depth charge containers into the helo, the DMEO supervising things with the WEO and Lieutenant Mayberry. Chops(S) and Kate Wallace were there, already wearing life-jackets, and someone had drawn side-arms for them from the armoury: a heavy pistol in a webbing belt hung from Wallace's hip.

There was a pilot, a Tornado jockey, he had met during the Gulf war. His view on side-arms was that if as aircrew you get close enough to fire a handgun then it's all over. You are buggered. At best you are going to get the shit kicked out of you. But you might live. So don't antagonize anyone. Surrender. He didn't want to think about what would happen to the helo crew if it went in amongst that lot. He looked at his watch. It would be light in about an hour and a half. In any other theatre common sense and tactical wisdom said to move out of the gunline and back to sea, where defence systems would have time to assess and meet incoming threats in good time, but that would increase the transit time for the boats. His intent was to stay as close as he could for as long as he could.

He moved though the officers' flat, much of it now a medical area, the wardroom an operating theatre and some of the cabins given over to post-operative care. He looked in on the rating who had been bitten by the snake. The wound was ugly. The area of the bite, the little finger and the forward part of the heel of the hand, was black and swollen. The man had been knocked out with drugs and Dr Bujould had taken opinion from her other colleagues, all of whom had seen and treated many snakebites. The view was strong. The flesh reacting to the powerful haemo-toxic venom was necrotizing. Dying, poisoned. It would have to come off or further infection and septicaemia could become life-threatening. The US naval surgeon, his table clear, was preparing to operate.

He had sent his assistants, Poppy and the Marine medic, out for a break and a hot drink. The medic was in the officers' galley with the anaesthetist, but when Bennett got back up to his bridge he found Poppy and her sister out on the wing. He had made Mrs Black the offer in acknowledgement of her position as the Ambassador's wife: if she wanted a few minutes away from the throng, the quietest place on the ship was on the narrow deck than ran back from the bridge wing. Maggie had a cup of tea, but Poppy was making do with a cigarette. She was tired, but the surgeon was good, he communicated well and he was easy to work with. The tough part had been keeping her mind on the job and not thinking about the man she had just met. It was odd. It was like a first date. One had asked, the other has said yes with a smile. That was it, but it was more. She knew it. She felt it. Instant attraction. A friend of hers once described it as 'woof'. It was like being sixteen again. She felt at home here: it was silly, really, but with her gear in Peter's cabin and wearing his clothes she felt very close to him. If she couldn't be with him, then this was next best.

'Hello, ladies. How are we doing?' Commander Bennett asked. He was wearing his cap and, except for the dressing over his eye, looked as if this was just another working day for him.

'Fine, thanks. Tired. But feeling better every time a boat comes alongside,' Maggie answered. He knew what she meant. Each arrival was one nearer her husband joining her. One nearer the end. 'What time is first light?'

'Just before five-thirty,' he said.

'The dawn comes quickly here,' she said. 'One minute it's like pitch and the next it's daylight.' She turned from her position looking out over the rail. Over his shoulder, a mile away on the shore, she could see the fires raging and the occasional bright lines of tracer bursts. The cloud was pink, reflecting the glow from the fires. Earlier the whole city seemed ablaze but now it was dying out to the south-east, round the port and the commercial area. It was the enclave that burned, the sounds of gunfire reaching out to them.

'Are we going to manage it? Get them all away before daylight?' she asked.

'We have taken a hundred in the last fifty minutes. There's only another seventy-six civilians to go. Then my people come off and we put to sea.

A rating opened the bridge door. 'Sir?'

Bennett went to the Clansman. They had done it. Moved back through the smoke and still burning bush and gardens and got themselves back on to the beach south of the villa. They had themselves positioned well, out of sight from anyone up the beach but set up so they could fire to seaward at the boats.

Their fire had ripped into a seaboat running into the beach, rupturing the inflatable sidewalls. As the boat had wallowed to a halt in the water a second burst of sustained fire had hit the coxswain, killing him.

Kitson had called for fire support, whatever *Beaufort* could deliver. Bastards, Bennett thought. Fucking barbarians. They're killing my people.

'Ops, Captain.'

'Captain, Ops go.'

'Ops, get the helo up. Target is south of the villa and will be marked with illumination rounds. PWO to the port thirty mill.'

'Pilot, as soon as the cages are up a couple of feet, bring her in closer. Another quarter-mile. Bring her head round. I want to bring the port thirty mill to bear. They are in range. We can keep their heads down. Buffer?'

'Sir.'

'Get down to the weather deck. Everyone over to the starboard side.'

Morris reached for the main broadcast system microphone. *'Do you hear there? Any visitors out on the weather deck, that is outside, on the port side, that is the left-hand side of the ship, please move across to the starboard side immediately.*

298

Crew will show you where to go. Clear the port side weather deck. Hoist parties, port side cage up. All boats in to the starboard side. I say again, all boats in to the starboard side.'

Bennett walked across and took the microphone from him. *'WEO to the bridge.'*

As crew shepherded those civilians on the port side across the ship's waist and into the relative safety of the seaward bulkheads of the citadel, the Principal Warfare Officer was taking the stairs for the deck. The crew who had been closed up on the 30 millimetre anti-aircraft gun for hours, bored and restless, would now get to do what they had been trained for. On a heavy sponson above the weather deck, in fact the same sponson where the seaboat was hauled inboard, was a twin-barrelled cannon. Largely exposed and on a powered swivel, it was designed for close-in air defence, but old-fashioned in that it required a gunner looking through optical sights to track the target and fire the weapon. The ammunition feed was limited. Unlike the hopper-fed Gatling guns, or belt-fed weapons, this gun consumed shells from a clip and consequently, although fully automatic and rapid-firing, it used what was in the clip very quickly. Ordinarily that didn't matter, as attacking aircraft passed by very quickly and the chances of ever needing a sustained burst of more than thirty rounds in its air defence role were remote. Therefore keep it simple. Use a clip. Nothing to jam. As the PWO brushed past the civilians being herded across and took the ladder to the sponson he was wishing the gun was something else. All day he had been wishing they had optical sights on a close-in defence system like Phalanx. Its six-barrel Gatling gun, at this range, could have cleared the beach of hostiles in a four-second burst. But they didn't. This was it. Big, slow, but if they could sight on the target it would be devastatingly effective. He had no doubt about that: 30-millimetre cannon with exploding ammunition could destroy aircraft and tanks.

The ratings on the hoists reported in. The port hoist was

clear and raised six feet, the starboard side was up another two feet, total four feet over the waterline, enough to let *Beaufort* manoeuvre.

'Slow ahead both. Midships the wheel,' Morris said.

'Slow ahead both. Wheel amidships,' the duty quarter-master replied. The WEO entered the bridge.

'WEO, I want to bring both thirty mills to bear. Can we move the starboard cannon across to support the port side and how long will it take?'

The WEO, although stunned at the question, knew that his Captain was serious. He was rapidly thinking it through.

'Hours, sir. We'd have to jerry rig some mounts. We'd need to set up a hoist of some sort, lift it, cable it across, or alternatively dismantle it and rebuild it over there. There is an alternative,' he offered.

'What?'

'The weapons have a limit to their arc of fire. We could try and alter that so we can fire them straight down the side of the ship. Bows on, you could bring both cannons to bear on a target dead ahead, obviously with an area equal to the beam as a dead zone.'

'Risk?'

'High. One mistake and the bridge wing would get it for starters. We would jerry rig a frame. Weld something that prevents the gun turning any further inboard or raising its elevation.'

'See if it's possible. Make it happen.'

'It will still take at least an hour on each side. I'll need both of them shut down. You won't have either for the period we are trying it.'

'No. Start on the starboard side. If that works, then let me know. For now I need the port gun.'

On the helicopter deck Lieutenant Mayberry had his engines run up and was about to engage rotors. In the back, alongside the drums of explosives, Kate Wallace's heart was pounding. She had only been in a helicopter once, as familiarization during training, and certainly never operationally. The side doors had been taken off and out of each side she could see the dark sea. She looked nervously at the bulk of the Chief Petty Officer (Sonar) and he raised a thumb at her. This was it. She had asked to go, to get to have a crack at the bastards, the people who had killed her mate, and she suppressed her nerves. She felt the anger rise again and lifted a thumb back at him. Let's fucking do it, she was thinking, let's fucking do it! The rotors began to turn, gathering speed, and she looked forward. The pilot, Lieutenant Mayberry, was in flight suit, life-jacket and helmet, cocooned in his little world with his observer, the lights of the instruments a dull glow back into the cockpit. Before, he had just been an officer, a two-stripe like the others. All that made him different was that he was the Lynx pilot. Suddenly her life was in his hands. He wasn't just another officer. He was one of the four of them in this fragile, vibrating thing, the guy who would get them in and get them out, and she realized that she knew nothing about him and she wanted to. He looked back at her and smiled.

'You okay?' came through the headphones. She nodded, raising a thumb. He nodded back, looked to the front, put his hand down and then the sound changed and they were up, hovering carefully, seemingly going backwards as the ship moved away under them.

On the port 30 mill the PWO looked out with a pair of binoculars. 'See it? Right of the flames, there's a building on the beach front there. That's where the fire came from.'

'I see it, sir,' the gunner said.

'Right, wait for the confirmation by illumination round.'

Sitting in the seat the gunner was looking through the rectangular plexiglass sighting reticle. It had an egg-shaped etching marked out in black with gradient lines coming in to the centre and was designed for leading an attacking aircraft, but it would do fine. Ashore, one of the SBS men had ranged with HE and when he thought he was on the target he fired a flare.

'That's it! Gunner has target, sir!' he called.

'*Captain, PWO. We have target.*'

'*PWO, Captain. Engage!*'

'Fire six rounds!'

The gunner pressed the trigger and the cannons opened up, a very short burst, three rounds from each barrel. They saw the strikes. He was on target, the explosive heads slamming into the beach wall in front of the building.

'*Fire for effect!*'

The gunner pressed his trigger and traversed the gun, its twin barrels pumping out anti-aircraft rounds. He blew the low seaward garden wall and the front walls of the house to pieces.

The SBS man had five illumination rounds left and, with Kitson and Lieutenant Gordon beside him, he waited for the call from the inbound helicopter, now out to sea behind the *Beaufort* getting ready to make her attack run.

'One run, then she holds, yeah?' the SBS man confirmed.

'That's correct,' Gordon replied. 'We'll hold the other stuff she has till we need 'em.'

'Hope they bloody work,' the man said. He looked at the XO. 'How good's your P1?'

In the dark Kitson smiled. 'He's good. Not as good as me, but he's good.'

The revised plan was for the Lynx to come in fast from the sea and drop one bomb on to the Ulima position down the beach. Then she would head back out to sea and loiter, airborne and ready to be called back in for another run wherever they needed support.

'Put the round back from the building if you can,' Kitson said, his tone hard. 'The thirty should have sorted out those at the wall. I want the others.' On his command the positions on the southern side would increase their rate of fire to hopefully drown out the noise of the helo.

The Clansman hissed and a voice came through. *'Ten seconds. Fire it!'*

'Beaufort one to three and four. Open fire.'

Out to sea the Lynx was on her approach. She had gone wide further out, slowly gathering airspeed, done a gentle long turn as Mayberry got his bearings and was now coming in, 130 knots, 200 feet, his right hand on the control column, his left ready, resting on the cyclic ready to pour on what power they had left for the egress.

The drum was going to go out of the right-hand side door and had been moved across so it was within a foot of the door sill. Wallace would arm the fuse and the Chief would push it out through the doorway with both feet.

'Ready. Five . . . four . . .'

Kate Wallace's heart was pounding, her hands on the pin of the first phase detonator, the wind rushing through the cabin. The beach was racing towards them, the fires reaching up, palls of smoke everywhere and on the ground tracer rounds speared pools of dark. She imagined crashing, but not dying, surviving, and seeing them come at her with machetes. She was terrified.

'Three . . . two . . . wait for it.'

Mayberry was concentrating fiercely. Keeping the aircraft at exactly the right height, knowing that the moment he hit the beach the warmer air, heated by the land and the fires would lift the machine. He got ready to push the nose down, the target racing at him, the illumination round, bright, white-green against the orange flickers, lined up to disappear under his right foot.

'One . . . Let it go!' he shouted, hoping like hell that the man who had shot down the American Chinook was down there. Get some, you fucker!

Kate pulled the pin, the Chief just extended his legs, and the drum, seven kilograms of Torpex surrounded with iron filings, chunks of metal, every bit of shrapnel the engineering department could find, dropped towards the ground, falling forward, tumbling as it went.

He jinked right, power on, turning as fast as he could to get back out over the water, dropping for the deck to lessen anyone's chances of time for a shot.

The bomb went off. Spectacularly. The explosion, off target by seventy feet, airburst closer to the ground than they wished, but went off with a blast that had ears ringing in the villa almost two hundred yards away. It blew leaves from trees, took the roofs from two houses, the concussion wave shaking trees half a mile away. The shrapnel, blasting out 360 degrees, embedded itself in concrete and wood, ricocheted off steel and killed and maimed whatever living, breathing things it struck, including a chicken which had so far survived being snatched for the pot.

Watching from the villa Kitson and Gordon were momentarily stunned. It was a Royal Marine nearby who spoke.

'Fuckin' 'ell! We'll have a few more of those!' he muttered.

'Signal the boats,' Kitson said. He was looking for the Lynx, looking to see that they had got clear. An airburst that size that close was skoshey. Very skoshey.

On the ship those who had seen the blast had big grins on their faces but Bennett's expression was more one of relief. It had been dangerous. High risk. But it seemed to have paid off.

'Beaufort one, helo.'

'Helo, one actual. Hell of an entrance. Looks to be effective, over,' Kitson responded.

'Roger. Thanks one. I need a change of underpants, over.' Mayberry's voice light, the relief real and rich, the satisfaction of hitting back feeling good and in the back Kate Wallace was smiling for the first time.

The Marines were withdrawing, again reducing their perimeter. The seven Americans were now in the garden on the southern side. To withdraw without leaving cover and fighting positions close to them they went with scorched earth, throwing incendiary devices into the three deserted houses. The fires caught and from now on for the next hours the heat and the smoke would prevent anyone using them to attack the old Italian villa. The Royals to the east and the north were moving back from their positions in the next few minutes. Men already there were cutting loopholes in the walls and Lieutenant Gordon and his sergeant had set out new positions with converging arcs of fire.

Conway and Buchanan, with their smaller reaction teams of armed ratings, were at the back wall helping the two Marines making the loopholes. As they withdrew the defensive line tightened and Gordon's command would all be inside the garden walls of the villa, close enough to shout to, to reinforce, close to the beach for the eventual withdrawal.

Suddenly a burst of fire raked their front. They dropped into cover behind the wall. The fire had come from the right, into the garden of the house behind the villa, the top corner above where the fires burned, between them and the handful of Marines who still manned the eastern wall facing back inland towards the Embassy compound.

'They're in!' Buchanan shouted. He was thinking quickly. They had breached the line. If they got themselves dug in there, had time to settle in and work forward, anything could happen.

'If they hold there we're in trouble,' he shouted. Two of the ratings and the pair of Marines had stopped digging loopholes and were shooting back.

'What do we do?' Conway asked.

'Counter-attack. We can't wait for the others.' He grabbed one of the Marines. 'We have to get them out of there. Hit 'em before they consolidate.'

The Marine shook his head. 'Wait for a section weapon, sir.'

But Buchanan was on his feet and moving, Godshall and Willard on his heels, down the wall to the corner. It entered his mind that that was where the snakes were, over the wall at that point, but it didn't seem to matter.

'Bastard sailors!' the Marine snapped in defeat. 'You!' he pointed at one of the ratings. 'Fuck off over to the lads there. Get one back here with a couple of LAWs and a Gimpy, right? LAWs and a Gimpy.' He looked down at his mate and pulled him to his feet. 'Come on, Bof.'

They went over the wall, one of the Marines laying down a withering rate of suppression fire and then following. The Marine pulled Buchanan back bodily, took the front over the twenty metres, his mate's fire ripping past them just feet to the left, and dropped prone, his weapon coming up as he did so. They were piling over the wall in the far corner, dropping into the cover of a garden shed, and he opened fire, pouring his rounds into it, knowing they would pass through the sheet metal and wooden planking like paper. The sailors dropped down beside him, bullets flying back at them, and the second Marine arrived and ran past, dropping down in front of them. Suddenly they were in the thick of it. Figures burst from the back of the shed, the volume of fire incredible, but much of it going upwards. One, lithe, young, came at them with nothing but a machete in his hands. Godshall, his magazine empty, rolled up to meet him and took the blow on his rifle and they fell to the ground, wrestling, fighting hand to hand. He blinded the fighter, driving his fingers into his eyeballs, gouging for the brain, and then, scrabbling in the dark, his hand found the man's machete and he finished him with it. He saw Buchanan go down, and waded in, swinging the heavy bladed weapon like a beserker. Baker beat a man back with his rifle butt and then got a mag in. The fighting was vicious, but the tide turned when Corporal Doughty and three of his section arrived. Their firepower made the difference and as the running attack faltered momentarily, his men pounced on those still in their position. The hand to hand was over quickly. No chivalry. No mercy. It was two to one, the Marines giving no quarter, using automatic weapons at inch range and fighting knives when there was risk of hurting a comrade. They closed up before the fighters could regather, but they were still coming over the wall.

'Pull back!' he yelled. 'Move!'

They withdrew to the wall, carrying their wounded, clambering over it in the dark under the supporting gunfire from the new loopholes, where a section weapon had opened up.

Baker was kneeling over Buchanan, his hands over the officer's wounds, trying to staunch the blood that seemed to be everywhere. Some of it was his own, he knew, but not this much.

'Get the medic, please. Medic!' He looked up suddenly. 'Willard?' he shouted, his voice breaking, tension, fear, adrenalin all there. 'Where's fucking Willard?'

Doughty didn't hesitate. He jammed a fresh magazine in his weapon and went back over the wall into the killing ground, the scene lit by fires and muzzle-flash. Godshall went to follow, but he was pulled back as Doughty's section poured fire in around him and soon Doughty was running back, Willard over his shoulder. Chops was there to take him, strong hands pulling them both back over the wall. A Marine down the line threw grenades and someone let loose with a LAW rocket. As always it was the queen of the infantry battle that made the difference. The withering fire laid down by the GPMG stalled the attack and when it faded there were many dead and dying out beyond the low wall, some of the forms lithe, youthful. No more than boys.

Chops had been round his lads, issued ammunition and was now sitting, his back to the wall, smoking a cigarette, the first in twenty years. He took a drag and looked at the exhausted man next to him, one of the Marines. He offered him the cigarette and the young Marine took it and inhaled deeply once or twice and passed it back. Nothing was said.

'Who was hit?' one of the ratings further down asked.

'Dave Willard's dead. Lieutenant Buchanan is back there

with half his chest gone. Kevin got something. A cut or something. He's okay.'

The man said nothing, the anger, the frustration building, thinking about these people they were fighting. They rampaged through the countryside, killing each other, hacked women and children to death, mutilated others. Fucking animals. Finally he sighted on one of the moving wounded out in the dark and fired twice. The figure shuddered and then lay still. No one stopped him. They all felt the same.

Godshall had something in his hand. He had ripped it from the neck of the fighter he had killed and somehow it had got caught in his kit. He looked down at it. A tiny red surfboard, complete with a skeg. He threw it away and looked down at his weapon, and began to clean dirt from the action. His shirt was gone, ripped away in the fighting, and in the flickering light from the fires the huge eagle tattoo was visible across his back. He had found chest webbing somewhere, taken it from the dead, and the bird was framed by the webbing straps. A few feet from him was Culverhouse, his shotgun in his hand. One of the SBS men had given him cartridges, SG shot, and he had been there in the awful mêlée at the end.

'How many of you lot left, then?' a sailor asked him. Chops turned round to listen, in case the rating was going to say something, blame this civilian by proxy for all of them, blame them for being in this poxy fucking shithole that had cost them so dearly.

'Dunno. Twelve or fifteen, maybe.'

The sailor, a PO, looked at him. 'You best be off then, son.'

'I'll stay.'

'Bollocks. Take your turn. Get yourself down the beach.'

Culverhouse smiled sadly. His turn had come up hours ago. He looked round what remained of Conway's little reaction team.

'Thanks eh . . . all of you. For everything.'

He looked at them and fished round in his pocket, taking

out three cartridges. He held out his shotgun. 'There's four in the mag and these. Take it. You might need it.'

The PO took the shotgun.

Lieutenant Gordon and Lieutenant Commander Kitson were appraising the situation. It was not good. Their luck had turned. The two Marines holding the eastern perimeter position had fallen back, both wounded, one seriously. Willard had died of his wounds in the seconds after Doughty got him back. Baker was wounded in the back, high up almost on his shoulder, a machete slash that had thankfully been turned by a webbing strap. Perhaps because he couldn't see it, perhaps because in relative terms it was slight, or for some other reason, he told Chalky to whack a dressing on it and went back to the wall, his countenance stolid.

Lieutenant Buchanan was laid out with the critically wounded Royal Marine, the American medic kneeling between them.

'Get on to the ship,' he said to Kitson. 'I need medivac asap. Get one of the doctors on a seaboat in to care for them on the way back out. Advise the surgeon. We have two.' He stopped talking to strip the cover from a saline drip needle with his teeth. 'Abdominals. One with a sucking chest wound. They're gonna need blood. Plenty of it.'

Conway was there. She looked at him. 'What can I do?'

He ignored her and kept working.

'Alabama?'

He looked up at her and down at Buchanan and shook his head imperceptibly. 'I've hit him with morphine. Hold his hand,' he replied softly. 'Talk to him. No time for a man to be alone.'

She took his hand and ran the other over his brow. A few moments later he opened his eyes and finally focused on her.

'Ha,' he said weakly. 'We la . . . in the face of danger.' It came out as a whisper, hoarse. 'Tex might get the skank after all.' He coughed and spat blood. The rating standing above holding the drip looked away. He was twenty years old and he had aged immeasurably in the last twenty-four hours, but he still didn't know what to do, what to say. He was embarrassed.

'Shhh, Jamie,' she said gently, like a mother talking to her child. 'You hang on now. We're going to get you back to the Beau.'

'I'll be all right. It doesn't hurt.' But his voice was changing. There was a quiver to it. 'I've been shot, Bob.'

'I know,' she said. 'Shhh. Don't talk. It's going to be okay. You're going to be fine.' Don't cry, she was saying to herself, don't let him see you cry. Get a grip of yourself. A few minutes later he managed a weak smile and spoke again. 'I'm tired,' he said softly.

He closed his eyes and she brushed his brow gently.

The medic looked across. 'Don't let him sleep.' He turned round, leaned over Buchanan. 'Stay with me, Lieutenant! Don't you go nowhere, now.' He tapped Buchanan's cheek. 'Stay with me, bro'. You fight this, man, you gotta wanna live! Hey!' He looked down at the chest, covered in a sealed plastic dressing. 'Nooo shit.' It wasn't rising. He reached for the neck to find a pulse. 'Yo, bro'! Come back now. You hear me! Don't you fuckin' die on me.'

There was no pulse. 'Shit!'

He turned back to the other patient, pulling off his thick issue spectacles and wiping the lenses, getting back to work.

This can't be it, she thought. Not this fast, not here, not now. Oh Jesus, no, please, not Jamie. Please God, he is my friend, my shipmate.

'He's dead,' the medic said, without looking back. 'I'm sorry.'

Oh Jamie, she thought, why you? She stood up, wiping her eyes, and picked up her rifle.

Aubrey Montagu was there as she came out. He had been fighting with his lads on the northern side and had just heard. He didn't have to ask. Her face said it all.

*   *   *

On the *Beaufort* the activity was feverish, the discipline and training holding the crew at a pace that would to observers seem like overdrive. It was with the stalwarts of the Petty Officers' mess that the strength lay, as it had always done. The boats were coming in on the starboard side, lining up, taking turns to unload. The ship was crowded now, bursting at the seams.

'*Do you hear there? Wounded coming aboard. All personnel with blood groups O or AB positive report to the sick bay at the double. I say again, all personnel with blood groups O or AB positive report to the sick bay at the double. Port watch to report first.*'

Crew, all of whom knew their blood groups, began leaving their action stations and moving down to the sick bay where the medical team had tipped out what equipment they had to begin taking blood.

People on the weather deck huddled in the lee of the citadel facing to seawards, not by choice but because, with the ship at action stations, all the operational departments were cleared to let her crew do their jobs.

Weapons artificers were working on the starboard 30 mill. They had completely removed the governor to allow the gun to traverse further inboard and the WEO and Tex, the DMEO, had a team welding a frame to prevent the gun traversing far enough to blow the bridge wing to pieces, or fire into the superstructure. The extended arc of fire would give them an extra thirteen degrees of turn.

Bennett put the radio handset down.

'Buffer. Find Mr Denny. Lieutenant Buchanan has been killed and I'm sorry to have to tell you, but Dave Willard was as well. I know you were mates. I am sorry. They are on a boat that is coming out. Ask Mr Denny if he would be so kind as to get a side party there to receive them, please.'

'It's not that simple,' Wisher said. There were just nine of them left now. HMA, the Embassy staff, young

Culverhouse. They were all in the loop, so Kitson didn't keep his voice down.

'Bullshit. There's too many dead. They are still coming. Why? What the hell are they after? My people are dying. Well not any more! Not on my watch! Find out what the fuck it is they are after and let's give it to them!'

He looked at his watch. It was 0450. Daylight in half an hour, he thought. Then we are fucked.

'Sir,' the rating at the radio called. 'Seaboats under fire.'

11

'Suspend seaboat ops,' Kitson said. He looked at the last handful, what would be the last boatload of civilians. Her Majesty's Ambassador William Black, Aitcheson, Tony Wisher, Ambassador Alberry from the US mission and Charles Davis, his number two, and young Culverhouse. The two ambassadors, both old-school in their thinking, had refused point blank to leave ahead of any of their countrymen.

'Sorry, gentlemen. It will be a while longer.' He crossed the few feet to the radio and squatted down beside the rating who handed him the handset. He asked for Mayberry, loitering in the Lynx, to be tasked.

'*One, he's ready. Which side, over?*' This was Bennett himself.

'*Not sure, Beaufort. We don't have time to recce. Suggest he covers all three on this run, over.*'

Kitson called Montagu, Conway and Gordon in and advised his intent, speaking loudly to be heard over the close gunfire.

'The moment he is finished I want that seaboat back in for the last group. Then all the boats in together. Cram them in. Stick twenty in Jones's lighter. I want forty men out in that first trip. Right?'

They all nodded.

'Then three fast Zodiacs come back in for the last twenty. As those twenty are withdrawing I will call in NGS. They only have seven HE left, so that must be to cover the withdrawal as the last men leave the walls. Any way we can slow their advance through the garden?'

'Possibly. I have a couple of chaps on that already,' Gordon replied.

'Good,' Kitson responded. 'No one and nothing left behind. Let's sort out who goes in the first bunch.'

'Your sailors,' Gordon said. 'Then the American lads. My people go off last.' He wanted a small, cohesive unit, highly disciplined, all trained the same way, with predictable behaviours. Of the people left, the ones best equipped to survive a fighting retreat were his lads. His recce troop, a composite of men from 45 Commando and the Special Boat Service: there wasn't a better 29-man formation in the fleet. In any case, he knew that all of them would have been most uncomfortable about getting into a boat as long as there was one sailor left ashore. Embarrassed even.

Kitson nodded with a bleak smile. Royal Marines. It was what Royal Marines did. First in, last out. Three hundred-odd years of ingrained tradition. The esprit de corps.

'Fair enough.'

Splif lay where he had fallen after running back out of the garden. He was hurt, he knew that. Blood was running down his face and it was in his eyes and he was also bleeding from a wound in the leg. He was still confused, but thought it must have been the grenades. He knew Bang-Bang was dead. He knew all the others were dead. As they dropped down the wall, he had ran forward but fallen over. Stoned on the dugee smokes, he had tripped, his own flip-flop catching on something. Everything happened so fast. He saw Bang-Bang drop his rifle and run in with his machete. Fearless Bang-Bang, the heroin and gunpowder scrapings racing through his blood, running in with his machete. He thought he was immortal, the amulets and charms protecting him. He wasn't. One of the whites killed him with his own machete. He had seen it in the glare of the flames and the flashes.

Money, they had said. Plenty of money. Enough for a car. These people had money. But they fought. They fought like no one he had ever fought before. Someone always ran, always saw the fight going against them and broke. That was the way it should be. He looked over to the fires glowing in the east. There, out there for ten miles across the city, was Ulima. Thousands of them. Why hadn't the whites run away or given up? They were only a small band by comparison. He had never seen such aggression, such courage. They had fought like men possessed by demons. Perhaps they had magic. He was confused. Wounded. Missing his friends. He was frightened. Someone moving up looked down at him where he lay and walked on. He clutched his weapon tightly. If they thought he was dead they would take it. He wished someone would stop and help him. He felt like crying, but had forgotten how.

Kate Wallace eased the strap round her waist and watched as the Chief pushed one of the bombs towards the door. He eased it into position and then pushed a second and then the third into place. They could be heaved out as necessary. He ran a strop round each, secured them with a quick-release knot and raised a thumb at Mayberry.

In the front he put power on and dipped the disc forward and they began to gather pace. This was going to be the hairy one. Three sides. Long looping turn, there was no way you could make it short at 130 knots in a rotary wing and keep up the air speed needed for the next drop.

The ship was looming up. Darkened down, the only illumination came from the muzzle-blast of something on the port side and on the starboard side, the seaward side, the blue-white light of what looked like arc welding. The other side he knew was the 30 millimetre cannon, the flash a full ten feet long each time one of its rounds left the barrels.

He could see the strikes ashore, bright flashes as the gunner raked the trees above the beach.

'Stand by. There's the illumination,' he said. 'Wait for it . . .'

The Chief pulled the strop of the first bomb and put his

feet against it; Wallace reached out and took the detonator pin in her hand. The split pin had been greased so there would be no resistance. The Chief's face was intense. The grin from the first run was gone now. They were frightened, both of them.

'Three . . . two . . . one. Leggo!'

He pushed the drum and it dropped from the door and as the helo swung east to begin its turn he got ready to slip the knot on the second bomb. There was a massive blast and a flash of light from behind them and he got a fleeting, lopsided half-smile from Wallace. Tracer raced up in front of them and, the turn complete, Mayberry stabilized the machine into straight and level, flying through smoke now.

'Target obscured,' from the observer. Dry-mouthed, but there.

'Get ready,' Mayberry said to the two in the back. 'Viz is shit. Can't see anything . . .' Down there somewhere in those flames and smoke was the second illumination flare, but he couldn't see it. Mixed blessing, he thought. They can't see us either. There! Blue-white in the orange! He lined up fractionally.

'There. Got it . . . two . . . one . . . Leggo!'

Into the turn, small-arms strikes on the fuselage, three thumps, the blast from behind them, close this time, the machine lifting with the concussion waves, settling, his heart pounding in his chest, checking the gauges and instruments, no warning lights, maintain height, long curving turn, there the flames again, more tracer rounds coming up. 'I have illumination. One o'clock,' from the observer. Where? There, see it. One then two. He lined up and as they went over it the bomb dropped from the side door and they ran for the sea.

It didn't go off.

'Port 30 mill target left side of the villa.'

They had four ratings doing nothing but lugging rounds

up to the gun now. The barrels would overheat soon, but Bennett didn't care. As long as they lasted long enough to suppress any enemy activity – he thought of them as the enemy, now, along that strip of the beach – then his boats could get in. Had the last bomb gone off it would have cleared them, but it hadn't.

'Pilot, can you get me in closer?' Bennett asked quickly.

'Shelves well, sir. I can get you to within six hundred yards of the surf line.'

'No. Make it four hundred.'

'I don't advise it, sir.'

'Noted. Nevertheless, make it four hundred yards, Mr Morris.'

'Aye aye, sir.'

'Seaboats are going in, sir.'

'Very good,' he replied. They deserve awards for this, he thought. The bravery this night. His lads. His ship. He was so proud of them.

'Gentlemen, I hope you don't mind but I want to get Buchanan and Willard back out to the ship,' Kitson said. 'They will be travelling in the same boat.'

Black was about to respond, but it was Alberry who got in first. 'We'd be honoured,' he replied.

'Let's go then.'

He led them down the sandy path to the gate, all of them crouched down low, and straight on to the sand. The first boat was nudging its way in, the coxswain with some considerable experience now, lying low in the scuppers, just his head peeping over the raised central driving position. Two rates bundled the men into the boat and another four men carried the bodies of Buchanan and Willard.

The bows were turned and the boat headed seawards, the coxswain finding the best power setting to get them away as fast as possible in the last minutes of darkness without creating a lovely white bow wave or phosphorescence in the water to betray their position.

The inflatable passed Jones and the yeoman heading ashore in the lighter, its inboard engine noisy by comparison. The last two Zodiacs were two minutes behind them.

C'mon, Kitson thought. We have a window, but not for long. There was a lull in the incoming fire. *Beaufort*'s 30 mill was still raking the bush on the right every now and then, but behind them and to the left the airburst bombs had done the trick. Anyone still out there was not wanting to draw attention to themselves. Ratings in small groups were moving towards the beach gate doubled over, past two Royal Marines who were laying booby traps along the rear and side walls of the villa. One was daubing words on the walls telling all comers that this was now a minefield. There were no mines, they didn't have any, but if it slowed the opposition down it would work. The same with the booby traps. The first to go off would have everyone in the area moving forward very slowly indeed, hopefully slowly enough to let the last boat get clear before anyone could set up fire from the villa.

The ratings carried their weapons, but had handed any full magazines over to the Marine lads staying till the last trip. The sun was almost up.

Conway darted into the villa to make sure it was clear. She flashed her torch round, checking each room. A familiar flash of colour caught her eye and she swung the torch back. There was a *Beaufort* zap on the wall and then another. She couldn't resist the smile that crossed her face, remembering the incident in London. It seemed a thousand years ago. Underneath the zap someone had scrawled 'Zulu 45 wuz 'ere.' Another said, 'Thanks for making my day', and it was signed RECCE TROOP.

Gordon had made his decision. There was only room for twenty in the last trip and he told Doughty to get his section ready to move. They would be in the last seaboat in the first wave. The tough little corporal began to plead his case, but Gordon moved away down the wall hunched over out of sight. The sergeant looked at him. 'Get on with it. Leave one Gimpy and go.'

Doughty, pissed off to be sent back to the ship, as he saw it, rounded up his exhausted lads and, lugging their second machine gun and four LAW rockets, they made for the last boat that was approaching. Fire was beginning to reach out from the shore.

They had done this a hundred times in training and the boat barely stopped. As it moved away two of the Marines were setting up the gun in the stern and began to return fire from less than a hundred yards away. The fire from the shore stopped abruptly and then started from a different position.

Further out, on the lighter crammed with ratings, the yeoman, clambering forward to do something, was hit. A bullet, flattened out, jagged and bouncing over the water hit him full in the neck. He fell forward on to his shipmates.

Chalky White caught him. 'Christ, Yeo! Ya great lump!' and then he saw the blood. 'He's hit.'

Conway and Chops clambered over others to get to him, looking for breathing, feeling for a pulse, Chops holding him like a child. Jones, kneeling at the stern steering the boat, shouted out to them to help him, but they were doing all they could. He knew the seaward side cage and weather deck would be crowded, so he came into the port side, rates leaping to man the davit winch to lower the port cage to water level. When they came alongside, under the noise and fury of the 30 millimetre cannon, the yeoman was the first into the cage and it was hoisted up. Jones, visibly upset, watched as his mate was carried away.

By the time Doughty's boat came in, that coxswain also opted for the port side. The odd bullet was hitting the ship, but the threat seemed limited after what they had been through.

The filthy, tired Marines, many with light wounds, their uniforms crusted in blood, sweat and dirt, piled out into the cage and the nearest raft. The lighter bobbing a few feet away was lashed to a line running back from the big life-raft that was still moored alongside, Jones still in it, and the much faster seaboat turned around it and headed back for the beach for the last pick-up. Doughty looked back at the beach, his first real view of it. The sky was pink. It was dawn. Full daylight in the next few minutes. Smoke rose up into the sky, and fires still burned for what seemed like miles. The only fighting seemed to be going on at the villa. It seemed the rest of the city had rolled over and given in. It would be carnage in there, he realized. Anyone caught in the middle of the two fighting forces as they had been would have been wiped out to a man if they hadn't dug in somewhere. The word was that the American Marines had arrived in Sierra Leone ready for tactical deployment by parachute. To his right and high above him, the 30 mill was pounding the shore, the sound almost deafening. Someone passed him a bottle of water, one of the ones they had been given ashore. He drank.

Down in the lighter Jones heard his radio go, and lifted it to hear better over the sound of the gun.

'*Beaufort Beaufort, seaboats under fire. Request immediate NGS. Two HE either side.*'

The Marines were ready to pull back. They still had guns in place, and the retreat of the men manning those would be covered by three other guns set nearer the beach. The boats had started taking fire, the nearest was hit. The fuel tank ruptured and the rating at the helm knew better than to stay with it and try and run it. He went over the side into the shallow water as more bullets hit the rigid hull and finally the whole aft section around the outboard burst into flames.

'*Gun bay, Ops.*'

'*Ops, gun bay.*'

'*Gun bay, load HE. Seven rounds.*'

'*Gun ready!*'

Out at the *Beaufort*, Jones saw the flames reach up. Without comment he darted forward and slipped the lighter's bowline. He moved back and as he was bending over to start the engine, Doughty crossed over from the raft where he had moved to let the cage go up. He was still humping his section's machine gun.

'Wait,' he said, then looking up, 'Oi! The LAWs!' he yelled. One of the lads already up on the deck dropped them to him, one by one, three of them, and from the corner of his eye Jones could see some else coming down a rope hand over hand. Tommy Godshall.

Doughty grinned. He had seen the sailor fight. He would do. Above them the main turret suddenly turned and the barrel dipped. It would be firing at point blank range.

Jones hit the throttle and without command or approval the three of them headed back for the beach, the lighter's engine running at full power for the first time. It didn't matter how much noise they made now. It was virtually daylight.

Lieutenant Commander Denny took the vertical ladder to the port TDS, the local area sight for the main gun, three at a time. He ran across to where the rating sat in the seat, peering through the sight. Breathing heavily, he lifted his binoculars and looked at the edge of the beach and the flat white villa.

'Listen carefully. Two rounds each side of the villa. We're way too close to drop them so it's point blank. On the left go for the road, first round fifty yards up by the burnt tree, then next left again by about fifty yards. Then straight away traverse the gun right and hit the garden between the houses on the other side right. We need to hit whoever is firing on the seaboats. Can you try and do that for me?' The rating nodded grimly.

Chops(M) on the other side of the ship was none the wiser. He had moved forward into the officers' flat to see how the yeoman was doing. The door to the wardroom was closed and civvies, medically trained people, moved round the area like they knew what they were doing. He walked away and as he came out of the heavy door on to the weather deck the main gun began to fire, an awesome whiplash blast that made the ears ring.

Two of Doughty's Marines ran forward up the weather deck to where a rating stood over the one light weapon that the ship had, a GPMG fixed to the rail with a G-clamp. The rating was moved bodily away.

'Oi, that's my job,' he protested.

'Fuck off.' One Marine cranked out the sights to their maximum, peered down the barrel and began to fire, short, measured bursts. The bullets would accurately travel the distance, no problem, but actually seeing something to specifically aim at was the issue.

The rating looked round. Chops(M) was suddenly there.

'They told me to fuck off,' he protested.

'Well fuck off, then,' Chops replied. 'Get the biggest pair of binoculars you can find and get back here at the double. Move it!'

Thirty seconds later he was back and Chops handed the other Marine the glasses. 'You'll need these.'

Either side of the machine gun other Marines were lying prone on the deck firing at the shore line.

Lieutenant Conway appeared, looking towards the beach and the old wooden boat that was powering its way in towards the besieged men. Her blonde hair was matted and filthy, her uniform crusted with dirt and blood, the bandage on her hand brown with the dirt of Liberia. She looked at Chops. 'What about the old bloke with the scope thingy on his gun?' Chops nodded and disappeared. She looked at one of the other marines. 'Got any more of those rockets?'

'Yes, ma'am.'

'You get 'em. Quick as you can. We'll take them up to the bridge wing. Okay?'

Gordon and Kitson were down at the garden gate. The last surviving inflatable was loaded and running out as they ducked for cover. One of the Marines had been hit in the legs as they loaded, the bullets coming from somewhere very close.

'Incoming!' Gordon yelled. This would be close, too. Terminal if the rate on the TDS screwed up, Kitson thought. There was a massive blast off to his right and then a second. He looked out and saw the Beau and felt something below the fear and the fatigue. Immense pride. She was in close, dangerously close to the beach, engaging with every gun she could bring to bear. Her 30 mill cannon roaring, a GPMG firing, other small arms, and as he watched the 4.5-inch main gun fired again. It recoiled, the barrel slamming back into the automated turret, a belch of smoke and then the sound reaching them. Either side of them it was a Dantean inferno, smoke and explosions, blackened burnt-out buildings and vegetation, the destruction of war.

He could see the lighter shouldering her way in towards them, a machine gun set up in her bows firing at something to their left. He looked back at Gordon's lads. There were fourteen of them still on the beach. Royal Marines were still deployed on the wall, four at the back and four on each side, their rate of fire constant. The lighter was closer. Plenty big enough for all of them. He could see the faces of the men crewing it. Jones kneeling in the stern. Godshall. A Marine. You ballsy brave wonderful bastards! 'Thirty seconds,' he said to Gordon. 'Last chance! Call your lads back in thirty seconds from now.'

Sarah Conway burst up the steps to the bridge, two Marines hard on her heels, lugging LAW rockets that banged against things as they moved. When Doughty had left Gibraltar thinking he was 'well tooled up' he was right.

'Permission to enter the bridge,' she called instinctively. She ran straight past the navigator's station and out of the port bridge wing door, the two Royal Marines after her. Bennett followed.

'Up there.' She pointed, jerking a thumb at the top of

the superstructure. She went to link her fingers, but with the bandaged hand it wouldn't work. The Marine looked at her, offering her wounded hand to help him climb. Silly tart, he thought, a rush of affection filling him. He did the lift, then boosted her on to the roof, passed up the five rockets and then clambered up himself. Ten seconds later they were kneeling on the bridge roof, the two Marines preparing the LAW rockets, Conway looking at the beach through her binoculars, her heart pounding. The lighter was almost there and under fire. One Marine slipped the tubes, extending the rocket's one-use launcher ready for action, while the other lifted the first to his shoulder and sighted. With its 500-metre range they were all right. Just.

'Wait till they run for the boat,' Conway called. 'Then go for it.' A couple of bullets smacked into the superstructure below them, but were ignored.

'Ready?' she asked.

'Ready!'

The lighter in the shallows began to turn, Doughty swinging his gun barrel to bear as it did so, Godshall firing the way he had been trained to, never more than two shots, picking his targets.

'Let's go!' Gordon yelled. 'Everyone move!'

'*Beaufort, NGS on my position. Fire!*' Kitson grabbed the Clansman and ran for the boat as fast as he could. Either side of him the Royal Marines were falling back, leap-frogging each other and fire from the ship was intense. His feet hit the water and he waded, to shouted words of encouragement from Jones. Men were piling into the boat on both sides and a strong arm reached down and grabbed the radio from him, the gunwale rising with the swell, bullets hitting the water round them, thumping into the thick wooden planking of the hull, splinters and chips flying off.

Something seared past his head, a flash of yellow white. A rocket, he realized. With it came the last of the main gun shells. At point-blank range they fell exactly where they were aimed and going off no more than forty yards away the sound was deafening, clods of earth and bits of brick and concrete showering down on them. One each side in the villa's own garden and the last straight into the villa itself. He pulled himself over the side and fell into the thwarts, on to a tangle of legs and kit and belt ammunition. Someone pulled him up and as he sat up he saw the last of the Marines retreating, it was the SBS men, moving backwards, covering each other as they waded to the boat. A gun thumped down beside him and began to fire and something else whooshed overhead. Doughty had handed over his gun and was extending one of the tubes he had been humping all night, others helping to get guns up on the side or shooting back with their rifles, the activity frenzied. Gordon came in over the side and at the front Doughty stood up and let fly with a LAW rocket. It hit the side wall of the garden where fighters, visible in the early light, were piling over. The high explosive head went off on impact and men fell with bits of breeze block and stone and leaves from the frangipani. Behind Kitson someone fell and then another. The last of them were in. Two more rockets came from the ship, searing past them, and with the 30 mill keeping heads down, Jones hit the throttle. Everyone except those with room to return fire at the shore, got down low in the scuppers.

As they moved into the lee of the ship one Marine, one of the men who had been hit and was holding his hand over the wound high on his thigh, looked at Kitson and punched the air with his other hand. He had a grin all over his face. Gordon was equally elated. He too looked at Kitson.

'That,' he said, 'was hairy.'

Jones, standing above them, conning the old boat into the cage, looked down at them.

'Hairy? I bloody near shat myself,' he said. 'I could murder a cup of tea.'

*　　*　　*

The weather deck on the seaward side was crowded with people. As the cage came up Chops(M) moved forward through the throng.

'Make way,' he growled. 'Royal Marines coming aboard.'

Oddly to those who knew him it seemed he said it with some pride, but then those who knew him, knew what he thought of Royal Marines, the same as he did of Pompey football club, thought no. No way.

A few who had been ashore in the last hours understood.

Jones called something to the coxswain of the last inflatable, who was preparing strops so the boat could be lifted inboard.

'Leave it,' someone called.

'Piss off,' he replied. 'It's someone's livelihood.' He looked at it fondly. 'Did us proud, it did.' He pushed off, rounded the stern of the *Beaufort* and then, after setting the throttle on the old lighter and lashing the tiller, he pointed it towards the beach where they had stolen it and set it running, jumping across to the seaboat as it moved off.

'Everyone aboard?'

'Yes, sir. XO is coming up now. Seaboat is inboard.'

'Ours or theirs?'

'Theirs, sir.'

Bennett grimaced. They had had six boats at one stage. Five of them were out there, sunk or tattered floating debris.

'Get the cages up. Secure for sea.'

Kitson stepped on to the bridge. He was filthy, exhausted, his eyes grainy.

Bennett smiled at him. 'Well done.' He looked back across the bridge. 'Mr Morris. In the log please. All civilians aboard and XO, shore party and Marines back aboard at 0537.'

Morris gave his orders and as the *Beaufort* turned and made her way seawards Bennett sat silent. Down on the weather deck they were jettisoning the cages they had built, cutting lines to the rafts dropped by the Nimrod that had been so useful. The deck party reported cages and rafts gone.

Kitson looked at his Captain, who was writing out a signal. Bennett nodded and looked back at his pad, ripping the pages off and handing them to a rating for transmission to Northwood via the circling AWACS Boeing overhead.

'Lieutenant Morris,' Kitson called.

'Sir.'

'A course to get us away from this dreadful bloody place.'

'Two-seventy degrees.'

'Up on the gas,' Kitson ordered, with some satisfaction in his voice. 'One-thirty on both. Steer two seven zero.'

The QM repeated the order, it seemed with equal satisfaction. Kitson moved out on to the bridge wing and watched the land fall away behind them. A rating came out, a fellow who normally worked in the officers' galley, a tray of mugs in his hands. Kitson wordlessly took one, as did Sarah Conway. Usually no food or drink was allowed outside the messes or wardroom, but this was an exception.

'Breakfast in half an hour in the Captain's day room, sirs.' Kitson nodded, patting his pockets. The rating reaching into his own pocket, took out his cigarettes and passed the packet to him. 'Hang on to 'em, sir. I got plenty below.'

'Thanks.'

The two officers silently sipped their drinks, leaning against the rail, Sarah Conway looking out to sea, letting the wind blow through her hair, blow out the dust and with it the smell of cordite and blood and fear and death. The next to arrive was Mayberry, still in his flight suit, the sweat stains under his arms discolouring the fabric. Orbs Montagu was last. Kitson looked over as he stepped out of the bridge and realized how little he had seen of the young Lieutenant in the rage and the dying of the night before. On the bridge Morris wanted to come out and chat, but he knew better. Better to leave them to it, to come to terms with what they had been through in the last twenty-four hours.

No one said anything. But they were all thinking about him, and felt him there with them. None of them wanted to think about where he really was, in a couple of black bin liners down in the fridge. Dead, but very much part of the kinship and closer to this small band than any who had fought from the ship. Kitson was suddenly aware of the division and knew it must be put to bed the moment they had the wardroom back. Get everyone shit-faced pissed, push Jamie Buchanan over to Valhalla the warrior's way and move on.

On the weather deck people were crowding up, many who had been below, to see the coast and the awful night slip away behind them. The sun was already warming and they were still on the bridge wing when the AWACS came down through the clouds and did a low pass, very low past the ship, waggling her wings as she did so, her own farewell.

'I am going to go down,' Sarah Conway said, 'have an hour-long shower and use a whole bottle of shampoo, but on the way I'm buying beer for the lads in the POs' mess. Anyone coming?'

'Yes,' Kitson said. 'Then eat and get some kip. You have the afternoon watch.'

The Commander at Northwood who had manned the desk throughout the night had caught odd snatches of sleep in his chair. The RAF fellow had gone home after the Nimrod had left the scene, but the Marines officer was still there, his feet up, fast asleep. The naval man looked over, envious of his ability to sleep anywhere. His CPO was coming across the quiet Ops room, a signal in his hand. The Commander took it and began to read, a smile crossing his face. It was a signal from *Beaufort*, stating the final casualty list, the supply position, fuel and ordnance expended, but the first

328

few lines were what he wanted to read. All friendly nationals were aboard safely. No civilian casualties. Shore parties were back aboard. She was at sea and wanting instructions on where to take the evacuees.

He advised Fleet Public Relations, got the fellow out of bed who would prepare statements for the media, and then phoned his boss the Chief of Operations, who in turn advised CinC and the Foreign and Commonwealth Office.

Finally he looked across at the Marine, who had just got off the phone to Royal Marines Condor at Arbroath.

'Come on, soldier. I'll buy you breakfast.'

Kitson knocked on the outer lintel of his cabin, given over to Bill Black, Maggie and Poppy. The curtain was pulled back. It was Maggie: he had hoped it would be Poppy. He wanted to see her again. The mild flirting and eye contact at the Embassy had all been fleeting and under unreal circumstances. Surely in the cold light of day the mood would have evaporated. It certainly would have in England. Naval officers weren't paid very much, spent long periods away from home. Not much fun for a girl.

'Sorry to disturb you,' he said. 'Could I raid my drawer? Get a clean rig and my shaving tackle?'

'Of course. Lovely to see you!' she replied standing back. 'This has been very kind of you, giving us your own space. Look, I'll take a walk. Bill is down with everyone.'

'No. It's okay. I'll only be a moment.' He began taking out clean clothing.

'I'm afraid Poppy borrowed one of your shirts and a pair of trousers. I hope you don't mind.'

He smiled suddenly. He liked the thought of her wearing his clothes. 'No. That's fine. There's more there if she wants them. Is she . . .'

'Assisting in the theatre. They're still at it in there. One more to go.'

Late that afternoon Tony Wisher went looking for Kitson and found him down aft. He indicated that he needed to talk. Kitson pointed to the bridge and met him there a few minutes later. They walked out on to the wing below where Sarah Conway had put her marines to fire their rockets that morning.

'I'm going out on a limb here. We owe you one,' Wisher said. Kitson nodded. 'And this conversation never took place.' The XO nodded again and Wisher began. 'You wanted to know what they wanted? What they were after?'

'Taylor's people?' Kitson asked.

'Not just the people,' Wisher responded. He talked for a few minutes and afterwards answered Kitson's questions before moving away.

Kitson thought about it for a few minutes, working to keep his anger in check. He couldn't act independently, but he could and would act. He went to find Captain Bennett and half an hour later sought out two of the civilians they had taken off the beach. By six he had what he wanted and knocked on the door of Commander Denny's cabin where US Ambassador Alberry was quartered.

'Captain Bennett's compliments, Ambassador. I wonder if you could join us for a few minutes.'

'Of course,' he replied, puzzled but willing.

Half an hour later he sent for his number three and Bennett issued his own orders.

The Embassy number three found Kreutz, the CIA man, and told him the Ambassador wanted to see him on the bridge.

Kreutz walked up the stairs. He couldn't see the Ambassador, but Kitson was there and the Captain was in his chair looking out of the dark windows.

'So,' Kitson said. 'Pleased with yourself?'

'No hard feelings, huh? Say, I'm looking for the Ambassador. I was told . . .'

'Nearly got away with it, didn't you?'

'What are you talking about?' The slick grin was back, his dark, ferrety eyes having taken in the fact that the Captain could overhear the conversation.

'The two men you brought out.'

'Now hold on. They are American passport holders.'

'American passports. Sure . . .' Kitson said sarcastically. His tone changed. 'That's crap. I'll bet you just knocked them out of the Embassy. You'd have access. You can create one in about five minutes. There's got to be a charge for that, and that is the least of it.'

'Look, I'm supposed to see the Ambassador. And for your information I don't disclose who we issue passports to, or the reason.'

'Ah. The reason. Yes. That's easy,' Kitson said. His voice had darkened, his tone like steel. 'You got them the passports so you could get them away from Liberia, with the loot.'

Two men moved up from the darkness behind Kreutz.

'What the fuck . . .' Kreutz snapped. 'I don't have to listen to . . .'

'Oh yes you do. The two men behind you are Royal Marines, now in their traditional role. Master at arms. Ship's police. The loot. Bearer bonds. From a country with nothing left to loot, except the future. The sweetener for the next five years of the ConLib agreement. Thirty million dollars to be paid into a Swiss bank for Samuel Taylor. Only Taylor didn't trust banks. Half in bonds up front. But Taylor isn't in power any more and for a cut of the action you were going to get his henchmen out. I'll bet they aren't even acting for him. They are probably doing a runner. What were you going to do? I'm sure they would never have got to spend the money. You might have. You would have killed them. Taken the money. Fifteen million. Enough to kill for. I saw the bodies in daylight. Thin. Young. Poor. They were coming to kill us to get the money. Wealth beyond their wildest dreams. And we were killing them and they were killing us. Primarily because of you.'

Bennett leant forward and took a call on the internal phone.

'You can't touch me. I have diplomatic accreditation and this is a pile of shit,' Kreutz snarled.

Captain Bennett stood up and took the three paces over to them. 'Not so. Your actions, your behaviour, were not only incompatible with your function, but you colluded, conspired and used the services and affairs of your office to further this endeavour. In so doing you undoubtedly contributed to the loss of lives. The lives of my crew. I am placing you under arrest.'

'You can't do that!'

'I can. I am the Captain of one of Her Majesty's warships on the high seas. *I am the law!* It may interest you to know that my Operations Officer, witnessed by the US chargé d'affaires and the British Ambassador, is taking a statement from the two men you smuggled aboard my ship. He found a black satchel in their possession. It was full of bearer bonds. We will check the serial numbers, which I am confident will match those handed over to Taylor's negotiators.'

'They won't talk,' Kreutz said confidently. 'You can't . . .'

'They are talking,' Bennett assured him. 'I suspect that Mr Bokia, or whoever it is, is right this minute demanding the extradition of the people who have run off with Liberia's wealth.' He paused for a second or two. 'I threatened to take them back. Let them answer to the new authorities.'

'You wouldn't do that.'

'Try me!' Bennett snapped. '*They* wouldn't!' A rating stepped up on to the bridge and handed Captain Bennett a slip of paper. He crossed to the soft light of the chart table and read it.

'My word against theirs,' Kreutz sneered. 'Think my people will believe me or a couple of corrupt niggers from some African banana republic? And anyway, you think Bokia is going to use the money for his people?' he snapped. 'Grow up! He'd whip it away as quick as anyone else. They will never believe you.'

'They will believe *me*,' Ambassador Alberry said, stepping from behind the blackout curtain that surrounded the chart table.

Bennett came back. 'My yeoman just died of his wounds. Consider yourself lucky. A hundred years ago I would have hanged you from my yard arm. Take him down,' Bennett said.

They made for Sierra Leone. The seriously wounded were helicoptered ashore to a waiting Royal Air Force C-130 tagged 'Aeromed One', fully equipped for trauma management, where a team of medical staff would care for them on the flight back to Britain. Chartered jets were waiting to uplift everyone, the port and airport with a heavy US Marine presence. Kreutz was handed over to US Military Police.

Kitson saw little of Poppy. The ship so crowded, the officers and crew extremely busy, with so little privacy their only half-decent conversation was on the bridge wing that evening and it was awkward, with crew moving round and people doing tours of the ship. He missed saying good-bye, too. When she left the ship with Bill and Maggie Black he was getting small craft moved from their seaward side to allow the bunkering barge in.

He was disappointed, but tried to shrug it off. She had left a note for him. Thanking him for his hospitality, with 'lovely to meet you' at the bottom and a little smiley face in the 'O' of her name. He also found something she had left in his cabin. He hoped it was hers and not Maggie's because as he fell into his bunk for the first time, he held the silk scarf to his face. He could smell perfume. And he hadn't put the shirt she had worn out to be washed. As long as it was there, folded where she had left it, part of her was still in his cabin. It was a nice feeling, the first time since his marriage had ended, and it made him realize how lonely he had been. The following morning the steward, thinking he was doing the right thing, had taken the shirt to be washed and Kitson, momentarily disappointed, acknowledged that life moved on. Another place another time maybe. But not this time. He would shake it off. Have to. Life was like that.

That night they invited the Captain to dine in the wardroom. The mess bills were considerable, Kitson working to rebond the wardroom and get them back to some normality, but when he got back to his cabin he lifted the scarf and smelled the scent of her. Soap and perfume and Poppy. He had only known her a little over forty-eight hours and he missed her dreadfully.

12

They had taken on new radios in Sierra Leone and within an hour of their being installed, electronics artificers running new coaxial aerial cables up to the damaged yards, messages began to come through from Northwood. Much of it was routine, but a handful were not. One was to advise Chalky White that his wife had given birth to their first child, another to a Wren rating that her father was dangerously ill. A third was from the Naval Police at Portsmouth advising that the Sussex Constabulary wanted to interview two of the ship's company on her return, regarding a serious incident in Brighton. Yet another signal Bennett read and crossed to the main broadcast system microphone.

'Do you hear there. This is the Captain. A signal has arrived addressed to the ship's company from CinC. It reads,' he paused, *' "Personal from CinC. Congratulations on a first class job under difficult conditions. You have upheld the best traditions of the RN. You were all magnificent. First Sea Lord and everyone in the service joins me in sending congratulations. Bravo Zulu. A safe and speedy trip home." '*

To the lads that mattered as much as anything. Bravo Zulu was a naval term for well done. Not often any ship got that from the First Sea Lord.

On the passage home the ship fell back into her routines, the time-worn schedules of training and maintenance giving her a feel of normality again. Only the blackened MCO, the missing faces and the presence of the Royal Marines who were hitching a ride home were there to remind them.

The POs' mess laid it on for the Marines. While Lieuten-ant Gordon, in borrowed kit, dined in the wardroom, his lads were back in action, Doughty and the sergeant holding up the pride of the Marines in a drinking game called Hawaii Five O. Three of their lads were already on the floor, officially missing in action and a fourth was singing karaoke with a bar towel on his head.

They were in the Channel, three hours from home and just on noon, when they saw a ship approaching. A Navy ship. As she got nearer Morris said, 'It's *Invincible*, sir. She's signalling.'

A moment or two later a rating darted in from the bridge wing. Morris took it.

'Signal reads, "The boyz done good. Welcome home."'

Bennett looked over at him. 'Say again?'

' "The boyz done good", sir, boys with a "z".'

'*Invincible* is saluting, Captain. She has dipped,' Conway, the officer of the watch, said.

'What?' Bennett asked, crossing to the bridge window and reaching for binoculars. *Invincible* was an aircraft car-rier commanded by a four-ring captain, a man Bennett had served under as a green two-ringer. They didn't salute mere frigates.

Morris dropped his binoculars on to his chest and looked across at Bennett. 'Company are mustered on the flight deck. Every man jack of them, by the look of it.' This was unusual. Highly unusual.

'All crew who can be spared topsides right now,' Bennett said. 'I want them to see this. Hold your course.'

As the huge carrier came closer and the *Beaufort*'s crew were coming up on deck, the carrier's course altered to bring her squarely abeam and parallel to *Beaufort*. She passed with her flags already dipped, and Chops Wilks snarled at the rating by the halyards: 'Wait for it.' Then, as he ordered his rating to dip their flags in return, they saw the *Invincible*'s crew do their own salute, a thousand hands coming up to touch the brims of caps and hats at once.

'Make to *Invincible*,' Bennett said, with a lump in his throat, ' "We thank you".'

HMS *Beaufort*, her superstructure battered and damaged, her sides still showing blackened surfaces from fire damage, was now approaching the Isle of Wight. Behind the Island was the Solent and home, the harbour and Portsmouth Naval Base. Bennett turned to Kitson. 'Not every day we get back from a deployment like this has been, Peter. Pass the word. Procedure Alpha, please.' Kitson smiled. Alpha was number one rig. Ship's company to man the rail on arrival.

'Do you hear there . . .'

Ships, naval or merchant, arriving in Portsmouth have their arrival time published in the local newspapers and announced on local radio. HMS *Beaufort* was no different, but instead of being buried with the other arrivals and departures on the inner pages it was on the front page.

Along the narrow entrance to Portsmouth harbour people were gathered to watch her come home. At the Round Tower, where many a captain's wife had stood to wave goodbye, the famous turret was crowded with waving people, some with banners, and the roads along the waterfront were clogged with cars that had stopped.

Bennett looked down the waist of his command. The lads, men and women, were out along the port rail, dressed in their number ones. Even those in the sick bay had dragged themselves up on to the weather deck: at a few points down the line there was flashes of white, slings and bandages, where there should have been blue. A flotilla of pleasure craft had taken up station either side of her, people waving. Suddenly there were dozens of them, boats of every shape and size, power launches, yachts, ribs. One yacht was flying multi-coloured bunting and had a huge

Union Flag flying from her mast; the strains of 'Rule Britannia' boomed from speakers set on her decks.

The lads had been expecting wives and girlfriends to wave them in as they would after any deployment, but nothing like this.

'Fucking 'ell,' someone muttered.

'Shut it,' Chops snarled. It was protocol time. It should have been standard stuff. They had been doing it for hundreds of years, but someone was bound to cock it up. They slid through the water, a fishing boat going out past them blowing her hooter. The cross-channel ferry *Pride of Le Havre* was approaching them, also making her way seaward.

Chops Wilks looked out. *Nottingham* and *Southampton*, two Type 42 destroyers tied up to Railway Jetty, were first coming up on the starboard side. Seemed to be a lot of people about.

Pride of Le Havre was running up abeam now, her huge engines pushing her forward, and someone on the bridge must have hit her foghorns because they blared out in a series of short hoots. And then again. Technically it was a manoeuvring signal, but everyone knew it was a welcome home for *Beaufort*. Passengers were crowding her open promenade decks, waving and shouting across the wind and her Captain had come out on to his bridge wing and was waving his cap. Behind the ferry three harbour tugs sat squat in the water, firing water into the air from their water cannons.

Except for a handful of ratings on the port side everyone missed it, but they didn't miss the next event. From nowhere, as they came abeam, *Nottingham*'s company had appeared and manned the rail. They had saluted with their flags the way they should have done and Chops didn't expect anything else, knowing their Chief as he did, but no one was expecting what happened next. As one, two hundred-odd sailors manning the destroyer's rail lifted their hats and cheered.

338

'Christ,' someone muttered, his chin lifting. 'They're cheering ship.'

For once Chops Wilks was silent. He had a lump in his throat and didn't trust himself to speak.

They weren't to know, but it had come down from the Naval Base Commander, a Commodore. A clear order. All ships will cheer HMS *Beaufort* on arrival. Further in, aboard Admiral the Lord Nelson's flagship HMS *Victory*, from which he had won the battle of Trafalgar, three retired navy men, now guides who took tourists round the ship, suspended the tours for a few minutes and stood aft on the quarter deck. As *Beaufort* passed them and saluted *Victory*, flagship home command, they returned the salute, but in fact were seconds ahead of *Beaufort*'s flag dropping. A breach of protocol in strict terms, but they were retired and this was what they wanted to do and none but the lads in *Beaufort* would see them anyway. Each ship they passed could see the hole in her side, the smoke damage, the battered shell-damaged funnel and shattered yards. They knew where she had been. *Southampton* was next. *Richmond*, *Beaufort*'s sister ship, followed and *Iron Duke*, another Type 23, loomed up. A couple of mine hunters were dwarfed by the bulk of the RFA *Black Rover* and the *Birmingham* berthed either side of them. Every ship of the fleet they passed on their way to their berth on Fountain Lake Jetty cheered them.

Now just inching forwards, her berth in sight, they could see the people gathered. Families who were allowed to meet ships after a deployment were there as usual. Normally there might be forty or fifty people. Not today. They were there in their hundreds surrounding the band of the Royal Marines and a group of what seemed to be dignitaries and television crews.

'Want to drive, Peter?' Bennett asked. They were on the bridge wing about to execute a lazy, very slow 180-degree turn that would bring them into the berth facing to seaward.

Kitson just looked at him. This was no place for any cock-ups. Half the Royal Navy watching. Whatever happens, the Captain remains responsible, which is why most choose to con the ship into her berth personally.

'Go on. It's good experience.'

Kitson grinned and took up the microphone. *'Select revolutions three zero. Starboard thirty . . .'*

The girl was waiting back from the main throng, a little self-conscious. He probably had other people there to meet him, family perhaps, maybe even another girl. She hoped not. But if he did, she would just melt away. No one would have seen her making a fool of herself. One of the others had told her the form. They would come ashore, greet people, then go back aboard, change into civvies and come ashore properly.

A woman who was standing beside her lit a cigarette. She was tall, sun-tanned with long blonde hair piled up. She blew out the smoke and looked across. 'Hi. Waiting for your man?' Her accent was not local, a bit posh even.

Tracy nodded. 'Yeah. Well sort of. Not sure. I've only met him a couple of times, last time they were in.'

'I met a few of them, briefly. Who's your chap, then?'

'Kevin. Kevin Baker.'

The woman smiled. 'I think I met him. Is he tall? Fair hair. Nice guy. You know, gentle?'

'Yeah, that's him,' Tracey replied shyly. She paused before asking, 'Where did you meet him?'

'Liberia,' the woman replied.

Godshall was expecting the police: the Captain had told him they would be there. He picked them out on the stand. Rozzers. They didn't look like the others gathered. No smiles. No waves. He had thought it through. If the waster Dave had taken out had pressed charges, then tough. He had it coming. His divisional officer had been Lieutenant Buchanan and now Conway had taken it over. She was

340

waiting with him, there to see he didn't try anything silly
and be his advocate until he was charged, if that was what
they were going to do. He had decided. He wasn't going
to fold and let Dave take the rap and he wasn't going to
shop him either.

The two police officers came up the gangway before
anyone went ashore. Lieutenant Conway was there to
meet them and swept them round to the side of the waist
away from the people.

'We are here to arrest David James Tomkins and Thomas
Godshall.'

Godshall stepped forward, his chin lifted, looking them
in the eye.

'I'm Lieutenant Conway, Divisional Officer. On what
charge?' Conway had requested this one from the Captain.
Asked for Godshall to be attached to her division. Orbs
Montagu had, as well. They both remembered it vividly,
his raw courage under fire, never flinching, always there
in the thick of it and volunteering at the end with Jonesy
to go back into the gunfire and get the last of the lads
away.

'Where's the other one?'

'David Tomkins, the other one as you call him,' she
replied acidly, 'is dead. Killed in action. Again I ask you,
on what charge?'

'It's serious.'

'It was a punch-up outside a pub. They were attacked,'
Conway countered.

'It's more than that. The victim died, never regained
consciousness. So it's manslaughter, possibly murder.'
Godshall's face dropped, but only for a moment. Fuck him,
he thought. He put the boot in and couldn't take it back.
I'm with you, Dave. Don't worry, my son.

'I see,' she said. 'Acting Petty Officer Godshall will of
course accompany you to help you with your enquiries,
but you should be aware of this.' She handed an envelope
to the senior of the two men. 'David Tomkins made a

341

deathbed confession.' Godshall looked at her quickly. 'It was to Captain Bennett and witnessed as you can see. He tells the story. They were attacked, but he admits striking a blow causing the attacker's head to hit the wall. The blow, he was aware, that rendered the attacker unconscious. He confesses to the act. This man was present at the time, but did not strike the blow.'

The policeman was reading the note. A statement, it was signed by the Captain and two others. 'I want to show this to my boss,' he looked at Godshall, 'and we'll want a statement from you. Got a contact number?'

No one had ever come to see him in before, so Baker remained on board and just watched from the rail. He still had a silly grin on his face. They had zapped the Royal Marines' kit. Riddled their stuff with *Beaufort* zaps. Then he saw her. Tracy. He was nervous. Maybe she was there to meet someone else. When she smiled and waved to him over the heads of a few other people he waved back. He carried on looking at her and eventually when he saw no one else with her he pointed to himself and mouthed, 'Me?'

She smiled shyly and nodded.

He punched the air, expelling the breath with a 'Yes!' and went for the gangway at a run. Chalky White watched him go. 'Lucky sod,' he muttered. Life was okay again. His wife wasn't there. She was still in hospital, but he would be going up to see her and their new baby daughter immediately.

There was twenty minutes of music and throng and relatives and placards before Kitson came down the gangway. He wasn't expecting his girls or their grandparents, but with senior officers there he thought he'd better show willing. He had just arrived at the bottom of the gangway when someone stepped out from the side. Blonde hair, blue blue eyes, the familiar perfume. Poppy. Her hair was up and she was wearing earrings and a necklace that dropped into the v-neck of her summer dress. She looked stunning.

'Hello, sailor,' she said. 'Looking for a good time?'

'Maybe,' he replied, a little-boy smile creasing his face. 'I don't do short time.'

'How long?' he grinned.

'Years,' she replied.

'Done,' he said and he kissed her.

Summary of awards to Royal Navy and Royal Marines personnel, gazetted in the *London Gazette* of 12/12/96, following the action to rescue British and foreign nationals, caught up in civil war, from Monrovia on 23–24 September 1996.

COMMANDER NICHOLAS EDWARD BENNETT RN
Distinguished Service Cross – for leadership

LIEUTENANT COMMANDER PETER JAMES KITSON RN
Distinguished Service Cross – for leadership

LIEUTENANT ANDREW ARGYL GORDON RM
Military Cross – for leadership

LIEUTENANT SARAH LOUISE CONWAY RN
Military Cross – for leadership

LEA CHERYL MARY SIMPSON RN
George Medal (posthumous) – for gallantry

CORPORAL MICHAEL EDWARD DOUGHTY RM
Distinguished Service Cross – for gallantry

LWA THOMAS GODSHALL RN
Distinguished Service Cross – for gallantry